THE WAY IT'S DONE . . .

"Busy."

She started, sliding forward a bit. "Pardon me?"

"Busy. Your calling keeps you *busy*. 'Actively engaged' sounds so"—he took a thoughtful sip—"frosty."

"Frosty?"

"Cool."

"Cool?" If he could see her well enough, he'd bet money her cheeks were blazing. "Constable, I'm neither frosty nor cool, or, or—"

"Frigid."

Flattening her palms on the table, she rose to her feet, her shadow washing over him. "I'm not frigid."

He paused, feeling an undeniable urge to challenge her. But no, he couldn't do that. Could he? "Prove it," he said.

"Okay," she whispered. "I will."

He lifted his head, jerked ramrod straight in his chair, searching Savannah's face for any indication that she was bluffing. Her clothes, her skin, her features were all obscured in gray and black, giving him no clue.

"Are you . . . joking?" His voice sounded as dry as day-old toast.

She released a pent-up breath and started to edge around the table toward him. "You said you could change my mind. Perhaps I can change yours. Are you willing?"

Through the shadows, he found her gleaming eyes, her slightly curved mouth. "No, it's too reckless. Too irresponsible."

"You're sounding like a father. Or a constable, Constable."

"I'm both, Miss Connor."

"I'll do it all. You don't have to participate. That should be enough to prove my case."

"I wasn't serious when I said that. I'm sure you're not, hell, *frigid*."

She leaned in, her hands sliding along the arms of the chair, her face fading out of view as it closed in on his. A scent, provocative and earthy, stole in with his stuttered breath. "You see, Constable, I'm always serious. And . . ." He watched her moisten her lips, so near he could almost taste her. "Close your eyes. I've heard that's the way it's done."

By Tracy Sumner

Carolina Rose

Tides of Love

When All Through the Night
(included in the *Christmas Kisses* anthology)

Published by Zebra Books

TIDES OF PASSION

Tracy Sumner

ZEBRA BOOKS
KENSINGTON PUBLISHING CORP.
http://www.kensingtonbooks.com

ACKNOWLEDGMENTS

I owe many people a nod of gratitude for this book, one written not so much under duress as after. . . .

To my World Trade Center colleagues, thank you for your support. Sometimes I felt you were the only ones who understood. Unfortunately, who *could* understand.

To my family—Hartsville and Columbia branches—for being there and believing in me. Brett and Emily, keep up the hometown marketing! I love you guys.

To my agent, Jennifer Jackson, and my editor, Ann LaFarge, for your unfailing encouragement and advice, some of which (on occasion) I resist taking.

Special, *special* thanks go to Jim, who ordered Thai and then did the dishes, night after night while I hunkered down over the computer. (Being the transplanted New Yorkers that we are, we tend to shy away from cooking.)

Finally, for me, two wishes for the coming year: continued good health for my ferret, Sammi, who's still hanging in there; and a national championship for my beloved team. Go Tigers!

Chapter One

North Carolina, 1898

Savannah knew she was in trouble a split second
before he reached her.

She also acknowledged, somewhere deep inside
herself, a tremor of fatigue. Although it was for
the good of the cause, being embroiled in one
predicament after another for the past eight years
had exhausted her.

Perhaps she should have done something to save
herself the embarrassment of a tussle with the town
constable, a man determined to believe the worst
of her. However, running from a challenge wasn't
her way, even though the uneasy prickle dancing
along the base of her spine had had her contem-
plating slipping off the rickety crate and into the
budding crowd gathered outside the oyster factory.
And she *had* turned, full circle, on her shaky perch
. . . only to falter due to nothing more than Constable Garrett's lack of proper *clothing*.

In the typical manner of the coastal community she had temporarily settled in—a Southern locale so foreign to her native New York that it often gave her the shivers—his shirt lay open to the waist, his ragged shirttail flicking his stomach as he advanced on her, dark, almost black hair whipping his brow with each lengthy stride. Tall, broad-shouldered, and lean-hipped, his physique belied his composed expression. Yet Savannah detected a faint edge of anger pulsing beneath the calm facade. She wanted to deny that the man's looks sent her heart racing.

Wanted to . . . but could not.

Flinging her fist into the air, she stared him down as she shouted, "Fight for your rights, women of Pilot Isle!"

The roar of the crowd, men in discord, women in glorious agreement, eclipsed her next call to action. *There,* she thought, pleased to see Zachariah Garrett's long-lashed gray eyes narrow, his golden skin pull tight in a frown. Again she shook her fist, and the crowd bellowed.

One man ripped the sign Savannah had hung from the warehouse wall to pieces and fed it to the flames shooting from a nearby barrel. Another began channeling the group of protesting women away from the warehouse entrance. Many looked at her with proud smiles on their faces or raised a hand as they passed. They felt the pulse thrumming through the air, the energy of being a part of a group, struggling, winning, losing, triumphing.

There was no power like the power of a crowd.

Standing on a wobbly crate on a dock alongside the ocean, Savannah let the madness rush over her, sure, completely sure to the depths of her soul, that *this* was worth her often forlorn existence. Change was good. Change was necessary. And while she was here, she would make sure Pilot Isle saw its fair share.

"That's it for the show, Miss Connor," Zachariah Garrett said, wrapping his arm around her waist and yanking her from the crate as people swarmed past. "You've done nothing but cause trouble since you got here a week ago, and personally, I've about had it."

"I'm sorry, Constable, but that's the purpose of my profession!"

He set her on her feet none too gently and whispered in her ear, "Not in my town, it isn't."

Preparing to argue—Savannah was *always* prepared to argue—a violent shove forced her to her knees. Sucking in a painful gasp, she scrambled between a pair of long legs and behind a water cask, having nowhere to hide in a town the size of a peanut. Dropping to a squat, she brushed a bead of perspiration from her brow and wondered what the inside of Pilot Isle's jail was going to look like.

Fatigue returned, along with the first flicker of doubt she had experienced in many a month. Resting her cheek on her knee, she let the sound of waves slapping the wharf calm her, the fierce breeze coming in off the water cool her skin. Her family had lived by the sea for a summer when she was a child. It was one of the last times she remembered being truly happy. Or loved.

Blessed God, how long ago that seemed now.

That was how Zach found her. Crouched behind a stinking fish barrel, dark hair a sodden mess hanging down her back, her dress—one that cost a pretty penny, he would bet—ripped and stained. She looked young right then, younger than he knew her to be. And harmless, which was as far from the truth as it got. He shoved aside the sympathetic twinge, determined not to let his role as a father cloud every damned judgment he made. Due to this woman's meddling, his townfolk pulsed like an angry wound behind him, the ringing of the ferry bell not doing a blessed thing to quiet a soul. All he could do was stare at the instigator huddling on a section of grimy planks and question how one uppity mite could stir people up as if she'd taken a stick to their rear ends.

No wonder she was some big-time social reformer up north. She was as good at causing trouble as any person he'd ever seen.

"Get up," Zach said, nudging her ankle with his boot. A slim, delicate-looking ankle. He didn't like her, this sassy, liberating *rabble-rouser,* but he was a man, after all, and had to admit she was put together nicely.

She lifted her head, blinking, seeming to pull herself from some distant place. A halo of shiny curls brushed her jaw, and as she tilted her head up, he got his first close look at her. A fine-boned face, the expression on it soft, almost dreamy.

Boy, the softness didn't last long.

Jamming her lips together, her cheeks plumped with the frown. Oh, yeah, that was the look he'd been expecting. "Good day, Constable," she said. Just like that, as if he should be offering a cordial greeting with a small war going on behind them.

"Miss Connor, this way, if you please."

She rose with all the dignity of a queen, shook out her skirts, and brushed dirt from one sleeve. He counted to ten and back, unruffled, good at hiding his impatience. That's what being the lone parent of a rambunctious young boy would do for a man, he reckoned. Just when he reached ten for the second time and opened his mouth to order her along, a misplaced swing caught him in the side and he stumbled forward, grasping Savannah's shoulders to keep from crashing into her. Motion ceased when she thumped the wall of the warehouse, her head coming up fast, her eyes wide and alarmed.

And very, very green.

He felt the heat of her skin through the thin material of her dress; her muscles jumped beneath his palms. Her gaze dropped to his chest, and a soft glow lit her cheeks. Blushing . . . something he wouldn't have expected from *this* woman.

Nevertheless, he stared, wondering why they both seemed frozen.

Zach was frozen because he'd forgotten what it felt like to touch a woman. How soft and round and warm they were. How they dabbed perfume in secret places and smiled teasing smiles and flicked those colorful little fans in your face, never *really* realizing what all that hoo-ha did to a man's equilibrium.

It was the first time he'd laid his hands on a woman since his wife died, except for a rescue last year and the captain's sister he'd pulled from the ocean. *She* had thrown her arms around him, shivering and crying, and he'd felt for her—sure, he had. Grateful and relieved and humble that God had once again shown him where the lost souls out on those darned shoals were.

He hadn't felt anything more. Anything strong. This wasn't strong either, nothing more than a minute spike of heat in his belly, nothing much at all. He didn't need as other men did. Not like his brothers or his friends in town. He had needed once, needed his wife. But she was dead. That life— loving and yearning and wanting—had died with her.

"Your mouth is bleeding," Savannah said and shifted, her arm rising.

Don't touch me, he thought, the words bubbling in his throat. Cursing beneath his breath, the full extent of his childishness struck him. She would think he'd gone crazy. And maybe he had. Stepping back, he thrust his hands in his pockets and gestured for her to follow, intentionally leading her away from the ruckus on the wharf.

Buttoning his shirt, he listened to her steady footfalls, thinking she'd be safe in his office until everything died down.

"I'm sorry you've been injured."

Dabbing at the corner of his lip, he shrugged. He could still hear the rumble of the crowd if he tried. No matter. His brother Caleb would break it up. They'd argued about who got what job in this mess.

Zach had lost.

"What did you expect, Miss Connor?" he finally asked. "People get heated and they do stupid things like fight with their neighbors and their friends. Hard not to get vexed with you standing up there, rising from the mist, preaching and persuading, stirring emotion like a witch with a cauldron."

She rushed to catch up to him, and he slowed his deliberately forceful stride. "Those women work twelve-hour days, Constable Garrett. Twelve hours on their feet, often without lunch breaks or access to sanitary drinking water. And for half the pay a man receives for the same day's work. Some are expecting a child and alone, young women who think they can disappear in this town without their families ever finding them. Their lives up to this point have been so dominated and environed by duties, so largely ordered for them, that many don't know how to balance a cash account of modest means or find work of any kind that doesn't involve sewing a straight stitch or shucking oysters."

She stomped around a puddle in their path, kicking at oyster shells and muttering, nicking her polished boots in the process. "If you can reconcile that treatment to your sense of what is just, then we have nothing more to discuss."

Zach halted before the unpretentious building that housed Pilot Isle's lone jail cell, getting riled himself, an emotion he rarely tolerated. He didn't know whether he should apologize or shake the stuffing out of her. "I'll be glad to tell you what I reconcile on a given day: business disputes, marriages, deaths, shipwrecks, the resulting cargo and bodies that wash up on shore, and just about everything in between. What you're talking about over at the oyster factory has been going on forever. Long hours, dreadfully long. The men may well get paid a higher wage—I couldn't say for certain—but they labor like mules, too. Do you reckon Hyman Carter is begging people to come work for him? Well, he isn't. It's a choice, free and clear." Reaching around her and flinging the door open, he stepped inside and, by God, expected her to follow. "What the heck can I do about that?"

Her abrupt silence had him turning. Savannah Connor stood in the doorway, bright sunlight flooding in around her, again looking like a vision of blamelessness, of sweet charity. She even smiled, closing the door gently behind her. Troubled, Zach reviewed his last words, racing through them in his mind. "Oh, no," he said, flinging his hand up in a motion his son knew meant no, flat out. "I'm not getting involved in this campaign of yours. Except to end it, I'm not getting involved."

"Why not get involved?" she asked, the edge back, her syrupy facade flying right out the window.

"Give me one worthy reason why. You're the perfect person to request a review of the factory's processes."

Ignoring her, he slumped into the chair behind his desk, dug his cargo ledger out of the top drawer and a water-stained list out of his pocket, and began calculating entries. He was two shipwrecks behind. The town couldn't auction property—funds they desperately needed—until he, as keeper of Lifesaving Division Six, completed the sad task of recording every damaged plank, every broken teacup, every poor soul's shoe. A cold, wet nose nudged his hand, soulful brown eyes pleading for attention: his boy's dog, who'd started coming into town with him around about the time he lost his wife. Funny, like the old fella had known something was wrong. Scratching a tender spot beneath Tiger's ear, Zach tried to get his mind on track and back to his accounts.

Work was good for the soul, he'd always thought. It had saved him a couple of years ago. That and his son. Besides, maybe Miss Connor would hush up if he didn't look at her.

Moments passed, the only sound the scratch of pen across paper and the occasional crunch of wagon wheels over the oyster-paved street out front. Tiger grunted and settled into a lazy pile at his feet. When the cell's metal door squealed, Zach started, flicking ink across the page. "What in tarnation are you doing, Miss Connor?"

Looking up from plumping the cot's skinny pillow, she flashed a tight smile. "Getting ready for a long night, Constable Garrett. You're writing"—she pointed—"'a summons for me in that little book, correct? What will it be? Disturbing the peace? Instigating a mutiny?" She shrugged, clearly to in crisis. Having met the man on only one occasion—an introduction rendered simply because she was his soon-to-be sister-in-law's best friend—she had heard his name a thousand times already.

Just when she'd devised a skillful argument to present for his inspection, a much better one strolled through the office door.

The woman was attractive and trim . . . and quite obviously smitten with Constable Garrett. Unbeknownst to him, she smoothed her hand the length of her bodice and straightened the rose-trimmed straw hat atop her head before making her presence known.

"Gracious, Zach, *what* is going on in town today?"

Zach slowly lifted his head, shooting a frigid glare Savannah's way before pasting a smile on his face and swiveling around on his stubborn rump. "Miss Lydia, I hope you didn't get caught up in that mess. Caleb should have it under control by now, though."

Miss Lydia drifted toward the desk, her clear blue gaze focused so intently on the man behind it that Savannah feared she'd trip over her own feet if she wasn't careful. "Oh, I didn't get near it; you know that would never do. If Papa heard, he'd have a conniption. But I *was* at Mr. Scoggins's store just a while ago and it was all anyone could talk about." She placed a cloth-covered basket on his desk. The scent of cinnamon filled the room. "Lands, imagine the excitement of a rally, right here in Pilot Isle."

Zach sighed. "Yes, imagine that."

"And"—Lydia glanced in Savannah's direction—"you've, um, detained . . ."

"I haven't—"

"Constable Garrett, if I may?" Savannah ges-

tured to the cell door she'd shut while Miss Lydia
stood in the threshold, hand-pressing her bodice.
"I promise to be on my best behavior. It's just so
hard to converse through metal bars."

"Oh, dear Lord." Zach yanked a drawer open
and fished for a set of keys he clearly didn't use
often. Stalking toward the cell with murder in his
eyes, he asked in a low tone, "What game are you
playing, Miss Connor?"

"Forewarned is forearmed, Constable."

With a snap of his wrist and a compelling shift
of muscle beneath the sleeve of his shirt, he yanked
open the door. "Out."

"My, my, Constable, such hospitality for a humble inmate." She plucked her skirt between her
fingers and circled him as if she were belle of the
ball. Belle of the ball was called for with Miss Lydia,
Savannah had realized from the first moment. The
bored woman of consequence needing fulfillment.

And a cause.

Savannah would gladly give her one.

"If I may introduce myself." Savannah halted
before Miss Lydia, her intensity diluted by a bashful
smile. "Savannah Connor. Pleased to make your
acquaintance."

Miss Lydia struggled for a moment, but her
inbred manners won out. In the South, they always
seemed to. "Lydia Alice Templeton. Pleased, also,
I'm sure." She gestured to the basket on the desk.
"Would you like a muffin? You must be starved,
poor thing. These are my special recipe. Cinnamon
and brown sugar, and a secret ingredient I won't
tell to save my life. Zach, oh"—she tapped her
bottom lips with a gloved finger—"Mr. Garrett
loves them."

"I'm sure he does," Savannah said, not having
to turn to see his displeasure. It radiated like a hot

brand pressed to her back. "And I would love one. I'm practically faint with hunger."

Miss Lydia sprang into action, unfastening and cutting, spreading butter, and clucking like a mother hen. Savannah admired women who could nurture like that. A born mother, when children scared Savannah half to death.

"Here, dear," Miss Lydia murmured, full of warmth and compassion. "Mr. Garrett, haven't you a pitcher of water?"

No reply, but within a minute a chipped jug and a glass appeared on the desk with a brusque clatter.

"Do you mind if I perch right here on the corner of your desk, Constable?" Savannah asked and bit into the most delicious muffin she had ever tasted. "Truly, these are good. Ummm."

"I win the blue ribbon every year at the Harvest Celebration." Lydia shrugged as if this were a certain thing in her life. "My father owns a commercial fishing company and my mother passed some time ago, so I take care of him now. I bake all day some days." She turned her hand in a dreamy circle. "To fill the time."

Savannah halted, a mouthful of muffin resting on her tongue. She couldn't stop herself—really, the urge was too powerful—from looking up. Constable Garrett stood in the cell's entryway, shoulder jammed against a metal bar, feet crossed at the ankle, those startling gray eyes trained on her. Trained without apology.

No, he mouthed. An honest appeal from an honest man.

She hadn't dealt with many honest men in her life, including her father and her brother. Also, she was confident she hadn't ever had as attractive an opponent. It was wicked to feel a tiny zing when she imagined besting him, wasn't it? Was that letting personal issues and professional ones collide?

Swallowing, she returned her attention to her prey. "You could find other ways to fill your time. I'm happy to tell you that that is precisely what I did."

"But—"

"My mother, also, passed away when I was a young girl. After that my life consisted of living in our home in New York City, making a life for my father and my older brother. They were helpless when it came to running a household, so I took over. My childhood ended at that time, but later on, I made sure I would have something to show for it."

"Ohhh," Lydia said, clasping her hand to her heart.

Savannah ignored the audible grunt from the back of the room and continued, "One day I simply found the endless duties and tasks, many of which I was uninterested in, to be so monotonous as to make my life seem worthless. I forced myself to search for meaning—a cause, if you will. I attended my first women's rights meeting the next afternoon." She failed to mention she had been all of sixteen and had nearly broken her ankle jumping from the window of her bedroom to the closest tree limb outside. After dragging her home from the meeting, her father had locked her in her bedroom for two days. Without food or water.

He hadn't let her out until that lovely old tree outside her window no longer stood tall and proud.

"Miss Connor, I couldn't possibly attend a meeting like that here."

Savannah dabbed a muffin crumb from the desk and licked her finger. "Why ever not?"

"It's not—I'm not . . . ." Lydia's voice trailed off.

"You're not resilient enough? Oh, you are. I could tell right away. Can you honestly say that you're satisfied with your life? What, tell me, are you doing completely for yourself?"

"Redecorating my father's stu—"

"That's for him. Try again."

"Cooking."

Savannah smiled and shook her head.

Lydia snapped her fingers. "Oh, I have one! I host an information-gathering tea in the historical society office one morning a week. Although Papa feels it's shameful for me to work, even when the position is entirely without compensation."

Savannah relaxed her shoulders, dabbed at another crumb, as if the news weren't simply wonderful. The glow of heat at her back seemed to increase. "And how do you feel about working?"

"I love it. I'm very good at keeping records and tallying donations. I raised more money for the society last year than any other volunteer, even though Sallie Rutherford's total arrived at five dollars more than mine." She leaned in, cupping her hand around her mouth. "Hyman Carter is her uncle, and he gave it to her at the last minute to lift her total past mine."

The wonder, Savannah thought, dizzy with promise. "Miss Templeton, this is a propitious conversation. I need a coleader for my efforts, and until this moment, I wasn't sure I would be able to locate the right woman in a town the size of Pilot Isle." She smiled, placing her hand over Lydia's gloved fingers. "Now, I think I have."

"Me?" Lydia breathed, hand climbing to her chest. "A coleader?"

Savannah nodded. "I have to govern Elle Beaumont's school in her absence. Teach classes and mentor her female students until her return. You may have heard that she's returned to university in South Carolina. Yet, I couldn't possibly live here and watch women live in a state of disability and not try to improve their situation. Women working exhausting hours for half the pay a man receives, for instance. Did you know about that?"

"The oyster factory? Well, I have to say, that is . . ." Her gaze skipped to the constable and back. "I haven't ever been employed. Not in a true position of payment. And the factory," she said, voice dropping to a whisper, "isn't where any ladies of, what did you call it, *consequence* are likely to pay a visit."

"As coleader of the Pilot Isle movement, you should make it your first stop. Let's plan to meet there tomorrow morning. Nine o'clock sharp. Bring Miss Rutherford, who even if she is a bit of a charlatan, might prove a worthy supporter. Too, she can gain access for the group without the burden of another impassioned assembly. Surely her uncle doesn't want that."

"Now wait a blessed minute."

Savannah glanced up as Zach's shadow flooded over them. Bits of dust drifted through the wide beam of sunlight he stood in, softening the intensity of his displeasure. No matter his inflexibility, the man was attractive, she thought. "A problem, Constable?"

"You're damn right there's a problem."

A soft gasp had him bowing slightly and frowning harder. "Beg pardon, Miss Lydia. I apologize for the language, but this doesn't concern you." He swung Savannah around on the desk, her knees banging his as he crouched before her, bringing their eyes level. Tiger scuttled out of the way, slinking into the empty jail cell. "It concerns *you*, and I remember telling *you* I wasn't putting up with this foolishness." He stabbed his finger against his chest. "Not in my town."

She drew a covert breath. Traces of manual labor and the faintest scent of cinnamon circled him. Savannah valued hard work above all else and never minded a man who confirmed he valued it as well, even if he smelled less than soap-fresh and his palms were a bit rough. "Are we prohibited from visiting the factory, Constable?" she asked, forcing her mind to the issue at hand.

"After today, you better believe you are."

She arched a brow, a trick she had practiced before the mirror for months until it alone personified frosty indifference. "My colleagues, Miss Templeton and Miss Rutherford, will attend in my absence, then."

"No."

She scooted forward until the stubble dotting his rigid jaw filled her vision. "You can't stop them and you know it. In fact, I'm fairly certain you cannot stop *me* without filing paperwork barring me from Mr. Carter's property. That takes time and signatures, rounding up witnesses to the dispute. However, I'm willing to forgo this meeting—during the initial phase, at any rate. For everyone's comfort." Sliding back the inch she needed to pull their knees apart, she decided that for all Zachariah Garrett's irritability—a trait she abhorred in a man—he smelled far, far too tempting to risk touching during negotiations. "Don't challenge my generosity. You won't get more."

"Are you daring me to do something, Miss Connor? Because I will, I tell you."

"Consider it a gracious request."

"You can take your gracious request and stick it . . ." Jamming his hands atop his knees, he rose to his feet. "Miss Lydia, will you excuse us a moment?"

Lydia cleared her throat and backed up two steps. Before she left, she looked at Savannah and smiled, her eyes bright with excitement. Savannah returned the smile, knowing she had won that series if nothing else.

"You must be crazy," Zach said the moment the door closed. "Look at the blood on your dress, the scrapes on your hands. Do you want Miss Lydia to suffer the same? The things you want her to experience are things her father has purposely kept her from experiencing, and for a darned good reason. You act as if I'm keeping her from some blessed garden party."

She gazed at the torn skin on her hands and the traces of blood on her skirt as she heard him begin to pace the narrow confines of the office. "It's a mockery to talk of sheltering women from life's fierce storms, Constable. Do you believe the ones who work twelve-hour days in that factory are too weak to weather the emotional stress of a political campaign? Do you believe Lydia cannot support a belief that runs counter to her father's? A child is not a replica of the parent. The sexes—excuse my frankness—do not have the same challenges in life." Watching him, his hands buried in his pockets—to keep from circling her neck, she supposed—she couldn't help but marvel at the curious mix of Southern courtesy and male arrogance, the natural assumption he shouldered of being lawfully in control. "Engaging in a moral battle isn't always hazardous to one's health, you know."

"Doesn't look like it's doing wonders for yours."

"Saints be praised, it can actually be rewarding."

Looking over his shoulder, he halted in the middle of the room. "Irish."

"I beg your pardon?"

"You. Irish. The green eyes, the tiny bit of red in your hair. Is Connor your real name?"

"Yes, why . . ." she said, stammering. *Bloody hell.* "Of course."

"Liar."

She felt the slow, hot roll of color cross her cheeks. "What could that possibly have to do with anything?"

"I don't know, but I have a feeling it means something. It's the first word I've heard dart out of that sassy mouth of yours that didn't sound like some damned speech." He tapped his head, starting to pace again. "What I wonder is, where are you in there?"

"I'm right here. Reasonable and—and judicious. Driven, perhaps, but not sassy—never sassy."

"You're full of piss and vinegar, all right. And some kinda' powerful determination to cause me problems when I have more than I can handle." He sighed. "And here I thought Ellie was difficult. Opening that woman's school and teaching God knows what in that shed behind Widow Wynne's, putting husbands and fathers in an uproar. Now you're here and it's ten times worse than it ever was before."

"Does every woman have to roll over like a dog begging for a scratch to its belly for men to value her?"

"That and a pretty face work well enough for me."

She hopped to her feet, her skirt slapping the desk. "You insufferable toad."

"Better that than a reckless nuisance."

"There's nothing wrong with feeling passionate about freedom, Constable Garrett. And I plan to let every woman in this town know it."

"If it means causing the kind of scene you caused today, you'll have to go through me first."

Savannah laughed, wishing it hadn't come out sounding so much like a cackle. "I've heard that several hundred times in the past. With no result, I might add."

"Guess you have." Halting before a tall cabinet that was scarred in more places than not, he went up on the toes of his boots and came back with a bottle. Another reach earned a glass. "With thirteen detentions, I can't say I'm surprised." She watched him pour a precise measure, tilt his head, and throw it back. "Did any of them happen to figure out you were working Irish underneath the prissy clothes and snooty manners?"

She lowered her chin, quickly, before he could spotlight her distress. *Working Irish.* A term she hadn't heard in years. Every horrible trait she possessed—willfulness, callousness, condescension—her father said came from the dirty Irish blood flowing through her veins. Her mother had been the immigrant who had trapped him in an unhappy marriage—a marriage beneath his station, thank you very much. And he had never let his family forget it.

"Would you like a medal for your perspicacious deduction, Constable?" she asked when she'd regained her composure.

He laughed and saluted her with his glass. "Heck, I don't even know what that means."

"*Astute,* Constable. Which you are—surprisingly so." She closed the distance between them and took the glass from his clenched fist, ignoring the warmth of his skin when their fingers touched. "May I?" she asked and drained the rest, liquid fire burning its way to her belly. Looking at him from beneath her lashes, she smiled. "The Irish like the taste of whiskey on their tongues, did you know that? O'Connor was my mother's maiden name. Her grandfather changed it to Connor when he came through Ellis Island. When my father kicked me out of his house the first time, I claimed the name, because he said if I must disgrace the family, I could disgrace her side of it. So I did." Handing the glass back, she said, "Now that you know one of my secrets, I should know one of yours."

He went very still, the arm that held the bottle dropping to his side. Before he pivoted on his heel, his face revealed such wretched grief that she felt the pain like a dart through her own heart. It wasn't enough to offer an apology for the offense. How could she when she wasn't sure what ground she had trespassed on?

Zach didn't speak another word that afternoon. Not even a parting threat about what he would do if he found her at the oyster factory the next morning. He didn't even look up from his cargo book when his brother arrived and was tersely asked to escort her home.

Her question about his past had sucked the very life from him.

"After she got released from jail, we had coffee she bought specially in New York City—about the best coffee I've ever tasted, too. And these hard, bready cookies that Savannah"—Lydia cupped her hand around her mouth—"I call her that now, you know—said she has to go to a place called Little Italy in New York City to buy. Can you imagine? And I'm to be her coleader. My goodness, I never would have thought anything this exciting would happen in Pilot Isle. Not in my lifetime."

"Your father?" Sallie Rutherford asked in a hushed whisper, pleating her skirt with shaky fingers.

"Oh, he'll shoot me dead when he finds out." Lydia fanned her warm cheeks, trying hard not to envision her father's certain fit of temper. "But I'm strong enough to handle him. Resilient, yes."

"And you're still planning to go tomorrow morning?"

She nodded. "With you."

"Oh, dear me, no. Dwight looks like he's sucking a lemon most days as it is. Do you want him to move back to his mother's for *good?*" Dwight Rutherford had married Sallie Smithe on the eve of his fortieth birthday, and any disturbance on the calm sea of his life sent him running back to his boyhood home and the welcoming arms of his mother.

"Savannah said there's nothing wrong with helping your fellow woman, Sallie. Why should we expect the men in this town to be happy about it, can you tell me that? It's a man's world; laws are men's laws; the government a man's government. We're merely set on changing that." Lydia felt sure Savannah would have been pleased to hear her parroting with such accuracy.

"Well, what about Dwight? And your father?"

"Oh, posh." Lydia chewed the last of her iced fruitcake with renewed enthusiasm. "They can take a big old leap off Pearson's dock for all I care."

"But the quilting meeting is—"

"Hang Nora and her weekly quilting meeting! I need you to get past the men your uncle will undoubtedly have guarding the gate. Plus, he won't curse too much with you in the room." Lydia dipped her linen napkin in a finger bowl on the table and patted the cool cloth against her lips. She ignored the beads of perspiration rolling down her back. Insufferable summers. "After the historical society calamity last year, you owe me. How can you even consider refusing?"

"Why, I never," Sallie sputtered with all the indignation of an affronted peacock.

Lydia drew a deep breath, testing the air to see if the roast she was cooking for dinner needed checking. "Savannah's going to unpack the rest of her belongings today. Books, pamphlets, materials to make signs. Paint and paper, all the way from New York. She also has badges for us to wear. Red with the words Freedom Fighter in gold right there emblazoned across it."

"Gold?"

"If you help us with this, you'll be a bona fide member of the Pilot Isle Ladies Freedom Fighters."

"My. . ." Sallie sank back against the plump cushions, a wistful look entering her eyes.

Lydia released a pent-up sigh, less frightened than good sense should allow. It was all—Savannah and the rally and the chance to live life for herself just this once—too rare an opportunity to let slip away. Besides, Zach Garrett wouldn't let them dillydally for more than a day or two. She needed to have her amusement now.

"I'll do it," Sallie surprised her by saying, quite clearly and without additional arm-twisting.

Lydia clapped her hands and giggled, giddy to the tips of her patent leather boots. "That is fine news. I'm thrilled and relieved. Gracious, now that that's settled, I must tell you what else happened at the jail. I shouldn't, but I simply must."

Sallie vaulted to a rigid position, eager for gossip. "I really shouldn't say . . ."

"Oh no, please do! It's been so dull around here since Noah Garrett ran off with that crazy Ellie Beaumont."

Too true, Lydia thought. The entire town had hungrily monitored the antics of Zach's youngest brother and Elle Beaumont, who, eccentric as she seemed to be, had snared the man she'd wanted since long before anyone could remember differently. And today, at the jail, the way Zach had looked at Savannah, just for a hint of a moment when he thought no one was looking . . .

Not with interest, no, no, *no.* More as though he'd been wound up like one of those newfangled toys she'd seen in the window of Dillon's Goods in Raleigh. *Agitated* was a good word for it, which was all well and fine because women often roused men to a fever pitch. Everyone knew that. It was just the way life operated. Except it never seemed to operate like that for Zach Garrett. Even when his beloved wife was alive, he'd been calm and capable and strong. Why, if Lydia felt half a heart in love with him it was *because* she'd never witnessed anything but calm, capable, and strong Constable Garrett—even with bodies from an ill-fated ship washing up on shore at his feet. That's who the entire town depended on.

She'd never seen him agitated. *Never.* Lydia wouldn't have guessed he had it in him.

Maybe there was something to this independence craze if it made a man sit up and take notice.

"Of course, this cannot go any further than this parlor," she finally said, tucking a wisp of damp hair beneath her bonnet. "And again, I shouldn't say, but I have to tell you that I've never seen such fire in Constable Garrett's eyes as I did today."

"*Fire*? Zach Garrett?" Sallie swallowed a bite of iced fruitcake too quickly and choked. "Are . . . are you sure? Why, he's so . . . *collected.*"

"Without a doubt," Lydia assured her friend. "And Savannah Connor lit the match."

Chapter Two

Remember, all men would be tyrants if they could.
—Abigail Adams

Having dinner at Constable Garrett's home the day after her detention, as he so elegantly referred to it, was the last thing Savannah wanted to do.

The *very* last, she amended as she leaned her bicycle against the front gate and did a quick review to make sure her clothing was in order. Damp from the ride, certainly, but in order. The evening promised to be awful enough without realizing midway through dinner that a bunched-up jacket had exposed the waistband of her bloomers to the constable's critical eye.

She lifted the covered plate from the bicycle's basket and started up the brick path, the front door looming before her. She halted at the bottom of the porch stairs long enough to record the sound of crickets in the bush beside her, and in the distance the rhythmic slap of waves against the shore. A peaceful place, Pilot Isle, beautiful and serene. If she didn't know herself better, she might imagine settling down in a town like this, in a place where she could grow old and make friends—true friends, not like the society ones she'd made in New York. Somewhere to stop on the boardwalk for idle conversation, a place where she would be a part of a community instead of simply part of a cause—which often felt like being a cog inside an enormous engine.

In the end, common sense won out. It made no sense to stand around waiting for a measure of comfort that clearly wasn't going to show. She had dealt with adversity all her life, starting with the moment her father got his first glimpse of her and realized, much to his disappointment, that a certain appendage was missing.

Her first knock was more forceful than necessary. The second sounded about right.

"Ma'am?"

She looked down as the door swung wide . . . and her heart dropped.

Constable Garrett's son. The boy was thin, tow-headed, and smiling fiercely. The kind of smile that spoke of capturing fireflies and dipping your toe in muddy puddles—innocence of a kind Savannah didn't remember and felt supremely uncomfortable being around.

"Coming in, ma'am?"

"Why, yes, I am," Savannah said and edged around him. "Rory, isn't it?"

"Yep," he replied around a mouthful of what looked to be yellow taffy. A scruffy-looking dog stood idle guard just behind him. "Everybody's here already, in the kitchen. Smell that? It's collards. They're good but they stink." He closed the door and gave her a little nudge down the hallway. "Pa said I could have a piece of candy before supper if I promised to eat all my string beans. Don't you reckon that's fair?"

Savannah halted beside a glowing gaslight. In return, Rory paused, tilting his head back and gazing at her through eyes identical to his father's. "Don't you reckon, huh?"

"Yes, well . . ."

"Pa said you don't fight fair, but you sure look like you do to me."

Savannah laughed softly, not bothering to cover it behind her hand. And surprise of surprises, Rory laughed with her, though of course he had no idea what she found so amusing. It felt, for the moment, somewhat *comfortable*. A new experience for a woman who had never had the opportunity to be around children.

The kitchen was warm and sweet-smelling, even with the underlying sour odor of cooking greens. The windows were open, yellow curtains with tiny daisies sucking in and out like a deep breath. Savannah stood on the threshold as long as she dared, letting Rory take the dish from her hands.

The scene shattered quite a few preconceived notions, starting with the revelation that her best friend, Marielle-Claire Garrett, a dedicated activist, was happily married. To a man unrelated to the cause. A professor of marine science, no less. In fact, Elle lay sprawled on her husband's lap, his arms wrapped around her waist as she struggled to rise. She laughed and punched his shoulder, fairly glowing with love. He grabbed her apron as she got to her feet, and tugged, forcing her to bend for a light kiss.

So it was true: she *was* happy.

Savannah glanced around the room and zeroed in on her nemesis. Zachariah, too, had an apron tied around his waist, one with pink rosettes and yellow stitching. In his hand he held a spatula, which he used to flip cornbread cakes and accentuate every third word or so. Hair a shade too long flicked his collar as he looked down when Rory slid Savannah's apple pie along the counter at his hip.

Zachariah glanced back then and caught her staring. And stared back.

He had a smudge of flour on the tip of his nose, a streak of it on his cheek. His clothes were pressed—Sunday attire, she guessed. His hair, black as night, shone from a recent combing. Had he actually dressed up for this evening? He must love Elle something awful, Savannah surmised. She shifted from one foot to the other, hating to acknowledge what the sight of him, surrounded by his family and standing in a kitchen that smelled so wonderful it made her yearn, did to her insides.

"Constable." She moved toward a table scattered with an assortment of pots, pans, and toys, making sure to keep her distance and her composure.

"Miss Connor," he said, the twist in his smile letting her know what he thought of their spending an evening together. In his home, with his son. No more than she thought of it, which she would thoroughly enjoy telling him. Except that Elle had planned this evening to introduce Savannah to everyone in her new family, and as a friend, Savannah must follow through.

She glanced in Elle's direction, discomfited to find all eyes trained upon her. And upon Constable Garrett.

The town gossips were obviously hard at work.

"Dinner smells wonderful," Savannah forced herself to say, with an affable nod in his direction. She would make it through this night or die trying.

Zach turned back to his cooking with a grunt.

Savannah felt her temper spark and begin to blaze. *Of all the rude—*

"Oh, I'm so thrilled to see you." Elle crossed the kitchen in record time, pulling Savannah into a fierce hug. She would not let her brother-in-law and her best friend, people she loved with all her heart, remain enemies. It just wouldn't do in a town the size of Pilot Isle. They could argue all they wanted at the jail or in front of the oyster factory; they could tear each other apart for the sake of independence and jurisdiction, but not at the first supper she hosted after her return from her honeymoon. "You look wonderful."

"You, too," Savannah said, stepping back. Elle had noticed before that Savannah didn't like being held; it made her wonder what her friend's life had been like as a child. "Really."

"I'm happy. Noah makes me happy." Elle looked over her shoulder and found her husband standing at his brother's side, teasing Zach about his flowery apron. After a brief series of introductions, Elle slipped her arm through Savannah's and said, "Let's take this outside." She led them out a back door and onto a wide porch, to a table set with blue-and-white dishes, many of them chipped. "Can you believe I'm saying that? A man has made me happy, my dear Vannie! *A man.* One of those uncompromising, inflexible beasts."

"I always believed a fruitful union was possible," Savannah said, seating herself across from Elle. "Many of the women working for the cause have wonderful marriages. Others . . ." Pouring a glass of water, she sipped slowly. "Others, well, not so wonderful."

Elle propped her elbows on the table and leaned forward. "But not you?"

"Me?"

"Don't you want to love someone, Vannie? And have him love you?"

"Ah, I recognize this. The stage where you're so blissfully delirious with love that you want *everyone* to have what you have."

Elle laughed and slid a saltshaker in a wide circle. "Would you think me demented if I agreed?"

"No, of course not. I'm delighted for you. You've spoken of nothing but this man since we met at university. On the quad near that old dogwood tree. Remember the conversations we used to have about your life here? Anyway"—she waved her hand to shoo away a persistent fly—"it isn't for me. Marriage isn't for me. Besides, it's not as if I haven't been courted. And experienced all the nonsense that goes along with that charming ritual."

"You can't mean Henry Bolton Finch the Third?"

Savannah smiled. "He had all the necessary equipment, didn't he?"

"Vannie, you were engaged for all of two days before he ran off with his butler's son."

"I was relieved, truth be told."

Elle sat back with a sigh. "I know. That's the problem. Suffering cats, I bet you never even kissed him."

"Oh, bother! Kissing is vastly overrated if you ask me."

A deep laugh sounded behind her. "Depends on who's doing it, Miss Connor."

Savannah tilted her head back, embarrassed, but damned if she'd show it. "I think I'd prefer to heed the testimony of a more reliable witness, Constable."

Zach shrugged and set a pan of biscuits on the table. As she watched him walk back into the house, she noted that his apron was absent. And that his trousers fit extremely well. "Ohhh, that man. What I wouldn't like to enlighten him about! Depends on who's doing it, my eye." She swiveled to find a wide smile crossing her friend's face. A glow of discovery lit Elle's cheeks. "Oh, no, you don't. Don't go getting any crazy ideas. I despise the man and he despises me. Don't you see that? I'd rather kiss a randy goat than pucker up to him."

"You think he's attractive."

Savannah pleated the tablecloth between her finger and thumb. "Well, yes, I suppose. A little. He's not the ugliest man I've encountered. So what?"

"So, every woman in town has been trying to get his attention since his wife passed away. Over two years now without a dash of success."

"He's capable and fair-minded. A leader, without doubt. Why wouldn't they try?"

"They're not interested in his mind, Vannie. Or his leadership skills, unless you mean the ones he'd use in bed."

Savannah looked across the table, into her friend's mirthful green gaze. "Is it so good?"

Elle nodded, humming beneath her breath. "Very."

"Worth all the trouble? The mess? The bother?" She had read about it, and in literal terms, it sounded a touch distasteful.

"More than you can imagine."

"But wouldn't it—I mean, couldn't the situation be unpleasant in some cases?"

"If you got the wrong man."

Smoothing the tablecloth with the heel of her hand, Savannah said, "But I don't like him."

"You like him enough."

"He doesn't like me."

Elle laughed softly. "He likes you enough."

Savannah glanced over her shoulder just to make sure no one was observing them, her stomach dancing. "What do you mean?"

"Vannie, let's speak plainly. I didn't wait until I got married. Noah's proposal came late in the day, do you understand? And I wouldn't change anything I did because it was wonderful."

"But you loved him."

"I do. And I did, yes. But love doesn't have to be there. For centuries, people have been experiencing passion without being in love. In fact, in this case, it would be a detriment. You don't want to get married, and Zach will never marry again." Elle nodded her head, fully convincing herself. "Why should two beautiful, loving people be lonely because of society's dictates when they could come to a reasonable agreement that would benefit them both?"

Savannah paused, never one to rally around society's decrees, especially when they hampered a woman's progress. "Do you honestly think sexual relations might aid my growth as a woman? Will I be stronger? I certainly never imagined I would *need* it."

"Mercy above, it's changed my entire outlook. I understand men much better than I used to, I can tell you that much. It simplifies the mystery."

"Truly?" Savannah finished the rest of her water and tapped the glass against the table. "That would be very helpful in my line of work."

"Plus, my *grandmère* always told me I needn't be married to experience passion."

"Ah, yes." Savannah nodded. "You're French. I sometimes forget."

The men stumbled out the door just then, their hands loaded with plates and tins, the smell of freshly baked biscuits drifting along behind them. They laughed and chattered, Rory dogging their heels.

All at once, Savannah was surrounded by men.

"You'll think about it?" Elle whispered.

Yes, she thought, noting the way Constable Garrett's shoulders flexed beneath his pressed cotton shirt. The way he smiled at his son, a flash of white teeth and firm lips.

She would.

The glass of wine had gone straight to her head.

A thick, sultry flavor colored her vision. The candles, sputtering in pools of wax and casting obliging shadows across the faces of those at the table, didn't hurt. In the balmy darkness, the sound of crickets chirping and the ocean rolling into the shore made a soothing distraction. The people surrounding the table looked beautiful: Elle and Noah, who touched with increasing frequency; Rory, who had long ago fallen asleep in his father's lap.

And Zachariah, most of all.

Savannah drew a deep breath, finishing the last of her wine. She needed to leave before she made a grave error and considered her friend's words too carefully. Before she could rise, Elle and Noah did, in one fluid movement, their hands linked.

"Let me get him to bed," Noah said, lifting Rory from Zach's arms and into his own. "Good night, Savannah."

Zach nodded, an amused tilt to his lips. "Fine. 'Night."

Elle grasped Savannah's hand as she passed. "I'll see you at the school in the morning. Zach will see you home."

" 'Course," he murmured, the smile still in place.

The tablecloth flipped in the breeze, the gentle snap filling the awkward silence. For a moment, the murmur of Rory's sleepy voice drifted from an upstairs window. Then it faded away.

"He's a bright child," she offered.

"Interesting observation from someone who doesn't like children."

She paused. The man didn't miss much. But it sounded terrible to admit the truth. "I like them; who doesn't like children? I simply am not *inured* to them. I was the youngest and have obviously never been married. Opportunities to fraternize with them have been limited."

"Fraternize. Inured," Zach said, draining his wine glass. "More of your substantial words."

"Is there something wrong with speaking well, Constable?"

Zach laughed, a lock of hair dropping across his brow, his gray eyes almost lost to the shadows. "About as much wrong with that as there is with enjoying kissing."

"I didn't say I thought there was anything wrong with enjoying it. I merely said I thought it was overrated."

"*It* being kissing, I take it?" he asked, leaning in, his elbows sliding onto the table for the first time that evening. She could have taken the man to a presidential dinner and he would have fit in.

"Yes. Kissing. Overrated."

"I could change your mind," Zach said, surprising the hell out of them both. Why would he take something as simple as this banter as a challenge? "I don't know that I want to, but I feel right sure I could."

"How arrogant. How typically male."

"I suppose." He shrugged and reached for the wine bottle. "More?"

She nodded, frowning now. "How do you know you could change my mind? It's been a long time since you . . . well . . ."

"Over two years." The pain was there, an ache in his chest he imagined he would feel every time he thought of Hannah. And he thought of her every day. Dreamed of her about as often. But lately, maybe only in the past week, he'd begun to realize that his life had not ended with his wife's. He either had to die or start living again.

Because of Rory, there really was no choice at all.

"Were you happy?"

Glancing across the table, he watched the flickering candlelight wash over Savannah. A soft glow highlighted the mass of shiny chestnut curls she was not capable of controlling. Long lashes brushed her fine-boned cheeks as she blinked slowly, watching him watch her.

With those looks, it was no wonder the men in town were buzzing about her.

"I was happy," he said, letting the wine trickle down his throat, hoping it would dull his heartache.

"What was she like?"

Zach closed his eyes and rested his head on the back of the chair, remembering. The crash of waves in the distance and the rustle of pine branches in the breeze soothed him. A little. "She was fragile. Like an angel made of glass. The kind they blow until it's so thin you think it'll break if you touch it." He had often been afraid to touch her, to hug her with even half his strength, but that was far too personal a memory to share. "There wasn't a cross bone in her body or an evil thought in her head. She was good . . . kind." He blinked, refocused. Savannah had moved forward in her chair, her arms propped on the table, her green eyes gleaming in the candlelight. "But she wasn't strong. I knew when I asked her to marry me that I would have to take care of her, that it wouldn't be the other way around. I accepted that; I wanted it."

"You wanted her."

Yes. He had wanted Hannah, had loved her intensely—something he had not felt for a woman since. But as the years of their marriage passed, and she seemed to wither under his care, he had often questioned whether he was the right man for her. If *any* man could be the right man for her. At the very end, he had almost decided that staying in the nurturing care of her family would have been best. He was a man, after all, and he had needed certain things—things Hannah had given freely but without genuine interest. Without fire or enthusiasm. It horrified him, made him feel guilty as hell, to think he'd loved a woman so completely, yet had very little in common with her in bed.

Conversely, the woman sitting across from him— uppity, proud, and sassy—was everything Hannah had not been. He sure as heck didn't like her . . . but he liked *watching* her. Watching swift, joyful smiles cross her face, hearing her gusts of uninhibited laughter and the way her mirth pressed her bosom against her crisp shirtwaist. She enjoyed life, or so it looked to him. He even imagined she might be an entertaining companion, maybe even *pleasant* on a good day. Just when he felt safe thinking that, she would turn and deliver a crushing line of superiority and irritate him so badly he wanted to spit. On her.

But she was intriguing, all right. He could not deny that.

"What about you, Miss Connor? Never felt the urge to shackle yourself to a man for the rest of your life?"

She straightened in her chair, her spine locking one vertebra at a time until she sat as rigid as a dried-up schoolmarm. "Me?" With a scant laugh, she took a hasty sip of wine.

Zach smiled, sinking low in his chair, balancing his glass on his stomach. *So, she doesn't want to talk about herself.* "It's a customary question, isn't it? I thought most women wanted marriage." Might as well enjoy her discomfort.

She sniffed. "I'm not most women, Constable."

No kidding, he wanted to say, eyeing her over the rim of his glass.

"Furthermore, I have a calling which keeps me decisively engaged for most of my waking—"

"Busy."

She started, sliding forward a bit. "Pardon me?"

"Busy. Your calling keeps you *busy.* 'Actively engaged' sounds so" —he took a thoughtful sip— "frosty."

"Frosty?"

"Cool."

"Cool?" If he could see her well enough, he'd bet money her cheeks were blazing. "Constable, I'm neither frosty or cool, or, or—"

"Frigid."

Flattening her palms on the table, she rose to her feet, her shadow washing over him. "I'm not frigid."

He paused, feeling an undeniable urge to challenge her. But no, he couldn't do that. Could he? "Prove it," he said, confirming that the wine had indeed distorted his reasoning. He and this temperamental woman had vowed to make each other's lives hellish unless they came to some agreement about the women working in the oyster factory. True, but this was more than he could honorably put *any* woman—

"Okay," she whispered. "I will."

He lifted his head, jerked ramrod straight in his chair, searching Savannah's face for any indication that she was bluffing. Her clothes, her skin, her features were all obscured in gray and black, giving him no clue.

"Are you . . . joking?" His voice sounded as dry as day-old toast.

She released a pent-up breath and started to edge around the table toward him. "You said you could change my mind. Perhaps I can change yours."

"Now, wait a blessed minute, Miss Connor." He waved her back with his glass, sloshing a drop or two on his trousers in the process. "You must know that I'm not a marrying man. Never, ever again."

She halted, surprising the heck out of him by throwing her head back and laughing, her body curving with it. It was a man's laugh and darned appealing, at that. "Oh, heavens, Constable, is that a call for marriage in *your* world? I've never been kissed well enough to get me in front of a preacher." Covering her mouth with her hand, she gasped, "Must be some—what would you call it—*mighty fine* kissing to make two people take vows."

"Tarnation," he said, feeling a frown bunch his brow, "it *could* be good. That's not out of the realm of possibility, you know."

"Prove it," she said around another burst of laughter. "Prove it, prove it, prove it."

He rubbed a hand across his chin, debating the

wisdom of having any more wine. Had he actually thought he was in control of this situation? "I don't know. This all seems crazy to me."

She gulped a breath and patted her chest. "My, from the fantastic entertainment I've witnessed in this town, I'm sure it does." Taking a step forward, she held out her hand, as if she were trying not to startle him or something. It was downright insulting. "Rightly, Constable, you asked me first. And I'm willing to go the distance to solve a disagreement."

"I bet you're always willing," Zach muttered, wondering if he'd lost his mind sitting in his backyard on a lovely twilit evening. Gambling with a woman who wouldn't back down if a tiger had her latched in its jaws.

"Are you willing?"

Through the shadows, he found her gleaming eyes, her slightly curved mouth. "No, it's too reckless. Too irresponsible."

"You're sounding like a father. Or a constable, Constable."

"I'm both, Miss Connor."

He watched her lips tilt and flow into a glorious smile. "Rory's in bed, safe and sound. The townspeople are in bed, safe and sound. And you're here, with a pragmatic woman who can take care of herself. Two adults and one magnificent challenge."

"More like a dare," he said and, damn it all, drained his glass.

She took a step closer, until her skirt brushed his knee. "Call it a dare if you like."

"No." His resolve slipped a notch when she crouched before him, the pleasing angles of her face flooding into view. She was much, much too tempting.

"I'll do it all. You don't have to participate. That should be enough to prove my case."

"I wasn't serious when I said that. I'm sure you're not, hell, *frigid*."

She leaned in, her hands sliding along the arms of the chair, her face fading out of view as it closed in on his. A scent, provocative and earthy, stole in with his stuttered breath. "You see, Constable, I'm always serious. And . . ." He watched her moisten her lips, so near he could almost taste her. "Close your eyes. I've heard that's the way it's done."

Chapter Three

The brain is not, and cannot be, the sole or complete organ of thought or feeling.
                              —Antoinette Brown Blackwell

Savannah held her breath, waiting, her pulse tapping against her temples in a potent rhythm, her fingers trembling where they gripped the chair. Who was this woman? This boastful, immodest woman challenging the most attractive man in town to a sexual dual?

Zachariah Garrett was right: she *was* crazy.

A moment passed; then he closed his eyes. *Dear God,* he closed his eyes.

She moved in, nearly resting in his lap, all the while keeping his lips in view. They looked firm and very nicely shaped. Harder than hers, most assuredly.

Closer. His breath smelled of wine and the cigarette she'd seen him smoke earlier in the evening. Pleasant, that, too. Nothing off-putting.

The gentle rise and fall of his chest beneath his pressed shirt. Whiskers on his chin and his cheek.

Long lashes, a shade or two lighter than his midnight black hair. Thank God those penetrating eyes
of his weren't trained on her.

And that it really *was* the way she'd heard it was
done.

She eased down, a lock of her hair falling forward
and skimming his cheek. She reached to lift it away
and found herself running her fingers along his
jaw, the edge of his ear, his eyebrow, almost as if
she sought to memorize the shape of his features,
the feel of his skin. Cupping his face, she brushed
her lips across his, her brain buzzing, her blood
thumping in her ears. His mouth was warm and
unyielding, just as he'd promised, the stubble
scraping her chin and cheek coarse and unfamiliar,
yet somehow quite agreeable.

She drew back, releasing a pent-up breath. A
quiver of movement in his shoulders as his hand
flexed, wrapping tightly around the stem of the
wineglass. Other than that, he gave no intimation
that he had felt her touch. Or enjoyed it in the
least. Perhaps she had done something wrong.

She tilted her head and moved in again, instinct-
ively understanding that this would bring her
closer, the fit more natural and possibly more *correct*. Furthermore, she felt a rabid inquisitiveness
to really know the feel of a man's lips on hers,
something to replace her less-than-considerable
accumulation of experience. Indeed, much was
based on imagination and hearsay rather than
actual practice. A brief taste wasn't nearly sufficient.

Lowering her lashes, she swallowed once, slid
her hand to the back of Zach's neck, and pulled
him toward her until their mouths grazed. Like
pieces of a puzzle, she maneuvered until the fit
was precise. She wasn't sure what to do with her

tongue; she'd read enough wanton novels to know she needed to use it. Once, twice, she rolled it across his lips, making sure to delve into each tucked corner, each ridge, each edge. It was a moist and much more pleasant experiment than she had expected. And for a time, this alone satisfied her.

However, there was more. She'd read that, too.

Carefully, she threaded her fingers through his hair and dabbed at the corners of his mouth, then along the seam, begging admittance. Coaxing his lips apart. He smelled faintly of starch, wine, and smoke. Delicious. Enticing. She felt his heartbeat thudding beneath her breast, felt hers race to match the rhythm. Finally charitable, he opened his lips, enough to allow her inside. The sweet, wet taste of him flowed inside her mouth. Further melting her with pleasure.

Although Savannah wouldn't go so far as to claim he participated.

So she tried harder to engage him, swaying against his chest, the heat of his skin burning through the layers of cloth covering her breasts. She explored the smooth edges of his teeth, the occasional brush of his tongue fairly shaking the ground beneath her.

More.

It was all she could think, all she could envision. And he knew. He *knew* . . . but would not relent. Her frustration built until she felt a dizzying wave of anger. Untangling her fingers from his hair, she shoved away from him.

"So you'll give up that easy," he murmured, his breath batting her cheek. "I'm surprised."

"Go to hell," she whispered, the weakness of her voice disquieting, especially when his sounded smooth as butter.

He laughed, his eyelids hanging low. "Come

back here. I'll try this time." He made a quick cross over his heart. "I promise."

On trembling legs, she pushed off the back of his chair and tried to stand.

Laughing again, Zach wrapped his arm around her waist and lifted them to their feet. Stunned, she stood in his embrace, her gaze searching his. She was unsure of what he wanted, what contest he hoped to win. Or whether they were still involved in any contest at all.

"I thought two were playing this game, Miss Connor." He trailed his finger down the edge of her jaw, cupping it gently. "Was I mistaken?"

Before she could answer—could unravel the muddled thoughts in her head enough to answer— he dipped his head and took possession, the arm at her waist clamping tight and bringing her flush against his body. She was a tall woman, but he was taller. She was fit, on the lean side, but he was harder. So solid, so muscularly sturdy in a manner his clothes deceptively hid. Being held by him, kissed, and *mastered,* taken under and swept away, enthralled her in a way she—an independent woman if nothing else in this life—could not have understood until forced to understand. From the tips of her toes to the ends of her hair, finally, a man's strength dominated her.

Suddenly, she understood why women wanted so deeply. Why they wanted *him.* If they sensed even one tenth of his passion, his power, his vitality, they would break his door down to get to him.

And this, she learned as quickly as any pupil could, was what had been missing before: Zachariah Garrett's full participation. In all fairness to the dare, she locked her arms around his neck and consented to a draw.

He murmured something low and unintelligible,

his wineglass dropping to the grass with a soft thump. The arm around her waist tightened, the other climbing, his fingers delving into her loose chignon and tilting her head as he deepened the kiss, drawing down on her bottom lip and sucking. Instinct had her following his lead, shifting to better accommodate, parrying each thrust of his tongue with her own, rising on the tips of her toes to better sink into him, to gorge herself in vast, voracious gulps. The frantic nature of their joining melted her stiff posture and her cocksure bearing, rolling through her in a languid, glorious wave of sensation and recognition. It was a peculiar time to realize she had built her sense of self around an erroneous ideal.

She was no different from other women.

He walked her backward in a frantic move; her bottom bumped the table, the wine bottle tipping and rolling into the grass. Still he hung on, challenging, demanding. In response, she plunged, heedlessly, recklessly attempting to sate her hunger. She realized that the more she took, the more she would need.

Bowing her head to break contact, she unlocked her arms from around his neck and shoved against his shoulders with all her pitiable strength. The table, lodged just beneath her bottom, kept her legs from liquefying like hot wax and spilling her at his feet.

He pulled back enough for a stray shaft of moonlight to illuminate the feral look in his eyes, the dull wash of color sweeping his cheeks. Their chests rose and fell in double-time, as if they had run a race. "I hope you're not expecting an apology, Miss Connor." The arm circling her waist tensed once before dropping, releasing her. "Not when you were knee-deep in the ring with me."

Edging away, she rubbed her hand over her tender lips, then up to the tangled droop of hair hanging past her shoulder. What a mess she must look. She had never been any good at putting it in those obtuse chignons. "This isn't"—she blew out a breath and edged a bit further away from him—"a scuffle. There's no ring. We're not adversaries. At least"—she waved her hand through the air, avoiding his piercing gaze—"not in *this*."

"Damn it," he said in a hoarse voice, his words clipped, "I knew you were trouble from the first minute I set eyes on you. A man has to go with intuition when he has nothing else. Gut feelings aren't reserved only for pretty little things in bonnets."

Crossing her arms over her chest, she stared at the ground, trying to ignore the way his voice made her stomach clench. She'd never liked the way he talked before now. The shaky tremors running through his words fortified her. For the first time in her life, she'd obviously had an amorous effect on a man—a rather positive outcome, as it was. Except that the man in question seemed moderately angry. Certainly, she had made men angry a thousand times before. Angry enough for them to throw her in a jail cell. Only, when a woman has a man look at her the way Zachariah Garrett had for a moment or two through the lazy shadows of a summer evening, she doesn't want him to snap right back to anger.

"I'm not trouble," she finally said, and by placing the table between them she gathered the nerve to look him in the eye. "A certain *joie de vivre*, perhaps, which has unquestionably embroiled me in diverse skirmishes in the past. I wouldn't—"

"*Stop.*" He halted his brisk pace between two towering pine trees and shot a sharp-eyed frown her way. "For the love of God, please. Stop." Bending down, he grasped his fallen wineglass, turning it in his hands. "Always, in my experience, troublemakers never know they're troublemakers. They go along causing problems and making everyone else's life hell, all the time thinking their actions are fine and dandy with the rest of us. Not a consequence out there that they're concerned about. I make my living dealing with them. Pilots who run aground because their bellies are too full of drink to steer clear of the shoals, men who can't handle their finances so I'm forced to auction off their houses and break up their families, busting up brawls every time payday rolls around. That's what I do in this town: clean up messes." He shoved to his feet, his eyes blazing. "So excuse me if I swear on the holy book that I can spot a menace at ten paces. And you, ma'am, are a menace to any unmarried man in this town. And by the way, I don't have a ghost of an idea what you said to me in French."

"Why, well . . ." She gestured broadly, frustration blocking clear thought. "I'm so glad to see you never have to clean up your own messes, Constable. My, how fortunate."

"I have plenty of my own, don't you worry. My life's been full of 'em. But just now, in the last months, since Noah came home to us, things are starting to settle. Starting to look right. You"—he pointed the glass at her—a rather lethal jab in her opinion—"are not going to put me on a path to destruction."

She stalked around the table, forgetting her need for a protective barrier. "How could I possibly set you on a path to destruction?"

He raised a brow, gesturing mildly. "I'm not going to marry again, Miss Connor. I did it once and it failed. *I* failed."

"I don't understand."

He shook his head. "You don't have to."

She halted, uncertain. Was he considering going further with this experiment? It was an intriguing notion, one that had her heart skipping beats, her palms perspiring. "I'm not looking for marriage, either. I have my own funds, my own life. I have no need for a husband. That is without question. As to the other, I won't tell. Discretion is key." In the event he wasn't talking about the future, she added, "What happened tonight is between us and no one else."

"Someone will find out. In a town this size, they always do." He tugged his hand through his hair, tussled locks falling back across his brow immediately after. "I have my son to consider and, blessed Lord, *you* to consider. People can't feel safe coming to me if my life is a great big mess."

"I know what I'm doing."

He rolled his eyes at that. She couldn't summon enough evidence to disagree.

"Granted, perhaps I don't know precisely what I'm doing, but I know who's responsible." She walked forward, stopping before him. "And it isn't you."

He lifted the glass to his nose and sniffed, probably wishing for another drink. "How do you figure that?"

"My life is my choice. Your life is your choice."

His straight, white teeth flashed as he released a sarcastic gust of laugher. "My life hasn't been *my* choice since I was twenty years old."

She didn't understand what he meant; she didn't know much about Zachariah Garrett other than his name and his occupation. Nothing but the trivial bits and pieces about the Garrett brothers that Elle had written to her over the years. If Savannah wanted more information, pressure was not the way to get it. He didn't play father to an entire town because he was a man easily led. "Then you're owed," she said with a small, negligent shrug.

He picked up her wineglass and licked a drop of wine from the rim, his eyes finding her over the edge. For some reason, his half-lidded look brought back the feel of his hands, his teeth nipping her bottom lip. "That so?"

"If you haven't ever done anything completely for yourself"—she moved in close enough to catch the peppery scent of his shaving lotion—"isn't it about time? I believe I'm due as well."

He lowered the glass. "Are we talking about the same thing here?"

She rocked back on her heels. "I agree that the details may require a spot of negotiation."

He laughed then, full-bellied, his glossy hair falling into his face. "Yeah? I'm not at all sure we're talking about the same thing; I'm not at all sure you even have a clue. But damned if I'm not willing to *negotiate.*"

Smiling, she smoothed her hand down her shirtwaist, strangely pleased. "Fine. Excellent, we're getting somewhere." Tapping her lip, she stepped out of reach, fearful she might give in to temptation and beg him for another kiss if she wasn't careful. "How about tomorrow morning? I'll stop by your office at, say, eleven. I'm having lunch at the restaurant across the way at noon with my committee. An hour should be enough time."

"Can't. Prior engagement."

She glanced his way, studying him to see if he was teasing her. "Truly?"

He nodded his head, but not before she caught the amused glint in his eyes. "Truly."

"Can you reschedule?"

"Hyman Carter is heading to Raleigh on business next week, and tomorrow morning is the only time he can stop by to discuss his situation."

She halted, whipping around so quickly she stumbled. "Hyman Carter? You're meeting with that man without alerting me? I must inform my committee."

Reaching out, he tipped her chin high with his finger. "I'm alerting you, Irish. But no committee. You show alone or not at all. And bring the sensible Miss Connor you've been telling me so much about, not the hellion." He blinked, gazing beyond her for a moment before refocusing. "Better yet, save her for the *negotiation*."

"What time?" Savannah asked, drawing back, breathless and disconcerted. Too disconcerted to reprimand him for using that childish and highly inappropriate moniker.

He shrugged, back to his good-natured self. "Ten or so."

They walked home in silence, her bicycle standing guard between them. Not an indecent touch passed. Nothing indecent at all occurred, aside from the graphic images exploding like last July's fireworks in her mind. Zach had refused to let her travel the two blocks to her rented room alone. Just imagine the nights she had walked alone in New York! If his gesture hadn't made her feel so warm, she would have laughed.

"Why," she asked as Zach stood outside the gate of the boarding house, waiting for her to climb the porch steps, "did you tell me about the meeting? I thought you weren't interested in helping me. I'm not sure I understand."

"Got to understand everything, huh?" He hesitated, clearly debating how much he should reveal. Finally, with a sigh, he closed the gate and started down the rutted path that served as a sidewalk. Stopping at the junction with his lane, the gleam of a gas streetlamp flooded over him, throwing his arresting features into dull relief. "Why, Miss Connor? I guess because your heart's in the right place, even if your lovely little head is in the clouds. Can't much fault anyone for being naive, though, now can I? Even a Yankee do-gooder."

She stayed on the porch, letting the gentle ocean breeze wrap its fingers around her, watching Zachariah Garrett disappear into the shadows. She wasn't sure whether to be affronted or gratified by his comments. If she was honest with herself, both. The man seemed to pull her in utterly divergent directions.

But she was smiling as she closed the door behind her.

Seeing his son take his first breath had been the most astounding feeling of Zach's life. Watching that miniature face contort and burst into color, hearing the impressive bellow roll from minute-old lungs. Of course, he had fallen in love immediately, forever.

It had also been the most frightening day of his life.

Tucking the sheet around Rory's scrawny shoulders, he moved the boy's thumb away from his mouth. It was an occasional habit, nothing more, but Zach had read an article recently about it changing the shape of a child's mouth. No good there.

Walking to the window, he lifted it higher, letting a nice gust of air into the humid room. Lord, if it wasn't getting hotter every day. He paused at the door, rechecked his direction, and settled into the rocking chair in the corner of the room. Moonlight spilled across the end of the bed, his feet, and lap. Resting his head on the back of the chair, he rocked in time to the sound of a cricket chirping somewhere close. It could be hiding in the room, for all he knew.

Hannah had lulled Rory to sleep every night when he was a baby right here, until he got too big and wanted only to scramble around on the floor, dragging his butt and legs behind him, chewing on every nasty bug or dust ball he could get his grubby hands on. Other than requiring that he watch what he dropped on the floor—something as simple as a button could be a dreadful hazard—and see that his son ate regularly and had clean diapers on his bottom as often as a person could make that happen, that first year or two of Rory's life had not presented any great difficulty. Then Rory's mind had opened up and the questions started. Excruciating questions. Where did stars come from? Why is the sky blue and not orange? What are oyster shells made of? By God, Zach had wished for Noah then—the professor, as everyone in town except his family called him—to ease the burden of lying all the time about stuff. Making up answers left and right. Caleb wasn't even as smart as Zachary was, so he was of no use in those instances at all.

Yes sir, it was a big responsibility raising a child. To Zach's way of thinking, there was no bigger and no more rewarding an experience. Unfortunately, it offered the best chance in life to suffer as if you were being roasted in Satan's den. Anything that hurt Rory hurt Zach ten times worse.

She had wondered—this odd woman he had kissed earlier in the evening—why he cautiously considered taking risks. She wasn't a parent and therefore couldn't understand that the weight of the world rested on his shoulders. The weight of *his* world. Zach glanced toward the bed, resisting the urge to tuck Rory's foot back under the covers or trace the shape of his toes just for the simple pleasure of touching him when the boy wasn't aware of it.

Zach's family, his entire *meaning,* lay snuggled beneath those covers, breathing in raspy little-boy breaths, probably dribbling spittle on the blue pillowcase, his fist clenched around a tattered rag doll.

Savannah Connor couldn't know that Zach had cried so at his wife's funeral because his family would never grow any larger than he did, because his wife and unborn child lay in the nicest pine box he could find on short notice in the dead of winter.

He *had* loved her. Of course, he'd been the worst sort of husband for her: too full of passion and eagerness and dreams. But he'd loved her, soul-deep. For pity's sake, he'd tried the best he knew how to care for her, to shelter her. Just as he had tried to do the best by his brothers after his mother passed away. By blind chance, he had come home that month, a pilot who could navigate every inlet and shoal in the Banks with his eyes closed, a young man seeking to grab the world by the short hairs, as cocky and irresponsible and fun-loving as any young man of twenty had a right to be.

Yep, he'd come home to a dying mother and two adolescent boys in need of he didn't know what, one with a temper he couldn't control, the other with a mind he didn't understand.

That had ended his cocky irresponsibility quicker than a fist against a brick wall.

He hadn't missed the rowdy life. Living in the

rank galley of a boat, eating high on the hog right out of port, then watching the supplies dwindle until he'd kill for a cracker that wasn't covered with mold. Working all hours until his back ached and his knees locked, staring at the damned horizon so long his eyes crossed.

For all the discomfort, a time or two he had missed the effortlessness of making decisions for *one*. The lack of a struggle to make sure he made the right decision.

So he had settled in Pilot Isle for good. He'd married Hannah and along came Rory. And his life was no longer his at all. Even if he loved them with everything he had to give—and he did—Rory, Hannah, Noah, and Caleb had exacted a price. A price he was willing to pay until the day he kicked.

Still, a price.

Then, today, surprise of all surprises, Savannah Connor—bold and brash and maybe a touch crazy—had offered him a mirror. When he'd looked into it, he saw that fun-loving young man staring back.

Lord knows, the temptation to take what she offered seemed more than he could refuse. Touching her had been like standing inside one of Edison's bulbs: the glow had dazzled, warmed, and enchanted him. He had been Zach Garrett and nothing more, kissing a woman for the unadulterated joy of it, feeling her nails lightly scratching his neck, her firm breasts flattening against his chest, her sweet breath stealing into his throat.

Lord, he'd forgotten the pleasure of a woman's touch.

Zach glanced at the door as the hinges squeaked. Just Tiger coming in for the night. He patted the dog's head as he passed, not bothering to stop him from jumping onto Rory's bed and plopping down with a tired sigh.

Rubbing his eyes with the heels of his hands, he breathed deeply of little boy, paint, and dog, wondering if Savannah understood the road she had started down. It was a treacherous road, a ruinous road for an unmarried woman. He was a bit older, and wiser by far, even though she was from New York City. The good deed would be to turn her away. Right now. *Tomorrow.*

Only, the wicked side of him, a side no one in Pilot Isle would have guessed existed, was hard at work building a wall around good intentions as Zach sat there wasting the night away. He had not been lonely those piloting years; he had learned things he had never considered bringing into his marital bed. Hannah had been too fragile, too sweet and innocent.

But Savannah Connor, oh, boy. That was another case altogether. Untried, he had no doubt. Gullible in her own way, he reckoned, but sakes, was she fearless. A fearless pain in the ass. He laughed as he thought it. Just as he'd once been.

Was it crazy to imagine he could find that young man with her, not for love's sake but simply for *life's* sake? For *his* sake and his alone?

Noah and Caleb told him, sometimes daily, that he had to move on, remarry and have more children. He didn't want that. He couldn't love that deeply or give of himself in that way again. Yet, he was tired, dog tired, of apologizing for wanting to live.

Smiling softly, he closed his eyes, imagining what it was going to be like *negotiating* with that hellion. . . .

And since he'd decided to take her up on her life-and-choices challenge, imagining whether she'd let him negotiate her right out of her fancy clothes.

Chapter Four

Getting along with men isn't what's truly important. The vital knowledge is how to get along with a man, one man.

—Phyllis McGinley

The next morning, Savannah lost her train of thought about the time she noticed the teensy half-inch scar running alongside Zachariah Garrett's bottom lip. It was pink, fresh enough to mean he had received the wound recently. If she hadn't known the man better, she might guess it was a brawling injury. Too wide for a razor nick.

"Miss Connor, are you still with us?"

She blinked and pinched her thigh where her hand rested beneath her parasol. Daydreaming during a meeting about the atrocities at the oyster factory. What would Miss Anthony, her mentor and the first woman to see any value in her as a freedom fighter, think of that? She would think that Savannah had unearthed her wayward impetuosity; that's what.

"I'm sorry; my mind drifted. Come again?"

Zach slid a dawdling look her way, the lazy grin on his face making her want to crack her parasol atop his head. He could kiss her feet and that's all he would kiss, the charlatan. He was no more a slow-talking Southern gentleman than she was a monkey's uncle. She had sat in New York state courtrooms with less gifted mediators. Without him, Mr. Carter would have been a blind man swimming in a sea of sharks.

"Mr. Carter has agreed to review his policies and submit a pay increase for female employees to his partner," Zach said, bringing her back to the issue at hand.

"How much?" She retrieved paper and a pen from her reticule. Licking the tip of her pen, she poised it over the page. "I'd like your hourly proposal and your monthly. I assume full-time workers will be compensated more copiously than part-time. This agreement will include my suggestion for minimal rest periods for expectant mothers, I take it?"

Hyman Carter glanced from Zach to her and back, a beseeching grimace drawing the edges of his mouth to his chin. Tufts of reddish-blond hair stood on end on his head, giving him a look of complete astonishment. Or perhaps it was her. She did occasionally have that impact on people.

"Gentlemen?" Tapping her pen against her knee, she smiled at Mr. Carter and kept herself from making a nasty gesture with her finger at the capable Constable Garrett.

"Hyman?" Zach coughed and dug a discreet elbow into Mr. Carter's ribs.

Hyman swallowed and fidgeted, knocking the toe of a polished boot against the worn plank floor. "Uh, well, you see, ma'am, Miss Connor, I'm going to have to sit a spell and figure on this. Draw up papers and talk with Mr. Henry in Raleigh. Mighty important decisions, all of these. Mighty important. And, well, uh . . ." He twisted his hat in his fist until she presumed he'd crushed it beyond repair. "I would like to keep these, um, talks in place, seeing as Mr. Henry and I wouldn't like any bad newspaper reports, you see. And everything we're discussing *is* for the good of the workers at C and H Oyster Producers. I'm not lost there."

"Indeed they are, Mr. Carter." Making a notation on her pad, she calculated a fair date in her head. "How about setting the next meeting for the fifteenth? That gives you two weeks to discuss changes with your partner and draw up any plans we need to review."

"Just us, you mean." He gave his hat another twist. "No, um, no committee of darned women or anything like that."

Savannah smiled, feeling the hook sink deep in Hyman Carter's hide. "No committee, no reporters, no further rallies. *If,* and I do want to stress the determined nature of my pledge, *if* changes are made." Sliding her writing materials into her reticule, she spanked the end of her parasol on the floor and rose, shaking her skirt for good measure. "Soon, of course, though I'm sure that's unspoken. We can't have women going into that factory for much longer with conditions as they are today."

Zach's gaze found hers. *You're winning; no need to kill the man,* it said.

"Thank you for meeting so promptly, Mr. Carter," she offered as he stomped past, huffing like a steam engine in overload. "I enjoyed it tremendously," she called as he skipped down the walk leading to the street, his coattail flapping. Turning her head, she smiled frostily as she passed Zach on the way out, proving she could be as gracious as any woman.

"Whoa, Irish, where in the world do you think you're headed?"

Kicking the door shut, he took two steps back and propped his bottom against it, crossing his arms to further the intimidation. His wide-legged stance, the way he held himself in perfect balance, told her he wasn't about to forget their negotiation. A sizzling burst of heat lit her stomach and rose to her face in seconds while she decided that she, wine, and Zachariah Garrett didn't mix. "I'm sure I have no idea what you mean."

He grinned, gesturing with his elbow to her face. "Oh, yes, you do. That flush in your cheeks tells me you know exactly what I mean."

"I've decided to renege on my offer due to your unscrupulous practices."

"Unscrupulous?" He puckered his lips and seemed to think on that. "Oh, oh, yes, I see. Because I didn't let you chew poor Hyman up and spit him out like a piece of gristle, I wasn't being honest." His gaze drilled into her, and it lacked all the rosy promise of a moment before. "You think because I talk slower than you do that I think slower? Irish, you've got an awful lot to learn about people."

"I can't help if I object."

"Object to what?"

"To your brazenness and your indolent grins, to your unhurried answers and your pointed observations. To your assumption of rightfully being in charge, even if you rightfully *are*. To the dreadful nickname *Irish*." She also objected to the slim fit of his trousers and the way he left two buttons on his shirt unbuttoned, allowing a patch of crisp black hair to show. And why did the hair on his head always look as though some woman had been running her hands through it? It was also a shade longer than was fashionable. However, she was charitable—he didn't have a wife, after all—so she would omit those grievances.

Laughing softly, Zach pushed off the door and headed for her, his stride seemingly listless when she knew it—knew *him*—to be anything but. She glanced around, drawing her parasol before her like a sword.

"Only one door. Better for keeping prisoners in, you know."

"Am I a prisoner?" she whispered, swallowing past a dry throat as he advanced, closing in on her.

Gripping her wrists between the fingers of one hand, he lowered the parasol and let it drop to the floor. The other hand rose, tilting her head until she couldn't help but stare into his face. "Do you want to be my prisoner, Miss Connor? Seeing as I know the town constable so well, I could probably make arrangements."

The blood beneath her skin heated to such an extent that Savannah feared her veins would melt. "I'm not sure . . . what I want."

His pupils expanded at her words; his eyelids slid low to hide it. His fingers traced her lower lip, her jaw, the rim of her ear.

"What are you doing?" she murmured on a soft sigh.

"I'm beginning the negotiation process."

She closed her eyes and, helpless, slid into his touch. "*This* is negotiating?"

"No," he said, a hot rush of air sweeping her lips. "This is."

The kiss wasn't slow this time. Or lackadaisical. Or hers to control.

After debating with the man all morning, she

understood his motives. He'd set out to prove a
point. His mouth shifted, settled . . . *persuaded*. With
regard to what, she didn't hope to comprehend.
She simply let the blossoming fever spread.

He had her. Though it wasn't fair the tactics he
used. Nor was it fair that he counted the seconds.
But damn it, was it fair that Savannah Connor presented every temptation known to man, and a couple of new ones besides? Unholy, that's how
wonderful she tasted. Warm and welcoming. Lush.
One part saint and two parts sinner. Zach breathed
her in, her scent potent enough to scatter his
thought *and* purpose.

Forty-five. Forty-five seconds more. Cupping her
cheek, he deepened the kiss, drawing her tongue
into play, teaching her what he liked and trying,
from the way she moaned, to record what she did.
If this went on longer than a minute—and dear
Lord, he wanted it to go on longer than a minute—
he would lose his advantage. That was the most he
could promise and hope to come up for air with
any sanity left.

Savannah sighed into his mouth and jerked at
her arms, seeking to bring them closer. Or to
escape. He held tight, careful not to hurt her. He
couldn't allow her to press herself to him as they
had for long moments the previous evening. And
he sure as heck wasn't letting her go. Not yet,
anyway. Already the soft heat of her threatened to
make him forget whatever the hell it was he'd been
about in the first place.

In spite of his efforts, he lost count, delaying for
a final suckle to her bottom lip and a lingering
series of kisses to the nape and back of her neck.

He was shaken when he released her, though he
hid it well. Holding her at arm's length, he found
her glittering green eyes with his, the naked hunger

he prayed to God that his own eyes concealed spilling forth. He turned away from that searching gaze, knowing that in a minute or two, his voice would return to normal and her fury would lock firmly in place.

It didn't even take that long.

"Damn you, Zachariah Garrett," she seethed, striding around him and placing herself in his path. "You can't kiss me every time you want to make a point. That isn't what I meant by negotiating."

Skirting her, he dropped into his chair, indicated the one on the other side of the desk with a nod. "Last night, I asked if you knew what you were about. You have no idea. Hell, I'm not so sure I do, either."

"You have a better idea than you let on," she muttered and reached for her parasol. He'd been hoping she would leave *that* on the floor. Glancing back at him, Savannah tapped her weapon against her thigh. "You won't play me for a fool like you do everyone else."

"What's the harm?"

"The harm is that every person I've stumbled upon in this pitiful excuse for a town thinks you're second in line to inherit God's kingdom. It's 'Zach this' and 'Constable that,' " she mimicked in a sing-song voice, waving the parasol around like a wand. " 'Call Zach if you can't find a room, Miss Connor.' 'Stop by the Constable's office if you need help ordering books for the school, dear.' 'Zachariah is better at telling you what a nasty rash is than any doctor.' " Releasing an unladylike snort, she flounced into the chair, her legs spilling wide. "Did you happen to let them in on the fact that you're a ruthless mediator, skilled enough for any court I've ever been in, *and* a flesh-and-blood man to boot?'' She tapped his desk with her weapon, three hard whacks. "I emphasize the word *flesh*."

Snatching the parasol from her hands, he leaned across the desk and drew a leisurely circle on her knee with the tip. "Look at you sitting there, practically spilling out of that chair. You're not a lady underneath all that bluster, are you, Irish?"

She batted the parasol away. "You're not an adorable angel underneath that wholesome-father facade, are you, Constable?"

He held the smoldering look until his lips began to tingle, until his body stirred inside the crotch of his britches. Savannah's chest rose and fell in an escalating rhythm, telling him she was as affected as he. His arm quivered with the compulsion to touch, with her damned umbrella, the puckered nipple he could see faintly jutting through her crisp white shirtwaist. If the office door had been locked, he would be frightened at what he might do.

Had he ever admitted his true, somewhat tarnished nature? Could he really be *honest* with someone? With that someone being a woman?

"I won't marry you even if we get caught buck naked in the middle of one of your blessed rallies," he said, figuring that was as good a place as any to start. He would not stoop to tricking Savannah into whatever it was they were starting. The lady had to be willing. "It's nothing personal. I just won't. Leave it at that."

She released a little shiver and scooted forward in her chair. "Naked? Will we be naked?"

"I don't rightly know, Miss Connor. The way things are progressing, it's surely a possibility."

"Hmmm . . ." Steepling her hands behind her head, she arched her back, drawing his eye and a tortured sigh he couldn't contain. Her brow puckered, then smoothed as she gained a bit more perspective into the weak nature of men. "Stipulation accepted."

"Don't think about telling Ellie, either."

She slapped her hands on her knees, almost coming up out of the chair. "I would so love to enlighten the world—that being Pilot Isle to you—about what a lascivious, shrewd bastard you really are. But I won't. Because of Rory, I would never."

Zach threw back his head and laughed until his eyes teared. "Lascivious, shrewd bastard? Some time, Irish, you gotta tell me where you learned some of this very unladylike language. I hate to mention this, but any scandal would do you more harm than it would me."

Sighing, she plopped her bottom back into the chair. "No talk of the past. Or the future. That's my stipulation. Don't ask me questions, and I won't ask you. Be whoever you want to be when we're together. Call yourself Jack, for all I care. Then we'll disappear into the sunset someday, each in our own direction."

What if I'm excited about being Zach Garrett for the first time in a long time? he wanted to ask, but that was more than he could reveal to a woman he didn't quite trust not to shoot him with his own bullets. "Accepted," he said instead.

"And stop calling me *Irish*. Make that another stipulation."

Wiping his eyes with his shirt cuff, he halted her with a raised brow. "Whoa, hold on, there. I thought these things went point for point. Sorta' like tennis, isn't it?"

"Well, yes, certainly. An unusual analogy, although acceptable. You know that quite well, from reading numerous legal texts, if my guess is correct." She flicked her fingers regally. "Fine, then, don't you have another stipulation tucked away in that dusty jar atop your neck? I'm not too fond of your charming nickname for me, that's all.''

"Am I to seduce you while calling you Miss Connor, then?"

Her eyes blazed, pupils expanding. "*Savannah* will do," she said, moistening her lips with her tongue.

He came around the desk in a fury, grasped her by the arms, and jerked her from the chair. "I've more experience playing this game than anyone thinks, true, but not so much that I can promise to control what I'm feeling for you." He brought her up against his body, allowing her to feel his aroused state for the first time. "It's been years since I've kissed a woman's breast, sucked her nipple into my mouth and tasted heaven. I want that with you. Hell, I want *you,* maybe more than I've ever wanted anyone—even Hannah, bless her soul."

She blinked, clearly dazed by his admission.

"Am I wrong in thinking you feel the same?"

"Would I have to feel the same?" she asked, glancing at the hands wrapped tightly around her.

Or would you force me? Her unspoken question.

He hauled her a step closer. "You would have to feel the same, damn it."

In response, she smiled, beautifully, sweetly. He almost wanted to believe there was an affable woman hiding inside this temperamental one. Almost. *There's one way to start finding out,* he thought, and lowered his head.

The doorknob jiggled, and Zach released Savannah so abruptly that they both stumbled before gaining purchase. A warning look was all he had time to issue before the door opened and his brother Caleb walked in.

"Zach, that damn door handle is about to fall—" Caleb's eyes widened at the sight of Savannah, standing in a puddle of liquid sunshine, looking fresh and untouched in her pink skirt and striped shirtwaist. She did look as pretty as a picture, Zach begrudgingly admitted. A lioness with her claws sheathed.

Caleb bobbed his head in apology and ripped his hat from his head, his hair flying into disarray. "Beg pardon, ma'am. I didn't know a lady was present."

Behind Caleb's back, Zach's brow rose.

Savannah sniffed. "It's quite understandable," she said and walked forward, her hand out. "I'm Savannah Connor, a friend of Elle's from New York."

Caleb glanced at Zach, shifting from one foot to the other. He had obviously heard plenty about the volatile Miss Connor from every man in town already. Finally, with a sigh, his brother grasped Savannah's hand, brought it to his lips and brushed a kiss across her knuckles. "Never accept a handshake when you can get a kiss, Savannah Connor," he said and grinned.

A slower-forming grin than Zach's, lips not quite as perfect, teeth not quite as white. But he was handsome and big. Solid. And he looked pleasant, like a lovable grizzly bear. She frowned at Zach over his brother's shoulder. Caleb was definitely the most charming Garrett of the bunch.

Caleb gave her hand back with a flourish, laughing as he turned to Zach, who rested against the jail cell, thumbs hooked in his pockets, one knee bent and resting on the metal bars behind him. A deliberately casual pose when she could see energy flowing just beneath the surface.

"You haven't forgotten about the picnic tomorrow, have you, Constance? On Devil Island?"

Zach tore his gaze from Savannah. "I haven't forgotten that blasted picnic. I'm bringing the coleslaw and the beans. The tent and . . . oh, I'll remember the rest later. I have a list somewhere. Rory and I'll sail over around noon or so. And don't forget your hat. Remember that awful sunburn you got last time?"

"Holy Mother Mary, Papa, I won't forget my blessed hat. Hey, though, what am I thinking? Why don't you put Miss Connor in that skiff and sail her over, too? A good way to meet a few neighbors, don't ya think?" Caleb glanced over his shoulder, his expression eager, boyish to the extreme. How dissimilar he and Zach were, she thought. "How 'bout it, Miss Connor? We can't promise much except a little fiddling and a silly game or two. And swimming—there'll be swimming. You can swim, can't ya?"

"Well, yes, I mean, a little. . . ."

Caleb slapped his hands together. "That settles it, another pretty girl in a bathing outfit. You've gotta come. Right now the men outnumber the women, and that's no fun." His voice dropped to a whisper. "Leave it to Zach here to never invite any women, so how 'bout it?"

Zach shoved away from the bars, swiping his index finger across his neck in a cutting motion and frantically shaking his head.

Savannah smiled, holding Zach's gaze. "I would love to go, Mr. Garrett."

"Oh, don't hold to the niceties." He waved his meaty hand at her. "Call me Caleb."

"Then you must call me Savannah."

"Pleased to."

Zach threw himself into the chair behind his

desk and dug the cargo book out with a clatter.
"For God's sake, Cale, save some of that sugar for
your coffee in the morning, why don't you?"

Savannah and Caleb turned in unison, looked
at each other, and laughed. "What's gotten into
you, Constable? My, how uncharitable you're being
toward a guest in your lovely town. Isn't being a
one-man welcome committee part of your job?"

Zach lifted his head, his eyes narrowing. "Thank
you for the reminder . . . Miss Connor." *Irish* was
on the tip of his tongue. She just knew it. "Of
course I'd be delighted to haul you out to Devil
Island for the picnic."

Caleb slipped his arm through hers and tugged
her toward the door. "Don't mind him, Savannah;
he's a stiff-Nelly sort of a fella. If you want to have
any fun tomorrow, darling, avoid Old Starchy;
that'd be my advice. Now, come on, you're late
meeting your gaggle over at Christabel's Restaurant."

Glancing into Caleb's amused gaze, she noted
that he indeed shared the Garrett grays. "How do
you know?"

"Ah, heck, in this town everyone knows everything."

She looked over her shoulder as Caleb ushered
her through the doorway. Zach sat still as a stone,
watching her with a cool expression. *Careful,* the
look said.

If she had an ounce of common sense, she would
heed his warning instead of leaving his office wondering when she'd get to kiss him again.

"I'm going to decline Caleb's offer about the
picnic."

Elle glanced up from her books, a pencil clamped

between her teeth. "Wgy?" She snatched the pencil out. "Why? I'll lend you a bathing costume. And I'm bringing enough food for an army. Noah and I are returning to South Carolina the day after to prepare for the fall semester, and I feel like we haven't spent any time together. Suffering cats, only time talking about this worthless school."

Savannah made a notation beside a student's name and struck through another whose husband had forced her to withdraw from classes. She planned to pay him a visit at his place of employment next week. "You love it. Don't try to fool me. Besides, I'm thrilled to have the opportunity; I'm hoping the school will revive my enthusiasm for the cause."

"I can't tell you how grateful I am that you came down here to manage *and* teach until I finish my degree in the spring. It's the only choice women have to better themselves in Pilot Isle. Closing the doors would have broken my heart."

Reviewing the small list of students, Savannah sighed. "Just don't expect me to make even an infinitesimal profit." She frowned, noting that some had paid for classes with an exchange of services. A seamstress and a piano teacher. "After books and materials, make that *any* profit."

Elle propped her chin on her palm. "You have access to the account. Use it."

"When did money cease to be an issue?"

Elle giggled, a sound Savannah had only heard her friend make *after* falling in love. If giggling was a requirement of being in love, she would choose not, thank you very much. "My darling husband supports my efforts to enrich the lives of the women in this town, Vannie. Of course, *he* called it a loan. I expect I won't have to pay him back."

"Hmmm. I imagine not."

"Savannah, dear? Have you—have you thought any more about our conversation?"

Savannah calculated a row of numbers and noted the total. "Pitiful excuse for a profit last month, Ellie. A dollar and ten cents. No, make that ... ten cents. I forgot to subtract the dollar you contributed to the women's fund in New York."

"I don't care about profits." She tapped her pencil on the coffee table. "Vannie, did you hear what I asked you?"

"A profit would allow you to put money back *into* the school. Buy better materials; hire another teacher. I don't necessarily mean profit to stuff beneath your mattress."

"*Savannah.*" Elle slammed the ledger shut, kicking a puff of dust into her friend's face. "We may not have time to talk in private at the picnic."

"I haven't thought about it." She reopened the ledger. "So there."

"Why not?"

"Constable Garrett's too"—she waved her hand in an absent circle—"controlling for my taste."

"Controlling?"

"Arrogant, too."

"Arrogant?"

Savannah sighed, realizing she wouldn't get any work done until they discussed this. Ellie, bless her benevolent heart, wanted to wrap everything up in a pretty package before she left town. "Nice idea in theory. Reality? We'd kill each other." *That may well find its way to being true.*

"I don't understand where you've gotten this impression of him from. Zach's not controlling or arrogant. He's wonderful. The kindest man, next to my darling Noah, that I've ever known."

Standing, Savannah kneaded her aching lower

back. "Don't act the affronted sister. I've seen a side of him you haven't. Trust me."

"Because you're quarrelling about the oyster factory and, and . . ."

"The oyster factory is only the beginning. When I secure that summit, I'll start climbing another. I have a quickly fashioned list of ones that need climbing in this town." A grin slipped into place as she imagined the verbal battles she and Zachariah Garrett were going to engage in throughout the foreseeable future. "I'm going to make his life hell."

Elle flopped back on the worn love seat, releasing an exasperated sigh. Savannah glanced around the room to avoid her friend's inquisitive gaze, noting that every stick of furniture in Vinecia Broom's parlor had seen better days twenty years before. Due to the drove of fishermen flooding into town for the summer, Miss Vin's Boarding House had had the only vacant room in town.

"I admire your tireless dedication, Vannie, but when are you going to start living for yourself?"

I started last evening, she was tempted to say. But she had promised Zach she would keep her mouth shut—a promise she intended to keep. One she felt very much like keeping, for some odd reason. Anyway, telling Elle that Zach had kissed her and that they were considering whatever it was they were considering was like telling his sister how he looked naked. Or his *mother.* Not an appealing thought.

Elle fiddled with the ragged tassel of a pillow, humming beneath her breath.

Savannah brushed her feet aside, perching on the edge of the love seat. "Spill it. You only hum when you're trying to devise a way to present your case. Remember when we got thrown in jail after that march down Fifth Avenue in 'ninety-four? You hummed the entire time you waited in line to speak to the judge. The other ladies thought you were close to having apoplexy.''

Throwing the pillow at her, Elle lifted herself up onto her elbow. "You're right. I'm sitting here wondering how to bring up a hush-hush subject when I've never worried about discussing anything with you before. But sex"—Elle's cheeks flushed— against her will, Savannah guessed—"isn't something women go around discussing like the weather.''

Savannah laughed. She couldn't help it. "Okay, okay, I'm listening. Please get this out of your system so we can have a pleasant day tomorrow.'' Settling in, she drew her legs to her chest and wrapped her arms around her knees. "A vulgar position for a vulgar discussion.'' She smiled. "Do you want to tell me how it's done? I know it's unseemly, but I confess to reading a naughty novel or two in my day. I understand the mechanics. The man puts his mem—''

Elle reared, plastering her hand over Savannah's mouth. "Vannie!''

She pried her hand away. "Oh, Ellie, when did you become so priggish? The other night—''

"The other night,'' she interrupted, sinking back on the love seat, "I had a glass of wine before you arrived. Then Noah kissed me and . . . oh, suffering cats, I was ready to give an introductory coitus lecture to every virgin in town!''

Savannah dropped her head to her knees and howled with laughter.

"Oh, it's funny, all right.'' She felt Elle roll off the love seat, her boots tapping against the floorboards as she began to pace. "But you'll get yours. Do it once, and you'll never be able to think of anything else. Every time he walks into the room, *boom,* like a bolt of lightning, there goes your mind flying right out the door."

A vivid picture raced through Savannah's mind: Zach flashing his heart-stopping smile, those long, slim fingers closing around her waist and drawing her forward. Into a roaring, uncontrollable blaze.

". . . if you change your mind."

Savannah lifted her head, squinting into a broad band of sunlight flooding in the window. "What?"

Elle paused, an expression of sheer frustration crossing her face. *"Juste Ciel,* I'm running out of patience." She pounded her chest with a closed fist. "I'm not going to be here to help you if you decide to seduce Zach. Caroline will have to help. Anyway, she's the natural choice. You'll have to make the first move because he's as close to a virgin as you'll find for a man his age. He's too noble to visit Madam Stella's outside town, and his marriage, while loving, wasn't passion—"

"Whoa, whoa, whoa!" Savannah cried, using Zach's expression without thinking. "What in heaven's name are you talking about? Caroline who? And Constable Garrett has a child. How can he be a virgin?"

Elle grunted and stalked the length of the parlor. "Close to one, I said. Close. He was very inexperienced when he married Hannah, and he hasn't done a thing, if you grasp my meaning, since she died. In a town this small, indiscretions travel as quickly as the pox. Zach's record is as clean as a baby's bottom fresh out of the bath. Because of that, he's liable to be rusty. That's where Caroline comes in. She knows men better than anyone in town. She can help."

"Saints' blood, Ellie, how could I fail to grasp *that?"* Again, a vision of Zach's hands flashed through her mind, his actions not the least bit rusty. "How do you know about this supposed inexperience? Did he tell you?"

Pausing in the middle of the room, Elle threw a thoughtful glance at the ceiling. "No. Hmmm. Let me see." Chewing her lip, she mumbled, "Honestly, he didn't. I guess Caleb told me. Or Noah. No, no, it wasn't Noah. He lived in Chicago then. And poor Hannah would have fainted before she talked about what went on in her bedroom. Couldn't have been her. Caleb, then."

"Basically, what you're saying is that this is pure speculation."

"What if it is? Take a look at the man. Does he look wild to you?"

Something must have crossed her face—a look that spoke volumes.

"That look, what is that look?" Elle threw herself to her knees before Savannah. "You've done something. What? Ohhh, you'd better tell me."

Savannah released a tense breath. She shrugged her shoulders, within seconds of giving up, when a soft knock on the parlor door deflated their conversation like a needle prick to a balloon.

"Mrs. Garrett?" a frail voice called from the other side of the door. "Your husband is here to escort you home. Are you decent, my dear?"

Savannah had serious doubts about Vinecia Broom's mental state, she truly did. "Decent?" she whispered. "What does she think we're doing in here?"

"You'd better tell me what that look meant. Pull me aside at the picnic. I mean it." Elle wagged her finger in Savannah's face for emphasis, then called out, "Yes, Miss Vin, we're decent.

"Or one of us is," she added with a heated glare thrown Savannah's way.

"I'm not her husband," Savannah heard Zach

explain from the hallway, giving her enough time to scramble for a less scandalous pose, though she couldn't have placed her hand on the Bible to swear Zach didn't get a peek at her bloomers.

He halted in the doorway, his gaze bouncing off her before landing on Elle. "That woman needs a doctor's attention. She thinks I'm Caleb . . . and your husband. How could she get it so mixed up?" His eyes found Savannah again, giving her a long, measuring study before sliding away. "Asking if you're decent. What did she think you were doing?"

Elle laughed a nervous titter of a laugh. "We were looking at lists of books for classes and talking. The school. So much about the school. Tireless, tireless work." Her calculating gaze darted between the two of them. "My, yes. My, my, yes."

Savannah wanted to kick her. She sounded as unbalanced as Miss Vin.

All at once, Zach frowned, drilling Savannah with a questioning glare.

She shook her head. *No, I didn't tell her.*

He looked doubtful.

And *she* felt choked for air, watching him tap his hat against his thigh, each ripple of muscle highlighted by his close-fitting trousers. His soiled vest hung open, revealing a cotton shirt dampened with sweat and clinging to the ridges and valleys beneath. What a fine specimen of masculinity he was. Broad shoulders, a trim waist, and surely a firm, flat tummy. Long legs and those magnificent fingers. How could anyone look upon a man like Zachariah Garrett and think *rusty*?

Elle leaned down and pressed a rather rough kiss to her cheek, whispering, "If you want to hide this, you'd better stop looking at him like he's a piece of chocolate cake just out of reach."

She nodded, her gaze leaving him for the first time since he'd entered the room. "Yes, I'm excited about the picnic, too. See you tomorrow."

Elle drew back. "Me, too. *Very* excited."

Ducking to avoid receiving more advice, and hoping to reduce the stinging heat of the Constable's gaze, she fiddled with the clasp on her boot, releasing a shaky breath when she heard the parlor door close behind them. Moments later, just when her heartbeat returned to normal, the door opened and Zach stepped inside. He leaned against it just long enough to let his gaze glide the length of her body.

Blinking dully, she could do no more than watch in amazed silence as he crossed the room in three long strides, circled her waist, and brought her to her feet, covering her mouth with his. She barely had time to register the faint taste of whiskey before it was over.

"I won't get to do that tomorrow, and I didn't want you to think I'd forgotten our agreement." His warm breath breezed past her ear, where he pressed a quick kiss before leaning down to pick up Elle's gloves from the loveseat.

"Tomorrow," she repeated, sounding breathless and feminine, and not at all like Savannah Connor.

He paused in the doorway, smoky eyes glittering. "Rory and I'll be by at noon to pick you up." Then he was gone, leaving only his teasing scent and a badly shaken woman.

Tumbling to the loveseat, Savannah placed her hand over her heart and pressed down to slow its frantic rhythm. *Rusty,* she thought, and began to laugh.

Chapter Five

Principles are a dangerous form of social dynamite.
—Katharine Susan Anthony

Zach directed Savannah to the flat-bottomed skiff moored next to the ferry bell. The two docked next to it were his as well. When you had a brother who built boats for a living and used you to test each new design, three seemed reasonable. In the early days of Caleb's career, Zach had ended up ass-over-teakettle in deep water more than once in a craft of poor construction. These were not too bad.

He hid his grin behind his hand and coughed as he watched Savannah peer into the skiff with an interest-and-uncertainty-laced expression. She watched Rory scramble in and fasten his skinny bottom to a plank seat, as he had been taught to do from the time he was a baby. Looking back, she cast a dubious glance at the hand Zach offered.

"Take it. I won't bite." *At least not yet.* "It may be a bit slippery, and your shoes aren't the most practical." The last part of the comment earned him a cross look, though she couldn't seriously argue. Bright blue with white lacing and a silly little bow, her boots looked expensive, made of some kind of soft leather. They'd be ruined after one dip in salt water.

"It's a bit smaller than the one I was in before."

"No doubt, princess."

She frowned but obviously decided his plan of action seemed best. Grasping his hand so hard he winced, she boarded the skiff as apprehensively as a sinner entering the caverns of hell.

City girls sure didn't belong on the water.

Damned, though, if he wouldn't take city over country any day, if this was the end result. She'd obviously borrowed an item or two of clothing from Ellie and mixed those with her own. Her outfit, a curious blend of tattered sea attire and contemporary fashion, gave Zach his first sight of her looking young, fresh, pretty, and terribly out of her element. Settling in behind her, he decided he felt more in control than he had when he'd kissed her.

With a billow of white canvas, the skiff sailed from the dock. Shading her eyes, Savannah tilted her head back, recording the progress of a flock of seagulls that had chosen to follow along.

"The gulls want food. A scrap of bait, maybe a shrimp. I feed 'em stale bread even if it has some green stuff on the edges. They don't care, 'cuz my Uncle Noah says they'll eat practically anything that won't eat 'em first." Rory leaned over the edge of the skiff, batting at the waves slapping the hull. "But we don't got none. Just stupid coleslaw."

"Young man, hand inside the boat."

"Awww, poop, Starchy. You're no fun."

Savannah lowered her head, but her laugher drifted out on the salty breeze, withering Zach's reprimand in his throat. Of course, Rory followed suit, giggling and holding his side, pleased to entertain. Zach gritted his teeth and grappled with the lines, ignoring them both. Damn Caleb and that stupid nickname, anyway. The boy was going to be a handful today, and Miss Connor, well, she looked good enough to eat.

Who was the handful on that end? Him . . . or her?

As Rory chattered away, telling "Miss Savannah" all he knew about the shoals and inlets, the island they lived on, and the one they sailed to, Zach noted that she listened with genuine interest if not ease. Even if she didn't naturally take to children, at least she didn't treat Rory like a blathering idiot. Actually, the boy knew far more about the area than she did and was probably giving a better tour than Zach would have done himself. They hadn't spoken more than five words to each other all morning and hadn't touched once, unless you counted his helping her into the boat.

He didn't.

He only wanted to count the times he touched her and her eyes darkened with pleasure. The times her breath crossed her lips in eager little pants. Heck, he would help an old crone into a boat as he'd helped Irish back there. Maybe he had held her hand a second longer than necessary, and yeah, he had leaned in and sniffed her hair. After years of loneliness, he'd be darned if he paid penance for as minor an offense as that.

Suddenly, Savannah shrieked and leaned over the side, jerking the skiff off course a notch. Zach's heart lodged in his chest as he yanked on the lines, anticipating disaster until he saw what she pointed at. A dolphin. Running alongside the boat, in turn diving beneath the waves and jumping high into the air.

"Constable, look!" she exclaimed, releasing a burst of joyful laughter, the wind ripping her bonnet off her head. A mass of hair the distinct color of mahogany tumbled into her face and came damn close to slapping his. Zach pictured that silken heap spread across a pillow, *his* pillow, and his stomach sank to his knees.

"Do you see him? A dolphin. How adorable."

"Yeah," he croaked, shifting on the hard plank to get away from those beguiling strands. "Adorable, all right."

"I think that's Lulu." Rory stuck his fingers in his mouth and executed a sharp whistle. The dolphin responded with a high-pitched squeal. "See? She's got a scar on her nose shaped jus' like a lightning bolt. Uncle Noah said it was probably from some fight with a killer fish. Like a shark. I've seen a shark up close, real close, when my pa caught it. We were fishing with sand fleas, which ain't the best bait, so he was hungry, I reckon."

"Fascinating," she said, propping her arms on the side of the skiff to record Lulu's antics. Zach had a hard time looking away from them, hanging over the edge of the boat, their faces coated with a constant spray of water. Rory patted her on the shoulder at various intervals, relating information about the shape of Lulu's fins and how she breathed—things Noah must have told him. His information sounded a bit mixed up to Zach, not quite right. If she noticed, she didn't let on, nodding and chatting, relaxing in the boy's presence. Except for Elle, his son didn't have a close relationship with a woman. Only four when his ma passed away, he must have missed that special tenderness a man just couldn't give. Or couldn't show. Or didn't have.

But damn it, Zach didn't want him getting attached to a woman who'd go trotting back to New York City the first opportunity she got.

"Son, you want to grab that rope by your feet and give it to me? We're almost there."

Clapping his hands, Rory grabbed the rope and scrambled across the seats. "I bet Ellie brung fried chicken. I'm starving."

"Brought," Savannah corrected without looking up, her face only inches from getting plastered by a wave. "I bet Ellie brought chicken."

"Brought," Rory parroted, dancing a jig. "Chicken, chicken, chicken."

Zach wrapped an arm around his son's waist and hauled him in between his legs. "Sit while I sail in, we might hit a rough patch."

"Naw, that sandbar is more over there." Rory stuck his tiny arm out. "Right, huh?"

Zach closed his eyes and felt a subtle shift in the wind, responding with a minor adjustment to the sail. "To the left about twenty feet, I'd say," he said, raising his voice to be heard over the slap of waves against the hull of the boat. He'd sailed the area for so many years—since he was Rory's age or before—that when he closed his eyes he could see the inlets and shoals in his mind, almost like a map. At one time, that map had brought him plentiful sums of money and minor fame in the commercial shipping community.

And for a while there, it had brought him women.

Zach opened his eyes to find Savannah's green gaze centered on him. Or more specifically, on his chest. Rory had moved to the side, doing another dance, and the wind ripped at Zach's shirt, exposing him nearly to the waist. He hoped that didn't offend her. Who knew? He never seemed to be able to guess which side of her he was going to get. She would see that the picnics at Devil tended to be casual, more casual than they probably ever got in the city. And summers in Pilot Isle, intensely humid and hot enough to fry an egg on the boardwalk most days, didn't make a man want to add more clothing just for modesty's sake. Raising a brow as he angled them in to shore, he asked, "Problem, Miss Connor?"

"No." Tugging her bonnet into place—it would help cover those pink cheeks—she let her gaze drift before he could make a move to cover up.

Savannah took a breath of salty air and tilted her head to let the sun warm her face. Continual beads of perspiration coursed down her back and between her breasts, but she didn't care. It was glorious, exhilarating. The rush of wind in her face and at her back, the swift dips when the boat crested a wave and slid home . . .

The heat of Zachariah Garrett's gaze.

She grasped the edge of the plank seat, digging her nails into the moist wood. She had never sailed with a man before—not a *real* man, just a puffed-up city version of one. Nothing like the windblown, sun-browned male working the sail's ropes with those stunning hands and muscled arms, looking as though he could maneuver the boat with his eyes closed. Which he had, for a moment back there. She fingered a splinter in the wood, wishing she could unbutton her dress down to her waist and let the wind rush inside, too.

She wished a lot of impractical things at the moment.

"This area is rather dangerous sailing, isn't it?" she asked, determined to dictate her interaction with the man. Their relationship must remain on friendly terms today: no heated arguments, no wild kisses, no errant touches, absolutely *no* depraved or impassioned behavior. She planned to schedule an appointment for those.

And until she felt secure in her decision, she would face the front of the boat, whatever that part was called, and avoid Constable Garrett's temptingly naked chest.

"Yes, ma'am. Surging ridges of sand all over out here, southeasterly from the north end to the tip of Cape Hatteras, then southwest to Cape Lookout Point, just over there." She didn't turn but rather imagined him rooted to the spot, arm extended, gaze scanning the glorious, vast horizon. When had she got to the point of being able to picture the man in her mind? "Shipwrecks often enough. Too often."

"I've read about them."

The sound of snapping canvas as they closed in on shore was the only reply.

After a moment of silence, Rory slipped in beside her and said, "My pa is going to let me go on a rescue someday."

"Rescue?" She smiled and shifted a fraction to the left, away from him. He was a lovely child, lively and polite. A typical little boy, she supposed. Only, she didn't handle children well. They seemed to sense her discomfort. Why Rory didn't was a mystery to her.

"Ya know, row out to gather the sailors from sinkin' ships. Pa needs volunteers all the time, 'cause people move and die or they're just plain lazy. So he needs me." Rory wiped his nose with his sleeve. "But I can't touch buoys until I'm ten."

"Twelve. If then." Zach hopped into the shallow water, slung a rope tied to the front of the boat on his shoulder and hauled them closer to shore.

"Ole Starchy," Rory whispered behind his grubby palm, his eyes twinkling. He had Zach's look about him, that mischievous, devil-may-care glow. She felt her heart thaw. It was with no real discomfort that she returned the smile and the whispered nickname.

"Come on, you two. Let's get a move on." Zach stood beside the boat, in knee-deep water, his hair in disarray, his mouth heavy with a frown. What he was displeased about, she had no idea and wasn't going to spend a moment trying to figure out.

Rory shouted gleefully and jumped over the side of the boat, wading to shore and taking off at a gallop. He obviously knew where he was going.

"You handle the shipwreck rescues?" Savannah asked when Zach reached to lift her from the boat.

"Hang on to me if you don't want to ruin those silly boots."

He slid one arm under her knees, the other around her back. Lifting her effortlessly, he trudged to shore. She gripped his back and shoulder, watching his face to see if that flat expression changed. The heat from his skin through his open shirt felt warmer than the sun's.

"Why are you so aggravated with me, Constable? May I ask?"

He rolled his eyes. "Like you need permission to be a nuisance. The boots, Miss Connor. How you thought those were appropriate I'll never understand. You'll be barefoot in five minutes; then we'll spend the afternoon digging splinters out of your feet or tending to burns from the sand, which is hotter than a lit skillet in some spots these days."

She stiffened. "Put me down. I can walk to shore *and* ruin my damned boots in the process. Better that than being carried like a damsel in distress. Excuse me if I don't fit that category."

"You don't have to ask twice," he muttered and

loosened his hold, allowing her to slide down his body and into the shallow water. After polishing his chest like a piece of tarnished silver, she didn't even feel the waves lapping her ankles.

"Run on up there like a good little girl," he said after a moment, his tone dark. "Go on; they're expecting you."

She nodded but didn't move, everything frozen except her fingertips, which tingled, urging her to use them for something wicked. One, the index finger of her left hand, had inadvertently worked its way through the open neck of his shirt and encountered bare skin. Savannah wiggled it, brushing a patch of hair.

"Go on," he repeated, giving her a weak nudge, his guarded expression turning hot.

Her heart skipped a beat as their gazes held, the buttons of his shirt pressing into her stomach.

His eyes were fascinating, effortlessly contradicting his blasé style, brimming with intelligence and a promise that he would not be easy to fool. Never mind his good looks; they overshadowed even the glorious beauty of the island.

"This is a good test for both of us, and we're failing." Forcing her from him, he swiveled around, reaching into the boat and coming out with a wicker basket.

She took a stumbling step back, struggling for composure that she didn't possess at the moment. "Fail? I never fail at anything."

Zach leaned against the boat to steady himself. The fingers wrapped around the handle of his dead wife's basket shook. His breath came a trifle quick for a leisurely sail to Devil Island. Didn't he know better? A family outing was no place to behave like a starving man suddenly presented with a king's feast. Mighty strange for a man who hadn't felt hunger pangs for over two years. And the boundaries were clear-cut.

He closed his eyes, drew a deep breath of air, and, blessed heck, smelled *her* scent on the wind. Turning, he grasped her elbow and hauled her to shore. "Do you want to be some sideshow for the entertainment of the folks in this town? They'll accommodate you, all right. We're bored quite often around here, as you can probably tell. A show would be good for all, 'cept the next day they won't speak when they pass you on the street. Not all folks, granted, but some."

"You think the censure of a bunch of small-minded people worries me? I would have renounced the cause the first week if that were the case, Constable. You might not realize it, but I'm made of much sturdier fabric."

"Yeah, yeah, why'd I know you'd spout some gibberish like that?" He let her go the second they hit sand, jerking his hand away so quickly he elbowed himself in the stomach. "Fine, Miss Independent. Be true to yourself. Live free and well. But what's that hardheadedness going to do for Ellie's school? You reckon riling every old biddy within five miles of Pilot Isle is going to help you get their granddaughters into typewriter class? This ain't New York, Irish, where scandal is as common as stray dogs. Not as much happens here, so we savor what we get."

She paused in the process of jerking off her boot. Clearly, this was a new thought.

"I'm sure Ellie would appreciate you driving her little school—already a pitiful business prospect as it is—straight to hell in a basket like the one I'm holding."

She tilted her head to see him past her bonnet's brim. "Are you trying to trick me?"

"Trick you into what?" He shoved the basket into her hands and waded back into the water. Bracing the lead rope around his shoulder and elbow, and with the help of an incoming wave, he hauled the skiff to shore. "I want you and you know it. Whether I like it or not—and I'm not sure I do, even though you're the first woman to spark my interest since Hannah—there it is. All out there on paper, so to speak." He shrugged. "Okay by me if you'd like to kiss me in full light of the entire town, ma'am. Okay by me. I can explain it to my family. Hell, I've decided it might be a good lesson for Rory to see me with someone."

"You want honesty, Constable?" A sodden blue boot hit the sand near his feet. Another bounced off his knee. At least her aim was poor. "I don't know *how* to play the demure, genteel belle. My father made a wise investment in 1883 that took me from an impoverished childhood in Brooklyn to the wealth of city living. It was enough to learn which fork was appropriate for salads and how to address the household staff without being too familiar, much less figure out how to charm and beguile at the same time."

Wedging the hull in good in case the tide rolled in sooner than he expected, Zach turned to find her standing with a closed fist propped on each slim hip, her expression defensive and defiant. Maybe it was because he was a father that he imagined he could see a crack in Savannah Connor's casing. Rory often threw fits, then cried like a baby from all the effort. Or maybe it was simply her toes wiggling in time to the angry thoughts in her head. Whatever it was, she looked far younger than her years, standing there on that dazzling sunlit beach, the wind tossing her hair into her face and pinking her lovely cheeks.

A part of his heart, a part he didn't have to give, threatened to leave him. He held on to it with both hands. "I can help you there. In Pilot Isle, it won't be so very hard to charm and . . . beguile. Easier than it is in New York, anyway." Plucking her tiny boots from the sand, he shook them out and headed up the beach. After a moment, he heard her follow him, the basket whacking her leg with each lengthy step.

"How?" she asked, puffing as she caught up to him.

He took the basket from her without breaking stride. "Simple. One, limit your battles."

"Oh, you'd just love that, wouldn't you? I *knew* this was a ploy to make your life easier."

Stepping in front of her, he cupped her chin in his palm, tilting her head so he could see inside that ridiculous floppy brim before either of them had a chance to think. "Do you want to explore this attraction between us?" When she was silent, he probed, "Do you?"

She nodded, bonnet ribbons slapping her jaw. Her eyelids lowered over her wide green eyes.

"Then consider that a battle, Irish. You chose to fight it. And because of who I am in this town, you may have to forgo another one because of that choice. Like, say, letting what we're doing be out in the open because, damn it, you don't care to hide or change or be accepted. Do you understand? You asked me to take something for myself, and I'm going to do it. I should ask the same of you. It may have a price, though. This is between us and no one else. That's the way it has to be for me. And for *you*, if you'd only get that through your thick noggin."

"How does"—she licked her bottom lip, sending his blood soaring—"that help me fit in and be a . . . lady?'' A frown tugged at her lips. "After all, I don't want to wreck Elle's school.''

Wiping away a drop of water from her cheek, he released her before he embarrassed himself and did what he was trying to tell her not to do and kissed her flat out in close proximity to the gathering. "You can't fix everything that's wrong with the world. That's wrong in Pilot Isle. And if some things"—he nailed her with a pointed look— "are more important, you have to make a decision which to go with. For instance, my number two suggestion is to court the mamas and grandmamas in town if you want their girls in your classes. Forget the men. Upset a wife, and the husband gets burnt dinners for two nights in a row and comes crawling to the jail blubbering like a babe. The angle is to court the women. And you can't court 'em if they think you're going to go around tempting all their husbands like a loose city woman. You have to make friends, be one *of* them. Not an enemy. *Not* a leader. Not all the time, you see? To do that, you'll have to attend some teas, a quilting bee or two—''

"Quilting!''

He laughed and stepped over a piece of driftwood, looking back to catch her if she stumbled. He would have offered his arm, but he couldn't risk touching her again. "Sorry but that's the agenda. Then, when you have some nagging problem you want to rectify—say, the need for more gas lamps along Main Street—you can rally the troops and they'll fall in behind you like loyal soldiers. If the cause is a useful one, you might even find help from the men in town. I'll help on that end if I can.''

She hummed a vague reply.

Zach paused as they reached a break in the dunes, dabbing at a bead of sweat trailing down his neck. The sound of laughter drifted by. He cocked his head; Rory was singing some song about apples and butterflies. Like it did at the strangest times with his boy, love pierced his heart like an arrow.

"*Does* Main Street lack sufficient lighting?"

It was with all his might that he kept a straight face. "Not nearly enough for women to travel safely after dark."

She glanced away, her bonnet flapping in the breeze. "I suppose I could work on that *and* the oyster factory improvements while teaching classes. Then move on to other issues once those are resolved. Not to forget, I also have articles to pen for a journal in New York. And of course, I need to establish a list of activities for this courting business." She grimaced. "A quilting bee and a tea should be a satisfactory start, right?"

"Yep, it would be. The church has a group who meet every Tuesday afternoon at Christabel's Restaurant. That's the most orderly gathering of ladies that I know of. Christa's here today and can tell you all about it."

"Church. My . . . well, it's been a long time since I've been to church. Most of the ministers in New York preferred I didn't attend."

"That notorious, huh?"

Her gaze found his—the first direct address she had given him since she climbed out of the skiff and into his arms. "I'm afraid so."

"Might be better to keep that story under your hat. And your arrest record."

She twisted her fingers before her lips with a wry smile.

"Yeah. And anything else . . . unseemly."

Untying the bonnet ribbons, she tugged it off with a sigh of pleasure. "I didn't have time for unseemly activities." Snatching her boots from his hand, she brushed aside a bunch of sea oats and threw a teasing glance over her shoulder. "But I plan to change that, Constable Garrett. *Soon.*"

That said, she trotted off toward the group while he stood there in the baking-hot sun trying to restart his heart.

Her stomach full of fried chicken, buttermilk biscuits, and Zach's surprisingly tasty coleslaw, Savannah rested in the shade of a large umbrella the likes of which she'd never seen, watching the Garrett clan cavort in the waves. Zach had Rory perched atop his shoulders and was dancing around in waist-deep water, trying to stay out of reach of Caleb, Noah, and Elle. It looked to be an ocean version of tag.

"Ever seen a finer bunch of men in your life? God's been mighty nice to the Garretts, I tell you what. Mighty nice."

Savannah shifted on the blanket to make room for Caroline Bartram. Tall and attractive and dressed in a vivid blue skirt and checkered blouse, she'd been introduced to Savannah as an old friend of Noah's who had recently moved to Pilot Isle with her son. The woman Elle had told her to ask for advice. *The woman who knew men.* "Where is Justin? Can he swim?" Savannah asked, hoping Justin was indeed Caroline's son's name. *That* introduction had occurred moments after Zach removed his shirt for his first swim of the day, and her mind had wandered.

"That boy can swim like a fish. He's under the tent back behind the dunes, fast asleep. When his belly is full, he needs a nap or he's liable to snap your head off. Grouchy, that's the truth. Rory's a more even-tempered sort, like his father."

Savannah smiled, thinking she liked Zachariah better when his temper ran hot. "I'm sure Justin's father was grouchy, too."

Caroline slapped at a fly buzzing in her face. "Could be true, yes. I have it down to either the congressman who shall remain nameless or Admiral Bastion, who only came into Chicago, oh, four times a year back then. He's in France for good, so no harm telling." Leaning back on her elbows, she sighed in contentment. "Both of them *were* a might testy after eating, now that I think of it."

Savannah swallowed the wrong way and choked, coughing until her lungs burned.

"Gracious alive, seeing as how you're with Zach and all, I thought you knew about me." Caroline slapped her back harder than she probably had to, sending Savannah scooting forward on the blanket. It wadded beneath her bottom.

"I'm . . . okay." She held up a hand, gasping for air. "And I'm not *with*—"

"Darling, don't bother saying you're not with the Constable. Maybe you're not yet, but you will be. The air between the two of you is warmer than this godforsaken sun beating down on my back." She plucked her blouse from her chest and flapped it. "Why I wanted to move to the South, I'll never know."

"I'm *not* with him," Savannah forced between stiff lips. Elle had been pestering her all day, and if she'd kept quiet then, she certainly could now.

Caroline laughed, a deep, knowing sound that made Savannah feel her denial had been a waste of breath. "Don't mistake me, Miss Connor. You keeping your business with Zach private is a smart idea. Anything else would damage you for sure.

Same for me. I was long gone in Chicago, so I came here to make a new start with my son. What I just told you about my boy's fathers is between me and my adopted family, the Garretts. I figured you knew, or I never would have said it so brash-like.''

Just then, to hammer the nail in, Zach turned and, seeing her watching him, winked.

Caroline dissolved into quiet laughter at her side.

''It isn't like that.'' When Caroline said nothing and continued to laugh, she continued, ''Really.''

''What is *it* like these days? Hiding away in this town, I'm out of touch.''

Savannah copied Caroline's casual stance and settled back on her elbows. Zach flipped Rory into the water with a splash and dove in behind him. He came up gasping, his hair slick and shockingly black against his flushed cheeks. Choosing not to answer the question but rather present a reason for considering *it*, she said, ''I like how soundly he's put together. The rugged way he walks, the solid way he stands, like he's impenetrable. I've never seen, I mean, he has genuine muscle, not padded bulk that comes off with his jacket.''

''Oh, honey, you're talking about city men. Men in Pilot Isle use their bodies in their work. There isn't any choice. Zach, for instance. A ship goes down on the shoals, he and his men are the ones in charge of saving them. That takes courage *and* strength.'' Caroline sighed dreamily. ''And isn't that a nice combination to look upon?''

Savannah tried to visualize Zach leading a group of men on a stormy sea, gigantic waves and bolts of lightning surrounding them. It was easy to do. He genuinely cared for people, and she couldn't imagine his being frightened at trying to help them. Across the distance, she watched his lips work into a smile as he hugged Rory to him, his eyes lighting up as the boy hugged him back. "He's a wonderful father."

"If you want children, you couldn't find a better daddy for them."

Keeping Zach in sight, she shook her head. "I'm dreadful around children. They don't like me." She shrugged. "Not every woman would make a good mother, Miss Bartram."

"Oh, that's true enough, I suppose. But you've a good heart, and I'm proof that that's all you truly need. All your work to help women, Ellie told me all about it. Only a first-rate heart can give that much to others."

"You always wanted children, Miss Bartram?"

Caroline released a low sigh. "I grew up in a shack full of brothers and sisters whom I loved dearly. I loved the noise and the fussing, the love. Justin's enough for me if that's all I get, but I would be happy with a gang of 'em running around. I have the money, but I think this time I need a husband."

"Yes," Savannah agreed, "it seems to be the way everyone would like the process to work."

"I've been meaning to stop by the school, but with all the rush with your rally, and Ellie going back to the university, I figured you had enough to do."

Savannah turned her head, surprised to hear the anxious tone in Caroline's voice. "Stop by the school?"

"Uh-hum. You see, my boy is starting school in September, and part of his homework until he learns to read good is for me to read *to* him every evening before bed. I tell him stories now, which works fine, but later . . ."

"How much can you read?"

Caroline paused, her voice subdued. "A little."

Savannah settled back, the sand warm and supple beneath her. Working her arms beneath her head, she yawned. "A little is more than enough. We'll have you reading any book you choose from the library before the first snow. Come by tomorrow at three-thirty and we'll begin."

"Thank you." She felt the light touch on her shoulder, then movement as Miss Bartram stood. "If you ever need anything, all you have to do is ask."

I may take you up on that, Savannah thought as she drifted to sleep. *I may indeed.*

Chapter Six

To understand another human being you must
gain some insight into the conditions which made
him what he is.

—Margaret Bourke-White

Zach found her there an hour later, curled on her side, sleeping as soundly as Rory had as a baby. Her chin rested on her spread fingers, and that glorious wealth of hair spilled like chocolate all over his favorite blanket. She'd unbuttoned the top two buttons of her dress to escape the sweltering heat, exposing a space of smooth ivory skin.

Squatting, he fingered the stockings she'd placed in a neat bundle by her side, remembering a minor argument with Hannah about her leaving them hanging all over the washroom.

What he wouldn't give for that now.

Pushing aside the familiar pang of guilt, he focused on the remarkable creature who had been suddenly, wondrously thrust into his life. He would never marry again, that was certain, but he could not live any longer in a deadening state of loneliness. Whether he loved the idea or not—he loved and hated it in turn—for the first time in years, he had a woman in his life.

She looked soft and vulnerable, and he almost hated to end the nap she seemed to need. Besides, the aggressive, demanding Savannah was bound to be the one to wake up.

"Irish?" He gave her shoulder a gentle squeeze, letting his fingers stray to her cheek. He glanced around and, seeing that everyone had gone back to the picnic site to prepare dinner, ran his thumb along her plump lower lip. She stirred but didn't wake, so he took one additional liberty and, not entirely certain why, slipped her stockings into his trouser pocket. Surely, she wouldn't miss them. "Irish, wake up."

She blinked and drowsily mumbled incoherent bits of nonsense. "Zachariah," she finally said— the first time she had called him by his name that he could recall. It sounded damned nice rolling out wrapped in her sleepy Yankee accent. "Hmmm?"

"We're going to move back behind the dunes. Once the sun sets, the bugs won't be as bad near the campfire. Dinner should be ready soon. Ellie's digging up the potatoes you buried in the ashes this morning, and Caleb's grilling the meat."

"I was having a dream," she murmured, pushing to a shaky sit, "and you were in it."

Zach grinned, awash in bawdy images. He'd done some dreaming of his own last night. "Yeah?" Lowering his voice, he whispered, "Tell me."

Suddenly full of vigor, which should have been a warning sign, she scooted forward until she was nearly sitting on his knee. "I was helping you find a ship that had sunk somewhere"—she waved her hand toward the ocean—"out there. It was very ominous and stormy. And hot, like it is today. Dreadfully hot. We pulled people into a boat and

... then I heard you calling me the name you're not supposed to and I woke up.''

Zach rose, disappointed as all get-out. Offering his hand, he said, ''Well, that's a nice dream and all, but kinda' ridiculous.'' Couldn't she have dreamed about him kissing her? Would that have been too much to ask?

''Ridiculous? I think it's wonderful!'' Ignoring his hand, she bounced up like a ball, and circled him as he walked toward the dunes. ''Now I know what else I can do. Truly, the gas streetlamp project is one I can manage from a distance. Lydia needs her own project to get her involved, and that one is perfect. Now, when does your life-saving group meet?''

Zach caught her as she came around the front. ''What in tarnation are you babbling about? You can't possibly think a woman's going to join the life-saving service.''

She thrust her chin high. ''I certainly do.''

''Of all the . . .'' Zach shook his head and stalked away.

Dogging his heels, she said, ''Can you give me one reason why not?''

''Lady, you're loony. I must be loony, too, to think we . . .'' He glanced at her, brow scrunching. ''Ah, blast.''

''I won't relent until you discuss this with me, Constable.''

They crossed the dunes at a trot, coming down into the picnic area Zach and his brothers had been using since they were children. It was a perfectly round, bare spot sitting equidistant between the dunes and the coastal forest. During the summer, the area remained the coolest due to partial shelter from a grove of loblolly pines. ''Forget it, Irish. I'll help you, but not with this.'' He sat on a piece of driftwood as far from the fire as he could get, put on a canvas shoe, and began lacing. Unfortunately, a small female blaze threw herself at his feet. "Go away."

"I could be a great asset to your group. Perhaps not during actual rescues but in another capacity. Surely, you can see the benefit of having a female crew member."

Damn, he loved watching her mouth form all those sassy words. It didn't seem possible for such dazzling lips to spill such stiff sentences. Or for such a nice-looking woman to be such a nuisance. "No. End of discussion. I know you're going to be angrier than a hornet when I say this, but life-saving is and always will be a man's job."

Behind Savannah, Elle looked up from where she squatted before the fire, digging potatoes out with pieces of driftwood. She shook her head, her eyes wide, a clear warning about the territory he had entered. Zach's temper ignited, a sizzling creep along his spine. Was he supposed to be scared of a woman who barely reached his shoulder and weighed sixty pounds less dripping wet? All she had over him was a quicker brain-to-mouth response.

Looking from Elle to Savannah, he tied a knot and jerked the laces to tighten it. "Throw a rally right here by the campfire if you'd like. My answer is no. And that, Irish"—he sent her the same cautionary look he sent Rory when he honest-to-God meant *no*—"is the final answer. I'm leader of the troops in this battle. Understand? You won't get anywhere, I'm telling you."

She threw her arms wide. "I *don't* understand. I can't understand excluding women from such an essential community task when you obviously need assistance."

He grasped her wrist and tugged until they were nose to nose, her tiny pink toes butting his shoes. "It's a horrible post, Miss Connor, rowing out to those wretched souls. I dream about the bodies and the debris . . . and the blood. Even in the moonlight, the sea looks red. And it has this peculiar smell, like metal. A very flat . . . awful smell." Swallowing, he thrust her away, marveling at how she seemed to crawl inside him to places he hadn't exposed to light in years. Angry, passionate places brimming with memories and uncontrollable urges. "Maybe you'd rather patrol the beaches during the dead of night and be the first person to hear a ship's stern tear in two. Hear the screams of men who know you won't make it to them as surely as you know the sharks will. That promises a good night of sleep for the next month."

Zach flinched when a hand covered his shoulder. Glancing up, he met Noah's troubled gaze. Caleb stood close by, too. And Ellie. Of course, they were worried. When had they seen him like this? Furious and belligerent, his voice raised, his fists clenched. Zach could count on his fingers the number of times he had lost control in front of his family. Emotional outbursts suited Caleb well, had all his life. Even the once placid Noah had revealed a remarkably passionate nature since returning to Pilot Isle.

Calm, capable Zachariah Garrett never, ever traveled that route.

A sizzling flash from the spit brought him back. With a deep breath, he shoved to his feet. In the distance, the drone of sand locusts hidden in the dunes united with the crackle of the campfire. The pungent smell of roasting meat swirled around him, carried along by a healthy sea breeze.

Savannah reached out and touched his knee, a

tentative brush of her fingers. "I'm sorry," she whispered, for his ears alone. The desire to haul her to her feet, strip that ragged dress from her body, and make love to her in the twilight of a warm summer evening tore through him. Intense longing of a kind he hadn't known since those wild piloting days swelled inside him. *God, to make her forget the cause, any goddamned cause, for one blessed minute.*

"Constable?" she asked, her voice full of remorse. Her shame made him angrier, with himself as much as with her. He'd have bet hard-earned money that at his age, a tempting bundle of sweet smells and soft skin wouldn't have had the power to turn him inside out like this.

"Miss Connor, when Rory ignores a no, I lay his skinny body across my lap and paddle his bare bottom till it's red as those embers over there."

He heard her indrawn breath and glanced down in time to see her flush before she dipped her head. If they'd been alone, he would have damn well explored that spark of awareness in her gaze.

"Separate corners, how 'bout it?" Noah stepped between them, arms raised, voice gentle, as if he feared setting off another round of fighting. "Zach, why don't you help me gather a few more pieces of driftwood? Savannah, you can help Ellie with supper."

Zach snorted under his breath.

Savannah jumped up and in, close enough for him to smell her undeniably unique scent. "I can cook, for your information, Constable. Quite well, in fact."

"Well, hoo-rah for men everywhere. A suffragette and a cook!"

Noah glanced over his shoulder. *Consulting with his missus,* Zach thought sourly. "It's all right; let's

take a walk. Get that wood. Unless you'd like to
do that, too, Miss Connor.''

"Now, Zach," Noah said in his stern preparing-
to-be-a-papa-someday voice. "Let's go find the others, tell them supper's almost ready."

Savannah watched Zach stalk from the clearing,
the stiffness in his stride setting off muscular ripples
in his shoulders and back. She liked the worn shirts
he wore that clung to him like a second skin.

My, he presented a handsome portrait of masculine fury.

"You simply must tell me what you've done to
whip Zach into such a frenzy." Elle came to stand
beside her, dusting her hands on her skirt. "And
who in the heck is *Irish?*"

Later that night, Savannah tiptoed from the
makeshift campsite, following the path leading
through the break in the dunes. Tilting her head,
she counted until she lost count of the twinkling
lights sheltered in the black velvet sky, more stars
than she had ever seen in one sitting. An owl
hooted nearby, a gull somewhere beyond that. A
respected marine biologist, Noah had identified
every sound for them after supper while Elle looked
on with her own stars in her eyes.

Savannah had left them sitting so close their
heads touched, their hands linked as if they each
couldn't bear to let the other go. Pushing aside
the pang of envy she hoped was a natural reaction
to witnessing such devoted adoration, she trudged
across the warm sand, the occasional chip of
quartz—another bit of information from Noah—
glittering in the moonlight.

They were due to sail back to Pilot Isle in another
hour, when the tide rolled in or out, whichever

made it easier, or safer, to get home. *Home.* A misstep to use that word. She had not had a true home since those ragtag Brooklyn days. Or certainly not since her mother's death, anyway. Her father had not had the heart to provide a home for the daughter he always wished had been born a son.

She wiggled her toes, relishing the freedom of bare feet and, too, the freedom of being Savannah Connor and nothing more for the summer. She wasn't sure when she would put on another pair of pinching boots or form another picket line and spend the night in a filthy jail cell for her dedication. Maybe never.

Peering through the shadowy moonlight, she found him sitting beneath a clump of sea oats, his back against the dune, hands stacked behind his head, bare feet propped upon a massive piece of driftwood. The wind tugged his shirt wide and pitched his crow black hair into his eyes. He looked vulnerable sitting there in the darkness, alone and silent. She wondered for a moment if he spotted her approach.

Sitting nearby, but not close enough to tempt either one of them, she pulled her skirt to midcalf and wormed her feet into the silken sand. Humid air whipped in from the east in gusts, and with an exhalation of surrender, she released her hair from the loose knot on her head.

"Lost, Irish?" His deep voice cut through the sound of the pounding surf.

So he did see her. Settling back against the dune, she gathered her thoughts. "Your family thinks we hate each other."

"Good. That'll keep them from asking questions."

"Do you—I mean—is this . . ." She shrugged,

sending grains of sand down the back of her dress. She had to ask.

"Wanting to wring your pretty little neck every other minute isn't enough to keep me from wanting to touch you, if that's where you're headed." He sighed, kicking at the driftwood. "Nothing seems to be enough."

"I'm sorry."

"For what?" Scooting close, he captured a strand of her hair between his thumb and finger. "For making me angry or making me yearn?"

Averting her gaze from the breadth of skin exposed by his unbuttoned shirt, she released a pent-up breath. "For my histrionics earlier this evening."

He seized her chin in his palm and directed her eyes to his face. "Say it again."

"I'm sorry," she whispered, stomach doing the familiar dance that must be what he called *yearning*.

He shook his head. "No. The big word."

She frowned, puzzled. "Big word? Oh. *Histrionics.*"

His attention centered on her mouth, recording every movement of her lips. "I love watching you talk, Irish. When we're in bed the first time, I want you to whisper one of those big words you love every time I slide inside you." He wrapped the strand of hair around his finger in a lazy rotation. "I don't care what they mean."

Her face colored, she felt it flame. Her lips opened, then closed, her brain powerless to string together a sentence, big words *or* small.

"You're afraid."

She shook her head. It didn't feel like fear in her belly. It felt like excitement.

"There's no need. We'll take it at your pace. You tell me when, where, and how much. Or how little."

"We'll be friends when it's over?"

A stray beam of moonlight spilled across his face in time for her to see his pause, his thoughtful deliberation. It made her feel good to know he tried to answer honestly. "I think so, yes."

Her eyes again dropped to his chest, the sprinkling of dark hair glistening. With perspiration or perhaps salt water.

Releasing her chin, he slipped his shirt from his shoulders and shook it from his arms. Lifting her hand from its mired position in the sand, he placed it palm-flat on his chest. "Go ahead. I think you want to. Hell, my good sense dissolved like mist on a sunny day the moment you stepped off the ferry. You might as well lose yours."

His head dropped back, his eyelids sliding low as she began to explore; the sand coating her fingers made an oddly pleasurable abrasion. His hair felt springy, sitting in tight curls close to his chest. She circled his nipples and watched them harden, feeling her own pucker beneath her borrowed dress. Zach's heartbeat thudded beneath the heel of her hand, his breath rushing forth in a belabored groan. Gaining courage, she traced each rib with her finger and drew her knuckles along the downy hollow trailing into his damp waistband.

He caught her there, his fingers trembling.

As she had told Elle, she understood the mechanics of intercourse. She'd made it a point to read every book about it she could get her hands on. Most of them were condemned by libraries and school districts over the years, many because of their blatant descriptions of the act of coupling. She had also studied anatomy at university. It was better than complete ignorance but still sadly, only illustrations in a book. She vaguely visualized what lay beneath the protuberance in Zachariah Garrett's trousers.

A teasing smile blossomed on her face. She waited until his eyelids flickered and lifted. "Protuberance," she whispered, then licked her lips to see if this added to his enthrallment.

The hand holding hers squeezed as he breathed, "If I kiss you now, I'll have you on your back in less time than it takes to say pro, pro—"

"Protuberance."

His gaze flicked from her lips to her eyes, then made an expansive sweep of her body. "And I don't want us prone just yet." His thumb covered the pulsing vein at her wrist. "Would you think I was plumb crazy if I said I wanted to take this very slowly?"

Laughter sounded in the distance, reminding her of where they were and how little time they had.

"It sounds quite rational to me," Savannah whispered.

"It isn't. Not to a man's way of thinking." Rolling to his back, he pulled her with him until she was balanced on her elbow at his side. "I haven't talked to a soul, and I surely haven't touched a woman, while being just plain Zach Garrett, in I can't remember how long. I want to be with you without being a daddy or an officeholder or the damned keeper of the cargo that washes up on shore." He sighed. "I just want to *be*. And dawdle, enough to enjoy every blessed second. Enough to show you everything and to remember everything."

"Sounds divine. So what's the hurry?"

"Ahhh, Irish, how can I explain that to you? Something you gotta experience for yourself."

"With your help, I presume."

He squeezed her hand, smiling his lazy smile. "Yes, ma'am. You can count on that."

Tugging free, she traced the scar on his lip. "You know I've never . . ." She dropped her hand to his chest. "Never."

He shifted to face her, and sand squeaked beneath him. "I know."

"I'm not scared." And she wasn't.

Much.

Zach laughed softly, his lips pulling back from his teeth. "I wouldn't presume to put *scared* and *Savannah* in the same sentence. Besides, there's nothing to be afraid of. I won't let anything happen to you, except wondrous things that'll make you float on a cloud for days. I make that promise. To protect you, to keep your best interests in mind. You can carry it with you now and take it when you go back home. At first I thought we were an awful idea, mostly because I suspected you were a virgin, and a bit because I wasn't sure if I wanted to—if I could—*live* again. But I know I want to be with you, I know I can take care of you in this." He scrubbed his hand over his face. "Jesus, I might as well face up to how good I am at that."

I can take care of you. When had anyone last taken care of her? Her mother, before her death.

Savannah realized the danger in his words. She needed to be able to hear them and remain unfeeling. She needed to be able to touch him, to be with him, and remain detached. Anything that warmed her heart to its core posed grave peril to her happiness. When she returned to New York, as she someday must, she didn't want to leave part of herself with Zachariah Garrett.

"I'm fine, Constable. Better than fine. I've been taking care of myself for years. I'm accustomed to it."

"Wouldn't it be nice, though, to relinquish power for a day or two? A week, maybe. Let someone else steer while you enjoy the scenery?" His gaze, sleepy and endearing, pledged that and much more.

What could she say in answer to that? Depending upon him enough to surrender control for even a moment went far beyond Savannah's expectations of a relationship with Zachariah Garrett—with any man. The breeze sneaked inside the open throat of her dress, drying the moisture on her skin. From the campsite, she heard her name being called. Then his. Time was running short, when she wanted the rest of the night to talk with him, to kiss him and feel his body pressed against hers.

To have him roll her to her back as he'd promised while she whispered big words in his ear, as she'd promised. To wake up with the sun and start all over again.

Attraction. She believed that's what Zach had called it earlier. Attraction. Warm and indescribable . . . *teasing,* if she had to choose a simple word. *Mesmerizing,* if she wanted a big one for him. His regard made her feel light as a feather, adrift on his prescribed cloud of bliss. My, what would the rest of it—the prone positions and the bedroom, the tangle of limbs she had read about—make her feel if his gaze held the power to scald to such an astonishing degree?

"Tomorrow," he said, pulling her to a sitting position and taking her hair in his hands. He combed his fingers through it once, twice, as tremors of awareness danced along her spine. Grains of sand filtered down the back of her dress, and she shivered.

"When?" She didn't have to ask what he meant . . . or where they would go from here. In her mind, she'd scuttled far past the point of return. Wasn't it past time for her body to catch up? "Where?"

"Noah and Ellie are returning to South Carolina day after next. They're taking Rory for dinner and ice cream tomorrow evening. After five, my night is free."

She smiled. "My last class is over at four-thirty." Caroline's reading lesson.

Bracing his hand on the dune, he leaned in and kissed the base of her neck. She swallowed hard, bright bursts of light scattering her vision. "The coach house above the school. I'll meet you there. Five o'clock. Four forty-five if I can make it. It's empty, and the door is unlocked."

Moaning softly when he took her earlobe between his teeth, she leaned into him, as pliable as runny clay.

"They're looking," he said gruffly, his arm snaking around her waist and pulling her into him, "and I don't want them to find us."

A second later, they scrambled apart as Caleb called their names from the other side of the dune. Zach slipped his hand over her mouth and gestured for silence. Grinning, she licked his palm, then bit down on the pad of one finger.

His gaze narrowed; he moved forward slightly. She could see his focus draining away like water from a leaky can. "Tomorrow, I'll make you pay for that," she thought he whispered.

She couldn't wait.

Chapter Seven

Tell almost the whole story.

—Anne Sexton

Dropping her bicycle by the garden gate, Savannah raced into Elle's school the next afternoon and slammed the door before anyone had a chance to peek inside. Ripping the veil from her head, she went to stand before the oval mirror hanging in the washroom. Saints' blood, was this a curse for her egotism? The price to pay for feeling beautiful for the first time in her life?

She brushed her fingers over her swollen cheeks, dabbed at the blister on the end of her nose. A tear trickled down her face, then another, the salt in them bringing pain and more tears.

Naturally.

Undeniably, hers was the most hideous case of sunburn ever seen in Pilot Isle. As Constable Garrett prepared to meet her in less than two hours, here she stood, covered in blisters and a flaming crimson stain. She shivered, gripping the washstand and praying the chills were part of this mess, not an additional curse for considering intimate relations with a man outside the holy bonds of marriage.

She bowed her head as a wave of nausea rolled through her, weakening her knees and making her wish she had worn her bonnet on the beach as Zach had told her to. *I'm fine, Constable,* she had snapped; *play daddy for someone who needs it.*

Oh, Lord, what would he say when he got a good look at her face? *I told you so,* more than likely.

She shook her head. As wretched as she felt, his censure would be enough to send her over the edge into complete and utter misery. She straightened, a method of deliverance popping into her mind. She would send a message through Caroline when she came for her class. An innocent lie about a forgotten meeting with Lydia. That would work.

From Rory to the life-saving crew to daily complaints from every person in town, Zachariah Garrett had a thousand ways to fill his time. He probably wouldn't care one way or the other if she canceled their rendezvous. As another wave of agony hit her, she convinced herself that any excitement about this afternoon had been hers and hers alone.

Zach checked his watch for the fifth time in an hour, wondering why days you wanted to pass in a blink always passed so blamed slowly. He'd swept the floor. Twice. Plumped up the pillows on the cot, checked the sheets to make sure they were clean, and changed the daisies in his mother's chipped vase. End of the month meant payroll time; the jail was certain to have a rowdy visitor or two any day now. Might as well look decent.

The cargo records were as up-to-date as he could

make them and not go stark-raving mad. The breeches buoys were in good shape, and everyone on this evening's patrol had been accounted for. And reminded—or threatened, as the case may be.

Slipping his watch free, he let the second hand complete a full circle before returning it to the small pocket at his waist. Twenty minutes and he could lock up the place, leave the key with Christabel in case of an emergency, and hightail it to the coach house. Dropping into his chair, he propped his feet on his desk, imagining what his sassy Irish belle might be wearing—or not wearing—when he arrived. It made for heady contemplation.

Leaning forward, he thumbed a dirty spot from the tip of his newly polished boots, approving of the effort. He'd gotten a quick haircut, too. And made sure to wear pressed trousers and the best-looking shirt he owned that wasn't reserved for Sundays. Even his underdrawers were starched. It wasn't comfortable, but it had to come across better for public viewing.

Damned if he wasn't excited. About seeing a woman. A sudden smile spread across his face. How long had *that* feeling been missing from his life? Put a little joggle in a man's step to know that a pretty woman waited for him on a delightful summer afternoon. It made Zach feel in the prime of life instead of miles past it.

He hoped Hannah looked down on him from time to time . . . and he hoped she approved of what he was doing. A couple of times during their years together, she'd told him to find someone else if anything should ever happen to her. Someone clever and vivid, all the colors of the rainbow, like he was. Of course, he'd scoffed at the idea. Imagine being with anyone except Hannah? He hadn't wanted anyone else, loved anyone else. She'd been the mother of his child, his sweetheart . . . his *wife*. If they didn't match up in all the ways people in love could, he'd never given it much thought. He'd been content.

Then God had chosen to take her. And his child. After a year or so of wishing he had died with them, he and God had made peace.

However, to this day, he didn't think he'd made peace with himself.

Savannah Connor, with her glowing green eyes and stormy nature, her naughty smiles and soul-stirring kisses, had promised to help him do that.

He was checking his watch for the seventh time when a gentle knock sounded on the door. Had she come here? Had she confused the location? His eyes drifted toward the freshly made cot in the jail cell. Not what he wanted for the first time they made love—if that came to pass today or ever—but it would do, he supposed, if need outweighed reason, as it often did with the woman.

He strode to the door, disappointment dropping like a weight on his shoulders when he opened it and saw Caroline standing on the other side.

"What can I do for you, Caro?" He mumbled a quick prayer that some catastrophe wouldn't keep him from his appointment. *Please, God, not now.* "Anything wrong?"

Caroline laughed, her rouged lips breaking into a wide smile. Resting her weight on her peacock blue parasol, she rummaged through her beaded reticule, muttering about a note inside a side pocket. "Here it is, praise be! I knew I stuck it inside that one." She slipped it into his hand with a wink. "It's from Miss Connor. I had a class scheduled with her today, but she's apparently busy and had to cancel and wanted me to give you—"

"Thanks." Grabbing his coat from the peg, he shrugged into it as he skirted Caroline. "Close the door if you don't mind," he shouted over his shoulder as he raced along the boardwalk.

Of all the nerve. Instead of facing him directly, bringing her fear or her displeasure—whatever had happened in the course of twenty-four hours to change her mind—to the forefront, she had sent a note. A goddamned *note*. Through a third party, no less.

A note that said . . .

Halting in the middle of the street where a carriage wheel came close to squashing his foot, he unfolded the crumpled missive and held it up to block out the blinding rays of sunlight.

It said, in unexpectedly feminine script:

> *Constable,*
> *I'm unable to attend our meeting this afternoon.*
> *I will call on you presently to reschedule.*
>   *Yours,*
>   *Savannah M. Connor*

He felt a slow, creeping burn of embarrassment. To think he had been anticipating their afternoon all day. Had felt a smidgen of excitement, even. Call on you presently to reschedule, would she?

They would see about that.

Shivering, she rummaged through a cedar chest in the corner of the coach house's bedroom. Noah's sweaters lay on top, but below she could see the tail of a green-and-gold knitted shawl. Reaching for it, she sniffed, the action stretching skin she didn't want to stretch—or touch—at the moment. There had been nothing in the school to warm

her, and Zach had said the coach house was unoc-
cupied. And strangely enough, or perhaps not for
Pilot Isle, unlocked.

Wrapping the shawl around her shoulders, she
returned to the main room, studying the oceano-
graphic maps tacked in neat alignment on the wall.
The others, composed of dotted lines and jagged
swirls, she guessed were called tidal charts. Brushing aside a spiderweb, she perched on the edge of
a settee that had once been dark magenta and was
now dusty pink, and waited for the sun to set.
Another hour, maybe two, and she could travel
back to the boarding house under the cover of
darkness.

She was dozing lightly, her cheeks throbbing in
time to her heartbeat, when Zach called to her
from the landing outside the front door.

"Go away," she croaked, certain she had never
looked or felt more miserable in her life. She'd be
damned if she'd let the world share her misery.
Especially him. Clearly, their *friendship* did not
extend to loving care in sickness and in health.

The doorknob jiggled. "Miss Connor?"

Stumbling to her feet, she crossed the room,
careful to stay in the shadows. She could see him
peering through a narrow, rather dirty window. His
hair: he'd had his hair trimmed, exposing nicely
shaped ears. Shaking her head in bemusement,
able to smile at the absurdity of the situation
despite her misery, she called loudly enough for
him to hear, "Constable, I'm ... indisposed."
There, that sounded like a dignified excuse. And
how could a man argue with a woman in—

"Are you alone?" His head banged against the
glass pane as he strained to see her.

A fevered flush, fueled by anger or sunburn,
crawled up her chest and into her face. Alone?

Saints' blood, did he imagine she had collected a string of men she wanted to seduce in his brother's coach house? "Of course I'm alone, you insufferable fool! I'm indisposed; didn't you hear?"

He tapped on the window with his knuckle. "Women like you are rarely indisposed. I lived with one for ten years who often and truthfully was, so I'm a decent enough judge. A girl like you, heck, would be just plain sick." Another sharp rap on the glass pane. "Now open the door and tell me what the hell is going on."

"No," she said, mortified to hear a sniffle threading the word.

A pause. "Irish, you okay in there?"

Oh, heaven! She knew the man well enough by now. He would walk away if she made him angry, but never if she were in need. Taking a deep breath, she heard the answer in her mind, and it sounded perfectly normal. "I'm fine, Constable . . . truly." Some performance, she thought, sagging against the wall. It had started weak and ended with a whimper.

The doorknob jiggled again, forcefully. "Open up, now. Whatever's wrong I'll fix."

That was what she was afraid of.

In the end, she unlocked the door, her shawl slipping to the floor. The scent of sunshine and soap traveled in with him. It heartened her to see that he had taken care with his appearance. His underclothes were probably starched.

He got one look at her face, and an expression of pity crossed his. "Ah, Savannah. Why didn't you tell me?"

She sniffed. "Because I'm . . ." A tear rolled down her cheek. "Ugly."

A soft smile played at the edges of his lips. "No, no. You're jus' ''—he shut the door behind him and retrieved her shawl from the floor—"well done." Taking her arm, he led her to the monstrous leather chair beside the settee and forced her into it. Tucking the shawl around her, he crouched before her.

Even in her sickly state, she couldn't fail to notice how well his trousers conformed to his thighs, the lean line of his hip. If she had to have a nursemaid, at least this one was put together nicely.

His gaze searched her face. "It's not that bad," he concluded after a moment. "I've seen worse." He laughed and dabbed a tear from her cheek. "I've *had* worse."

"Truly?" Another sniffle surfaced, this from a woman who hadn't cried any of the thirteen times she'd been arrested. Not once.

Nodding, he placed the back of his hand against her brow. "You've a bit of fever."

"Probably," she agreed, feeling weaker by the moment, as if his ministrations sapped her strength.

She could have sworn a flash of amusement lit his gaze, though he quickly banked it. "Sit back; close your eyes." He pressed her shoulder into the worn leather. "I'll see what we have around here to take care of this."

Her eyelids low, she heard him walk into the small kitchen, open cabinets, a drawer. He clicked his tongue in displeasure, then snapped his fingers. The universal signal for success.

For a moment, she dozed, the late afternoon sunlight drifting across her face. She found the sound of him moving about, whispering beneath his breath and occasionally cursing, strangely comforting.

His touch drew her from her light slumber. She blinked, his handsome face flooding into view.

"What is that?" she asked, nodding to the bowl in his hand.

"Baking-soda paste."

She felt her nose wrinkle. Painful. "Yuck."

Grinning, he replied, "Yes, ma'am, but it'll cure what ails ya."

He had a son. And more than likely, experience with cuts and scrapes and sunburn. She closed her eyes and leaned forward. "Okay."

While he related a story about Rory getting locked in the coach house as an infant, he smoothed the cool, immediately soothing mixture on her face. For a man, he really did have a gentle touch. Nothing like she had ever known. She couldn't imagine Daniel Webster Morgan, her father and vice president of the second largest bank in New York, touching her with this amount of tenderness. And her brother? She had seen the way he treated his wife and two young children: as if they were cattle to be herded through life.

"I'm sorry about this," she whispered, shrugging faintly.

He paused, his fingers stilling at the edge of her mouth. "Why?"

"Because. . . ." She sighed, pleating her skirt between her fingers. "I can't—we can't . . . well, you know. I can't be appealing."

With a sweeping glance down her body but no comment, he continued his nursing until the gritty paste covered every square inch of her face. "Maybe, once I get some of these windows open and let a little fresh air in this hothouse, we can simply talk. That's enough for now."

She blinked. "Really?"

His eyes did the sweep again, but his voice was neutral when he replied, "Really."

"What did you think earlier?" She wrinkled her

nose and reached to scratch. When his magic salve began to dry, it itched like the devil.

"Hands off." He interrupted her movement. "No scratching or we will have a mess on our hands." Tipping her chin up, he ran the rough pad of his thumb along her jaw. "Does this hurt?"

"Hmmm?" Her lids had drifted low, his touch relaxing and invigorating all at once. Her knees certainly wouldn't support her if she had to stand anytime soon. "What?"

He released a peppermint sigh into her face. His finger quivered against her skin. "Where else are you burned, Irish?"

Her eyelids fluttered. Her hands rose. When she began to unbutton her shirtwaist, his eyes grew round as coins. She spread the material aside, baring her neck and the faintest hint of her chest. "I left it open yesterday because of the heat. Stings a little bit."

He sighed, shook his head, chuckled. She had no idea what he found amusing. The situation, her, or himself. "No blisters, at least."

She cast her eyes down, unable to see. "Lucky me."

He raised a brow without commenting, stuck his finger in the bowl, and began to dab the paste on her skin with light, diligent strokes. When he reached the top edge of her camisole, he sat back on his haunches, his expression vexed. "You want me to do this, or should you? The pink runs down some into, past"—he gestured vaguely—"past your whatsit here."

She couldn't have said before this moment what her answer might have been if asked such a personal question. Half the time since arriving in Pilot Isle, she figured she had gone crazy to let things go as far as they had with Zachariah Garrett. But she trusted him. There. He was so bloody sincere and understanding—if he wanted to be—and so, so *dependable*. She could say no anytime; she felt relatively certain he would back off.

Moreover, the medicinal treatment had been his idea. If you considered the facts, it seemed like rubbing salve past her "whatsit" was his responsibility.

Thrusting her chest out, she smiled, hoping it seemed innocent rather than cunning. "Go ahead, please. That stings, too."

He muttered something rough, but his touch was gentle. Unbuttoning another button, for a total of three, he spread her shirtwaist farther apart. Her camisole straps he slid close to the edge of her shoulder. She didn't watch him, but she heard his breathing sharpen, felt a moderate increase in the force he exerted. Her nipples, she was finding, had a mind of their own. Beneath the thin camisole, they puckered tight as Zach's fingers came within inches of brushing them. It was delicious, exposing this previously virginal four-inch patch of skin. What would it feel like to be completely naked?

"You're loving this, aren't you?"

She cracked an eyelid to see him squatting there and ... well, *glaring* at her. "Pardon me, Constable?"

His lips curled, a subtle set of dimples she hadn't noticed before flaring to life. Bracing an elbow on the arm of her chair, he leaned in. The soft puff of air hit her neck and sent a shiver racing in the opposite direction. Then he aimed lower, making sure to reach everything hidden inside her shirtwaist's folds. It worked, hardening the paste *and* making her nipples ache. Eyes wide, she rocked forward, sending a fleck of dried paste to the floor.

"What are you"—she swallowed to moisten her throat—"doing?"

"Just tending everything that stings, ma'am."

She eyed him, not trusting his innocent smile any more than she trusted hers. But turnabout was fair play, after all. Sitting back, she struggled for a modicum of dignity with her face, neck, and part of her chest covered in baking soda goo. She felt sure she looked less than attractive. "You didn't answer before. What did you think I had done when you came here? You seemed irate . . . when I sent a note."

Setting the bowl on the floor, he dragged a nearby chair over, swung it around, and straddled the seat, folding his arms along the back. His gaze never left her as his brow wrinkled in thought. "I thought you were either playing with me, like you'd changed your mind and couldn't come right out and tell me that, or . . ." He rested his chin on his wrist and regarded her with a wary expression.

"Or," she prompted, her skin beginning to feel as stiff as new leather with a layer of mud on top.

His gaze drifted. "I figured you had a man up here with you."

She couldn't contain the spurt of laughter. "A man? Saint's blood, Constable, when would I have had the time to find him?"

"I've heard a couple of the fellas in town say they're planning to ask you . . . ah, heck." He slapped the chair back on its hind legs. "Mark my words: you'd better be careful."

She did laugh then, cracking his handiwork. "What about me sitting here half naked with you? Is that your idea of me being careful?"

His gaze locked with hers. *I'm different,* he wanted to say. But that was a mighty hard declaration to make with a respectable erection filling his britches, and the chair he grasped like a lifeline the only thing keeping him from jumping on her. The paste he had slathered everywhere he could get it helped keep him away. She looked a tad unsightly. And beautiful despite the mess. "This is different," is what he finally came up with. *Great, Zach, just great.*

"Different? Do tell."

"I can control myself. Some of the men interesting in asking you to supper at Christabel's or out for a walk along the wharf may not be able to. They see a pretty woman climbing up on a dad-blamed crate, shaking her fist and riling up the whole town, they hear that clipped accent and the snappy words, and think, she'll be a hell of a time in bed. You're confounding the lot of 'em." *Didn't this happen in New York City? How naive was she?*

"Is that what you thought the first time you saw me? A hell of a time in bed?"

"Irish, I haven't put *woman* and *bed* in the same sentence for over two years. Thinking or speaking." He pulled at his lower lip, trying to recall the first time he had laid eyes on her. "Blast, what did I think? Was it, 'looks like she's gonna be a damned nuisance'? Yeah, that was it. I remember *distinctly*, to use one of your favorite words. Dis-tinct-ly." He'd also thought, *slim ankles, round bottom, magnificent lips.* And glorious hair. Oh, the woman had a fine head of hair.

Later, though. Those had all come later.

He watched her caked-up, robin's red cheeks crinkle with displeasure. "If we're only friends, why worry if another man is up here with me? Isn't that permissible? Are we establishing restrictions, Constable?"

"No!" He leaped from the chair, reaching to steady it as it rocked from side to side. *"No."* Strid-

ing to the window, he flicked the curtain aside,
gauging how much longer until sundown. Knowing
women the tiny bit he did, he reckoned one whose
face looked like hers wouldn't want to leave her
hiding place before dark. Opening the window, he
breathed deeply of the fresh air pouring into the
room. "That isn't it."

"Then what *is* it?"

Jealousy? Close. Mixed with a healthy dose of
rage. He rather felt as if he'd discovered Savannah
Connor, uncovered this tremendously valuable
treasure that no one else truly understood. Other
men saw her beauty, sure, who wouldn't? But did
they see that she was funny and bright and so
incredibly earnest that it made your teeth ache?
Did they see the yearning in her wide emerald eyes
when she looked at a child as if she was afraid to
touch them for fear they'd reject her? Did they
hear the passion in her voice when she talked about
all those darned women she thought she was helping?

He had. And he didn't want any of the salty
bastards in town to hurt her, is all. A piercing dart
of guilt pricked him. Was it so dreadful for him to
feel something for another woman? Nothing like
love, but . . . respect and concern? Did that mean
he didn't love Hannah any longer? Did it mean
she was finally, truly gone from his life? Even if it
meant all of those things, he didn't think he could
help . . .

Glancing at Savannah, he studied her as she
wiped her face with the rag he'd brought from the
washroom. A feeling like the one he often felt when
he looked at Rory swept over him. Affection and
contentment and misery wrapped into one mighty
cumbersome bundle. Boy, that just beat all. Why
her? Why not Mrs. Brand, who'd been widowed

for longer than he had and had made her interest known on more than one occasion? At the spring picnic and last month at the Gillards' wedding reception. Why not her?

He grunted. Something about Savannah Connor got to him. That was about as simply as he could put it.

Sighing, he turned, propping his hip on the window ledge. So he cared about her in a friendly fashion. Wasn't that better if their relationship should become intimate? Better that than nothing and pretending just to get close to her. He had never been good at feigning feeling, even during his wild days. What you saw was what you got. It hurt him more often than it helped, but it caused less confusion.

Besides, it was useless to try and hide anything. The old Garrett protective instinct was kicking like a healthy mule. No doubt about it, he knew that feeling.

"I don't want you to get hurt," he snapped, mostly directing the statement out the window. "Anything wrong with that?"

Her eyes appeared above the limp rag—stunned, if her expression told the right story.

"My mother died when I was twenty. I came home from piloting to find myself instant papa to Noah and Caleb. Lord, they used to fight something awful. About the most opposite people you'd ever want to meet. Body size, looks, interests—all of it." Pushing off the ledge, he paced to Noah's desk and fingered a letter opener he remembered his brother having as a kid. "One day, about ten years back, Caleb lost his temper and got into a scrap with Noah, who ran off, hurt and angry. I gave them both bad advice, and Noah didn't come back until last year. For ten years, I didn't know if he was dead or alive. Nothing. But I did know I had failed them. Caleb, Noah, and my ma.'' Then there was Hannah. That failure was too hard to talk about, too painful by far.

He traced the letter opener along a jagged scratch in the desk. ''I hardly had time to grow up before I was taking care of people. My mother, my brothers, my wife.'' He wiped at the moisture on his brow. ''And of course, Rory. Add to that the entire town and every crew that sails inside my boundaries. So if I throw some of that caring your way, I mean to tell you that that's just the way it'll have to be. If we are, or we become, involved. 'Cause I won't be able to change it.''

Savannah folded the washrag into a tight square, her lips pressed to hide what he suspected was a smile. ''What would you compare this caring to? Friend? Sister? Mother?''

Nodding, he clicked his tongue against his teeth. ''The first one sounds good to me. The last two kinda' make me feel funny.'' His gaze sharpened. ''Is that fine? It's not insulting, is it? I mean, I'm not good at lying, and we both know we're not in—''

''Whoa, whoa, to use one of your favorite words.'' Savannah walked across the room, halting only when the tips of her shoes touched his boots. Extending her hand, she smiled. Despite the gritty white smudges on her face, she looked gorgeous. ''*Friends* sounds lovely. Nothing more, nothing less. When one of us wants out, we tell the other. No pretenses, no games, complete discretion. End of story.''

Zach tilted his head, studying her, thinking it sounded too good to be true. When had any man ever had a relationship with a woman packaged up neat and tidy as this one? It sure sounded nice.

Even—no, *especially*—the *friends* part. He had friends, of course, and family, but . . .

He'd be damned if he wasn't plumb tired of Caleb's teasing about his getting married again. What about Christabel sending her unattached women friends to the jail with cakes, cookies, and those simpering smiles? And he loved Rory to death, but a person couldn't expect broad levels of companionship from a seven-year-old. Come to think of it, he couldn't picture a soul he acted himself around. That man who didn't feel like being Mr. Responsible all the time, who wanted to be, well, *normal.*

Before he changed his mind, Zach took her hand and sealed his deal with an Irish devil.

He lay in bed later that night, estimating how long it would take a tolerable case of sunburn to heal. Two days? Three? Had to give her at least that much time. The dead skin needed to peel off and the color on the new fade backing. Even if Savannah wasn't in pain, she wouldn't feel pretty. And there wasn't much you could do with a woman who didn't feel pretty.

Especially what he had in mind.

Acting the friend and keeping his lustful thoughts to himself, he had escorted her home under cover of darkness, the glow from what Savannah agreed were too few streetlamps lighting their way. She had told him about her family in New York—bits and pieces, nothing substantial, as if she couldn't bear to talk about it for long. Her father and brother sounded like narrow-minded bullies. Zach had kept his opinions—and the sorrow he felt for her—to himself.

Actually, once he stopped trying to catch a

glimpse of her trim ankles below her flapping skirt, or the curve of her breast when she was looking the other direction, he had really enjoyed talking to her. He hated struggling to fill every moment with meaningless chatter. Savannah wasn't bothered by brief lulls in conversation. Men couldn't think as quickly as women when it came to talking. It was one of the reasons Zach avoided social functions. Avoided women, he supposed.

She had told him about an article she'd written for this women's journal, something about a proposal for the vote in South Dakota or Utah or somewhere out west. With her eyes shining and her hands flapping to punctuate each comment, he had found himself thinking, *Lord, she's exquisite.* Most of it was just imagination at this point, but he imagined a lush body with a surprising bit of muscle thrown in. A flat tummy. Long legs. From the looking and touching he'd done, he was pretty sure about those two.

And her breasts . . . ah, he had missed breasts. Cupping them, tasting them, drawing a taut nipple into his mouth and rolling it between his teeth. He didn't understand exactly what was so fascinating about nipples. But he understood that he felt it.

Dimming the lamp, he rolled to his side. The crackle of paper reminded him. Tossing the magazine to the floor, he sighed in the darkness. The article Savannah had written discussed the possibility for more equal partnerships between men and women after the turn of the century. It was the one she had danced in the street with excitement about. She had insisted he take it home and read it, and had even run inside while he waited on the walk outside Miss Vin's, avoiding the curious glances and knowing smiles. He'd have to be careful about escorting her home too often. She would have to be careful, too. He grunted. *Yeah, right.*

They had, however, discussed how to proceed with discretion. That was a start. The plan was to meet at the coach house. After all, it was empty, and if Noah was ever in town and planned to use it, Zach would know right away. Savannah said she would check her calendar and send a note to the jail a day before with the exact time.

Laughing, he stacked his hands behind his head. Maybe the note would be scented.

Heck, forget scented paper. He hoped he could *wait.*

He hadn't felt like this over a woman—itchy and feverish and impatient—in a long time. Maybe ever. A positive change from his feelings before Savannah had arrived: restless, cranky, and dissatisfied. Hannah had made him feel loved and secure but never antsy. Whatever Savannah Connor had done to him, whatever spell she'd cast, he hoped she could undo. Her loving had better contain some kind of a strong antidote.

She was too smart not to realize what she was doing to him, wasn't she? Those big words that burst from her dazzling lips weren't just for show. Though she was a curious mix, he had to admit, of innocence and experience. She seemed to know things, things he figured a woman was simply born knowing. Other things brought a completely blank look.

Savannah's article rolled to the front of his mind. Along with it came a considerable twinge of guilt. Was what he was planning to do going to keep her from having a chance to marry? Maybe even with an eligible male in this very town? Men still liked to wed virgins, he assumed. Dr. Leland had been searching for one high and low since Elle broke his heart.

Savannah was about the last one left in town.

Puffed-up, arrogant peacock, the doctor was. Not a friend of any Garrett, but he and his tailored pinstripes might be the type to suit a citified woman like her. On the outside, it wouldn't seem that way. Why she'd agreed to test the water with *him*, he couldn't say. His education ran an inch to her mile, and he surely wasn't the handsomest fella she'd had the pleasure to meet. Not counting all that, she actually seemed as attracted to him as he was to her. Maybe that saying about opposites had a kernel of truth to it.

Picturing Savannah in the snappy green skirt and shirtwaist she'd worn today, looking fresh as a flower even with the baking soda paste slathered on, he couldn't help but wonder what it would be like to undress her. In response, his body temperature skyrocketed. "Oh, hell," he groaned and kicked the sheet to the floor.

Stalking to the wardrobe, he tugged on a pair of dirty trousers and a ragged shirt he kept for garden duty and painting. A walk along the wharf would calm him. It always did. Being near the water, enveloped in a thick, salty mist, tasting it on his lips, feeling it coat his skin, made him breathe easier. It made troubles fade into the distance when his mind was filled with the roar of the sea.

He must have spent a hundred nights since Hannah's death sitting on that scarred dock and staring into inky-black waves. At least this time a goddamn nightmare wasn't driving him from his bed.

Getting Savannah Connor *into* it was the problem.

Chapter Eight

A sip is the most that mortals are permitted from any goblet of delight.

— A. Bronson Alcott

"Zachariah Garrett, you gotta stop that woman. She's causing a ruckus over at my house. A ruckus, I say!"

Zach sighed; the ale barrels found on the beach during the last shipwreck were drying up like a puddle in the blazing summer sun. Lord have mercy, what had the woman done now? "Festus, what's the problem?" He held on to his calm smile, jotting the initials *S.C.* in the margin of the cargo ledger. Underlining them twice with enough force to tear the page. As if he didn't know.

Festus Bellamy, owner of Pilot Isle's net shop, stood in front of Zach, the belly drooping over his faded trousers and bumping the desk with each word. "That city woman. Something has ta be done about her!" Festus slapped a crumpled wad of white calico on the desk; the lock of hair falling into his face was as red as "that woman's" nose had been two days earlier. He looked as if he had run the half mile to the jail from the way he was huffing—a feat Zach would have paid two bits to see. "Maybe this is fine and dandy in New York City, but it ain't fine here. Alvin came and told me, and I went on home, tripped over my own feet trying to get there before my Shirley got involved in that woman's business. I made her get inside and get back to cooking my dinner. But not before them women wasted all my black furniture stain and went to the store for more. On *my* account, yes-siree. Painting some kind of signage to hang up somewhere or another. I can't tell you the mess they're making, clucking like a bunch of hens and stomping all over my fresh-sodded grass."

Spreading out the cloth, Zach squinted, making out one word in smeared black stain—a word that chilled him to the bone. *Vote.* "What is this?"

Festus blew a tense breath through his nose. "One of them fabric signs. I grabbed it outta my senseless daughter's hands. Imagine my fine, upstanding Shirley getting mixed up with that crazy city woman. After all Elma and I have done for her. Piano lessons, a new dress every time she asks for one, and don't let me start on all the hair gigs and girly fripperies I buy." Slipping his thumbs inside his braces, he yanked, then let them slap back against his chest. "This has got to stop. You know I can't be a part of a disruptive predicament, being a businessman myself."

Zach shoved back his chair, feeling the urge to throttle Savannah Connor. Or kiss her silly. "I'll handle it. I'll handle *her*. You go on back to your store."

"You'd better get over there. Got your son painting away like some miniature soldier in a female camp."

Zach paused, his arm jammed halfway down his coat sleeve. "My boy's over there?"

Festus tapped the tips of his fingers together and rocked back on his worn-down heels, his smile growing. "Oh, yes. Oh, yes. Got him in the middle of the pack—like wolves, they are. I swear that city woman nearly took my head off when I told her my Shirley wasn't about to take classes at her damned school. I can't guess what they're learning over there."

"Typewriting," Zach muttered, slamming the door behind him.

"Uh-oh. He's spittin' mad."

Savannah paused, a black dribble running down her paper. Rory stood beside her, still as a stone, his paintbrush stuck in the middle of the letter *L*. Blond hair dried by salt and sun hung like crisp wheat past his brow, tangling with lashes as delicate as a spider's web. Red specks of paint sprinkled his cheeks, giving the appearance of a rampant rash. Tiger had somehow gotten involved and bore a streak on his head and one paw.

"Who?" she asked.

Rory stretched his skinny arm, his index finger rising to a point. "Pa."

Savannah felt the prickle of awareness before she turned. Zach crossed the yard at a furious stride, threading in and out of the small clusters of women and cloth posters without missing a beat. Without tearing his gaze from *her*. Idly, she noted the blades of moist green grass sticking to his boots, the slight sheen of perspiration on his brow, wondering why she felt nothing but excitement. Not a solitary trace of fear. "Rory, you'd better go stand with Miss

Caroline. I think your father would like a private word with me.''

His gray eyes were drawn into narrow slits, his brows angry black slashes above them. A shadow of day-old stubble lined the jaw he clenched as he came toward her. Cheeks flushed and fists bunched, he looked "spittin' mad" indeed.

And more devastating than any man she had ever seen.

"He's gonna cuss," Rory warned in a calm tone, resting his paintbrush neatly on the edge of the paper and climbing to his feet. "But it won't last long."

Savannah laughed, amused and charmed. "Yes, more than likely." Brushing his hair from his eyes, she made a mental note to tell Zachariah his son needed a haircut. "Run along, now, so you don't have to witness my scolding."

Rory left her with a brave wink, as if to say, *he's all bluster, don't worry.* It was the first confidence in her twenty-five years she had shared with a child. The flood of delight spreading through her almost made her miss what Zach's arrival did to her once-steady heartbeat. She smiled, though, in spite of his glower, in spite of the rattle in her chest. It lifted her lips and her mood.

She was delighted to see him. Was this what missing a man felt like?

He didn't say a word or politely return her greeting, just took her upper arm in his callused grip and hauled her around the side of the house and into a lean-to storage shed.

"Unhand me at once, Constable," she panted. Struggling to break his hold, her gaze located his in the semidarkness of the enclosure. "This is reprehensible behav—"

Interrupting with an abrupt movement, he

backed her into the shed's wall. She saw his eyes
for a moment in a slash of sunlight: wild and so
dark they looked black. Then his head lowered,
blocking vision and thought. When his hands tangled in her hair, tilting her face to better fit her
mouth to his, she didn't pull away. Rather, she
stretched up on her toes to crowd him, to claim
him, her arms circling his neck and holding on
for dear life.

Finesse forgotten, he thrust his tongue into her
mouth, his hands kneading her scalp, sending a
delicious rush of awareness through her body. Her
nipples hardened, her stomach jumped ... and
for the first time, the area between her thighs flared
to life, demanding attention. *Hmmm*, she thought,
remembering the pictures in her books and
squirming against him, *I'm beginning to see how this
might work.* Hungrily she followed him move for
move, battling to deepen the kiss with her budding
skill. She recalled what he liked and set about using
it for her benefit.

She had paid attention.

Gentle bites to his lips, her tongue tracing the
edges just after. Hands sliding into his hair and
tugging. Nails gently digging into his skin. A murmured plea against his lips, his animal growl of a
reply.

If God had asked just then, she couldn't have
said where she stood or what day it was. Perhaps
what year. Anything outside that world, outside
him, ceased to matter. Dazed, she recorded it all:
the intense wall of heat surrounding them; splinters from the lean-to pricking her through her
cotton shirtwaist; the smell of turpentine and dirt;
Zach's rough-tipped fingers on her face, her neck,
her shoulders. His coffee-scented breath, his low,
sultry murmur.

Him.

She could not quell the nagging voice telling her that this kind of recklessness, this complete acquiescence, spelled nothing but trouble.

Her hand slid over his, down his arm, fingers digging into his shoulder. "Sweet heaven," she gasped as his lips trailed down her neck, latching on to her earlobe. "Zachariah, stop. Stop, please."

Yet she swayed into him, rolled her head to the side to give him access. Who would have guessed that ears were this sensitive? When his tongue dipped inside lightly in a warm, wet, surprisingly decadent swirl, her knees buckled. Clutching a fistful of his shirt, buttons cutting into her palm, she dropped her cheek to his chest, inhaling a breath of soap and sunshine.

"When?" he asked—a ragged appeal. Almost pleading. "The coach house?" He shivered in the heat, releasing a harsh breath all but into her face. "I can't take much more of this, Irish. I'm stopping myself from exploring places I shouldn't. Taking this past the point of no return. But it's an itch I can't keep from scratching much longer." Almost angrily he returned to her mouth, nibbling, teasing, his tongue memorizing each peak and valley as if his dutiful attention meant anything.

Pressing her palm flat over his thumping heart, she leaned back in his arms. "How do I look?" She tilted her head back and forth in the narrow shaft of light, hoping he could see her entire face. "Am I healed? Am I ghastly?"

He blinked and opened his mouth, shut it . . . shook his head. It would be a lie if she said his befuddled expression didn't send a burst of satisfaction straight to her toes.

He recovered, frowning, then yanked his hand

through his hair. "You're driving me crazy, woman."

Me? When he didn't answer, she realized she hadn't voiced the question but simply stood lazily in his arms, letting his attention steal her breath as cunningly as a cat stole a baby's. "You might say I look fine, or some such encouraging statement." She stumbled back in her haste to free herself, getting angry for no good reason. "A minimal courtesy."

He grasped her wrist before she could storm from the shed, and in one quick move lifted her chin with the same hand holding her captive. A dangerous adversary lay beneath Zachariah Garrett's winning smile and tranquil demeanor. Her attraction to him felt primeval, instinctual, like a maiden in need of a warrior's skill to survive.

"Courtesy is what you're wanting? I don't know how to be courteous, so I'll just be honest." His eyes glowed in the dim, dusted-filled light, a feral blaze. "You don't look *fine;* you've never looked *fine* to me. You're so goddamned beautiful it makes my heart hurt. Makes air get all blocked up in my throat. Is that encouraging enough? Even with that mess on your face and it shining brighter than a baby's irritated bottom, I couldn't see anything else even if I tried. Jesus, do you think I came roaring over here to kiss you in some"—making a quick sweep of the shed, Zach kicked a bucket at his feet, sending it into the wall—"blessed shed on the side of Festus Bellamy's house? With a gaggle of women out there waiting to see if we come outta here kicking and screaming?"

His blunt words, each one more startlingly than the last, stripped away fear, suspicion, and hesitation until she fairly glowed. "Why did you kiss me, then?" she asked in another one of those womanly whispers that didn't sound like *her*. A woman whose father found her lack of feminine grace and penchant for trouble such an enormous disadvantage that he suggested she begin using her mother's maiden surname. The push to change it legally had come a year later. The occasional *Times* article about her enraged him much less from then on, even though everyone in New York knew Savannah M. Connor and Savannah Morgan were one and the same.

"Why?" she repeated when he failed to answer, standing there with a confused glower.

He growled a reply, waiting a long moment before he answered. "I don't know. To stop the flow of words?" His hand went up, an admission of uncertainty. "I came tearing around the corner, wanting only to paddle your bothersome bottom ... but you were standing there in the sunlight looking so sweet, which I know darned well you're not. And you smiled when you saw me. You kinda' lit up." He looped his finger in a crazy circle. "And your hair. I like it, hanging on your shoulders like that. It's"—he shrugged, looking terribly uncomfortable—"nice."

She lifted her hand, not able to keep from touching it. "My chignons, I'm afraid, have always been a rather weak invention."

Reaching, he twirled a strand around his finger. "When you meet me tonight, leave it."

She nodded. "Okay." She felt sure, deep inside. Trust made the impossible possible, the complex simple. At least that was what she assumed allowed this decision to be so ... *effortless*.

Zach stepped back clumsily, a man who made few graceless movements. Clearing his throat, he scuffed the toe of his boot through the dirt. "What did you say?"

She released a faint laugh, his sheepishness utterly charming. "I'm meeting you at the coach house. Tonight. With my hair down."

Rubbing his hand over the back of his neck, he gauged her sincerity with a hesitant appraisal. "Have you been drinking?"

Her laughter grew warm and full. "No, no." She shook her head, wrapping her hand around her stomach and holding tight. "Of course not."

"Is it some female trick to make me forget about putting a stop to this nonsense?" He jerked his thumb over his shoulder, indicating her industrious sign making.

She felt a flicker of anger. "We're not doing anything you *can* put a stop to, Constable."

"Ah, Irish, you know that's not the truth of it."

"What harm is there in painting posters? It's for a rally next week—nothing in your precious town, I might add."

He clicked his tongue against his teeth. "So that's what the telegram was about."

The missive that she had tucked into her penny pocket burned like a hot coal through the material of her skirt. "Saints' blood, as if the need for posters for the Raleigh delegation is grand gossip."

"Irish, you know how few telegrams we receive in the span of a week? They're *all* big news around here." He shrugged, unconcerned. "Whatever it's for, make 'em stop. Or I will."

"Why?" She resisted the urge to stomp her foot.

He muttered something she was relieved she didn't hear. "Because, damn it, you're on a man's private property, and he's not agreeable to having a 'gaggle of women,' as he calls it, painting up a storm in his yard and charging furniture stain to his account."

"His daughter—"

"Shirley doesn't pay the bills. Her name isn't on the deed for this place." He paused, letting it sink in. "Understand?"

It almost pained him to watch her stiffen up and swallow her hurt behind an overconfident smile. There wasn't anything she could do—not immediately, anyhow, and maybe not in her lifetime—to change what was a man's world, a man's *right.* Or to change the powerlessness of being a woman.

She knew it. He could tell by the slight droop in her posture as she walked from the shed without looking back to see if he followed. It pricked his conscience to be the person to tell her a nasty truth she had likely heard a thousand times before.

As he stood there feeling like an ogre, she went to each group, squeezing shoulders and giving encouraging pats on the back. Women rolled up the dried posters and gently folded the others, gathering spare fabric and cans of stain, all the while throwing looks his way. Ones he wasn't at all used to. They were downright hostile.

"This is part of the deal, you know." He trailed after Savannah like a pup, feeling the insane need to explain as she shook out brushes and dropped them into a rusted bucket. She gave him nothing but a cold look and silence, the most frustrating combination known to man. "Pick and choose your battles, remember? I can't help who I am in this town, or that people come to me to clean up messes. Settle disputes. Law is law, after all." He sighed, defying the impulse to touch her on the arm or hand to show he wasn't really as angry as all that. "I can't give in even if I want to, don't you see? I don't have an official reason to and I don't want to shed any more nosey parker light on me and . . . well, you."

She stilled, a paintbrush slipping from her fingers. Her hand lowered, sinking into the tall stalks of grass, grasping them. Her eyes were wide and very green when they met his. "Even if . . ." Her lips lifted in a soft, awfully agreeable smile. "You mean you don't want to run us out of here?"

"Well, no." He flapped his hand around, indicating the women and the mess. "How can a little painting on faded old calico harm anybody? What's a few signs in the scheme of things? But I can't let you and this exhibition of liberty stay here. Festus has every right to order you from his land. And every right to ask me to see that it happens."

Really, she had a remarkable smile when it was sincere. "But you're not enjoying it." She placed the remaining brushes in the bucket and rose to her feet, shaking out her pretty blue skirt.

Enjoy it? Hell, this reminded him of fighting with Noah and Caleb when they were boys, guilt leading him to the general store for taffy and chewing gum an hour later. And Hannah? He hadn't ever fought with her that he could recall. "Why in the heck would I enjoy this?"

She turned but not quickly enough to hide the anxious look, the frightening memory, spilling into her eyes. A chill raised the hairs on the back of his neck. Fury at a faceless person rendered him speechless for a moment. "Who enjoyed it, Irish?" he finally asked, blood thumping in his temples, his face heating as it did when someone threatened his family or he saw a puppy being kicked.

Ignoring him, she walked to a group of stragglers standing in the shade of a large pine tree. Obviously, they awaited further instruction. "Ladies, Constable Garrett has so kindly offered his yard for us to conclude our poster project." She smiled, a smug one versus the sincere kind he preferred, her earlier distress evident only in the faint paleness of her cheeks. She must have known he wouldn't call her on it. Besides, it did return the familiar expressions to everyone's face. He found he favored that over the hostile glares.

Savannah extended her hand. "Deal, Constable?"

He cursed beneath his breath, not about to shake her hand in front of twenty gawking women. Stalking halfway to the street, he spun around to find her watching him from the edge of her regiment. Rory had saddled up next to her, drops of paint covering his face, shirt, and short trousers.

"Yes, yes, use the blamed yard. Take my son while you're at it and let him join the fight." She had him over the proverbial barrel this time.

He would return the favor tonight.

Zach arrived at the coach house early.

Impatience—eagerness, if he faced the truth—had him dropping off Rory with Caroline an hour before he had told her he would. Under the guise of a night patrol, he'd promised to return when he could, telling Caroline it would take at least three hours or so. Maybe four. Rory had run into the house with a succinct goodbye, his friend Justin's new cast-iron truck already filling his mind. Caroline had told Zach to let the boy stay the night if it came to that, saying two were about as easy as one. As a father of a trying six-year-old, he sure didn't believe that.

But . . . all night staring into those wide green eyes, kissing those incredible lips, and sliding inside that extraordinary body? Damn, it was a tempting notion.

As he lit a row of candles sitting on the window ledge, he realized he had no idea what the night might hold, no idea how far Savannah planned to go with this game. He blew the match out before it burned his fingers, and headed to the kitchen in search of a corkscrew. Jesus, he hoped Noah had one or he was in trouble.

"Bring wine," the paint-spattered note tacked to his bedroom door had said. No signature. No teasing banter to strengthen his resolve. He'd never purchased wine in the past, mostly ale, and if Christabel had found his abrupt request strange, or his knocking on her office door in the middle of the afternoon, she'd kept it to herself.

How had Savannah found his bedroom? Rory must have shown her. That, or she'd poked around while the others were outside painting. Either way, the image of her sitting on his bed and touching his clothing, sweeping her hand across his pillow, and maybe sniffing the sheets flustered and excited him. He could have sworn her scent lingered. It was all he could think about as he showered and changed into fresh clothes.

Locating a scarred wooden-handled corkscrew in a drawer crowded with utensils, he worked the rusted spiral end into the cork and gave it a good tug. He had never been with a woman in his bedroom. The one he shared with Hannah during their marriage was on the second floor. Noah and Ellie used that room now when they came into town. Or guests, the rare times he and Caleb had any. It was better that way. Part of the past put firmly into the past. It had helped with the nightmares, too. Besides, the third floor was basically an attic, quiet and dark. It fitted his mood most of the time.

Or had until recently.

He liked the privacy the steep staircase provided, and the far-reaching view from the window over the roofs of nearby houses. In the distance, if he squinted, he could see blue-black waves with frothy edging rolling into shore. Rory wasn't allowed up there alone—a bone-breaking tumble down the stairs or out the window was not something Zach wanted to risk. Also, the room provided complete privacy.

That in mind, maybe he could take Savannah up there someday. Zach smiled, brushing a sliver of cork from the counter. Sneak her in the back door or have her shinny up the trellis.

It had shaken Zach to see her with Rory this afternoon. His son and—he hoped—his soon-to-be lover. Pouring a measure of wine, he took a fast sip. Both of them had been covered in paint and sunshine, a gusty sea breeze ruffling their hair and clothes. They had looked like a picture, squatting there in the grass, pleased smiles on their faces. His chest tightened, knowing Rory would never have another mother when the boy clearly longed for one. If Zach was capable of making that significant a commitment again, he would.

Even without love, for his son's sake.

He would if he could. God knew it, had been told during many a prayer. Zach had pledged his life to his family and this town. He would do anything to help a person in need, do anything to improve his son's life or Noah's, Caleb's or Ellie's life.

But he would not marry again—could not bring himself even to imagine it. When he thought about marriage for more than a minute or two, as he did now, he started to feel physically sick. The burden of guilt and sorrow, weighing his shoulders down as surely as a three-foot-thick plank from the hull of a ship, amounted to more than even the capable Zachariah Garrett, leader, life-saver, brother, and father, could endure.

Draining the glass, he held off pouring another. He didn't want drink, regret about the past, or fear of the future to ruin this night or cloud his reasoning. Better to keep a clear head when dealing with a woman like Savannah Connor. Flat out, in any confrontation, she would stand toe to toe with him, as bold as any man.

Grabbing the bottle and an extra glass, he carried them into the main room. Even with the leather chair and the small settee, you couldn't exactly call it a parlor. The massive desk sitting in one corner and Noah's maps and charts tacked to every bit of available space made sure of that. Not to mention the bottles and metal instruments lining the shelves, the stacks of books crowding the floor.

Stretching out on the settee, Zach kicked his boots off and let his feet dangle over the scrolled edge. Stacking his hands behind his head, he stretched and yawned. Would she show? He closed his eyes and inhaled deeply, smelling spiced candle wax and something fishy from one of Noah's specimen bottles.

He hoped like hell she would.

Savannah approached with hushed steps until she stood over him.

He lay sprawled on the settee, one arm folded beneath his head, the other hanging to the floor, his long, slender fingers curled as if he held something in the palm of his hand. Candlelight cast flickering shadows across his face, highlighting the moist sheen on his cheeks and brow. A bottle of Claret sat nearby. Two glasses—she reached for both and sniffed—one used—stood next to it.

The sound of chirping crickets drifted in the open window, mixing with his whispery breaths.

His eyelids fluttered and he murmured softly, his fingers drawing into a fist. Slipping her boots off, she went to her knees beside him, her gaze wandering down his body. The chance to study him while he slept provided a far greater temptation than she could deny.

Zachariah Garrett was a beautiful man. More beautiful, she thought, because he didn't seem to know. He had unbuttoned his shirt for relief from the heat, exposing a light dusting of springy curls she wanted to feel against her skin. His sleeves were rolled to the elbow, leaving his muscled forearms bare. She brushed her finger over a protruding bone in his wrist, down the vein to his middle finger. A sprinkling of black hairs, neatly trimmed nails, a ragged cuticle. Her finger moved to his stomach, trailing lightly over the flat plane, pausing. Her hand, spotted with furniture stain she hadn't been able to scrub off, contrasted sharply with his white cotton shirt. She released an unsteady breath and let her eyes drift past his belt.

Her breath caught in her throat. Her hand twitched.

"Touch me, Irish," he whispered, his arm rising, his hand covering hers and tugging gently.

Startled, she glanced up. Thankfully, his eyes were closed, his lips pressed in a tight line. She watched a line of perspiration trickle down his neck and into his shirt collar before returning her gaze to his face.

She was curious. Frightened but curious. Healthy—curiosity was healthy. And natural. Completely natural. She remembered that much from the books. Relaxing her shoulders, she gave the silent signal and let Zach guide her.

Hard. And long beneath his wash-worn trousers. "My," she breathed, impressed despite her trepidation. This wasn't a child's toy or soft, like ... like a banana. No, my, no. Resting against the side of the settee, she examined the shape, tracing and squeezing gently, feeling it twitch and grow. *Amazing*.

He groaned, a sound unlike any she had ever heard. Primal and quite gratified. His hips lifted, a slight shift. She shot a quick glance at his face, not sure what to do, what he wanted. His eyelids fluttered again, his pupils so large and round they seemed to spill over. "I'm going to kiss you, then ..." Sliding the hand holding hers behind her back, he pulled her atop him. Her hair fluttered down, sheltering them like a curtain.

"Then?" She arched as he kissed his way from the open collar of her shirtwaist to her jaw.

He framed her face with his hands, his gaze drilling into her, giving her a chance to say no, to back out. He had no idea, she marveled, that she desired their union as much as he. She licked her lips, her heart thumping hard enough for him to hear, she felt certain. "Then, Constable Garrett?"

A lazy smile curved his mouth, his eyes half closing as he drew her lips to his. He tasted of wine, mint, and smoke. "Then, Miss Connor ... I'm going to do *everything* else."

She loved the feel of his mouth on hers, had loved it from the first. Soft yet firm, insistent yet gentle. However, this kiss was different from the others. Lying prone on a hard, flat body while being lured deeper and deeper into a blissful dream seemed akin to throwing rubbing alcohol on an already raging fire. Feeling his arousal lodged between her thighs—an area demanding attention itself recently—and the strength of his arms surrounding her only increased her need. She feared not the act but losing herself in it.

He was proficient at lovemaking. So far, anyway. As colors burst behind her eyelids, a rush of pleasure making her scalp prickle, she moaned softly against his lips, willing to revise her verdict. Gifted. Steady. Deliberate. Measured, when she wanted to rip his clothes off, tug at his hair, and will him to go faster. *Move to my breasts, my nipples,* she wanted to scream. *And please, God, ease the ache between my thighs.*

How, after all these years without, could he maintain such endurance?

Yet his eyes when she raised her head and looked at him were blazing with need and passion, fear and trepidation—a mass of contradiction. The competent leader held her hands just above her head with one of his while the paternal caregiver murmured gentle words in her ear. The covert lover unbuttoned her shirtwaist with an ease born of experience while the considerate friend stroked her shoulders and back in a calming rhythm.

She squirmed, pushing off the end of the settee with her toes and sliding up his body. She thought she might like to feel his mouth on her nipples, doing all the things he did so well to her lips.

He laughed softly and gripped her waist to still her advance. "Now why would I imagine you'd be patient?"

Through the flickering shadows, she watched his amusement build, felt her irritation follow. "After twenty-five years of wondering, to hell with patience. For you, it's been some time. Don't you, aren't you . . ." Her words drifted away, her face heating.

Tucking a strand of hair behind her ear, he pressed a kiss to her throat. "I've missed this more than you can imagine. Mostly the simple, basic beauty of it that people take for granted. The smell of flowers on a woman's skin. Something sweet. Something a man would never smell like. The softness, the dips and hollows. The differences—I guess that's what intrigues a man. Slim wrists and ankles, fine bones, and delicateness. Long hair and the way it shines in the candlelight. Yours is the finest I've ever seen." He sighed, a contented release, his fingers skimming her back in resolute circles. "So as long as I can hold on, I'm going to. There's so much I want, too much to pack into one night. I hope you agree. I don't plan on this being a one-night event for me and you."

She arched like a kitten under his touch. Her nipple grazed his stubbly chin, puckering into a tight bud inside her silk camisole. His eyes met hers: indecision there. She shoved hard against the settee, but in the end he held on.

"Please," she whispered.

"There's time, Irish." Taking her earlobe between his teeth, he sucked and nibbled. "We'll make it, find it."

"You want . . ."

"Hmmm . . . to caress the back of your knees and calves, kiss that soft patch of skin on the inside of your ankle." His fingers returned to her shirtwaist, freeing the remaining buttons until it hung open. "I want to see the shape of your hips without cloth covering, the length of your legs against pale sheets when you open yourself to me." He worked her camisole straps down her arms. "But if this is all we do, that's mighty fine, too."

Flattening her hand over his heart, she lifted enough to see him in the dim shadows. "It is?"

Arm going around her waist, he rolled to his feet, carrying her with him across the room. She gazed at his face, her feet dangling inches from the floor. It seemed the height of vulnerability.

"Uh-huh," he murmured against her neck. "Stop me if it feels wrong. Or too sudden."

"You won't" —she shivered as he found a particularly sensitive spot just above her collarbone— "be angry if I do?"

"No." Halting beside the bed, he let her slide down his body until her toes grazed the cool pine. Her knees threatened to buckle. She swayed into him, and he held on. Bringing her hand to his neck, he pressed her fingertips against the pulse drumming there. His eyelids looked heavy, his eyes clear and beautiful. "Never doubt how much I want you, 'cause I do. More, I think, than I've ever wanted anyone." A fleeting shadow passed across his face—a remembrance of his wife, Savannah guessed. "But you have to make this decision. I can't make it for you. If we were courting, it'd be different. As it is, I can protect you only as long as you stay here. I'm not set on doing anything to jeopardize your future. I won't allow you to do that to yourself."

Another woman might have been insulted. To Savannah, it sounded like the greatest grant of freedom.

For a woman who had fought for independence her entire adult life and had not found a man to share even friendship, a compassionate, considerate, handsome one entering her world at this stage and desiring her as Zach did seemed a gift from God.

"I want this," she vowed, holding his gaze so he knew she meant every word. "I want *you*."

Chapter Nine

Sin makes its own hell, and goodness its own heaven.
—Mary Baker Eddy

Except for the jerky release of air from his lips, Zach made no sound. He didn't want Savannah to know how close he was to splintering apart at her feet. No matter how much she would have liked to think they were equal in this partnership, he understood that the responsibility sat on his shoulders. A virgin couldn't be expected to run the show.

Lifting her by the waist, he set her on the bed, the ropes protesting with a muted squeak. She watched him in heart-pounding silence as he tugged her shirtwaist from her shoulders and down her arms, careful to keep from ripping the delicate lace front. Crouching before her, he inched her skirt to her knee and reached inside, his fingers brushing her thighs. Dear Lord, her skin was soft. And she smelled like the highest level of heaven.

She made a sound: a whimper or a low sigh.

His gaze met hers. He worked hard to keep his passion from showing. "Your stockings," he said huskily and began to roll them down her leg. "Unless you'd rather."

She shook her head, then let it fall back until it dangled from her neck like a rag doll's. That marvelous wealth of glossy chocolate trailed over the cream bedspread, just as it had in recent dreams. On the way down, he paused to explore the moist hollow behind her knee, the round calf, the slim ankle he had caught glimpses of the day of their picnic. Underneath her clothing, she was more delicate than he'd pictured. More feminine, though he figured she would argue if he told her.

Captivated, he kept his touch light, fearful of moving too quickly . . . and recorded every inch of her.

"My stockings," she whispered. "I lost a pair at the beach." She shivered, sighed. "Save those."

Using both hands, he massaged her feet, skimming the stocking over her toes and to the floor. He didn't mention that her misplaced pair sat in the top drawer of his bedside table. Instead, he lost track of himself removing the other one, stopping every few seconds to kiss what he exposed. He was powerless. She had the thighs of a woman who walked often, firm and sleek. Like an athlete or something. Unique, like no thighs he'd ever seen. Or touched. Her legs, long for her height and well shaped, lay spread before him, open to his eyes and his body, a mind-boggling invitation.

Placing a last, lingering kiss to a spot on her knee that she seemed to respond greatly to, ignoring the upward shift of her hips and her murmur of encouragement, he stood. The room smelled of her. He breathed deeply; his hands smelled of her. She lay sprawled on the bed, her arms thrown wide in surrender. After a moment, hearing only the sounds of their raspy breathing and the distant call of an owl, her eyes opened, held.

"The rest?" he asked, gesturing to her skirt and chemise. She had worn a minimal amount of underclothing in preparation for their evening. *That* didn't help his meager fortitude.

"Ummm, yes." She lifted her hips to help him, eager as a child. He wasn't about to ask a second time. She was sure—at this point he had to believe that—of what was going to happen.

Her skirt hit the floor, her chemise a silky flutter behind it. He took a gulp of air and rocked back on his heels. Her breasts were larger than he'd thought. No, not larger, *rounder*. Lord, though, her nipples were the icing on his fantasy cake. They were the color of a pink sunset the day after a furious storm, and looked to be hard as an acorn right now. He reached to palm one, then the other until she squirmed and quivered, lifting her hand to cover his. He loved nipples better than anything on a woman, hands down.

Before he could taste one, test his acorn theory, she sat up, placing her hands on his belt and working the strip of leather from the metal clasp with refreshing confidence. He closed his eyes, not wanting to see his erection straining toward her when he had no control over it. Luckily, she was as relentless as he, pausing to investigate his arousal in between unfastening each trouser button. A finger down the length, a half circle around the throbbing head. When she leaned in and kissed his belly, her magnificent breasts jiggling and his trousers dropping to the floor, he called her off with a desperate oath.

She tipped her head, smiling into his face, her hand snaking in to cup his testicles. Scooting forward, she wrapped her legs around his thighs and drew him closer, all the while continuing to fondle. Their groins were inches apart, inches from irrevocable contact. Did she realize what the heck she was doing?

"You're crazy, Irish, I'll give you that," he said, the rasping voice not his own. His hand tangled in her hair. He had to touch her somewhere or go crazy. "But I like it."

She squeezed, testing his weight in her palm, her thumb moving to the vein running along the underside, nearly knocking the breath out of him. He couldn't remember a woman—not even the occasional prostitute he had sampled as an immature young man—touching his *balls.* Cupping them so tenderly and with such interest. "I'm simply undaunted, Constable. To you, heavens, to most men, that does appear senseless. As if women don't experience the same curiosity and impulses." She laughed, releasing him and moving her hands to his hips. He felt her smooth, round nails digging in as she drew him forward.

She nodded to his jutting member. "I know where that goes, if you're worried. I've seen illustrations a number of times. I can't guarantee it will fit, but I know where it goes."

He grinned and lowered his body to hers, pressing them down into the mattress. He was relieved that she had some knowledge of the act, even if when sounded ridiculous. "Pictures? What kind of pictures?"

She adjusted her legs until they were hooked over his calves. "A book from Asia." Lifting her hips, she angled, searching for a good fit. "A book of . . . positions."

He felt a burst of pleasure at her words and her touch, praying she didn't feel scared to death by the hard length pressed against her. He couldn't account for how stiff he'd gotten, or do anything about how sharply it contrasted with her softness. Shifting his hips from side to side, he lodged himself in her moist folds, joining them like two interlocking pieces of a puzzle.

Jesus, he had missed this.

"A position like this?" he asked, flicking his tongue out to catch her nipple.

She stroked her way from his shoulders to his buttocks, pinching and pressing, murmuring praise for a part of his body he'd damn near taken for granted. "Like this, certainly. And more." Sucking a patch of skin on his shoulder between her teeth, she said in a garbled rush, "Sitting. Standing. Sometimes in a chair; I remember. In the water."

He jerked as if she'd scorched him with a lit match, lifting his lips from her breast. "You'd do that? In the water?"

She hummed an affirmative, enthusiastic reply that she would, of course, make love to him in the water. Her lids lowered, her chest lifting in rapid jerks, coming closer to his lips with each exhalation. *Well, hell,* he thought; he had lived on an island his entire life and never really figured on making love in the ocean. Though it sounded like a damn fine idea now that he'd found an agreeable woman.

He snapped back to find her deep-green gaze fixed on his face, a teasing smile curling her lips. "Is this the point where I whisper big words in your ears? To get you in the mood?"

Circling her nipple with his tongue, he worked his hand between their bodies. He stroked her sex, watching closely for her reaction when he gently worked his middle finger in as far as it would go. Her muscles clenched around him like a wet leather glove.

"Saints' blood," she breathed. "Are you certain you'll . . . oh, don't stop. Don't . . . stop."

"I will fit, and I won't stop." Was she demented? Stop when she had begun to follow the motion of his hips and the thrust of his finger, matching step for step his rhythmic cadence? It was an instinctive dance, sex without entry. Sometime in the past, a long time ago, he'd thought the bump and grind could be almost as good. *Almost.*

Capturing her lips beneath his, he invited her one step closer to bliss.

With a husky murmur, she agreed to come.

Their kisses grew reckless, their touches bold. Inflaming, inciting. A damp tangle of arms and legs, they explored each other from one end of the bed to the other. Zach imagined he had logged enough information in his brain to identify her without opening his eyes. The endearing chip on her back tooth, the tiny mole on the side of her breast, the inch-long scar on her belly. Her scent. *Oh, yeah.* Partly floral, married with an earthy something, a scent he could spot in a greenhouse full of fresh blooms.

He got the chance to focus on his favorite area when she rolled on top, her taut nipple bumping his chin for the second time that night. Capturing it in his mouth, he kept her still as he rolled it beneath his tongue, sucking and nibbling, feeling it pucker against his lips. Damn, was there anything in this world better than a woman's well-loved nipple?

"Now." Arching her back, sending her nipple in deeper, she gasped, "Now, Zach, now."

Hands coming up to cradle her face, he set her back a bit. "What'd you call me, Irish?"

She blinked, clearly dazed, more bewildered than he'd ever seen her. "What?" Her hand came up to push a tangle of hair from her face. Her fingers trembled against her temple. "Did I say something?"

Laughing, he rolled her to her back and settled inside her thighs. The sheets had come partly off the mattress, and what was left on the bed was a wrinkled mess. Perspiration trickled down his back, and hers felt right slick, too. A summer storm had blown in some time since they arrived and was sending a fierce sheet of rain against the windows and a ripping breeze into the room. The air, humid and salty, felt good skating across his skin. Hell, he hadn't heard the storm begin. It could have been hail, thunder, and lightning for all he knew. Remarkable.

Savannah Connor's brand of loving was unlike any he had experienced.

Confirming that belief, she reached down and guided his shaft damn near where it needed to be to finish the job. "I'm ready. For pity's sake, Constable, let's go."

He dropped his brow to hers, smiling softly. "Oh, yeah?"

She wiggled her hips, sighing. "Definitely," she said, ruining the act when her voice fractured. Vengeful, her hand circled him, stroking industriously as she struggled to fit him into place.

He couldn't contain the tortured groan that spilled free, even as he thought he might be able to hang on long enough to tease her a little more. "Find it, Irish. You're mighty close." And damn if she wasn't. "But you still need *me* to bring it home. Independence isn't all it's cracked up to be, is it?"

She giggled. Knowing she wasn't a giggling kind of girl, he should have taken note. "What if I promised more than big words?"

"I'm listening." Listening while he counted to

twenty and back. Or maybe thinking about fishing would do the trick.

"More than positions were detailed in my books, you see."

Goddamn. His fingers clenched, fisting around the sheet. She'd struck gold. "Hmmm . . . like what?" Teasing her was starting to feel like a fool's errand.

Stretching, her fingers walked across the mattress. Grasping a pillow by the edging, she slid it beneath her raised bottom. Then, one trifling boost, aided by the long legs anchored around his bottom for support, was all it took to have the head of his manhood edge inside her just the slightest amount. Enough for both of them instantly to feel as if they'd jogged a mile uphill. With hundred-pound packs on their shoulders.

"My mouth," she whispered raggedly into his ear. Her breath smelled like apples. And maybe peppermint.

Fingers tangling in her hair, he tilted her head for a kiss. "This lovely mouth?" His tongue brushed against her lips, teasing, tasting. "Where?"

Her hands cupped his buttocks and shoved, driving him a trace deeper. "Where do . . . you think?"

As she arched her back, her plump breasts flattening against his chest, he decided he was getting sick of this game. "I have no idea," he said between clenched teeth. Jesus, he could feel a climax building deep in his sex, and he wasn't even a tenth of the way inside her yet.

"My, your vision . . . astounds." Her nails scratched their way up his back. "On . . . this, of course. Or over. The sketches were . . . extremely detailed." She laughed, but it turned into a rabid moan as Zach lost his grip—literally and figuratively—and slipped in as far as he could, her maidenhead the only thing keeping their pelvic bones from knocking together.

Hobbling up onto his elbows, he stared into her face. *"Whoa."*

She didn't open her eyes but simply flashed a feline smile. "I feel utterly stretched out, Constable. Tingly and moist and, well, stretched. The books didn't mention this."

"Forget about those blamed books!"

Her eyelids lifted. "You mean my suggestion is a dreadful one?"

"No—yes." He frowned, backing up, not wanting to rule it out. No man wanted to rule *that* out. Struggling to regain control of the situation, he glanced at her lips, swollen and pink from his kisses. It wasn't a dreadful idea, actually. However, if he began to fantasize about her putting her mouth there, he wouldn't last another five seconds.

She smiled as if she'd read his mind, and shifted for better purchase. He slid in a bit deeper, angry, for some goddamn reason wanting to be the man here.

"Slow down, will you? Can I lead this dance? There's pain in—"

"Lead it," she interrupted, her hands tangling in his hair and bringing his mouth within reach. "I know it's going to be painful." Her tongue stroked his lower lip and slipped inside his mouth. "I'm sure you'll make up for it next time." Her lashes fluttered, her eyes focusing on him. "I trust you."

Well, that did it. When had he ever been able to turn away from someone who looked at him with such confidence?

Savannah held her breath as his jaw clenched, his arms tensing, muscles twitching. Then, before she had a chance to congratulate herself for speaking the truth while figuring in the back of her mind that he would respond out of duty if nothing else, he was kissing her, murmuring soft words against her lips as he worked his hips from side to side—the most deliberate, devastating entry she could imagine. His arms snaked around her and seized her bottom, pulling her up and in. She gasped at that bit of trickery, her heartbeat thudding in her chest. "Sneaky devil."

"Just . . ." he sighed into her ear, adding something else too low for her to hear. ". . . keep up if you can."

Hooking her legs more securely around his, she grabbed his hips, making bloody sure she "kept up." Push. Pull. Lift. Lower. Clench. Release. It all seemed rather elemental. And animalistic as they whispered battle calls and challenges, tangling the sheets around their ankles and edging across the bed. The sharp prick of discomfort passed quickly, as did the feeling of being torn in half from the groin up, when he slid all the way inside. Ever considerate, Zach felt her flinch and leaned in to kiss away her hesitation.

He seemed obsessed with her breasts—or more specifically, and to her delight, her nipples—and a nib of flesh between her legs that she had until this moment found no use for. *He* found it, teased it, circling repeatedly while telling her what he was going to do to her, tossing her in over her head in less than a minute. The orgasm—she believed that was the word for it—ripped through her with the speed of a tornado. Had she cried out? Screamed, even? Opening her eyes, she found Zach staring at her as if she'd certainly done something . . . *loud.*

"Did I . . ." She licked her lips and swallowed. "Did I make a noise?"

He smiled, pausing on the upswing. "Oh, yeah."

She could feel him pulsing inside her. As she watched, he pressed to the hilt, then retreated until she thought he would pop out. Again, the gradual charge. And again. Her vision blurred. White. A burst of blue. Gray, like his eyes.

"I'm embarrassed," she said, clutching his shoulders and lifting to meet each plunge.

He withdrew. "Never, Irish. Never hold back with me."

A deep thrust followed his appeal. Arching her back, she surrendered. She felt his release of control. In his reckless kiss. In the trembling hands that cupped her face. In his labored breaths and the words he spoke. Meaningless phrases, low curses. Smoky eyes fixed on her, then closed tight in ecstasy. They were an amazing study in contrast. Her nipples, his wiry chest hair. Her soft tummy, his hard, flat one. Hip to hip, he urged her to follow him.

"You there, Irish?" His voice sounded raw, tense.

"Yes," she whispered, unsure what he asked for. "Right here."

He suckled one nipple, rolling the bud beneath his tongue. When he bit gently, she couldn't contain her choking moan.

"Come on, come with me." His breath washed across her breast, urgent, fervent.

She hummed low in her throat, her body lifting, stretching. . . . If this was another orgasm, it felt wildly different from the first one. Her body flushed and she whimpered, flexing her bottom, her hips, clutching him to her. He had quit worrying about her pain or his direction and pounded into her, bumping them to the edge of the bed. Her head slipped over, and he reached, cradling it in his big hands, not pausing for a second.

"Zachariah?" Her body quivered, sizzling ripples spreading from her furrowed brow to the heels of her feet. The colors had returned to tint her vision.

"Right here, Irish." She felt him brace his elbows on the edge of the mattress and dig them in deep, slowing his movement until he rested against her. She wanted to shout in fury, ask him what in Eve's ghost he was doing. The feelings were fading fast, her vision returning. Then he shifted his hips from side to side, rubbing. *Rubbing.* The same spot, that useless nub he had introduced her to before. Better than his finger, oh . . . yes.

This was perfection.

She focused on the expansive feeling of penetration. His rasping exhalations hitting her cheek. The snap of the curtain in the breeze. Rain plinking against glass, and the scent of their bodies thick in the air. She tried not to get attached to the idea of experiencing this too often, because when it hit her this time, she nearly fainted. Blood pounding in her ears, her harsh cry just after, her scalp prickling, every place he touched almost painfully sensitive. Wave after wave until she fought to catch her breath, her wits.

The arms holding her trembled, squeezed tight.

She drifted back, blinking. With a final, consuming thrust, Zach jerked and rose to his knees, cursing softly. Lines bracketed his mouth; grooves swept from the corners of his eyes. He dropped his head to his hands and released a harsh breath through his fingers. His shoulders shuddered.

Rising to her elbow, she swayed, swirling black dots making the room go dark. Admitting defeat, she flopped back, throwing her arm over her eyes. "I feel . . . shaky all of the sudden. Dizzy." *Complete. Resplendent. Satisfied.*

The mattress dipped as he dropped upon it.

"That makes two of us." His voice sounded like glass being ground beneath a boot heel.

"Why did"—she flipped her hand in a droopy circle—"you, um, disengage? Did I do something wrong?"

He sighed, looping his arm around her waist and dragging her into the crook between his armpit and ribs. Her head found a perfect resting place. His heartbeat skittered beneath her ear, his pleased laugh a distant rumble in his chest. "Jesus, no. *No.*" He yawned, his hold relaxing, fingers splaying across her stomach. "Everything right." He kissed the top of her head, saying, "I withdrew for protection." A whisper of air ruffled her hair. "Yours. And mine."

Savannah lay in the warm cocoon of Zach's embrace, their bodies twisted in a moist tangle. She glanced at his stunning features serene in slumber, lit by a moonlight flood, and deemed her first sexual experience a rousing success.

Yet for all she was grateful that Zachariah Garrett was the man she had chosen, she felt strangely bereft.

"Are you sure no one's up?" Savannah asked, glancing anxiously at the star-filled sky, judging sunrise to be less than two hours away. Her body felt boneless, her mind dazed. It was a wonder she had been able to make it down the coach house stairs. "At the oyster factory or on the docks?"

Zach offered his hand to assist her across the wooden walking bridge and onto the narrow strip of shoreline tucked away in a secreted corner of the wharf, unsuccessfully trying to hide a smile at her state of bewilderment. "On Sunday morning? No, ma'am. Preaching doesn't start until ten. Businesses open after that, if at all. Folks don't rise until, oh, eight or so, usually. This is a day of rest.''

She didn't know about the "folks" of Pilot Isle, but *she* didn't feel rested. She felt grumpy and sticky and disheveled. It would take an hour to untangle her hair. And her clothes? A rip in her skirt and a button missing from her shirtwaist. She looked a fright, while he looked as tidy as a trolley car first thing in the morning. Gritting her teeth, she wondered how men managed to do that. Have stubble on their face and wrinkled clothes on their body and still look . . . *good.*

She threw the man beside her a covert glance. Good enough to eat, in fact.

Bringing their clasped hands to his lips, he pressed a kiss to her knuckle. "Now, don't pout."

She kicked at the sand, a wave rolling in and washing against her ankle. "I'm not pouting." Not really, not when he held her hand so tenderly. She had not held hands with a man before that she could recall, certainly not without gloves serving as a barrier. "Really."

He smiled, a flash of white teeth. "I've practically raised three boys. I know pouting when I see it."

"Well," she said, shrugging, "we had time." Now they were frittering it away walking on the beach.

Arm snaking around her waist, he hugged her to him, laughing against her neck. He nibbled on her jaw, her cheek. "Wasn't twice enough? Next time I'll make sure I haven't spent the entire night beforehand patrolling the beach and getting maybe a half hour's sleep."

For a long moment, she let her cheek rest on his chest, listening to the sea slapping the shore and the steady rhythm of his heartbeat. Lukewarm gusts of air pummeled her back, salt spray coating each exposed piece of skin. She denied the desire to curl into Zach's body, seeking shelter. Take what he so proficiently gave. Dependence of that magnitude was simply not to be borne. Not for Savannah Connor, visionary, social reformer. However, didn't a woman reside inside her? And when would *her* time come?

If her life consisted of shucking oysters or adding columns of numbers for eight, nine, ten hours a day, could she stay locked in Zach's embrace, close her eyes and let him hold her while the waves lapped at her feet and the world around them faded into the distance? Would that—would *he*—be enough?

With a nod of acceptance for what simply was, and what was not, she stepped back, walking to the water's edge to avoid his perceptive gaze.

This would be the hardest part of their association, she suspected.

The time after.

When her body thrummed from lovemaking—and half her mind and a sliver of her heart, if she admitted it—lay in his hands. It wasn't love, this intense longing she felt in the pit of her stomach, but she believed a woman had to give part of herself to do what she and Zachariah had spent the night doing. How could she shed her clothing and her inhibitions, her autonomy and her virginity, without part of her heart being involved? Lovemaking was not the place to "stand alone," though this had been her motto for years.

Zach came to stand beside her, his shirttail whipping against his lean stomach, his gaze fixed on the twilight blue horizon. She had kissed him there, explored each rib and hollow, run her tongue around his navel before he pulled her atop him.

That had been an interesting lesson.

He bent over, picked up a rock, and, with a

torque of his upper body, skipped it across the waves. Helpless, her gaze recorded each flexing muscle.

"How many lovers have you taken, Constable?" She swallowed, coughed lightly into her fist. "It seems like you ... well, like it's an adequate amount."

He tilted his head, gray eyes glowing with what one could only label masculine satisfaction. My, she had done something this evening to please him. Stooping, he selected another gleaming rock and let it fly. Three, four, five skips before he answered. "I don't know."

Wiggling her toes in the damp sand, she tangled her fingers in her skirt. "Don't know number-wise, or don't know, didn't keep count?"

Crouching on one knee, he glanced up, his hair falling across his brow. He knocked it aside, but it blew right back into his face. "The last one. I didn't *want* to count."

"Because you had a woman waiting here for you?" Savannah knew from some tale she'd heard in town that Zach had met his wife when they were children, then gone off to seek his fortune as a pilot before coming back to a dying mother, two soon-to-be-orphaned brothers, and a woman expecting him to make her his wife.

Another rock went flying, his aim not as good from his hunched position. "Not so much. Not entirely."

Deciding she wasn't preserving her dignity by standing, Savannah dropped to the sand, a wave instantly rushing in, soaking through cloth to chill her bottom. "I don't understand."

He shot her a bemused look that said, *why do you have to understand?*

She shook her head and shrugged.

Anchoring his hand in the sand, he angled in beside her, crossing his legs Indian-style.

They sat in silence, watching flashes of light in the distance from a thunderstorm at sea. "I didn't count," he finally said, "not so much out of guilt but because" —he sighed— "she knew."

Savannah inhaled gustily. "You *told* her?"

Zach's shocked gaze flew to her. "Hell no, I didn't tell her." Looking away, he drew a vicious circle in the sand. "But she knew. I was four years older and a heck of a lot wilder, although no one seems to remember that. I sailed away when she was no more than a child. And no, Miss Nosy Britches, she never asked when I got back. We just got married . . . and didn't talk about things like that. Ever. We didn't talk about relations and, and . . ." He struggled, the circles in the sand getting bigger. "Hannah was so sweet and delicate. Gentle. If you've ever seen a doe in the woods on a snowy day—I saw one once hunting in the mountains when I was a kid—she was like that. She never raised her voice or stomped her foot. I don't think I ever remember her yelling at me or the boy."

Savannah felt her heart sink but pasted on a plucky smile. "She sounds perfect."

Zach reached for a firefly as it floated by, blinking madly. "She wasn't. She was good and kind, but she wasn't made to be a wife, I don't think. Birthing Rory was hard on her, terribly hard. And she didn't really seem to like living away from home, from the comfort of her family. Our entire marriage, she spent half her time there, coming back to my house when it made her happy to do it. Or made me happy, I reckon. I didn't complain. How could I when she was so naive, so innocent? I think Rory even understood from the time he was a baby that his ma wasn't as . . . *strong* as some of the other mothers in town.'' He yanked a sandy hand through his hair. She stopped herself from brushing the grit from his face, especially since he was talking about Hannah.

So she nodded in lieu of a reply.

''Even when she was older than you are right now, she seemed''—he shrugged a broad shoulder—''young. But I was young once, too. When I left. Seventeen to her thirteen. And full of passion for life, excited by every blessed thing. I guess I couldn't help myself: the women, the drinking. I knew the sea so well it attracted all sorts. Hell, I was a kid. What did I know? Though I didn't ever do anything to my knowledge that hurt her or my family. It just never seemed to be like that between me and Hannah. Like the two people, rowdy Zach and kind Zach, weren't connected, and she only knew the one.''

''You did an excellent job sheltering her from the wicked truth. Trust me.''

''Yeah, maybe. But I failed her in the long run.''

Savannah peeked at him, his windblown beauty affecting her like a blow to the head. She wanted to lighten his mood, steer him away from distressing memories. Even though curiosity ate at her, she didn't want to cause him more pain. ''The entire town thinks you're a saint. I'm ill from hearing everyone lionize you. I'm sure Hannah felt the same.'' She rested her head on her drawn knees, releasing a gust of laughter. ''And Elle thinks you were a virgin when you got married.''

''Jesus Christ,'' he said, disgusted, stabbing his finger in the sand. ''You must be joking.''

She shook her head, her shoulders shaking. Her eyes pricked with tears as she gasped, trying to regain control. After all the things Zach had shown her, and his huskily murmured promises to show her more, she couldn't imagine thinking the man had no experience. Truly, it was preposterous. One hot look and she had known. How could another *woman* fail to see it? She could understand the men being daft, but . . .

"I almost wish you'd told her what we were planning now. All the nasty details." He cleaned his hand on his trousers with a vicious swipe. "What man spends five years sailing in and out of every port in the Carolinas, washing away his loneliness with cheap ale and whatever friends he can find, and *doesn't* lose his virginity?"

"Zachariah Garrett, humanitarian, town constable, and all-around nice guy, that's who."

With a rueful smile, he rested on his elbows, studying her with his penetrating charcoal gaze. She felt a nagging lick of desire in the pit of her stomach but squashed it. Obviously, he felt two times was enough. That she thought it wasn't was consistent with a lifetime of unladylike behavior. Just ask her father.

"Is that all Miss Ellie had to say, Irish?"

Deciding to see if he was as steady as he appeared, Savannah swiveled around on her wet bottom and drew her skirt to her knees. Her boots and undergarments were in a pile by the bridge. Heaven help her if anyone came along and found them before they left. Feeling wicked, she propped her bare foot on his stomach and wiggled her toes.

Because she was looking closely, she caught the slight narrowing of his eyes, his fingers clenching in the sand.

"Maybe that's not all she had to say," she replied with an airy wave.

Licking his thumb, he leaned in, rubbing hard on her chin. "Care to enlighten me? That word should be big enough to spark your interest."

She wiped her chin, forcing back the rising tide in her mind, in her body. The tide telling her to crawl over there and climb on top of him, appease every impulse still standing after the night they'd had. The only ones that *were* still standing, he had propped up on two feet with all those sly suggestions.

"A dab of paint," he said in reply to his touch. Casually, as if he didn't need to touch her again, he lay back. But after a moment, his hand circled her ankle, his thumb caressing a particularly responsive spot. "What else?" When she didn't answer, he tugged, bringing her bumping against his side.

She dug her heel deeper in the sand and contemplated him across the short distance, shifting only when a shrieking gull flew past, signaling the approach of daybreak.

The end of their night together.

She drew a breath of air so thick it felt hard to swallow. Her heart ached for a split second before she regained control of it. "Elle told me to take it easy," she blurted before she had the chance to ask any foolhardy questions or make any impetuous statements. If she pushed Zachariah Garrett for promises that he could not, in all honesty and with noble intent, make, he would put a halt to their affair faster than one of the ladies down at the factory could shuck a bushel of oysters. "She said you were rusty."

He dropped his head back, laughing. "Rusty? I'll be damned. That much is"—he squeezed her ankle again—"*was* true. Other than that, I think they have the wrong fella."

She flopped to the sand, relaxing into his touch, her clothes thoroughly ruined now. A thousand stars twinkled from black velvet folds, more than you could ever see in a city sky. "Yes, it appears most don't know you at all. You're a shrewdly intelligent, very cunning diplomat who is seen by everyone in this town as a priest without the appropriate neckwear. An angel without detectable wings. They're blind as bats, the lot of them."

"So you're not falling for that angel business, huh?"

She closed her eyes, the night mist cooling her overheated skin. Zach's hand had worked its way to her thigh. "No. I'm afraid I've ... seen the light." And everything else he had to offer.

Sand squeaked; then she felt him flooding over her body like a wave, knee to knee, hip to hip, chest to chest. Hands cradling her head, his lips found hers, the urgency in the kiss warming her insides like a shot of spiced whiskey.

"I've decided two wasn't enough," he said, and set about proving how far from an angel he was.

Chapter Ten

No matter how hard a man may labor, some woman is always in the background of his mind.
—Gertrude Franklin Atherton

Heart pounding, the dream returned in a series of flashes: Hannah's shrill, weak cries, his lungs burning as he raced for a doctor, her crystal blue eyes wide and unseeing, her arm hanging off the bed, fingers trailing on the cold floor. The ending was always the same.

Zach drew a hitching breath and let his head flop back to the pillow. The salty sting of tears pricked his throat and he swallowed thickly. For a moment, he had awakened and imagined someone slept beside him, someone warm and sweet-scented. Before he had the chance to align his thoughts, a sharp burst of pleasure expanded his chest.

Savannah.

Blinking, he rolled over, searching for the round indentation in the pillow, the wealth of glossy hair spread across his sheets.

He wasn't going crazy, he reminded himself as he had so many times since she arrived in Pilot Isle two weeks before. Savannah Connor was real. Flesh-and-blood real. Not simply a product of his dreams . . . or his loneliness. And while she was here, she was his.

It took another moment to realize that he lay on the cot in the jail cell and not in what he had come to think of as "their" coach house. He never had nightmares during the nights—or rather the stolen hours in the middle of them—that he spent with her there, in what had become a frequent occurrence. Wrapped around Savannah's body, exhausted from loving her, he slept better than he did after a shot of whiskey, even better than after a late-night walk on the beach. If not for the sunset-to-sunrise patrols like the one he had finished at daybreak, he would consider himself well rested for the first time in two years.

Stretching, he slung his legs over the side of the cot, untangling himself from a blanket he hadn't remembered throwing over his body when he'd ambled in at dawn. Strange. Rising unsteadily to his feet, he scratched his day-old beard and sniffed. Coffee.

Skirting Tiger, who lay on the floor in a sluggish puddle, he walked toward his desk and the chipped yellow mug, covered with a napkin to hold the heat inside. A note lay beside it. Zach squinted, unable to make out the script. Glancing over his shoulder, checking to see that he was alone, he went around his desk, opened a small side drawer, and took out a pair of silver-rimmed spectacles. He stared at them with such strong distaste, he could *feel* the sneer twist his lips.

Dad blast, when had he become old enough to need spectacles?

Wire arms hooked unfamiliarly over his ears, mug of lukewarm coffee in one hand, he began to read and sip in time.

> *I stopped by to schedule the final meeting with Hyman Carter and his employee delegation. Please let him know that I'm available tomorrow afternoon. The coffee is from Christabel's; I hope it stays warm. You were too fatigued to wake. Long night with the patrol, I imagine. I pitched in as any able-bodied citizen, even a temporary one, of the town should and entered the latest figures into your cargo book as well as I could manage without your participation. I recorded the stack of lists and placed them in the envelope marked "input figures." I believe this is a perfect job for someone on my committee. You're overworked as it is.*
>
> S.C.

> *P.S. If Mr. Carter needs to meet in the evening I'm also available tonight.*

Zach took a sip of coffee, gripping the mug to keep his fingers from trembling. For a split second, he considered walking down Main Street, poking in every shop until he tracked her down. Dragging her back and locking the door behind them. That cot wasn't in such bad shape as all that.

Hell, it had been two days since he'd seen the woman. Or more specifically, since he'd touched her. His heart kicked as a picture of her on the beach that first night popped into his mind. Waves lapping her feet, her long legs spread, her eyes a clear, green invitation.

Get a hold of yourself, Zach.

Flopping into the chair, he thumped the mug

on his desk. Did he miss Savannah? Was that it?
His body did; he knew that much. Heck, once it
realized what it had been doing without, it seemed
to have unlimited vigor. And enthusiasm. Jesus, he
got hard every time she was within spitting distance.

But missing . . .

Did she feel the same? She had come here this
morning on an unscheduled visit, rare for a woman
who lived and died by her damned appointment
book. Covered him with a blanket—tattered and
none too clean, but still. *And* brought him coffee.
It made him feel suspicious and . . . wonderful in
a way that scared the hell out of him. No one
had taken care of him since, well, since never. His
mother had two infants to worry about not too
many years after he came along. He'd helped out,
doing chores and tending his baby brothers until
that job defined him. Thirty years later, it still
defined him.

Then, suddenly, someone came along offering
to help *him*. First the cargo ledger. What would
be next? Scheduling the men for beach patrol?
Shopping for his groceries? Sliding the ledger into
view, Zach studied her entries. The ink glistened,
barely dry. Orderly figures, not a period out of
place. Everything written in her neat, flowing
script. He did a quick calculation. All tallied perfectly. Of course.

Smart as a whip, the woman was. Zach didn't
buy that weaker sex bullshit for a minute. She could
outfox darn near every man in town, and from the
fearful looks on their faces when she stepped into
a room, they knew it. He'd wondered on more
than one occasion if she was *too* smart for him. Not
that this thing they had was going anywhere beyond
Elle's return from university. So forget brains for
the time being. Physically, there wasn't a better

match in any universe, his or hers. Boy, there was no
way there could be. He hadn't imagined a woman
existed who would fit him in bed the way Savannah
did. He could suggest any foolish old thing, like
having sex in the ocean, and she'd get this clever
look in her eye, wheels turning as she figured out
how to do it. He gathered, from the sounds she
made and the words she said, that she felt the same
way.

Still, it rankled to be with a woman who ate books
like candy and whose vocabulary included terms
he often didn't understand. Though he had quit
teasing her about it, because watching her mouth
form those fancy words excited him almost as much
as watching her take her clothes off.

He studied the cargo ledger, took another swig
of lukewarm coffee. What was he worrying about?
Between passionate descriptions of what they
planned to do to each other, there were plenty of
assurances on both sides that when it ended, it
ended. Savannah wasn't establishing any roots she
couldn't yank up quickly. A telegram from New
York arrived nearly every day.

Zach pushed aside the coffee mug and the nig-
gling voice telling him that he sometimes didn't
feel so final when he said final. Heck, who was to say
he and Savannah couldn't continue this affair—if
that was an apt description for the most thrilling
goddamn experience of his life—even after Ellie
returned? Maybe Savannah would want to stay, help
out with the school a little longer. Or visit. Often.
Caleb and Christabel had been doing whatever it
was they did for years now, without a vow in sight.
Of course, Caleb had asked, but Christabel didn't
seem to want marriage.

Not every woman wanted marriage. Savannah
repeated those five words like a darn parrot until

he believed her, or believed her as much as he could. He trusted her when she said they weren't going too far or letting things get out of control.

Shoving the ledger out of his way, he propped his elbows on the desk and dropped his head onto his hands, trying to massage away the tension. Blazes, Irish gave a good massage.

He sighed and wiped his damp brow on his sleeve. Darned hot summers.

Out of control. That's the way *he* felt when he was with her. Hungry. For her touch and, frighteningly enough, for her mind. Lately, he found himself wanting to ask her all sorts of useless questions. About her family, what growing up in a big city had been like, and, most disturbing, about the man who'd hurt her. The bastard who had enjoyed arresting her, which still caused her face to pale. Zach had come to think of her as his in an entirely horrible, masculine way. He would never, not on his life, tell her. He could imagine the explosion. No matter, he did feel possessive, and anyone who hurt her . . .

His fists clenched. Suffice it to say, the thought made him angry as hell.

He glanced at the cargo ledger and shoved back his chair. About time to run on over to the restaurant and pick up lunch. On the way, he'd sniff around town and see what kind of trouble his Irish was stirring up. He ignored the kick of anticipation in his belly.

Meanwhile, Savannah sat in Caroline's parlor, in a circle of women industriously stabbing needles through cloth. Some worked on quilts, others on church dresses. Lydia, behind on her chores, sat with her hand stuffed in a sock, darning a hole in the toe. They cast pitying looks at her, although she could sew, thank you very much. A skill taught to her by her mother during her childhood, one her father had frowned upon after they moved to a modest mansion in the city. They had servants for those duties, he had told her time and time again. Therefore her needlework was, to use Ellie's word, rusty.

Dipping her head, she smiled—secretly, she hoped—feeling a warm zing in the pit of her stomach. Picking at a loose thread, she suppressed a frustrated sigh.

It had been two days since she had seen Zachariah.

Actually, not two full days. She had stopped by the jail this morning and found him sleeping on the cot in the cell, his hair salt-crusted, his cheeks and nose windburned. Seeing him lying on his back, one arm thrown over his eyes, the other stretched across his stomach, it was all Savannah could do to restrain herself from sliding in next to him and hugging him close. But the door was unlocked, and truly, their relationship did not include cuddling on a cot in the middle of the morning. That seemed like something you would do with your husband or possibly a true love. She and Zach had firmly defined their liaison. Love, it was not. If she found herself unable to turn away from him at times, studying the way he wagged his fingers while he talked, or the tiny dimple by his mouth that flared to life at odd times and only with sincere smiles, she would admit to suffering from an impressive case of infatuation.

Savannah glanced at the faces of the women in the sewing circle. Wouldn't the unmarried ladies gathered here be infatuated with him if they had the chance to see him as she did?

"Prissy's taking a red velvet cake over to the jail this afternoon," Lydia said, nodding at the light laughter that followed her statement. "Darnella will be heading that way tomorrow morning with her scrumptious cheese biscuits. You know what that means."

"Church dance coming up," a gray-haired woman whose name had slipped Savannah's mind chimed in. One of the younger women in the circle was her granddaughter, she did remember that much. "Time to start harassing the unattached men, yep. An autumn wedding would sure liven things up."

"Wonder if Zach will ask one of them? Never any good at taking the bit in his teeth, that one. Stubborn." This from Christabel Connery, Caleb's "friend" and owner of the town's only restaurant. She snapped a length of thread with her teeth and continued, "Prissy's not his type, anyway. Too much chatter and not enough thinking behind it. She would drive the man crazy. Darnella is a pretty girl, though. Maybe that's enough to entice."

Until Zach's name was mentioned, the conversation had been monotonous, the gossip harmless. Savannah leaned forward and smiled warmly, striving for the poise of one involved in a meaningless tête-à-tête but not genuinely interested. "How agreeable. A dance, you say?"

Lydia dabbed a piece of green thread against the end of her tongue and worked it through the eye of a needle. "Hmmm, yes, next Saturday. What with days getting shorter before we know it, and cold weather rolling in, we like to have a dance while the evenings are still pleasant. Donations are taken at the door, a cake raffle and quilt exhibition held before the fiddlers arrive. All funds go to the church. For one thing, we need a new red pane in the stained-glass window over the vestibule. A bird, poor beast, lost its way and crashed right into it last winter. Cracked it something awful. Have to go to Raleigh for the repair, you know, and everything in that city is steep." She knotted her thread and turned with a broad smile the likes of which made Savannah extremely nervous. "Many a marriage has come about because of this dance, Savannah, dear."

Savannah jabbed her needle through her embroidery sample and straight into her thumb. Wincing, she raised it to her lips, murmuring, "You don't say." The taste of blood filled her mouth.

Sensing a tenderfoot among them, the ladies starting barking like a passel of hungry dogs. They dispensed advice about what to wear, how to fix her hair—she needed help with that, everyone agreed—and how to catch a man. Talk of rallies or independence, women's schools, or shorter hours for workers at the oyster factory was not recommended.

"Wonderful, wonderful concerns," Lydia said, "but not fit conversation for charming a man, dear."

Christabel smoothed her finger along a neat row of stitches. "Too bad you and Zach dislike each other, Savannah, cause he's a plum one just waiting to be picked. The Garrett men are handsome, no doubt about it. And Zach the best of the bunch." This seemed an odd comment coming from an intimately close friend of Caleb Garrett. Except for a few soft giggles, the women let it pass.

"We don't . . . *dislike* each other." She drew a breath of cinnamon-scented air. Cookies sat in an alabaster blue dish on the mahogany side table. "Simple disagreements, nothing more."

Christabel checked her stitching and grinned.

"Spitting like cats whenever you're together. What about that argument last week in the restaurant? I thought I was gonna have to separate you like two fighters in a ring. Zach has never, to my mind, let his anger get the best of him. I'd prescribe far corners for you two."

Savannah squirmed on the settee, crossing and uncrossing her ankles. That particular argument had been silly. With Zach in the wrong, of course. Hyman Carter's daughter had every right to attend their meetings regarding the oyster factory amendments. The man had no sons and was sure to leave part of the business to his daughter. It wasn't Savannah's fault the girl came to her without first consulting her father. That it was such a surprise to the men in the room to see Mirabelle walk in the door was not her concern. The woman was twenty-nine years old and not in need of a keeper.

"I heard about it, too," Lydia said with a sigh. "I agree. It's terribly out of character for Zach to get so cross. The two of you are a bad mix, unfortunately."

Such a "bad mix" that they had met at the coach house an hour later for an extremely passionate encounter. Zach told her afterward that he would argue with her every day if the result could be the same.

The gray-haired grandmother cackled, slapping her wadded cloth against her thigh. "Something strange about a man not looking for a wife after a couple of years of being alone. Bless Hannah's heart, the dear girl, but living is living. And men *are* men. You would think the Constable would like comfort only a woman can give. We know he isn't receiving any, not even"—her voice dropped to a whisper—"*out* of town."

"Strange indeed," Caroline agreed, with a sly glance thrown Savannah's way.

She stared at her row of uneven stitches, avoiding the shrewd gaze of her newest student. Caroline was reading better with each lesson. A very bright woman, she didn't miss much.

"Magnus wants to ask you to attend with him; he told me so himself yesterday evening," Lydia said, checking her material for tears. "He's as suitable as a new penny. A mite stiff, true, but suitable just the same. Savannah, you would make an excellent doctor's wife."

"Me?" she asked, wishing she had not accepted an invitation to what was turning out to be a hellacious exploration into the world of proper sewing circles and small-town gossip.

"Of course, you," Lydia laughed, waving away the ridiculous question. "You have so much vigor and initiative. Magnus has noticed, of course. That's why he thought to mention his interest to me, since I am the cochair for our oyster factory project." She leaned over and gripped Savannah's cold fingers. "Since we're such good friends."

Savannah fiddled with her sample, at a loss. Who would Zach take to the dance? Did their agreement include any stipulations about courting? She couldn't remember their discussing that issue. Couldn't he have asked her to attend the dance with him? What could that have hurt? A kind gesture to introduce her around, nothing romantic about it. Did he think she could not keep her hands off him for one evening? No one in town with the exception of a woman who had a rather scandalous past herself had an inkling that anything was going on between them.

When Savannah really thought about it, his resistance was quite insulting.

"You know," Savannah replied, squeezing Lydia's hand, "I believe I would like to attend the dance with Dr. Leland. Since I've only met him once, could you talk to him for me?"

Lydia squealed and danced around in her seat. "Oh, to introduce two young people and hope for more to come of it! I would be truly honored, Savannah. This is simply so exciting."

"Yes, exciting," Caroline said in accord with the amenable nods and murmurs. But the look she gave Savannah was anything but agreeable. Downright worried, if Savannah read her student's furrowed brow correctly.

And later that evening, she caught up to Savannah as they walked through the door, taking her elbow in a brusque grip. "You know what they say about playing with fire, darling. Be careful."

Savannah nodded but said nothing, holding her chin high. She wasn't playing with fire.

Was she?

That evening, Zach locked his office door and started down the boardwalk. The sun was close to setting and most folks were home having supper, surrounded by family and friends. An occasional wagon bearing fish or lumber swayed past. Fireflies flickered and crickets chirped. It was a peaceful evening in his town.

Rubbing the back of his neck, he suppressed an anxious twitch. He felt anything but peaceful. He'd received a letter of thanks from the wife of a sailor whose body washed up on Devil Island last month, and had spent two hours writing a compulsory, saddening reply. How did you say "you're welcome" for delivering a husband's body home to his family? Dear Lord, it made him want to rage at the gods even to reckon on it.

He thumbed his aching eyes. The headaches were getting worse. Every afternoon, the pain started on one side of his head, creeping behind his eyes and sitting there, pulsing with each breath he took. By the time he went to bed, they were hot and watery, too tired to focus. Savannah had been massaging his temples and had told him he should see a doctor. She had mentioned the possibility of the need for spectacles once, too, he remembered. And she had said he would look cute in them. *Cute.*

Sighing, he pulled the pair Dr. Leland had ordered direct from Raleigh from his shirt pocket and angled a wire arm behind each ear. He wrinkled his nose, testing the still-foreign weight. They didn't feel too bad. He wondered how they looked. Before he picked up Rory from Caroline's, maybe he could stop by Miss Vin's and see if Savannah had a moment to take a peek at them. He had thus far avoided wearing them in her presence. Plus, he had a little present for her. Nothing much, just a fountain pen she had been admiring in the general store window the other day. She'd oohhed and aahhed over it like women do but hadn't dreamed of buying it. For some incredibly insane reason he didn't want to ponder, he had returned the next day and bought the darn thing for her. And here he was carrying it to her like some randy youth taking his first woman out to dinner.

Taking a quick side-hop into the street, he skirted a wheel rut, tossing his yarn-wrapped bundle from one hand to the other. At least thinking about Savannah made him forget that awful letter he'd had to write.

Speaking of the devil, he saw a flash from the corner of his eye. His belly tightened in the way it did whenever Savannah was near. He watched her skip off the boardwalk in front of the post office, dodge a shallow puddle, and cross the street at a brisk pace. She didn't look in his direction. He squinted, tipping his spectacles. Obviously, she wasn't interested in *his* whereabouts, even though he'd been guessing about hers all day long.

Her smile glowing like an electric bulb, she halted before a red safety bicycle angled against the side of Captain Willie's Net Repair and looped her basket through the front handlebars, her movements efficient and vigorous.

Well-defined hips. A glimpse of one trim ankle. Standing astride, the pedals resting against her calves, she smoothed a pair of leather gloves over her hands. A twist and snap at each wrist. A rounded bottom adjusted to the seat. Lifting it indecently off the seat to gain speed, she pedaled down the street.

His chest hitched; he released an edgy breath. Crushing his package in his fist, he continued in her direction. No faster, no slower. It wasn't as if he was following her. He couldn't be faulted for taking this particular street, the quickest route home. Besides, what did he have to worry about? Other than that argument in Christabel's last week, they rarely spoke in public.

With a shell-scattering lurch, Savannah turned suddenly but steadily and headed straight for him. Zach halted to a dead stop, a small cloud of dust billowing around his feet.

A smile curled his lips as a slow burn of sexual awareness lit him from the inside out. She'd known he was behind her all along.

Now she would play some infantile game, like trying to make the arrogant town constable scramble from her path. He blinked and gave his spectacles a shove, daring himself to twitch. She would beat him at this game if he let her. Darn it, he didn't care how resourceful she was. How capable. She was still a hellion at heart, and she always would be. Cheeks pink, dark strands flapping about her face. Bloomers, or whatever the heck you called those female britches, swelling in the wind. He grunted, inconspicuously bracing his knees.

He would be damned if he'd move a muscle.

She pedaled faster and faster, pump, pump, pump, knees lifting, circling, a laugh tearing from her. Jesus, she was even crazier than he'd imagined!

She laughed again, as unable to restrain the sound as she was the giddiness flowing like blood through her veins. Of course, she had known he was behind her. If she were an eighty-year-old woman and Zachariah Garrett entered a room, the air would thicken like molasses, the polish on the heart-pine floors brighten to a high sheen.

It might infuriate her, but it was true.

Getting closer, she searched for the difference. *Ah, spectacles.* How attractive and wise he looked in them. And stubborn. *That* astonished her. Zach defied her as no man ever had. Most were terrified after one encounter . . . or irate enough to stay out of her way. Yet this man seemed to like her, very much in certain circumstances. Why, he often told her she was *beautiful.* Beautiful. Savannah Morgan Connor, beautiful. The thought nearly made her heart stop.

Standing tall, legs spread, hands fisted, Zach faced her with an expression somewhat like that of a boy standing down the town bully. She laughed softly. Didn't he know she would rather slam into a tree than harm a hair on his maddening head? Obviously not. The man did take things very seriously. Honorable people were like that.

Digging in her heels, spraying shells and dirt, the tail of the bike fished to the left. Sliding to a stop inches from him, she smiled broadly. She had perfected this trick only in the past month.

Zach relaxed his stance, rolling his shoulders. Shaking shell particles from his canvas shoes, he stepped around her without a word.

She stared after him, her chest heaving. Closing her lips with a snap, she pedaled forward until she rode alongside him. "I wasn't close to hitting you, you must know that. I had absolute control."

His steps lagged; he cast her a lingering sidelong look. Though she could only see half his mouth and one dark brow, she did not misread the cynicism in his expression. Blowing out a strained breath, she cycled ahead and circled. Two rings around him as he walked along the street. Was he going to travel the entire way home in silence?

Wrenching to a halt, she blocked his path. "Want to try it?"

He paused, flipping his package between his hands. Taking a step back, he let his gaze travel over the bicycle, skepticism evident in his lock-kneed stance, his arched brow. Shaking his head, not once looking at her, he moved on.

My, the spectacles looked fine on him. "Scared, Constable?" She drew alongside him.

He laughed, full of masculine bravado. "No, Miss Connor, I'm not scared."

"Come on. You're a little tall for this model, of course, but it will do in a pinch."

"Thank you, but no."

What game was he playing today? Wasn't he the least bit pleased to see her? She glanced around. No one was on the street, no one to see them talking and spread it around town. "You've ridden a bicycle before, right? No one is on the street to see your attempt.''

"I've ridden one. Absolutely." He glanced at her, a dying ray of sunlight glinting off his spectacles. "Once or twice."

She snapped her fingers, one hand navigating from the middle of the handlebars. "Then you must remember that it's like sailing on wheels."

His stride slowed to a hesitant shuffle, then stopped altogether. His gaze jumped to her, to the bicycle, to the ground. Before he could crush it, she saw a glimmer in his eyes, a definite spark of interest. Taking advantage of the opportunity, she braked and hopped to the ground. "Here." She grabbed his package and shoved the bicycle at him, not giving him a chance to refuse.

His mouth opened and closed as if he wanted to protest, but his hands latched on to the handlebars.

"Wait." She rose on her toes, as high as she could, and skimmed her fingers through the soft hair curling over his ears. He had parted his hair on the side, slicked just enough to notice. Enough to keep it under control as he liked. The scent of pomade and smoke drifted to her on the swift sea breeze. She swayed toward him just the slightest bit, her eyes locking with his.

His pupils widened behind the wire frames. He tried to step back. *Gentle, Savannah.* A spooked horse, this one. "Your spectacles. If you fall." She slid them down his nose as the clamor of daily life faded to a strong heartbeat pulsing in her ears. The sun burst apart in the sky; the wind died a sudden death at her feet.

Without their glass guardian, his eyes looked irritated and red, the skin around them stretched taut, a web of tiny lines spreading from the edges. Heavens, even when he looked about ready to drop

from exhaustion he was a handsome man. *Beautiful.*
She knew that Zach—any man, perhaps—would
raise a resistive hand at the use of that particular
word. Although why not use it if it fit? His features
were shaped by a sculptor's hand: the patrician
nose flaring at the nostrils, the square jaw.

As she stared, her breath left her.

If she struggled past the controlled blankness
he wore so often like a mask, past the secreted
intelligence—in itself an incredibly strong barrier—she found emotions dwelling there, colorful
and varied. She knew this, though he didn't always
let her witness it. Zach never allowed her unlimited
time to search. That was why she forced herself to
lie awake in his arms until his breathing slowed,
his chest rising and falling in a gentle rhythm. Then
she looked her fill.

As she had this morning in the jail. She had
watched him for half an hour before forcing herself
to leave his side.

As if on cue, he blinked and dropped his gaze.
To her lips.

Heat swept her cheeks. Her mouth and her nipples seemed to fascinate him. Dazed, she licked
her bottom lip, wondering if she had a spot of dirt
on it, perhaps.

The bicycle tottered in his hands. Zach angled
his head, leaving her arm suspended in air, his
spectacles dangling. He scooted the bicycle to the
side. "Don't drop those. They're new," he said in
a strained voice.

She swallowed, forcing a laugh. It sounded thin
and frantic. Nudging the flap aside, she placed his
spectacles with extreme care in her pocket. Her
hand trembled. She yanked it out and into a tight
fist.

Glancing up, she found him balanced on one

foot, his other resting on the left pedal. He looked shockingly tall standing over the diminutive bicycle, the smallest ladies' model in the Sears and Roebuck catalog. His hands closed around the handles, shifted, searching for the right position. He glanced at her when he pushed off, a boyish gleam in his eyes, a self-assured smile twisting his lips. For a moment, it seemed as if he hoped to impress her.

He wobbled a bit—quite a bit, at first. After all, crushed shells were much harder to navigate than the packed sand where he had ridden before. She winced as his knees cracked the handlebars with each rotation. Rising off the seat, he circled faster, wobbling less. At the end of the street, he turned. Only a faint shimmy rocked the bicycle. He rode well, better than she would have guessed. Another talent to add to the extensive list.

"You're doing wonderfully," she shouted and waved.

He grinned in reply but kept a straight course. Didn't he see the half-hollow—last week an oozing crater from a violent storm—five feet in front of him?

Like a clock striking the hour, the piddling weight in her pocket chimed an alarming bell.

"Zach!" She rushed forward, but the course was set. The rubber tire met air, then the round bottom of the hole. The bicycle made an awkward little leap, landing with the front tire at a crooked angle. The back end, traveling faster, jolted like a drunkard from a deep sleep. The bicycle pitched one way, then careened off the road and over the sidewalk, directly into a huge azalea bush in the Reverend Tiernan's yard.

The soft hiss of spinning wheels and the crunch

of azalea twigs beneath her boots sounded as she reached him. "Zach? Are you okay?"

He lay on his back, limbs and pine straw scattered across his chest and neck, an angry red scratch on his right cheek, his hair sprouting from his head in spiked tufts. Saints' blood! If he wasn't dead, he was going to have a fit when he got a good look at himself. Dear heaven, if anyone came along before he cleaned himself up . . .

"Zach?" She dropped to her knees, slinging his package to the ground. "Zach?" His chest rose in a series of rapid jerks, but other than that, he did not move a muscle. Why had she encouraged him? Perhaps he wasn't an especially athletic man, too serious for tennis and croquet. She had never seen him do anything physical except sail and . . . make love. He was excellent at both of those.

Searching for injury, she ran her fingers down his arm, over his elbow, tracing the bones in his wrist. Everything in proper alignment, for all she knew. Dropping a trembling hand to his chest, trying to remember where that bloody doctor's office was, she felt the first rumble. Then another, followed by a release of smoke-scented air. It might have been a sigh, yet it sounded remarkably like laughter. She frowned and settled back, flat-footed.

A low chuckle broke the silence. Zach brought his hands to his face, his eyes still shut tight, and laughed behind them.

"Are you demented?" she snapped and threw his package at him. It landed in the grass beside his hand. Was he trying to scare her to death, playing dead like a dog struck by a cart's wheel? Although she *had* gotten to touch him. That was always nice. But she hadn't enjoyed it the way she would have if she had known he was uninjured.

He rolled his head back and forth, branches and pine straw stuck in his hair.

He would buy the farm if he held a mirror right now, she thought, forgetting her earlier pleas for his well-being. The man didn't like to look foolish. "Stop laughing. Do you want someone to walk by and think you've lost your senses?"

Her comments only seemed to make him laugh harder. She glanced at his head, searched the little she could see through his spread fingers. Black hair, mussed to death, but no blood. Perhaps he had a concussion. She'd had one after falling off a wagon during a rally and couldn't recall the reason she had fallen off for hours. When her memory returned, she had hidden from the authorities the fact that a man had dragged her off the cart and into the street. Already they thought the rallies were dangerous business.

Maybe Zach didn't remember anything. That might explain his strange behavior.

"Constable, do you remember what happened?"

"I remember thinking, that woman is the biggest nut in the cake. A right shoddy doctor, too. You nearly broke the bones in my wrist."

She gasped, jumping to her feet. "Biggest nut? Why, I never!"

He swiped a thumb beneath each eye, mustering a fresh cluster of fury in the pit of her stomach, and elbowed to a sit. Touching his cheek, he winced. He moved gingerly, his gaze finding hers. "Maybe *I'm* the biggest nut for going along with your tomfoolery. Riding a blamed bicycle at my age! Rory would have paid all the pennies in his bank to see this spectacle."

"Tomfoolery? You old, old . . ." she sputtered, grabbing the bicycle handles and attempting to retrieve it from the bush. "Many people in New

York City ride them. It's not like tippling whiskey on the back porch, to cite your vernacular—which you've done as well, I'm sure.''

She glanced back, noting the rip in his shirt, near the shoulder. The material flapped, held against his chest by a black suspender. Dark curls poked out, taunting her. She swallowed, remembering how she had run her fingers through them two days ago in the shimmering darkness of the coach house.

Viscous, scorching need roared through her body like a Pullman car on tracks.

"What if I have?" She yanked the bicycle with all her might. It didn't budge. Of course, she hadn't counted on having to struggle to keep air in her lungs while she did it. All because of a scant amount of chest hair.

Zach groaned and got to his feet. Brushing her aside, he hoisted the bicycle from the bush as if it were merely a nuisance, certainly nothing requiring strength. His suspender snapped when his shoulder flexed, a button flying into the grass, the strap flipping to his waist. Their gazes met and he smiled. A slow, sheepish smile. "I wasn't that bad, was I?"

Savannah paused, her rage thawing. Often she felt these pangs of warmth around the general region of her heart when she was with the man. A teasing smile or a slow wink seemed to carry enough weight to throw her into a significant state of confusion. And Zach used each weapon mercilessly: in the mercantile two evenings ago, with barrels of dried beans standing between them; during a meeting with Hyman Carter last week, causing her to forget her argument and stutter like some inept lunatic. Though the worst yet had been in church on Sunday. Everyone's heads had been bowed during a prayer. She had looked Zach's way only because she thought—well, felt *sure*—he wouldn't be looking hers. God couldn't consent to a woman's experiencing a powerful surge of lust while attending a religious service, could he?

Restless and bewildered, and determined to ignore whatever this feeling was, Savannah feigned annoyance and assessed the damage to her bicycle. The basket was smashed flat as a pancake—lucky only a few pieces of mail were inside—and the handlebars were bent on one side. "You were appalling, Constable," she said, finally answering.

"Not so bad for my first time, I don't think."

She stumbled, her trousers flapping against her knee. "*First* time?"

He nodded, eyes wide, a whisper of amusement in them.

"Of all the fool ... the first time ... without your spectacles?" *Oh*. Perching the bicycle against her hip, she yanked them from her pocket and slapped them into his hand. "And you think *I'm* a nut?"

Slipping the wire arms behind each ear, he made a small adjustment to the narrow bridge resting on his nose. They really were an attractive accessory. He must have followed her advice about the headaches.

"No, not a nut." He tilted his head, seeming to consider his words. "You disregard common sense."

"Common sense? Is that what keeps you from riding a bicycle until you're nearly a doddering old man?"

"Thirty-four is hardly an old man, Irish. You should know I still have plenty of get-up-and-go if I need it." He tipped her beneath the chin, his fingers lingering longer than necessary. "Want to test my fortitude, teacher?"

"Humph," she whispered and looked both ways to see if anyone loitered on the street. They were alone, yet she felt conspicuous. And warm. And fidgety.

A fat raindrop hit her cheek; another, her nose. She tilted her head to the sky, tasting salt and sea. A rumble of thunder sounded in the distance.

Expecting the clouds to burst open at any moment, she jogged ahead, the bicycle bumping her side. She caught a glimpse of Miss Vin's faded blue shutters ahead, peeping between dense oak and elm branches. Heaven, she wanted to lock herself in her small, tidy room until she regained control. When she had started this affair, she made a rule that she must never go to the coach house in an emotional state. Sound decisions were made only when one was in control of one's emotions.

"Good night, Constable," she called, struggling to open Miss Vin's front gate while keeping the bicycle upright.

"Hold up, there." His hands covered hers. He stood so close, she felt the muscles in his chest bunch when he lifted the bicycle over, felt the curve of his forearm when he slipped his arm around her between waist and ribs and nudged the rock pulley. The gate swung wide, creaking all the way. She ran, turning only when she reached the top of the porch stairs. Zach stood just inside the fenced yard, inspecting her through his attractive wire rims.

A loose shutter banged the side of the house, startling her. Savannah lifted her hand to her heart, baffled and a tad frightened. She closed her eyes and forced air in, then out. A twig snapped. Smoke and pomade drifted into her nostrils.

Zach stood two steps below, his gaze searching. She worked hard to keep hers from dropping to his torn shirt—a difficult choice. What presented the least temptation? A tiny sprig of chest hair, or those beautiful, reflective eyes?

"Irish, there's something." He fumbled in his pocket, extracting the wrapped package she had assumed was a toy for Rory, effectively drawing her gaze to the black suspender dangling past his waist. A thin crease ran along the front of his trousers. She shivered, desire rocking her where she stood. Raindrops danced lightly across her skin.

He handed it to her, then swabbed with a curled fist at the line of blood coursing down his cheek. "Just a little something."

Ignoring the package, more from apprehension than embarrassment, she lifted her hand. "Your face."

He shook his head, his expression telling her not to act on the impulse. The wind howled, the loose shutter sounding a persistent beat. "Open it," he said, while distant bursts of thunder rumbled and the air grew heavy with a storm's promise—grew heavy with whatever encircled them.

Glancing down, she released the yarn bow and removed the brown paper wrapping. The warm spot surrounding her heart swelled, filling her entire chest. "The pen I saw in the . . ." Her words trailed off as tears pricked, stinging from the effort to hold them back. When had she last received a gift from a man? Her father had stopped giving her presents on her twelfth birthday, saying she was getting too old for trinkets and baubles that she did not seem to know what to do with anyway.

Blinking, she shook herself, remembering their situation and Zach's probable rationale for feeling the need to compensate. "Thank you," she said softly, taking a deep breath and looking up. "But this isn't necessary."

Alarmed by whatever it was he saw in her gaze, his thoughts scattered. He took a step back and down, hasty, awkward. "Nothing much. I saw you mooning over it and . . ." He shrugged; his spectacles slipped. "No real reason, I just thought you might like it."

"I love it, but I can't possibly accept it." She thrust the gift, wrapping and all, at him.

A spark of annoyance flickered in his eyes. "Can't accept it? Why not?"

"It isn't proper for you to give me gifts, Constable."

"Let me get this." He rolled his shoulder angrily, wincing from an apparent bicycle injury. "It's proper for me to take you to my bed but not to give you some stupid present?"

She gulped a breath, irritation shoving affection aside. "It is not proper to give me gifts *because* of our"—she glanced over her shoulder and back—"relationship. We must not let this get out of control. Where does it end if we allow for the exchange of gifts?"

"Control is a big issue with you, isn't it?" He snorted, bumping his spectacles high. "Being careful to protect your reputation, and mine, doesn't mean we can't do anything outside of that darned coach house." He raked his hand through his hair, sincerely, she could tell, trying to see where he had blundered. "Would it have been better to give you the pen there? So you could walk home, stick it in a drawer, and wait until you got back home to use it?"

Taking a step down, staring eye to eye, she jammed a finger in his chest, close to the rip. "If we're allowed to speak outside the coach house, why didn't you ask me to the church dance coming up?" Propping her hands on her hips, she prepared for battle. "There wouldn't have been any undue scandal attached to Saint Garrett doing a good deed such as inviting the new lady in town to the dance, now, would there?"

Zach's lips worked, but no sound popped out. Hair blew into his face, obscuring his puzzled gaze.

He had never thought of it, had not once considered asking her. Savannah had convinced herself he didn't ask because he couldn't, not because he didn't want to. It was irrational, everything she was feeling, yet . . .

Her blood surged. Red tinged her vision. She pressed her lips together until they stung, not knowing what would roll out if she opened them.

Zach gestured in the direction of the sea in confusion, the brown paper wrapping fluttering in the breeze. She could hear waves faintly crashing against the shore. "I never take anyone to that silly dance. Not since Hannah."

She jammed her toe against the step, the irate haze clouding her mind. "Who are you really protecting, Constable? You say it's me when I think it isn't me at all. Your wife is long—" Her foot halted midjam, the rest of the sentence stolen by her startled oath.

He stiffened, his gaze freezing like a shallow pond in winter. "I don't need any goddamn reminders about the past, Miss Connor."

Lightning struck close by, shaking a glass pane in Miss Vin's front window. They glanced at the darkening clouds, then, warily, at each other. Like a crystal vase hurled against brick, the day's agreeable promise had utterly shattered.

Zach stared at her a minute, then stuffed the rumpled package into his pocket. "Hyman and I are set to meet on Thursday. Sorry, but I can't make it tonight," he said and marched across the yard with a stiff-shouldered stride, the bicycle jaunt and their shared laughter forgotten. Slapping the gate wide, he never looked back.

She dropped to the top step, a burst of rain spilling from the sky and soaking her clothes and hair. She had planned on spending the evening in her lover's arms, listening to the ping of raindrops bouncing off the coach house roof as they made slow, sweet love. Instead, she sat alone in a humid downpour, an apology sitting dully on her tongue, guilt lying heavy on her breast.

Chapter Eleven

*One cannot be always laughing at a man without
now and then stumbling on something witty.*
—Jane Austen

He was drinking too much, Zach thought, raising his glass to his lips for what must have been the fortieth time that night. The ale was lukewarm and bitter, but not a bad darn remedy for what ailed him. His intake had gone beyond what it should, what he usually allowed it to. The unfamiliar vagueness in his mind and unsteadiness in his step were a glaring indication. The circle of men surrounding him knew it, too, if the amused glances thrown his way meant squat.

They assumed his being rooked into asking Darnella Watkins to the dance was the reason for his testy mood. He hadn't voiced one word to correct the mistaken assumption, even with Darnella's brother George, who had warned him to tread lightly when he stopped by earlier this evening to escort her to the event. Anyway, Darnella had come fluttering out on the porch in a mess of pink silk

and lacey gewgaws before he got the chance to say
a blessed thing in reply to her brother's threat.

Tread lightly? Was dancing with Darnella once
when he first arrived, then leaving her to giggle
and chatter with the crowd of women circling the
cake table while he drank with the men circling the
ale barrel, treading lightly? Was furtively watching
Savannah Connor strut back and forth across the
sawdust-covered dance floor in Magnus Leland's
arms treading lightly? Eyeing her over the rim of
his glass, he reckoned George would probably say
it wasn't.

She looked magnificent, damn her. Radiant.
Like a star thrust into a dark box. Strange, because
her clothing was more informal than the stuff she'd
worn when she first arrived. A sensible choice for
summer living in a seaside town where days were
hotter than Hades and nights muggy as all get-out.
But it did limit one's choices. Though the long,
full skirt clung to her hips better without the frou-
frous and flounces of her city wear, showing shape
where shape was. The woman didn't need frills.
She shone without it.

And her hair . . .

Zach sipped slowly, judging. Candlelight from
the multitude of sconces surrounding the dance
floor cascaded over the gleaming mane clasped at
her neck with a delicate flower fastening of some
sort. Wasn't much like Savannah to do that—fix
herself up, that is. He had a good idea one of the
ladies parading around her and old Magnus every
time they got within range had placed it there.
Gazing into Magnus's face, she said something and
they laughed, her lips slowly pulling back from her
teeth in a smile pretty enough to bring a preacher
to his knees. Zach felt a reactive tightening in his
gut, one the likes of which he had tried repeatedly

to squash throughout the five long days since their argument on Miss Vin's porch.

If you could call that confused tangle of heat, fury, and remorse an argument.

Quietly he ducked outside the tent and, leaning his hip against a nearby tree, inhaled a breath of moist air. Eyes closed, he listened to the steady pulse of the night: the rustle of leaves on the branches above his head, and the chirping crickets in the azalea bushes lining the church's walkway.

It had terrified him to see her tears the other day. Swimming in her eyes and making them look like a clear, green pond after a storm. He had felt as shocked as he would if an oar caught him across the back of the head. The fountain pen had been an impulsive bit of, of . . . *nothing*. A gesture without real thought, a kind word cloaked in a meaningless gift. He never imagined it would *touch* her. Whatever emotion had made her eyes go all watery . . .

Lifting his face to the moon, Zach sloped his back against the tree trunk and drained his glass. A faint headache pulsed; his spectacles were a dead weight in his pocket. Somehow, crazy as it seemed, wearing them reminded him of *her*. Damn, he was losing his mind.

Losing his mind and allowing guilt to eat him up. Again.

He couldn't bring Hannah back. For himself or Rory. Couldn't change what had happened during their marriage, or how she had died. He had been a lousy husband, in the later years not patient or prudent enough. Still, Hannah had loved him, and he had loved her. He had. But they hadn't been . . . *alike*. How better could he explain it, even if he'd never admitted it to anyone but himself? When he had come home from piloting and suddenly had such responsibility, he had dug a hole and settled in, lock, stock, and barrel. Husband, father, brother. Without looking back or questioning his choices.

He and Hannah hadn't discussed the future until they were knee-deep in it. If memory served, he recalled catching her a time or two staring at him across the kitchen table with a quizzical look on her face. As though she wasn't sure who he was.

As though she wondered where *her* Zachariah Garrett had run off to. The boy she'd loved. He should have told her that life changed a man. Responsibility changed a man. Love changed a man. Years changed a man. All of those things had turned him into something she didn't recognize. They had not shared common interests, simple though that may be. Most especially, his *need* had been frightening to her, almost unwelcome. Wearisome. Was it crazy to imagine that Hannah would have been happiest with the pristine purity of their childhood affection?

Nothing like the raging passion he shared with that Irish hellion.

Regretful memories stiffened his spine until bark dug painfully into his back. He shook out his shoulders, telling himself to let go. Savannah was right, even if her way of enlightening him wasn't the best. He needed to forgive himself, damned if that wasn't the truth. His life was far from over. However, in the process of self-pardoning his sins, he didn't want to go and get bamboozled by the excitement of being with Savannah. Didn't want to go and fall in love with her.

Wouldn't that be a hell of a mess?

His eyes snapped open as a burst of laughter sounded from the tent. *I wonder if Magnus is making her laugh,* he wondered because he couldn't help it. The linen flaps of the enclosure were gathered

at each pole with a length of tassel, allowing the
evening breeze to waft through. The covering still
providing protection from rain should the clouds
deliver what they promised. Sweat beaded his skin;
he wiped it from his brow with a clenched fist.

Wasn't jealousy a novel emotion?

It had just been so long since he'd had a relationship like this with a woman: sex and friendship,
a reasonable amount of caring, extreme respect,
laughter, and the tiniest bit of sharing. The mix
worked right well if a man kept his wits about him.
That was the key: rational, sound decision making.
Savannah certainly had a firm hold on *her* wits.

Or so he'd thought until that bout of near-tears.

The ale he had drunk swam in his head as he
wrestled with a question he'd found no answer for
in the past five days. He leaned back against the
tree to steady himself and asked again.

What would he do if Savannah—a woman he
would have bet his meager savings wasn't one to
be susceptible to base emotion—fell in love with
him? It didn't seem possible, did it? He wasn't really
good enough, clever or wealthy or handsome
enough. Stomach churning, he sucked in a stabiliz-
ing breath. It scared him to death to feel his lips
turn up at the notion, his heart start to pound.
Jesus, what would it be like to feel that strongly
about a woman again?

Feel like it about a woman who fit him like a
glove in more ways than one.

He shook his head. *No.* Never again. As long as
he and Savannah continued on this course, both
of them happy with what they had, he felt sure he
could handle it. But if the scales tipped in either
direction, oh, Lord . . .

He wasn't at all sure about that.

"Zach, you'd better get in here," Caroline whispered urgently, peeking around the closest opening in the tent and beckoning him with a curved finger. The dim light cast shadows across her face, but he could see she was frowning.

Sighing, Zach wiped his eyes and shoved away from the tree. He never settled more disputes than at the church dances. "What is it?" he asked when he got closer. He didn't much want to get in the middle of a ruckus tonight.

Caroline shrugged, fiddling with her skirt and shaking her head.

With a flash, he knew. *Savannah. Trouble.* Did two words ever fit together as nicely as those?

Stomping inside, he pictured a long night ahead.

His angry oath reached her about five seconds before his firm grasp on her shoulder did.

Savannah turned at the insistent touch, pasting a smile on her face. "Hello, Constable. Mr. Carter and I were just discussing a point he isn't willing to negotiate."

The men standing around her laughed; the women tittered nervously. Someone in the crowd— it sounded a lot like Caleb—called out asking if Zach could handle her. Saints' blood, that wasn't going to sit well with the man.

Zach ducked his head, his hot gaze finding hers. "One night? One night of peace? Is that too much to ask?"

Free to study him closely for the first time that evening—truly, the first time in days—she couldn't help but see the exhaustion chalking grooves alongside his mouth and eyes, the shadows beneath his dark lashes. He looked drained but handsome enough to light a fire in her stomach. "Where are your spectacles?" She avoided his questions.

"To hell with my spectacles." With a firm nod to Hyman Carter, he dragged her outside the tent and into the night. He didn't let her go until they'd reached a storage shed of some sort. The cool air slid over her warm cheeks, lifting damp strands of hair from her brow. She couldn't contain her sigh of relief.

"You've been drinking." He sounded like her father, reproachful and disappointed.

"Yes. One swig, as you so delicately refer to it. Is that permitted?"

"How the heck should I know what's permitted?"

Watching anger brighten his eyes, she couldn't help but note that the emotion seemed at odds with his calm expression. "Are you incensed about my choice of escort? Is that the problem?"

Startled as if he'd been shot, he stumbled back. "I don't care who escorts you anywhere, Miss Connor. Although Magnus is a complete ass, if you ask me."

Not that it wasn't what she had expected him to say, but it hurt just the same. Plucking a piece of moss from the wooden wall at her side, she twirled it in a slow circle. "Oh, yes. I remember. No rules, except discretion and honesty."

"Exactly," he agreed, his voice low and furious.

She waited a beat, letting his scent drift her way. Ale, if she wasn't mistaken, and the ever-present hint of smoke. He didn't wear cologne, apparently, and didn't need to to smell like a slice of heaven. In addition, damn it, he looked splendid, although his navy trousers and crisp white shirt were obviously store-bought. Dr. Leland's tailored wear should have appealed in comparison, but dear heaven, Zachariah looked leagues better, and would if he had showed up at the dance in a potato sack.

"Can you swear you'll go back in there and behave, Irish? Rory would give me less trouble if he were here. One reason children don't attend."

Brushing the moss across his cheek, she watched his eyes darken, the fingers still clutching her arm tighten. She wondered what she could do to get him to meet her at the coach house after the dance. "One point I need to clear up first. Am I to understand that I can go to bed with the complete ass tonight and still meet you at the coach house, say, tomorrow evening? Is that permissible?"

The kiss came so quickly that Savannah couldn't have prepared for it if she had wanted to. Or push him away, which was highly unlikely. His lips covered hers, his arms snaking around her waist, shutting out the sounds of the night and the cool caress of the sea breeze. She arched into him, tilting her head and allowing him boundless access. Her hands were on him, under his shirt and skimming his back with light scratches in less time than even she knew she needed.

He backed her into the shed wall and reached for her breasts, cupping and lifting, his thumbs seeking her nipples through thin layers of cloth. Finesse often departed when faced with this degree of hunger, she had come to understand. She loved it. They had passed the point a couple of weeks ago of taking forever to get past the kissing.

"Not here," he whispered against her lips, his hands sliding up her neck, cradling her face and tipping it high. His lips traveled past her jaw, nipping and kissing and sucking, the sensitive spot behind her ear the tender patch below her left shoulder.

She shivered, the ground dissolving beneath her

feet. Swaying into him, she felt his arousal pressing against her hip. It lay at an angle, she recognized, beneath his trouser buttons. It was a heady thought to realize how well she had come to know him. Every tantalizing inch of him. And if that was not truly the case, she was willing to investigate further. "Where?" Her sigh of pleasure nearly obscured the question.

"Jail." His breath washed inside her ear as he lifted her by the waist, nestling his erection between her thighs and rocking his hips from side to side.

She whimpered, sliding her legs apart as far as she could with her skirt hindering her. It wasn't far enough. "When?" Her voice sounded petulant even to her own ears.

He pulled back slightly, his gaze dazed but shrewd. "Tonight. After the dance." His lips were a wet, urgent whisper across hers, then were gone. "Unless you have a previous engagement with Dr. Leland. I can always see if Darnella is available." Another kiss, deeper this time. "Or Prissy, if that fails. She makes a terrific red velvet cake."

Savannah dug her nails into his shoulders, pleased when he burrowed into her with a muted groan, pressing her against the wall. She didn't love this game of his, but she would play. "I'll kill you if you touch her. *Either* her." This much she felt was true. "Although you can eat all the red velvet cake you'd like."

He smiled, his eyes very dark in the moonlight. "Then we agree. I would hate to injure the only doctor we have in Pilot Isle."

She rubbed herself against him as best she could, closing her eyes with a purr of pleasure. His trousers pleasantly chafed, his hardness throbbing against her. If she could only move an inch to the left, life would be perfect. "Hmmm . . . I can't have you harming such an important citizen, now, can I?'' She nipped at his lower lip and sighed. ''What kind of citizen would that make me?''

''The jail,'' he repeated, sliding back into another kiss as if he'd forgotten his earlier admonition. ''Midnight.''

When she left him standing in the shadowy night, his gaze burning into her back, her skin blistered from his touch, she was humming.

''You're late.'' She sent the chair into a gentle twirl, dragging it to a stop before him.

Zach might have collapsed like a house of cards at her feet if he'd had his spectacles on. As it was, he stumbled to a halt, squinting to see what little she wore.

Her chemise.

No stockings, no dress, no shoes, no petticoats. Hair trailing down her shoulders. A sliver of moonlight exposed her chin and one round breast, her nipple stabbing through the gauzy material. She grinned like a cat, sliding forward in the chair. His obsession with her nipples had evidently not gone unnoticed.

Dropping her arms over the sides of the chair, she welcomed him with a shameless smile. Reaching back, he fumbled with the lock. The dull clunk echoed in the tiny enclosure. Crossing the room, he unfastened his shirt buttons and shrugged out of it and the undershirt beneath. He held off unbuttoning his trousers; Savannah liked to do those.

Crouching before her, he rubbed his thumb along her lips. ''What's with the chair?''

Leaning in, she sucked the tip into her mouth. ''Remember the dream I told you about last week?

The one that you, well, interrupted the telling of?"
She chewed on his knuckle. "Noah's desk."

He nodded, unable to utter a coherent response
with her lips wrapped around his thumb. Didn't
need to reply, anyway. As if he would ever forget
knocking Noah's books to the floor, propping her
up on the desk, and . . .

"We were in a chair in the dream," she whispered, a crimson blush coloring her cheeks. "I
wasn't sure it was possible, but . . ."

"It's possible."

"Have you ever?" She gestured to the chair.

"Not in this one."

Her eyes flared with equal parts envy and interest.
"I'm open to tutoring, if you have the time."

"I have time." He popped the snaps on her
chemise, leaving the material in a silken sprawl
open to the waist. Ignoring her gasp, he stayed her
hands on the chair arms. Damn it, she wasn't going
to direct his every move this time. She was good
at orchestrating the entire process; he would give
the woman that. Her blessed books had helped,
he supposed.

"Let me take my chemise off." She fought his
hold, but he didn't let her win this round.

He shook his head, bending, pressing a kiss to
the underside of her left breast. It had been days
since he'd touched her. His hunger—and hers—
could wait. He wanted to *explore.*

"Zachariah," she said on a sigh.

He lifted his head, arching a brow.

"Zach." She jerked at his grasp, to no avail.
"Zach, please."

He smiled, feeling wonderfully cheerful. Gener-
ous, even. "Did you let him kiss you?" He intentionally directed his exhalation in the general direction
of her nipple. "Touch you?"

Dropping her head back, she rolled it wildly against the back of the chair. "Of . . . course . . . not."

Relieved that her devilish green eyes were hidden from sight—eyes a man could find himself tempted to sell his soul for while looking into them—he leaned in, seizing the chemise in his teeth and drawing it away from her nipple. His lips bumped the erect nub once, not intentionally. She moaned, but it hurt him as much as it hurt her.

"Ohhh, you're going to play games, I see. Bloody hell."

"Actually," he mumbled around the cloth, "I'm feeling rather charitable."

She arched, sending her nipple into his chin. "How . . . charitable?"

He left the cloth in a wad at the side of her breast. Moonlight glistened across a portion of her face and body, highlighting each perfect swell and valley. Her skin glowed, her hair trailing over her shoulders as she squirmed. Had he ever seen a more beautiful picture in his life? "What can I say, Irish? I'm open to suggestion. It *has* been almost seven days."

She lifted her head, eyes dazed. "Suggestion?"

Leaning in to kiss her, he lingered until she shifted, begging for more. "Anything you ask for."

The shrewd look that crossed her face made him laugh softly, a burst of hunger clenching his belly. It gratified him to see that this wasn't part of *her* plan, even in the face of having an erection hard enough to whittle wood with.

"Anything?"

"Humanly possible, that is. But I choose the speed."

Her head flopped back. "I knew there was a catch. You'll go at a snail's pace."

He traced the hollow beneath one of her ribs with his tongue. "Snails are good lovers, I've heard."

She laughed, bending with the sound, the vibration beneath his palm pleasantly gentle. "Oh, Zach, you're crazy."

And you're crazy about me, he almost said. His lips opened to release it. Then, the statement stopped him cold. He stared at Savannah, rocking back on his heels. All those months since Hannah's death, he had naively imagined he no longer needed a woman's love. Did he need it after all? Could he return it? That might be the more crucial question. How had he missed this? Maybe because it wasn't an issue until Savannah stepped into his life.

"Zach?"

He blinked, pulling himself back, forcing aside the fear chilling his heart. Back arched, chemise wadded in wrinkled folds, she gazed at the ceiling, chewing on her bottom lip, concentrating, as he could see. Her arms were motionless beneath his. She no longer struggled.

"Take off your clothing. I want to try something I mentioned once before."

She wanted to try something she had mentioned before? Ah, Lord, there were lots of options there. They talked almost constantly while they made love, much to his pleasure. He didn't remember talking much in the past, and he liked it. He released a gust of air; his arousal intensified. Wordlessly, he removed his clothing. It didn't aid his resolve that she watched him the entire time with those glowing feline eyes. Her gaze strayed below his waist and stayed there.

"Is this something you read in one of those books?" he asked.

A smile curved her lips. She nodded, her gaze lifting to his face.

He held out his hand, preparing to escort her to the cot that had had clean sheets every day since Savannah arrived in town. He changed them himself, smiling with each tuck and fold as he imagined what he might do on them. Now he was going to find out.

She shook her head and stood, dancing around his hand. "Sit."

His brow shot up as an idea popped into his mind. A very pleasing mental picture. Jesus, if she did that . . .

"Sit, Zach."

With a final, questioning glance, he sat, trying hard not to blush at the indignity of it all.

"Hands where I had mine, eyes closed. If you watch me, I'll get nervous and lose my train of thought."

He knew how she felt, but he was too intrigued by what she might do to him to comment. Tipping his head back, he lowered his eyelids and relaxed his body until it slid low in the chair.

He felt her hair first, sliding along his thigh, slick and heavy. The scent of pine drifted from it, making him think of the forest in winter. Then her lips were at his knee and rising higher. "Are you sure, Irish?" A shiver raced up his spine. "You don't have to do this."

Boy, he wanted her to, though.

"Hmmm, you taste like soap." She released a breathless laugh. "Clean, capable Constable Garrett."

"Is that good?" His words were barely loud enough to be heard. He tried again, then was sorry when she halted, her breath hitting his knee.

"With you"—she ran her tongue along the inside of his thigh, stopping to lick a scar he'd got from a swordfish on his fourteenth birthday—"it's all good."

He let her go, too flattered to argue, too weak to resist. Why resist when he desperately wanted what she offered in the first place? As she got closer, mouth and hands working in tandem, stroking and licking and scratching, he gripped the chair until the muscles in his arms bulged. When she finally touched him there, with her *teeth,* he gasped and buried his hand in her hair. "Holy Christ, where ... did you ... learn that?"

She breathed on him, a teasing sigh that made him stiffen to a painful degree. *Think of fishing, Zach. Sailing. That new rigging on the skiff. Anything.*

"A book," she said, lips skimming the tip of his shaft. "I read about it in a book. Is it okay so far?" Her tongue eased out, giving a hesitant lick.

Sucking in a swift gulp of air, he mumbled a reply, past the point of engaging in real conversation. Better she understood she held a man in her hands at a time like this—and that they were helpless as babes.

She held him captive, teasing without meaning to, going at his snail's pace despite her earlier objections. And his. When she fumbled, he fit her hand around him and showed her how to move it. When she flicked her tongue along the ridge running along the underside, he let his groan of pleasure break free to show her it was, as she said, *all good.* Damned good. The best.

His hand stayed in her hair, the other rising to join it. When she united her mouth and hand in perfect rhythm, he knew he was short on reserves. Then a lock of hair brushed his and he nearly shot from the chair.

"Stop," he gasped, hands sliding to her shoulders and lifting. "I can't ... it's too ... much."

He opened his eyes in time to see her rise from between his legs. That alone was almost enough to send him over the edge. Her lashes lifted, a pleased smile spreading across her face. "You liked it?"

"Yes," he whispered, his voice raw.

"There's more." A statement, as if she knew.

"There can be."

"Now?" She went to move below.

Zach shook his head and settled her astride him, her legs hanging over the sides of the chair. "I can't wait. Not this time. Not after days away from you."

She placed her hands on his knees and leaned back, awaiting a reaction. He tried hard but must have given up something, because she laughed. "Later, then."

Hands going behind her bottom, he slid her forward until he could suck her erect nipple into his mouth. He had to touch her or die. "Can you remember the dream, Irish?"

"Umm, oh, yes. I remember it well." She thrust her hands into his hair and held on tight. "We were in the leather . . . chair in the coach house. It was dark, rainy. Candles lit." Sighing and shifting on his lap, she inched her sex tantalizingly close. "I was on top. Sitting. Then moving."

His tongue circled her areola; he bit down gently. "Like this?"

Swaying, she rested her brow atop his head, her breasts brushing his face. "Close," she whispered in his ear. Gasping, she blew a sweet breath into his face. "Oh, yes, that's good, Constable. Bite down a little harder."

"This any closer, Irish?" Letting her nipple slide free, he scooted lower in the chair, bringing their hips into alignment. Hands on her bottom, he lifted. "Like this. See?"

Her gaze met his. Her lips were swollen, her cheeks flushed. She looked amazingly beautiful, and the tiniest bit unsure. A dangerous combination, he had learned.

"Guide me," he instructed, beginning to think they'd better start this. That, or he would make a big fool of himself and lose control before he even made it inside her.

Her lashes fluttered as she looked down. "Seems the same as me on top in bed."

She did as he asked without another comment, wrapping her hand around him and adjusting the fit. When she had it right—more by feel than sight, he was sure—she sighed and sank slowly down his length, wriggling along the way. Just to drive him wild.

Closing his eyes, he prayed for restraint, picturing every toy in Rory's room.

"Do that thing I like again," she panted, ruining his strategy by pushing her nipple between his slightly parted lips. Sucking the taut bud into his mouth, he latched on, doing what she liked as charged. Hands on her waist, he helped her establish a maddening, steady rhythm. And kept her from making him climax before she did.

She caught on quickly, locking her knees in place beside his buttocks and hanging on to his shoulders. Doing a slow rise and fall, sliding down just before he popped out. She laughed seductively, wiggling at the bottom. "This is perfect. Oh, I can see why they put this in the book . . . on an early page. Better than the bed. More—oh, more *leverage.*"

Dear God, he wasn't going to make it long if she

kept talking about . . . oh, hell, if she talked about anything. "Slow down, Irish. I'm going to lose it."

Bending, she sucked his earlobe into her mouth and swirled her tongue inside. "Lose it. I want . . . you to. You can . . ." she exhaled gustily, "pay me back in other ways."

Their last encounter in the coach house had included her first introduction to the joys of oral coupling. Obviously, she had liked it if she was willing to go that route. "No. I couldn't leave you like this."

Her muscles clenched around him. "I can feel every inch of you. Every glorious . . . inch." Her eyelids fluttered; her breathing escalated.

"That's not fair," he said between clenched teeth. "And you know it."

Pressing her lips to his, she sent her soft laughter into his mouth. The kiss grew reckless, mimicking the movement of their hips, each thrust and retreat. She teased with her tongue as his hands traveled her body, squeezing her breasts, testing their weight, thumbs working her nipples.

"I'm wet," she whispered, drawing back to watch him with a wicked smile. Seducing by degrees. "And all because of you."

His eyelids lowered as colors flashed behind them. He couldn't think of a thing to say or do. His hand strayed below her waist to bring her closer to climax. She blocked his move, saying, "Think of yourself. Later. You can take care of me later." He felt his scrotum rise and tighten, felt the orgasm build as she continued to suggest and tease, murmuring in his ear. She'd gotten the best of him, he realized, heat flooding his body. Surrendering, he shouted and shivered and bucked, pouring into her.

When his vision cleared and he regained the

ability to carry weight on his trembling knees, he moved them to the cot and "took care of her." Tormenting her until she begged for release and agreed that a snail's pace wasn't so bad after all.

It was only after she fell asleep, her body tucked against his, her hand spread across his stomach, that he realized he had not withdrawn.

Once again, he had failed to protect someone he cared about.

The sound of the lock's tumblers turning woke Zach. Groaning, he glanced up, squinting into the dazzling sunlight. His eyes adjusted slowly, his mind just behind. He recognized the weight pressing into his side and the scent at once. *Savannah.* It felt good to wake with her by his side. Darned good.

But a moment later he was sorry. Once he realized where they were. And how much trouble they were in.

Magnus stood in the doorway of the jail, and as Zach watched, Caleb and Caroline pushed in behind him.

Chapter Twelve

It's all right to tell a wife the brutal truth, but you've got to go sort of easy with your lady-love.

—Zoe Akins

"I'll be damned if you and your brothers aren't good at stealing my women," Magnus snarled and took a hasty step into the office. Savannah groaned, sinking deeper into the thin mattress, remembering that the good doctor had once been engaged to Ellie. A vase that she thought held nothing but a withered carnation hit the floor, spraying glass. "I guess she wasn't so hard to steal, though, huh, Constable?"

Savannah burrowed under the cot's scratchy cover. Saints' blood, were they ever in a fix! Zach was going to have a conniption.

The man in question smoothed the blanket over her, making sure she was tucked in. Thank God he had put his pants back on last night. Unfortunately, *she* was the naked one.

"Couldn't you have gone out of town for entertainment, Garrett? Or had Miss Connor already been through the paces? I wondered, being a city woman and all.''

The cot creaked as Zach shot to his feet. "Shut your mouth, Leland, or I'll shut it for you. I would enjoy it, so don't goddamn tempt me.''

Savannah lifted the edge of the blanket and peeked out. Yes, Zach was making those threats. Of course. It was his voice. However, even her antics had not triggered that violent a tone before.

"Don't worry, Zach, old boy, I wasn't thinking of marrying her, either. I simply would have tried to get her into the same situation you did." He chuckled darkly. "A more luxurious bed, granted, but the outcome would have been the same.''

Savannah slammed her eyes closed, knowing Zach too well. She heard the pop as his fist connected with Magnus's jaw. They rolled to the floor, from the sound of it; then another crack echoed in the room before Caleb and Caroline began shouting for them to break it up.

"Magnus, get the hell outta here. Now, or I'm gonna whip your doctoring ass. My skinny brother here might not be able to do it, but I sure can.'' Savannah peeped out in time to see Caleb shoving Magnus out the door by the scruff of his stiff collar. Turning, he offered his brother a hand up, pulling him to his feet. Zach scowled and shook off the assistance the second he could.

"Skinny? I ought to split your lip for that, you ungrateful son of a bitch." Zach rubbed his hand over his face with a grimace of pain, massaging his jaw.

"Only one of us needs a busted mouth right now, Constable. Gonna be a frightful amount of rumor traveling as it is.''

Zach glanced back, but not long enough to catch her eye. An abbreviated grunt was his only reply.

Caroline walked around the room, gathering clothing and boots, mostly of the feminine variety. The sympathetic smile on her face held no I-told-you-so tone, as it could have. She had warned Savannah not to play with fire, and look at the mess surrounding her because she had ignored good advice.

Caroline entered the cell, closing the metal door behind her. Looping a sheet she'd found in the corner over the bars, she provided a means for Savannah to dress in privacy.

Savannah's heart warmed with the gesture even as everything else felt cold as ice. "Thank you," she said, pleased to hear that her voice sounded calm. On the other side of the curtain she heard Zach ask Caleb where the fire was and why the hell they'd busted into the jail.

"We were worried," Caroline whispered, throwing a look of caution toward the men. "No one had heard from either of you since the dance."

"Did anyone suspect?" Savannah fastened her chemise, frowning as she noted one metal snap was missing.

She smoothed Savannah's skirt with her hand. "I did, of course. And Magnus, perhaps." Caroline laughed, clicking her tongue against her teeth. "Caleb wouldn't have believed Zach had bedded a woman unless he saw her tangled up with him."

"Like he did, you mean."

Caroline held the skirt out with a hesitant smile and a shrug. "Could be worse things that happen to a woman than marrying Zach Garrett."

Savannah laced her skirt strings, straightening it as best she could in its rumpled condition. "I'm not marrying anyone, Caroline."

"Oh, dear," Caroline murmured, frowning at

the floor. "This will be a problem, after all. Caleb thought it might."

A strong tug ripped the sheet from the bars. Savannah watched it flutter to the floor, her gaze traveling the length of material to find Zach clutching the other end. His look screamed murder and was directed at her.

"Get that look off your face, Constable. It takes two to waltz, remember?"

He stalked forward, grasping the bars instead of her neck. "What the heck do you imagine Magnus Leland is doing right now, Irish?"

"Oh, gee." She tilted her head, pouting her lips and tapping a finger on them. "Having a cup of coffee at Christabel's? Or," she said, sighing dramatically and thumping her chest, "I imagine he may be telling everyone in town that he caught us in your office tangled up like two cats in a sack!"

Flinging his hands from the bars, he paced to the desk and gave the already wobbly leg a swift kick. Caleb stood to the side, trying hard not to burst into laughter.

She turned to Zach's brother with a scowl. "What do you find so bloody amusing about this situation, may I ask?"

He grinned then, covering his mouth seconds too late. "My brother has returned to the world of the living, ma'am. I, for one, am a very happy fella. Magnus Leland can jump off the lighthouse landing for all I care. The Garrett family has been spinning like a top for years and it's finally stopped at normal."

"Shut up," she and Zach said in unison. Then they glared at each other for a long moment, wanting to share nothing right now. How she could find him attractive at a time like this, with his hair mussed and his face stubbled and a cross glower on his face, she would never know. His eyes were bleary from not wearing his spectacles, and his cheeks were red from something—maybe her kisses. He had a scratch on his neck, and his shirt lay in a wrinkled puddle on his shoulders. Still, he looked breathtaking, enough to make her wish Caroline and Caleb would leave them and what they had found was a quite suitable cot for love-making.

She sighed, shoulders slumping. Her excessive attraction for Zachariah Garrett rendered her a hopeless case. Truly hopeless. And look at the muddle she'd gotten herself into. Worse than any in New York, far worse.

"I'm not getting married," she repeated when the stillness began to make her fingers tremble and her stomach dance. Everyone was looking at her as though she had some momentous decision to make. "Ask Zach if you don't believe me. He said he would *never* marry again." She glanced over and found him watching her with an expression so grave that it made her toes curl into the cool pine floorboard. "Right?" The word slithered out, dry as dust.

For the first time in his life, she'd wage, Zach seemed to have no counsel to offer.

"Your morality is in question, Constable, not mine." When he remained silent, she slammed her fist against the cell door. The burst of pain had her gritting her teeth and saying between them, "I won't do it."

Zach perched his rump on the desk and pressed his fingers to his eyes. She could see the headache twisting his brow. "Reason with her, will you, Caroline?" That said, he left the office, slamming the door behind him.

"I hope he doesn't consider that a proposal, the

arrogant, intractable ..." She continued muttering as she slipped her boots on, wadding her stockings into a tight ball in her fist. That was all she had brought with her, and all she would take home.

She felt Caleb and Caroline communicating over her head. Her blood bubbled over. "Stop it, you two. It won't work. I won't do it."

"Savannah," Caroline said, slippery as butter as Caleb crept from the office—going after his brother, she supposed. "Why don't I walk you home. I know a back way. And darling, for a spell it might be better if you stayed with me and Justin. Miss Vin isn't likely to want the biggest scandal in ages residing in her upstairs bedroom."

"That bad?" Savannah dropped her face to her hands. "Heaven, why did I have to do this in the smallest town I could find?"

"It never happens in a good place—at least, it hasn't for me." Caroline gave her hand a squeeze, then helped her search for hairpins and a piece of underclothing she'd yet to locate.

As they walked home, using side streets and back alleys as Caroline had promised, she got an earful. At least the advice was coming from a woman who'd seen and done more than she had.

"It don't matter what Zach said before the fact, missy. He's far too respectable to let this lie like sleeping dogs and the rest. You must realize that." She nudged her front gate aside with the toe of her leather boot. "There's no help for it. It's the whole lot of 'em, honorable as preachers—even Caleb, though he likes to imagine he's the wild one."

Savannah *did* realize it. That was the thought making her knees wobbly. "I explained to you all that it was Zach's morality in danger of defilement, not mine. I don't give a rip, as Rory says, what anyone in this town thinks of me. I won't be here long enough to care. If I can make sure Ellie's school survives the scandal—and I *will*—then everyone will be fine."

Caroline glanced back as she opened the front door—unlocked, of course. Her eyes were sad, troubled. "What about Rory?"

Savannah squinted, blocking a broad ray of sunlight with her hand. "I don't understand."

Crooking her finger, she escorted Savannah down the paneled hallway and into a darkened back bedroom. Two small bodies lay huddled beneath a thin sheet, cooled only by the robust breeze floating in the open window. Rory was lying with the sheet half over his face, his lips twisted into a lopsided smile. Perspiration dotted his nose and cheeks. His chest rose with a stuttered breath that might have been a sigh, falling into a childish snore.

Savannah's heart pounded hard as she stood there wrestling with the terror of being trapped.

"You and Zach might be okay, but what about him?" Caroline had stepped beside her, her hand going to brush her son's hair from his face. "Trust me, honey. The sins of the father fall to the child. I should know. My boy Justin is just starting to recover from mine."

Savannah's hands trembled and she bunched them into fists. She sank to the settee in the corner, a tear welling and trickling down her face. "It won't work. He'll never have room in his heart for anyone but Hannah." She scrubbed her face and gave a clicky swallow.

Caroline sat beside her, kicking her feet up on a tasseled ottoman. "So that's the trouble."

"Not really. It's simply an assessment." She

closed her eyes, dropping her head back when her stomach threatened to crawl into her throat. "We had an agreement." Now, didn't *that* sound stupid?

"Unfortunately, agreements are usually null and void when you're found in a compromising circumstance."

Savannah waved the statement away as she would shoo a fly. "We talked about the possibility. Zach said he wouldn't ask me to marry him if we were found naked in the middle of Main Street, or something like that." She sniffled, appalled to hear the sound come from *her* throat. "If I remember correctly. And I was content with that agreement. Truly."

Caroline flopped her head back and howled. "Old Starchy said that, did he?" She gasped, laughing so hard she choked. "And you believed him? Lordy, that's a good one." Slapping her thigh, she struggled for breath. "Naked in . . . the street."

It was a good one, wasn't it?

Curling into a ball, Savannah tucked her fist beneath her chin. The sound of crickets chirping outside the window and Rory's and Justin's gentle snoring lulled her nearly to sleep. She felt a blanket cover her, fingers skimming her brow. Murmuring her thanks, she slid low on the settee, hoping to dream of Zach looking at her just as he had the night before. With uncomplicated desire and anticipation in his slate gray eyes.

Instead, she dreamed of his cherished wife and unborn child . . . and the love he could never give.

Fear had him by the tail and was dragging him along, kicking and screaming.

Leaning his shoulder against the door frame, Zach settled his gaze on the woman sleeping in a

tight curl on Caroline's settee. Her arm had spilled
free of the covers, her fist curled and tucked beneath her chin. Her hair had long ago come loose
from that little flower clip she'd had it in last night;
it flowed over her shoulder and chest, the wispy
ends brushing the floor. A startling contrast to the
blazing yellow carpet. She looked lovely lying there.
Innocent and young.

His hand shook as he tugged it through his hair;
his stomach churned. Four shots of whiskey,
Caleb's remedy for darn near everything, hadn't
done much to relieve his mind. He felt a mite less
panicked, but other than that . . .

Liquor never really provided any answers. Hadn't
he preached that to both his brothers on more
than one occasion? Noah especially, when he was
falling in love with Ellie. Caleb, on the other hand,
tended to let rage lift the glass to his lips. Love
never seemed to bother him.

Love. Zach reached to the side, pulling a leaf
from an overflowing ivy-looking plant and spinning
it between his fingers. He watched Savannah's chest
rise with a whispery breath, a frown weighing her
lips. She murmured and shifted, the fist beneath
her chin clenching. A nightmare? Zach let out a
rush of air between his teeth, his shoulders tensing
with the effort to resist going to her. Dear Lord,
if he married Savannah Connor, she would be his
responsibility. To comfort, in sickness and health.
To love, or do the best he could to reach that place.
He understood exactly what it meant to be married.
Maybe he'd never explained it to her in a good
way, a way she would really sit down and chew on.
Really think about without getting her hackles up
about the lack of independence and all.

Hell, they hadn't exactly talked about their pasts

as much as he had come to think they should. He knew next to nothing about her.

Maybe he should have explained to Savannah this morning that he agonized *because* he knew what it was like for God to place another's life in your hands. Marriage was a life-long, fundamental commitment. A vow that brought misery and bliss, belonging and loneliness, freedom and imprisonment. So many wonderful things, so many damned frightening ones.

He remembered the anguish of failing all too well. Once burned, twice shy, was that the saying? Not that he'd failed in the actual marriage, but in holding someone so dear you didn't let them suffer. Or die. He had slipped up somewhere. Hannah had paid for his sins. It wasn't a rational thing to think, but he did just the same.

His son, by God, was not going to pay for them. That much was certain. And Savannah could be pregnant after last night, whether she realized it or not. She wasn't going to pay for his sins, either. He'd taken her virginity, and now it was time to settle up.

Zach rested his head on the door frame, steadying himself with a deeply drawn breath. He did not want to marry again. For lots of reasons. Many he wasn't keen on picking apart, but there you had it. No matter. As it always seemed to happen in his life, another duty—a fascinating, infuriating, gorgeous one that he'd confess if forced—was about to fall to his shoulders.

He had spoken to the minister about a ceremony early next week.

There was no choice; everyone in town knew where he and Savannah had been found this morning. Zach felt a slow sizzle of fury, visualizing what would happen when he got his hands on Magnus Leland. He would; that was a fact.

If he weren't so pole-axed by the turn of events, he would have enjoyed the wide-eyed glances thrown his way from the women he'd passed on the street, the titters behind lacey hankies and cupped hands. The spark of interest in their gazes. Virgin when he married Hannah, his behind. At least people wouldn't continue to think he was perfect. Saint Zachariah. Protecting that image took too heavy a toll on a man.

Savannah whispered an incoherent something in her sleep. His gaze drifted back to her. Jesus, his knees got weak every time he looked at her, his breath a painful hitch in his chest. Seemed like a good thing for a man on the verge of marriage to be feeling. Instead, he'd rather feel nothing— stone-cold *nothing*. Because he wasn't going to love Savannah Connor. He wasn't going to; that was final. Hannah had been his *wife;* another woman would always come in second. Besides, if someone he loved slipped away again, he didn't think he could take it. For Rory's sake, because he was the only parent the boy had, he had to take *everything* that came along.

How was he going to protect himself, though? Lord, considering how Savannah mixed him up and drove him to the brink, and loved him more passionately than any woman ever had, maintaining a tough heart around her promised to be mighty hard.

She thought the problem was standing before a judge and saying the words. Words? Who gave a damn about words? What about sleeping in the same bed every night, touching a toe or a wrist— simple, devastating contact when it was too hot to spoon? What about sitting in companionable silence every morning in a warm, coffee-scented kitchen? What about sharing the load of raising a growing boy? Seeing him change and mature? Seeing each other change and mature?

Zach swallowed, tears pricking his eyelids, making him blink and tremble.

Oh, God, he was scared. Bone-deep, the kind of fear a man can't shake off like an old jacket. He needed some time to figure on this, to come to terms with having a wife again. Without love this time around. Although it wasn't all gloom and doom. He cared about Savannah. Watching the light play across her face, he felt that ache in the pit of his stomach. He desired her like no other woman. Ever. And he truly wanted her to be happy. Wanted to protect her, which wasn't an unusual sentiment for him.

Weren't those important things? He could make her happy. Maybe. Possibly.

If he tried.

If they didn't discuss things too deeply—he and Hannah hadn't discussed important issues like love and marital relations and the future—they might survive this marriage without killing each other.

Chapter Thirteen

Any intelligent woman who reads the marriage contract and then goes into it deserves all the consequences.

—Isadora Duncan

The ceremony passed in a blur, like gray images flickering across the screen in the darkened picture theater Savannah often visited on Fifth Avenue. With only an hour's practice at being a wife, she stood at the edge of a boisterous crowd, greeting guests while scanning the crowd for Noah's tall form. He had promised to bring her a glass of wine. A robust floral aroma wafted from the bouquet clutched in her hands. Wrinkling her nose, she held back a sneeze, not wanting to hurt Ellie's feelings by admitting she sometimes suffered from allergies.

Thrilled by the upcoming celebration, her best friend and future sister-in-law had taken the first train from South Carolina after receiving the announcement telegram and had set about organizing everything. Cakes and casseroles and dishes of vegetables covered four tables sitting just outside the same tent used for the church dance. A fiddler played a lively tune from a makeshift stage not more than twenty feet from where she stood. After hearing the gossip, the Reverend Tiernan had left the tent standing, realizing, even if Savannah and Zach did not, that this wedding would be the most exciting and well-attended event to occur in Pilot Isle in years.

Hurry up with that wine, Noah, she thought, nodding her head and smiling as another well-wisher paused to offer advice on how to keep Constable Garrett happy. Those, in particular, had helped her decide to capitulate to weakness and drink until she forgot whose wife she was. The last time she'd seen him, Zach appeared to be employing this approach. She had lost sight of him some time ago amid the backslapping and congratulatory toasts. At least with every drink, his smile seemed less forced, his stance less rigid.

What had she done by agreeing to this? She had questioned herself over and over since the moment she stood next to a man she desired above all but did not love—and was sure would never love her— and repeated vows before God. *Marriage.* To Zachariah Garrett. Saints' blood, what a frightening thought. Dizzying, exhilarating, terrifying. Of course, she had resolved absolutely nothing in the past week, except agreeing to this blessed ritual after two heated arguments with her fiancé. Other than that, there hadn't been time for much contemplation, thank God for small favors. With one visit after another from her students and giddy members of her committee, family friends of the Garretts, and nosy neighbors, time had sped by like a runaway freight car. Fittings for her gown and trips to the mercantile for new clothes for Rory and Zach, the men in her life now, had taken all but the last minute or two. The only spot of truly good news was that the school had had a substantial increase in enrollment. A married teacher was much more attractive—and safer—than an unattached, city-bred one.

Savannah bowed her head and stepped away from the endless line of guests waiting to speak to her. She smiled and wagged her bouquet, letting them know she would return. Her veil slid off without much fuss, allowing the moist air to caress her face for the first time all day.

Elle, Caroline, and Christabel had done a wonderful job of decorating. Blooming flowers of a variety she did not recognize cascaded gaily from woven baskets hung from thick tree limbs. Unlit candles sat in sconces waiting for the sun to set. The grass beneath her feet rippled in the late afternoon breeze as she strolled toward the sea. Caroline had helped her find a suitable gown in record time, with able assistance from the town's seamstress. In fact, everyone in Pilot Isle had offered to help with more enthusiasm than the future bride or groom had shown.

A wedding! What merriment!

Savannah sighed and shook out her skirt, deciding it was a rather lovely, if not entirely appropriate, selection. A voluminous tea gown with a wide lace collar and flowing gigot sleeves, it was buoyant enough to be comfortable in the oppressive heat. Although she had worn more beautiful clothing or nothing at all on occasion around her hus—*Zach*—she had witnessed a spark of approval in his eyes when he saw her walking down the church's narrow center aisle.

Had she banked her significant appreciation? No need to give him the upper hand.

Savannah brushed aside the stalks of sea oats and crossed the dune. Heavens, he'd looked magnificent standing at the end of the sun-filled aisle, hands clasped behind his back, his gaze steady and sure. Only she had seen the hint of nervousness. From the straw boater atop his slicked hair to the polished boots on his feet, he looked like something from her dreams. Never had a man looked more attractive than he did that morning, dressed in a light linen jacket, striped trousers, crisp white shirt, and shoddily knotted Derby tie. Tall and proud and capable.

If she wasn't careful, Zach would begin to look like the hero the rest of the town thought him to be.

Sinking to the velvety sand, her thoughts got more depraved by the second. Tossing aside her bouquet, she pressed her hands to her flaming cheeks and tried to think of something else. But *oh*, she missed his touch. The feel of his hands on her body, his lips and teeth sucking, biting. The smell of him, of *them*, clinging to the coach-house sheets, her hair and clothing. Since their relationship had been exposed, moments alone had been few and far between. And any, quite honestly, had been consumed with furious arguments. Zach had proven to be insufferably formidable. And tenacious. Once his mind was set, Savannah's proven tactics hadn't budged him one inch in her direction.

She laughed, digging her fingers into the sand. The tactics her opponents in New York had feared worked for naught in Pilot Isle. It was preposterous, and a little frightening, when she considered that her adversary was now her husband. Gracious, how would she prevail in any battle if he understood her stratagem so well? During their most recent skirmish, she had tried to sway him by igniting their ever-present passion, using every brilliant trick he had taught her in the process.

Accepting what she offered, he had taken a little more than she counted on giving in Caroline's parlor, with the pocket doors wide open. Enough to have her panting and clutching his shoulders or face, slithering to the floor. Delighted, she'd had a glimmer of hope that she might get herself out of this mess when he abruptly pushed her away—his breathing rapid itself—telling her with a clever smile that more of that would come after the ceremony. And not a second before.

So here she was, living in Pilot Isle, North Carolina, new mother to a six-year-old boy, and wife of the handsomest, most exasperating man she'd ever met. Throw in two brothers-in-law who treasured her, they said, for bringing their brother back to life, and you had a full family. In the end, her choices had indeed been limited. She had married Zach mostly for Rory's sake. Somehow, that sweet boy had slipped into her heart without her knowing it. Heavens, the way he'd looked at her in the church, holding her hand as he waited for his father to finish repeating his vows, had brought tears to her eyes.

She had also done it in part for Zach, since character and honor meant so bloody much to him. And finally, secret of all secrets, she had done it for herself.

Stacking her hands behind her head, she settled back, the sand warm and soft and soothing. A furtive smile crossed her face, one she hadn't allowed to show all day. She didn't love Zachariah Garrett. She *didn't*. But—and this was something she had told no one, not even Ellie—she wouldn't have married him if she knew without a doubt that she

could not love him. It hadn't happened; of that she
was certain. But she felt . . . *something*. And at the
oddest times. When his lips lifted in a frustratingly
smug smile, when he gestured with his hands about
a subject that excited him, when he looked at her
as if he . . .

She closed her eyes, fading sunlight caressing
her face, a splash of color behind her lowered
eyelids. When he looked at her as though he
accepted her for who she was. That in itself, and
from a man, was most unusual.

What exactly did she feel for Zachariah? Well,
he infuriated her half the time, and the other half
they were naked. Who had time to figure out what
one was feeling with all that going on?

The kiss was gentle. Relentless. Wet. Light, then
increasing in pressure, coaxing, teasing. Savannah
woke in gradual degrees, tasting salt and sunshine
and the smoky trace of liquor. The featherlike
brush of his tongue, slow and languid. Again. And
again, until her hands rose to find him, fingers
burying themselves in his hair. He murmured or
sighed against her lips, his body warm and solid
by her side.

She blinked, rousing herself from the dream.
Dying rays of sunlight flooded around the man
hovering above her, throwing his face into indistin-
guishable shadow. But she knew from the sound
of his breathing and the scent lingering on her
lips.

"How long do we have?" Hand cupping the nape
of his neck, she drew him back to her.

Zach's mouth was warm and firm, persuasive
enough to have her trembling and demanding
more. "Not long. The toast. . . ." For a moment,

he lost the battle, leaning over her and pressing her back into the sand. The hand cradling her head tightened, lifted, bringing her deeper into the kiss. "Sleepyhead."

"I've missed this," she said against his lips.

"Tonight," he returned after a moment.

She settled back. Golden light surrounded him, searing her eyes. It almost felt as if she sought to capture a sunbeam.

"Tonight?"

He smiled, that much she could see. "Did you doubt it?"

She had. He seemed to have an ideal for a wife in his mind, in his *heart*—one she was sure didn't hold any resemblance to her. How could she possibly tell him that?

"Irish, if you think you'll be in my bedroom for more than five minutes"—his lips trailed down her neck to her collarbone, where he lay a possessive kiss—"and still have a stitch of clothing on, you have sadly miscalculated."

"I thought you might—that is, I assumed you . . ." Arms flopping to her side, her statement petered away.

Wedging his elbow into the sand, he peered down at her from an angle that silhouetted only half his face. "What?"

"This marriage." She shrugged, sending a dusting of sand down the back of her dress. "It isn't real. Or rather, I wasn't certain you wished to legitimize it."

She felt him stiffen. "Isn't real?"

Touching him, she trailed her fingers along his jaw. For all his calm control, he possessed a healthy temper. "You swore never to marry again. And now you have."

"Yes. Now I have."

She sighed. Men always needed a woman to spell it out. "Our relationship ... I wasn't sure you wanted it to continue."

His mouth, the half she could see, lowered in a frown. Then he laughed, but it held no amusement. "You thought we would have a celibate marriage?"

"I didn't know."

The hand at her hip clenched into a fist. "Why the hell would we do that?"

Dare she? "Hannah."

His head snapped up. After a stunned moment, he shoved to his feet.

She caught him at the water's edge, her hand tugging his sleeve. Waves rolled in, dampening his trouser bottoms. Obviously, he had left his shoes by the dunes. "I have to be able to speak her name without you retreating from me. We can't live like that."

Turning his head to look at her, his beautiful eyes expressed an emotion she didn't recognize. Something distant and confined. "You can speak her name. I'll answer any question you ask." His gaze returned to the sea. "I don't have any secrets. What you see ..." He shrugged off the rest.

"It was perfect." *She* was perfect, Savannah wanted to cry. But she found she couldn't bear to hear him agree.

Shoving his hands in his pockets, he rolled his shoulders. The sinking sun lit the ocean with a hundred crimson points of fire. Overhead, a gull dove into the misty wind in search of food. "It was far from perfect. I've told you that before."

"You were happy."

"Content." He nodded. "Yes."

She could tell he didn't like to delve deeply into these areas, but to ignore them would go against her very being. "Contentment isn't a state of existence I've had much experience with. Especially—oh, you see, I'm not very good with men," she admitted in a reluctant whisper. "At extreme odds most times. Even with the ones in my own family." Family she had failed to notify about her pending marriage, but that was another issue altogether.

He turned to her, his hand going to her chin and lifting. The chill had evaporated from his eyes. "Maybe they expected something you weren't willing to give. You can't spend your entire life apologizing for who you are, Irish."

She swallowed. "You don't expect more?"

His gaze traveled away, then slowly back. She could see him weighing his answer. "Let's just say I'm willing to negotiate."

"You think we have a chance to be . . . content?"

A smile played over his lips. "I'm hopeful."

"Most of the men of my acquaintance would not agree. They would tell you to run for the hills. My father would weep for you."

Laughing, he said, "I'm not expecting harmony every hour of the day, if that's what you're thinking. I have a little boy in the house, remember? That creates its own level of bedlam."

She shook off his hand, walking forward until the waves lapped her ankles. "I don't know how to be married, Zachariah. I don't know how to be content."

His hand slipped into hers, and they stood shoulder to shoulder, gazing at the flaming horizon. "I'm not trying to recreate what I had, Irish. So this is new for me, too. I'm as scared as you are, maybe more so."

"Scared? You?"

He squeezed her hand. "Don't go believing all

that stuff you hear in town. I'm not picture perfect.''

''They're used to us bickering. What will they think when we come back smiling?''

Turning her to face him, he pulled her close. ''I can think of a couple of things.''

''Saints' blood. How embarrassing.''

Throwing back his head, he laughed. ''Embarrassing is getting caught tangled up like—how did you phrase it? Two cats in a sack.''

''Are you sorry?''

He considered, then shook his head. ''Unbelievably, this has actually helped my image. I've saved you from spinsterhood. A life of abject loneliness in an unfeeling city. Everyone tonight has been patting me on the back for my selflessness.''

''What?'' Somewhere in the back of her mind, she realized he had dodged her question. But she could not let the spinsterhood comment pass. ''They're insane if they believe you've—oh, that is so insulting. The idiots.''

Guiding her up the beach, he wrapped his arm around her shoulders and held on tight. ''Sweetheart, paste a smile on for those idiots, if you please. I have a sainthood to uphold.''

Sweetheart. The endearment took the spark right out of her.

Their truce didn't last for long.

Thinking back on it, Zach remembered standing with Caleb and trying to figure a way to leave his wedding reception as soon as possible. . . .

He glanced at Savannah, noting that she looked half-cocked, her hair hanging down her back, her feet bare, shoes God knew where. Also, he thought he spotted a tiny rip in her sleeve. Unable to check the urge, he let his gaze travel from her wiggling toes to her lopsided smile. The dress . . . ah, he didn't know how to express how beautiful she looked in it. Her wild hair and flushed cheeks only made him think of how she looked after they made love.

As he stared, the usual response occurred: pounding heart and a subtle, or not so subtle, shift below his trouser buttons.

"Constance, if you want to take advantage of that lusty look you're giving Savannah, you'd better do something quick. She's a wee bit tipsy if I'm a good judge." Caleb swayed, not so steady on his feet himself, knocking into Zach's shoulder.

"Who would be a better one?" he replied, agreeing, though he wanted to argue just for the sake of arguing. As soon as Savannah finished a drink, someone filled up her glass. Zach had poured out one in the grass when she wasn't looking, but he couldn't manage that trick all night.

"She asked me if I'm sorry that we had to get married." Zach blurted it out because the question had been lingering in his mind. More truthfully, his lack of a real answer had been lingering.

Caleb sipped, swallowed. "Are ya?"

He watched Savannah smile at Ellie, her lips lifting from her straight, white teeth. They looked moist, as though she had just licked them. "I don't know." Raising his glass, he eyed her over the rim. "I'm confused, I reckon. Everything's happened so damn fast."

"Holy Mother Mary, Zach, let the past go, will ya? Life ain't to be lived for the dearly departed. Enjoy it. You have a pretty woman by your side, in your bed. Trouble with a capital T, right enough, but darn if some of what Savannah's got don't make up for that."

Zach felt the familiar stirring of anger. "I would have liked to choose for myself; is that too much to hope for at my age?"

"Choose what? To be alone? You *were* choosing that."

Rage roared through his mind, the wine consumed all evening swimming crazily in his head. Turning, Zach thrust his face close to his brother's. "Marriage is serious business, Cale. And maybe you don't see it, but lust and love are miles apart. Yeah, okay, you were *right*. Does that make you happy? In the end, I couldn't live like a goddamn monk. But now . . ." He flung his hand out, sending wine across the cuff of his shirt. "I have a . . . I have a—"

"Wife," she whispered, the brush of silk against his wrist and the teasing scent in his nostrils telling him what a big mistake he'd made. "You have a wife."

Zach's gaze shot to his brother's. The panicked expression he saw reflected there surely mirrored his own. "Cale." He tipped his chin to indicate the need for privacy. Caleb bowed his head in Savannah's direction, a plea for understanding, and stumbled away.

"You could have told me the truth when I asked you."

Closing his eyes for the briefest second, he waited for his stomach to quit churning. The sounds of laughter and music barely filtered into his mind. Damn if the woman didn't jab the needle dead center from the get-go. "I did tell you the truth," he said, swiveling to face her, praying to God she wasn't crying or something worse—whatever it was women could do that was worse than tears.

Her expression held nothing more than a healthy dose of resentment. Not a tear in sight. "You most certainly did not," she said between clenched teeth. The slight unsteadiness in her stance and the slurring of a word or two were the only indication of her inebriated state. She held herself together pretty well for a woman.

"I didn't lie."

She drew a gusty breath, releasing it to the starry sky. "Yes, fine, Constable. You did not, indeed, lie. You simply avoided the question."

He began to feel his own resentment flare. "What the heck do you want from me, Irish? Huh? Can you tell me that? I'm doing everything I can here."

Her eyes locked with his. Lord, they were green tonight. "I want honesty."

"You . . . have . . . that."

"Prove it." She swallowed. "Are you sorry?"

He didn't know why he and Savannah had to talk so much. Why she wanted to know what he was thinking all the time. Sometimes he wasn't thinking *anything*. Nothing at all. Anyway, he and Hannah had never talked about feelings. They had just *been*. It seemed dangerous, like swimming through a pack of sharks, talking about stuff like this.

"Are you?" She took a step forward, her voice cracking. The wind tossed a lock of hair into her face. He had to shove his free hand into his pockets to keep from reaching. "Are you?"

"I don't know," he burst out, practically shouting. "I never counted on you—on *this*. I had it all planned. The rest of my life planned. Now . . . now. . . ." His knuckles whitened as his fingers tensed around the glass.

"You don't have room for anyone else in your heart. Do you realize that?" She shook her head in resignation. "I do. And why it hurts, I'm not certain."

"Heart?" He took a stumbling step back.

Savannah laughed when she got a look at his face. She couldn't help it. Incomprehension dominated his features, making him look like a man thrust into a maze with no exits. It was foolish of her—all of this. He was right. What did she want from him? "You've done the proper thing by me, Constable. You don't have to worry." There. That sounded rather composed.

"What the hell does that mean?"

"It means we, you and I, we can't . . . shouldn't . . ."

He took her arm in a firm grip and hauled her behind an oak tree as thick and round as the water casks sitting on the dock. "You're nuttier than I ever imagined if you think I can live in the same house, sleep in the same bed, and keep my hands to myself. All I've been doing the past hour is waiting to get out of here so I can get you home and rip that damn dress off you."

Oh. Her knees trembled and she shoved her bottom against the tree trunk to steady herself.

His lips came down hard on hers. "Let's go back. *Now.*" His glass bounced off the ground as his arms circled her waist, drawing her against his body.

"What if I . . . become pregnant?"

His arms fell away as he dropped his brow to the tree. His labored sigh nearly made her feel sorry for him.

"Your method isn't foolproof, you know. Accidents do happen. And that last time at the jail, we didn't even utilize your crafty . . . technique."

"I don't have all the answers. The truth of it is, I never, ever, in my deepest imaginings pictured myself with more children."

"Is the notion an appalling one?"

"Terrifying, more like."

Her hand covered her stomach in an unconscious gesture. "Terrifying. That doesn't sound very optimistic."

He was silent for a long moment. "*You* expect too much, not me. I'm up to my ears in confusion here. Care to give me a little rope?"

She shook her head. "I don't agree about my expectations. I think I'm being completely rational."

"You want me to fall head over tail in love with you, Irish? Is that it?" He braced his hand above her shoulder and glared down at her. "That make you happy?"

Yes. My, wasn't this a disturbing development? Well, so what, she thought. What woman didn't want her husband to love her? Even if she didn't love him. "I want you *not* to be sorry," she hedged instead of giving the truthful sort of answer she had demanded from him.

"And until I can honestly tell you I'm without a goddamn doubt *not* sorry?"

She shrugged, wine-muddled thoughts bumping together in her mind. Backing against the tree as far as she could, feeling the bark pricking her back and ruining her dress, she kept silent.

"We *are* married," he snapped. "It's real. Sleeping together at this point isn't gonna alter a blessed thing."

"Oh, yes, please use that matrimony angle when it's convenient for *your* argument."

He threw up his hands and spun around. Kicking his glass a good distance, he snapped his gaze back to her, his eyes glowing. "Why are we arguing? Can't we just go home and forget about this? Why all this talk is necessary is beyond me."

Glancing down, she studied her nails, neatly trimmed and filed thanks to Caroline. "I don't need your love, Zachariah. I understand that's outside the realm of possibility." That much was true.

He had advised her of that in clear terms from the beginning. Too, want and need were not always related even if they felt as though they were one and the same. "Yet I'm uncertain about continuing where we left off when you're exhibiting signs of resentment toward this marriage. I heard what you told Caleb—what you felt you could not tell me."

He rubbed the back of his neck furiously. "Wish you'd forget what you heard, but I'd have to be out of my nut to imagine you would." Turning with a careless smile she wouldn't have been able to dredge up if she tried, he said, "Fine, Irish, I give up. You want a platonic—that's the word for it, right?—a platonic relationship, I'll give it to you."

Slipping her hands behind her back, she gripped the tree trunk until her knuckles cracked. If she went to him now, she would never know as she lay there after their lovemaking, listening to him breathe and watching the moonlight play across his skin, whether he wished she were not his wife. Before, the after had been so *good*. He had wanted her by his side, pulling her in and telling her not to leave. Somehow, being his wife made a difference, in heart or gut, wherever this tortured feeling was coming from— one she had not counted on feeling.

How could she possibly bear to accept less than what they'd had before?

When she failed to reject his offer, Zach cursed beneath his breath and stalked toward the tent and the still lively crowd. "I'll have Caleb escort you back," he threw over his shoulder and disappeared from view.

She dropped her face to her hands and let the tears fall.

Chapter Fourteen

One faces the future with one's past.
                                    —Pearl Buck

Dawn broke as Noah searched the wharf the next morning. A brilliant burst of red and gold colored the waves slapping the dock he stood upon. He paused to look, never happier than when he gazed out upon a calm sea—apart from the times Ellie looked out with him.

He smiled, remembering how he would have resisted the feeling of love charging through him a few months back. For Christ's sake, times changed, though, didn't they? It looked as if he was set to repay a favor and help his brother see that his life was changing just as everyone's did. Plans were beneficial—highly—but God didn't always feel the need to follow them. Besides, everything that had happened to Zach in the past month had been for the better.

Noah thought so. The whole Garrett family thought so. If he had created Savannah Connor in his lab, he couldn't have come up with a better formula. Attractive, intelligent, spirited. So what if she was a handful? His Ellie was just as troublesome, and thus far it had only made his life enormously interesting. Outrageous behavior didn't hurt in the bedroom, either. He'd tested that hypothesis many times over.

It seemed as though his cautious older brother had shocked them all and tested it thoroughly himself.

Grinning, Noah glanced around once more before heading back into town. No sign of Zach here. He tugged his hand through his hair, knowing where he was bound to find him. Bless it, he dreaded going there. That was why Caleb hadn't come along: because they both knew where they were bound to find their brother. Noah laughed behind the hand he dragged over his mouth. Caleb had always had this absurd fear of cemeteries. And spiders. Wasn't that asinine?

To be fair, though, if he was doling out hard knocks, he had to give himself one for leaving the burying ground as the last place he searched.

A horde of whalers passed him carrying try-pots in their hands, nets slung over their wide shoulders. The thump of barrels being unloaded and the ring of a bell announcing a ship's arrival in the harbor faded into the distance as he took a back alley that looped around the church. Shouldering through a throng of fishermen heading to the docks, he crossed the vacant field between the chapel and the graveyard.

Knocking the wrought-iron gate aside with his boot, he searched the shadowy corners of the fenced-in square of land. A wisteria vine wrapped around a tree root nearly had him pitching to the ground face first. Grumbling, he steadied himself and, rounding a corner, stopped dead. Zach sat with his back against the largest oak tree in the place, head tipped back, eyes closed.

"What a surprise." Zach's tone was harsh but sober. Noah had to be thankful for that, at least. "Cale decided to stay home, I'm guessing. Spiders and the deceased aren't his favorites."

Noah ducked beneath a low-hanging limb and crouched down, settling back against a tombstone. The slab of marble was the only refreshing thing about the morning. A wall of heat surrounded him even in the shade, and it wasn't six-thirty yet. "Yeah, he felt he'd better stay around the house in case Savannah needed something."

Zach's lids lifted. "So she went home?"

"She's your wife. Where else would she go?"

Looking away, he rolled to his feet. With his back to Noah, he leaned into the fence, his hands clutching the top rung with a corded grip. "Who knows you best, Noah?"

Noah shifted, searching for a comfortable spot. "Besides you and Caleb?"

"Best." He shrugged a shoulder. "Just . . . best."

He wasn't sure where Zach was heading, and he didn't want to get caught saying the wrong thing. The strategy he and Caleb had devised once they realized their brother wasn't coming back was to find him, bring him home, and lock him in a bedroom with his wife. Seeing that the two of them hadn't been able to take their eyes off each other the night before, he didn't see how that plan could fail.

"Well?" Zach asked, angry and impatient.

"Ellie, I guess. If you factor in every aspect." He ripped a weed from the ground and trailed it along his trouser leg. "Consider the matter from all sides."

Zach snorted scornfully. "Like any good scientist would."

"Yeah." Noah smiled, thinking of her. If he had his druthers, he'd be in a warm bed cuddling with his willing wife. "Yeah."

"You're pitiful," Zach said, glancing back. "Pathetic."

"Not bad being in love. I recommend it highly."

Zach's smiled cooled, his hands flexing on the fence. "Did you think I was a virgin when I married Hannah?"

Noah choked, coughing until his lungs ached. *"What?"*

"Your blessed wife did."

It took another breath or two to get his voice back. "Ellie thought you were *what?*"

"Never mind, never mind." He crouched down until his eyes were level with Noah's. "Does it please you knowing Elle can see you like no one else does? That she sees the man behind the mask?"

"Hmmm, yes, I think so. Isn't that what love is all about?"

"Bully for you, then. But what if a person's not *in* love?"

Noah hid the smile itching to curve his lips, realizing amusement would send his brother tearing out of there quicker than a cat with its tail on fire. "If you're not in love but have found someone who understands you better than anyone else, then I guess you've found a . . ." He paused, wanting Zach to believe he sincerely considered the question. ". . . good friend."

Zach sat back on his heels. "That makes sense."

Noah coughed to cover the laughter. "Doesn't it?"

"A good friend. That's one step closer to not being sorry."

Noah had no clue what that meant. "Excuse me?"

Shaking his head, Zach dismissed the query. Placing his hands on his knees, he rose to his feet. "I have to go."

He had almost reached the fence before Noah had time to stand. "Zach," he called as his brother kicked the gate back on its hinges. The man sure was in a hurry to get to her.

He turned, impatience chalking grooves by his mouth. "Yeah?"

"Whatever you're feeling, you're not betraying Hannah, you know."

He frowned, apparently not as sure of that as Noah wished he were. However, thoughts of his first wife didn't stop him from sprinting down the street after his second.

"Wait, let me get my finger out of the way." Savannah snatched her arm back, narrowing her gaze until she watched Rory through her lashes. She flinched when the hammer struck. Silence. Opening her eyes, she smiled, smoothing the embedded nail with her knuckle. "We'll have this finished in no time." Her hand settled atop his bowed head, fingers sinking into the snarl of flaxen curls.

Gray eyes skipped her way. So like his father's that they nearly brought a fresh wave of tears. *No more*, she told herself. *No more.*

A shrug of impatience jerked the thin shoulders and the head beneath her hand. "Vannie, let me do the next one by myself. No one wants a tree house a girl builded."

"Built." She tapped his nose, which he had wrinkled with the insult. "And why not?"

"Aw, you know why. It'll fall down."

She threw up her hands in defeat. Only six years old and already a full-blown male. They must be born with it. "I guess I can help you pick out the curtains, then."

Smiling, he laughed softly. A charmer already.

"Don't jest, young man. I'm the only one out here helping you build this thing."

Rory studied the nail embedded between his feet. "Pa'll be along any minute. He knows we're nearly done."

Savannah tugged her sleeve from where it had caught on a jagged sliver of wood, and glanced around, heart pounding at the thought of seeing Zach. Maybe she could hide up here for a week or two until they settled things between them. That would silence any gossip about their having a rocky start to their marriage *and* give her time to figure out what in the world to do about desiring a man the way she desired this one.

She could live up here if she had to. The structure had three walls and a solid floor. No door or windows yet, but with a couple of pillows and a blanket, it wouldn't be half bad. Many hotel rooms had fewer amenities. She hadn't been too thrilled about Rory's sitting up there all by himself, so she'd climbed up with him, which was not as easy as it looked even though the tree house sat only eight feet off the ground.

"Rory, you up there?"

Savannah swayed, so startled she nearly pitched over the side.

Edging on his belly as she'd instructed, Rory hung his head over the side missing a wall. She grabbed his ankle to ensure he didn't jiggle right off. "Right here, Pa! Come on up! I got a couple boards nailed and ready. I don't know if I have 'nuff nails, so bring some.''

"In a few minutes, son. First I have to talk to Miss Savannah. Have you seen her?"

Rory laughed freely and deeply, as only a child could. "Uh-huh. She's up here nailing in nails backward like a girl." He glanced back as soon as he said it and winked. Lord, how like his father he was, the scamp.

"There?" Zach called. "She's up there?"

"Yep. I'll get her." Rory wiggled back. "Your husband wants to talk to you."

"Thanks," Savannah murmured wryly. Shading her eyes, she moved to the ladder and descended two rungs. A strand of hair whipped into her mouth. Shaking it off, she leaned out, her bare foot dangling.

Sunlight glinted off glass. He wore his spectacles.

For a long moment, he stared. She could tell by the tilt of his head, although the wide brim of his hat effectively concealed his features. She thought he dropped his gaze to her bare foot. Feeling wicked and aiming for retribution, she wiggled her toes.

Not so scandalous, actually. They were covered, even if only by a tattered pair of stockings.

Zach shook his head, glanced at the sky, and groaned softly. "Are you trying to kill me, Irish?"

It was then she noticed the bouquet of flowers he held in his left hand, partially hidden behind his back. Warmth flooded her. If he was coming to apologize, as it appeared he might be, even if he wasn't completely sure about having married her, she was willing to give in. Sleeping in his bed the previous night, with every creak of the old house waking her, surrounded by his scent and his things—the daguerreotype of his brothers sitting on his chest of drawers, and a picture Rory had drawn tacked to the wall—loneliness had taken on new meaning.

Setting the bouquet aside, he held out his arms. "Come on down. I've got you."

Two more rungs, then she turned on the last one, holding on with one hand. The tiny leap into his arms wasn't hard to do, knowing that this man, her husband, would catch her. Though alarmingly, it was the first time, as Zach's arms circled her, his muscles tensing as she slid slowly down his body, that she wondered if the tight feeling in her chest meant that she loved him . . . and had for some time.

He stopped her downward progress when her mouth reached his. "I see you slept in my bed."

His breath washed over her, his scent sharp and spicy. He had shaved and brushed his teeth for this meeting. She smiled, wondering if he was planning to kiss her or simply tease her with the thought of it. "I did. Punishing myself."

He liked that answer. "Yeah?"

"Uh-huh."

Letting her slide the rest of the way down, directly over his blatant arousal, he whispered in her ear, "How soon can you make it up there?"

The belt of lust that hit her was so intense that she pitched forward in his arms. Zach clutched her to him, tightening his hold. "Three minutes." Thinking fast, she amended, "Maybe two."

He laughed, his eyes flooding dark. "Give me five. I have to get the boy down from that blamed tree house and send him off with his uncle."

"Which uncle?" she breathed.

He rolled his lips over hers in a brief, bone-melting kiss that sent another blossom of heat across Savannah's cheeks and straight down her body. If she didn't climb those steps to his bedroom in the next few minutes, he would have to carry her up.

"Sweetheart, whichever one I can find in a hurry."

"I think my leg . . . is permanently numb. It's been a long while with no feeling."

Savannah flung her arm out, groaning. "You think you've got troubles? Mister, who fell off the bed?"

Zach laughed weakly. "I tried to catch you. I really did." He wouldn't mention—because it didn't sound entirely civil to his way of thinking—that her skin had been too slick for him to get a good hold.

"Sell *that* story in town."

Pulling her atop him, he asked, "How much do you think they'll pay me for it?" Late afternoon sunlight poured in through the window, spilling across her back and shoulders. With her skin flushed from exertion, her lips swollen from his kisses, it seemed hard to believe that this amazing woman shared his ardor, his bed . . . and now his name.

Stacking her arms on his chest and her chin on them, she smiled. "A story about the downfall of the prince of Pilot Isle? I imagine I could get quite a tidy sum for that." Her breasts lay heavy and warm against his chest, a definite enticement if he'd had the power to do more than lift his pinkie finger.

Muted passion softened her mouth and lit her eyes the color of dewy stalks of grass first thing in the morning. When he'd reached the room to find her naked and waiting beneath the covers, their encounter had been spectacular to say the least, even in its haste. The second time . . . Zach stared into her eyes, struggling to bring the picture of her face when she climaxed into his mind. The feeling as he stroked in a slow rhythm, invading her, had scared *him*: intimacy of a variety he wondered if he had ever felt before. He could not remember such a feeling with Hannah.

Guilt rode hard on the thought, though he resisted its pull. His vow to himself in the burying ground this morning had been to allow Savannah Connor Garrett into his life if not his heart. Zach was a man used to honoring promises.

"Look at this mess," she said, gesturing at the room, drawing him from his troubled reverie. His shirt hung from the wardrobe door; his trousers had somehow made it to the top of the chest of drawers. Conversely, her clothes lay in neat puddles from the door to the bed.

"Your flowers." He gripped her waist to keep her from repeating her topple to the floor while he peered over the side of the bed.

She giggled, a sound that never failed to amuse him coming from such an independent lass. "Remember tickling my, um, you know . . . with the iris leaf?"

Rearing back, he felt the smile pull. "Is that a blush?" He brushed her cheek with his thumb. "Have I managed, after all my strenuous effort the past three weeks, to finally embarrass you?"

"I'm not embarrassed." She ducked as she said it, tucking her cheek against his chest. "The flowers are beautiful," she continued after a slight pause. "I've never received any before unless you include that lovely spray sent from a delegation of freedom fighters in Maryland in 'ninety-six. Or no, was that from the Ohio contingent in 'ninety-five?" She squirmed while trying to figure it out, kicking his temperature up a notch. "I sent them 'Fight for the Vote' pamphlets and arranged for one of our senior representatives to assist in leading a rally in their hometown."

Brushing his lips across the crown of her head, he inhaled sunshine and roses. "Hmmm, if you like them *this* much, I'll bring them home every blessed day."

Her mouth brushed his chest, an innocuous kiss close enough to his nipple to have him tensing. "My father sent me roses once. In all honesty I should mention those."

Zach bit the inside of his cheek to keep from rushing in. Every time he brought up her family, she shied away from the subject, using the blatant misdirection quite typical of her. "What occasion?" There, that didn't sound too meddling.

She rubbed her chin back and forth as if she was scratching an itch. Zach wanted to tell her to quit moving or damn it, he wasn't going to be accountable for what happened. "My graduation from the Peterman School for Young Ladies."

Zach's burst of laughter ruffled her hair. "Like where they teach you how to hold a teacup and fold a hankie in one of those stupid little squares?"

"Of a sort, yes," she said, her voice dry as toast. Maybe a bit amused. "I completed the program a month late due to a minor infraction that required an additional summer term. Crossed the finish line, as they say, last in the class. Although my father was elated I made it through at all. Hence the roses. They died before my train pulled into Penn Station, the poor things."

"What kinda' infraction had them giving you extra work? You forget to hang up your clothes or get caught reading a naughty book or something?"

He felt her smile on his chest, her cheeks plumping with it. "I got caught sneaking in the window of the bedroom I shared with Velma Manchester after curfew."

"Heck, that doesn't sound so bad. Probably out with your girlfriends getting ice cream, right?"

She trailed a finger along his collarbone. "Well, no. The headmistress, LuAnne Peterman Brice, daughter of the school's founder, nearly ran down Adair Alton McBee the Third with her buggy as he dashed down the drive after helping me climb the oak tree outside my window."

Zach's laughter died in his throat. What was this? Hands going to the sides of her face, he tilted her head where he could see her eyes. "You were out and about with some young buck after . . . what time was this?"

Savannah squinted an eye in a show of recalling. "Ten o'clock or there about. Had to be. Curfew was eight-thirty."

He didn't like the sudden tightness in his chest or his juvenile interest. But he asked anyway. "Did you kiss him?"

An iniquitous grin lit her face and eyes. "Of course, Constable."

He reached for her but she rolled away, dancing off the bed and across the room. Pushing back the covers tangled around his ankles, he stood. It gratified him in a purely sophomoric way to see her gaze travel the length of his body, halting at his waist and holding.

"My, you're unflagging . . . *enthusiasm* steals my breath, Zachariah."

"I'd like to find another way to steal it," he said, moving closer, purpose in his step. She backed up in response, into the chest of drawers. His pulse hammered in his temples; his fingertips tingled.

He flexed his fingers, letting her see. "Nowhere to go, sweetheart."

Her hands stole back to grip the curved edge of the dresser. Damn, she looked beautiful standing there in all her naked glory, chest thrust out, bottom hitched against the top drawer.

Boy, he'd never open that thing again with the same thoughtlessness.

"Adair's kiss was terrible, truly horrible." A breathless denial.

He advanced a step. "With a name like Adair, I'm sure it was."

"There's no need to prove anything, I can assure you."

"Who says I'm out to prove anything, Irish?" He'd gotten close enough for her sweet scent to tease his senses. "I'm not a proving sort of man."

Glancing left, she scooted toward the door. Where she thought she could go without a stitch of clothing on, Zach couldn't say. "Harmless, that's what I told Mrs. Brice and my father. Basic adolescent inquisitiveness. Surely you understand."

"Oh, I do. Felt it a time or two myself."

Her gaze swung back, a flash of temper present. "Do tell."

"Naw, now, what kind of gentleman"—he reached her, his arm sliding around her waist before she had a chance to bolt—"would that make me?"

Her chin rose high, the light of battle sparking in her eyes. Her breath hissed out in a disjointed pant. "Maybe I'm not interested in a gentleman."

"Ladies never did anything for me either." His hand flew out, sweeping the contents of the dresser to the floor. Lifting her up, he moved inside her open thighs, the height too perfect. "You sure?" he asked, sliding her to the edge. In more ways than one, he hoped. "Last chance."

She held his gaze, her legs wrapping around his and tensing. His heart threatened to pound right through the walls of his chest. By God, he'd never dreamed a woman like this existed. Maybe it was only a dream.

"In case you're wondering, Constable"—her lashes lowered, concealing the fire—"I'm ready."

Cupping her bottom and jamming his knees against wood, he thrust home in one smooth stroke. She gasped, her arms snaking around his neck. "Perfect, wonderful, amazing," she told him.

Lord, he thought, trying to put the brakes on his desire, this woman was more real than any damned dream.

Chapter Fifteen

A man has only one escape from his old self: To see a different self in the mirror of some woman's eyes.

—Clare Boothe Luce

Zach flipped through the pages of the cargo ledger, briefly checking each entry. Savannah had recorded all the latest figures in her neat script just this morning over a shared breakfast of coffee, biscuits, and Christabel's delectable strawberry preserves. As expected, every sum totaled perfectly. She had a fine head on her shoulders, his wife did. Brightest candle on the mantel, as Ellie had once said.

The burst of pride in his chest was no less than he should feel. It wasn't every day a man met—or married—a woman like Savannah. Not that every man could handle a woman like her. She was a troublemaker undeniably, and a habitual one at that. Argumentative and dogged and too smart to let you fool her into taking your side. Yet, in the five weeks since their wedding, life had sailed along as smoothly as a ship on a calm sea. Teaching classes at the school and writing articles for publications up north kept her mighty busy. Not to mention the fussy changes she was making to the house—changes he welcomed if it made her happy.

Closing the ledger, he chuckled softly. Her glove lay on his desk; he lifted it to his nose and inhaled.

He tried his best to keep her busy, too. He slept well, anyway. A definite benefit of marriage. Exhaustion always made him sleep like a log. Darned right, he and Savannah were good at exhausting each other.

The jail's front door flew back on its hinges, the accompanying gust of wind sending papers flying. Zach flinched, squirting ink across the page of his writing pad. "What the heck?" Dabbing at a splotch on his desk, he cursed beneath his breath. "What is it?"

"Come quick, Zach. We got a problem on our hands." Toby Malard stood in the archway, breathing heavily and wringing his callused hands. His head nearly brushed the ceiling; his shoulders filled the doorway. A working fisherman for years, he now owned his own boat and had a modest office in a building on the wharf. Caleb was working on a design for his second vessel.

Zach shoved back his chair, reaching to catch it before it hit the ground. "Jesus, a ship didn't beach on the shoals, did it? Let me get my gear. I thought in this weather we'd have no trouble for a few—"

"Forget the gear. It's them women! You gotta do something about them women. Madness down there, I tell ya. Sheer madness."

Zach halted, his belly curling into a tiny ball. *Holy Mother of God.* He could feel his peaceful existence slipping away like a puff of smoke in the wind.

"Where are they?" No need to ask who. Or who the leader was, in any case.

"Down by the lab. Something about hiring women to work there. Female scientists—have you ever heard of such a crazy thing as that? I didn't even think there *were* women scientists, but your wife assured me that there were. 'Indeed,' she said. Indeed: can you imagine a more snippy answer than that?" Toby slapped his hands together, words tripping from his mouth. "It gets worse, I tell ya; it does. Ellie's on one side of the arguing and Noah on the other. If'n Caleb got himself married, I bet his wife would be down there nipping at everyone's heels, too. Ain't there no peace for any of the Garrett men? You're doomed, I say. Doomed!"

Leaving without his coat, deciding this matter could be handled quite satisfactorily in shirtsleeves, Zach slammed the door behind them. "Peace? Peace is highly overrated in my household." He patted Toby on the back as they crossed the street, headed in the general direction of the docks. "I'm glad another man, and my brother at that, gets to share my pain."

"That's cruel," Toby whispered, turning wide eyes to Zach.

"Isn't it?"

They dodged hulking carts loaded with barrels of fish and oysters, and wagons with lumber piled high. Dust swirled, reminding Zach that they needed a good, hard shower. He heard the melee before he got into actual sight of it. Shouting and a whistle blowing: it sounded like a stampede. Boy, Savannah could stir up trouble better than anyone he had ever seen.

"Can't you control this, Zach, being constable and such? You're her husband, isn't that right? Law-bound to manage her. I can see why Noah can't manage Miss Ellie. Too nice, that boy, too tolerant—always was, if you ask me. But you?'' Toby sighed, shoving his hands deep in his pockets and hunching his shoulders. "It's a damn shame. Makes me scared of getting hitched, it does.''

Did they think Savannah would stop because she married the town constable? The thought made Zach laugh out loud.

Shouldering through the throng of protesters, he left Toby and his disillusionment behind. Taller than many of the men, he scanned the crowd, able to locate the gorgeous instigator pretty quickly. As if she'd gotten a jab in her lovely behind, she jerked, her gaze finding his quickly, too. The familiar tingle raced down his spine and lodged firmly in his belly.

He wondered about this connection they had, the way they each sensed when the other stepped into a room. It happened time and time again. In the mercantile yesterday, for instance, as he dug through bolts of cloth, looking for a swatch the color of her eyes for a quilt she'd been working on. The hairs on his neck had risen, and sure as the sky was blue, she stood inside the entrance with the same dazed look on her face that he reckoned sat on his.

The quilting still threw him for a loop. He hadn't pictured Savannah being able to sew or do anything normal females did. The first time he walked into their parlor and watched her putting together strips of cloth like a darned puzzle, well, it was safe to say he'd been surprised. And warmed, deep in his heart. Against his better judgment.

Kind of how he felt when he watched her with Rory. Only that was a much fiercer blow. Working on that blamed tree house or tucking the boy into bed each night with a story. Making cookies: another surprising talent.

His son had clearly fallen in love even if his father hadn't. Zach didn't know quite what to do about that. He just didn't. The boy needed a mother, and some days he wondered if his wife didn't need a son. Confusing. And a bona fide threat to his heart if he looked too closely.

As with most things, he hoped the answer would come to him.

He held Savannah's gaze as he made his way to her, daring her to look away as he shoved aside bodies and ignored advice about how to control a wife and teach a little brother to do the same. All the men agreed, from the scant bit he let himself soak in, that Noah's disposition made him a sure-fire failure as a husband of the stern variety. That left it up to Zach. Prince of Pilot Isle. Saint. Protector.

Everyone felt he could rise to the task.

Except Caleb and Noah. They would laugh until the tears fell if asked whether Zach could control his wife. And Ellie, of course. She knew better. Oh, and Caroline. Christabel, too. No fooling them. Other than that, his reputation was intact.

Reaching Savannah's side, he dragged her into an empty pocket at the edge of the crowd. "Today's dilemma, Mrs. Garrett?"

She started, her lashes fluttering the way they did when he pleased her without knowing he was going to. Then a smile broke through, confirming it. It was the first time he had called her that. Why he picked this day to do it, he couldn't say for the life of him. "Thelma Thompkins came to me after trying to secure a position at the lab. She has a marine science degree, you understand, from a respected university. And after reviewing a list of employees for the lab, I noticed that there wasn't a woman among them. Your brother promised to give the matter his attention."

He tapped his foot, relatively sure she wouldn't be able to see the impatient motion. "And?"

"And that was a month ago. Without a trace of improvement. So, I marched right up to Noah's office this morning without delay. Do you know he hasn't even scheduled an appointment with Miss Thompkins? He had the gall to admit that fact right to my face."

"Did you need all this to prove the point?" Zach gestured to the crowd of women, a modest one in the scheme of things, and noted the placard tacked to the warehouse wall that said "Unfair Practices" in tidy black lettering. "Couldn't you have just come to me? Let me talk to Noah?"

Her back shot up, ramrod straight. Her chin soared high. "Man to man, you mean? The way disagreements *should* be settled?"

"Now don't go getting riled, will you please? I already have a nagging headache and a meeting in an hour with—"

"Where are your spectacles? If you wore them half as often as you—"

Taking her by the shoulders, he shook her. A light shake. Gentle. Nothing more than he would do to Rory before taking a switch to his backside. Since he couldn't do that with his wife . . .

The first second, she only looked livid. A flaming crimson slash covered both cheeks. Then she blinked, gave a woozy little sigh, and toppled over like a child's top after it has finished spinning.

He caught her, of course. Held her against his chest for one heart-stopping moment while trying to decide what to do. With her still in his arms, he lowered her to the ground, the crowd swarming in around them. Chaos erupted while he prayed for a fresh whiff of air to reach them. The accusing looks thrown his way by the members of Savannah's blamed committee didn't escape him, either.

Brushing aside her hair, Zach peered down at her face. Fear crawled into his throat, sent a chill down his spine. Her skin was pale as moonlight, her long lashes resting against the dark crescents beneath. She looked worn out. How had he missed that? Was she overworking herself with the school and that doggoned article writing? Or was *he* the cause, he wondered with a sinking heart? Half the nights, they didn't get to sleep until the wee hours of the morning.

He whispered her name to no avail; she was out cold. Her skin felt chilled against his palm.

Elle elbowed in next to him, dropping to her haunches. "What happened?"

He shook his head, mouthing an answer that didn't make it past his parched throat.

"It's the heat, I'm sure. *Juste Ciel*, these summers! It happens at lots of rallies. Don't worry." Turning, Elle doused a lace handkerchief in a barrel of putrid water sitting by their side. "This stinks to high heaven, but it may do the trick." She bathed Savannah's face and neck, calling her name. Sure enough, Savannah moaned, lifting a hand to bat away the rag. After a moment, her lashes fluttered.

"What the heck," she whispered, "is that putrid stench?"

Zach glanced at Elle. They shared a relieved smile. His hand shook as he pulled the moist cloth from Elle's grip and dabbed his wife's brow. "Irish, can you hear me?"

Her eyelids flickered, held. "Of course. I'm just . . . what happened?"

"You fainted," he and Elle said at the same time.

A small smile curled Savannah's lips. "I don't . . . faint. *Ladies* faint." Her words were soft, the power to utter them louder obviously not present.

"Inside," Zach whispered, indicating with a jerk of his shoulder that Elle should fashion a path through the crowd for him to carry Savannah through.

Savannah was light, a perfect weight in his arms. He didn't remember carrying her more than the distance from his bedroom door to the bed ever before. She tucked her head neatly beneath his chin without a whisper of complaint and didn't utter a peep as he carried her across the street and into his office. He could hear her ragged breathing though. Her complaisance troubled him more than anything else.

"Get the doctor," he ordered to someone, anyone, as he settled his wife on the cell's cot. "*Now.* And shut that damned door." Half the town had followed them over and stood crowded outside the jail's entrance.

"No." Savannah tugged his sleeve, the mattress squeaking with the movement. For a moment, their gazes met in remembrance. It amazed him to see yearning cross her face. That she could think of such a thing in this condition. *What a woman.*

"Yes." He tugged the thin sheet over her. Removing her hand, he shoved that under the cover, too.

"Not Magnus." She closed her eyes and sighed. "I couldn't bear it."

Elle popped her head into the cell. "Zach?"

"Who, then, Irish?" In his gut, he knew she would know someone to suggest.

"Macy Dallas. Her father was a physician in Texas. She studied with him until her father passed away last year."

Zach had met Miss Dallas once. After church or in Christabel's. She and her mother had moved to town just after Savannah under rather mysterious circumstances. "Does she . . ." He licked his lips, knowing this was going to come out wrong. ". . . have any *proper* credentials?" At least he hadn't said *real*.

Savannah dropped her arm over her eyes and pressed her lips tight. "Zachariah Dalton Garrett, do you want me to scream loud enough to have every person outside that door piling in here thinking I'm getting the beating of my life? Or would you prefer I lie here and shut up?"

Zach turned to Elle, who had bowed her head to hide a smile, he'd bet a dollar. "Do you know where Miss Dallas lives?"

"Are you going to tell him or should I?" Macy asked, settling back in the chair Zach had pulled up next to the cot earlier.

Savannah sipped her iced tea, debating the options. She pursed her mouth; the tea was too sweet for her taste, but it was how everyone around here made it. Okay. One choice: to tell her husband—the same man who had yet to tell *her* without a doubt that he wanted to be married to her—that she was expecting his child.

She knew her condition would come as a great shock to him. Saints' blood, what did he expect? She had told him his withdrawal method didn't hold water any better than a can with a big, fat hole in it.

Or, second choice, she could hide beneath the proverbial covers and let someone else, maybe Ellie, do her dirty work for her.

"Savannah?"

She glanced at Macy, whose expression dripped kindness. Her gaze moving to Elle, Savannah decided *that* look could only be described as thrilled. Flopping back to the cot, suddenly despising the squeak that could have been the very one to get her in this mess, she snapped, "He's not going to be happy, so you'd better let me do it."

"What man wouldn't be thrilled by news of a new baby?" This from Macy. It didn't pass Savannah's notice that Elle had nothing to say.

"One who's still in love with his first wife, that's who."

"Savannah!" Elle gripped her arm. Perhaps a squeeze to tell her to keep the family secrets in the family?

"Oh, la, forget I said that." She waved her hand before her face, her eyes closing. "I must be delusional."

Elle drew a sharp breath and, without a saying a word, rushed the undoubtedly distressed Macy Dallas out of the cell. "What are you babbling about?" she asked in a furious whisper once they were alone.

"My dear misguided friend, are you saying you believe, without one speck of doubt, that Zachariah Garrett is going to throw his arms to the heavens and shout 'Halleluiah!' when I deliver the news about our upcoming delivery?"

"Oh, darling." Elle sighed and grabbed her hand, wrapping it warmly in both of hers. "Can't you take what he can offer at present and wait for the rest to come?"

A tear slid from the corner of Savannah's eye and down her face. She rubbed it away, determined to hold herself together. At least her condition explained the recent bouts of sleepiness and her

tendency to cry. It had alarmed her to think she
was losing her touch and turning into a *woman*.

"He looked for all the world like a man in love
when he carried you over here. You should have
seen the terrified look in his eyes. No matter what
you tell me, I'll tell *you* that I didn't imagine that,
Vannie. I couldn't have." She wiped a tear away
from Savannah's cheek before Savannah could do
it herself with a rough swipe. "Can't you make
believe it's all there until it really is? He needs time,
that's all. Just time."

"If it were you, could you pretend? Would half
Noah's love be enough?"

Elle looked away before Savannah could see the
truth in her eyes.

"What if you had none of his love at all?" Savannah struggled to a sit, resting her back against the
wall. "You know, Ellie, I left the reception because
he couldn't tell me he was at least content—no,
no, not even content; simply *satisfied*—with our
marriage."

"But he came after you. Noah told me he did."

Savannah arched a brow to say without words
why he had come after her. Her face flushed just
after, in the event Elle missed her meaning.

"That isn't all you have," Elle protested.

"Are you so certain of that?" Savannah twirled
a lock of hair around her finger, sincerely interested in what her best friend had to say. Maybe
there *was* something she had missed. "How do
you know that isn't all we have? Remember, my
condition can't be used as justification."

Elle leaned forward, peeking over her shoulder
before speaking. "The way he looks at you. Zach
hasn't given a woman more than a passing glance
since I've known him. Except for—"

"Hannah," she filled in.

"Yes. Fine. Hannah. But he never *stared* at her, God rest her soul, with a look that could melt glass. He looked at her more like, like a brother would look at a sister. The ones he gives you are far from sisterly."

This made her feel a bit better. Savannah bobbed her head, a decree to continue.

Elle shrugged. "And he's happier."

Savannah pinched the bridge of her nose, willing away an impending headache. "Happier? Is that the best you can come up with?"

"Hellfire! How do you feel about him?" Elle jumped to her feet and paced the length of the narrow cell. Her skirt flapped against her ankles as she gestured wildly.

Proprietary. Since coming to Pilot Isle, Savannah had come to think of Zach as her . . . well, not her property or anything too terribly demeaning. But as *hers*. Perfectly natural, considering her intense level of infatuation and the incredible heat they generated when they were in the same room.

"See? You can't tell me any better than he would be able to. My advice? You have to make a leap. Both of you. Love is a grand leap off a cliff without anything to soften the fall. Do you understand? You feel horrible and scared, but you do it because the outcome is worth the risk. I can't give you certainties, and I'm scared to death that's what he's looking for, too. You're both the most hardheaded, though, seemingly reasonable, people I'll ever hope to meet."

"A certainty of what? That I won't leave him?"

Elle shook her head, glaring at Savannah. "No, silly, certainty that you won't *die*. That this *baby* won't die. How do you think he'll feel once you tell him, envisioning losing another wife and child all over again? It may be irrational, but he can't be blamed for thinking it."

Savannah unraveled her hair from her finger, gazing at a point above Elle's shoulder. My, that made sense. It didn't relieve the ache in her heart, but it gave her something to work toward. A time-line of sorts. Shaking her head, she glanced at her friend. "I can't give him that assurance, either. He wouldn't know until . . ."

"Until everything turns out okay."

Savannah mashed the heels of her hands to her eyes, the headache pounding now. "So you're suggesting I give him time. About eight months' worth?"

"Can you do it?" Elle dropped to the edge of the cot, eliciting another cheery squeak.

I'll try, she thought. But she didn't feel sure enough even to put the promise into words.

Zach tilted his head, the sails above him filling, fat and lazy. His angles were off a bit, but he'd had good trim on each tack, enough to skip the boat across the narrow pass like a smooth pebble. Clos-ing his eyes, he inhaled a lung-stinging breath. The weather was a welcome surprise. A burst of moonlight shone on his face, shoulders, and back. He squinted against the silver diamonds glinting off the water's surface and off his spectacles as he studied a group of rowdy seagulls drifting alongside the stern.

As the dense shrub thickets and sea-oat-topped dunes of Devil Island came into view, he shifted to a starboard tack, bringing the skiff close to shore. Flipping off his shoes, he rolled his trousers to his knees and hopped over the side, a groan slipping out at the water's bite.

Halting, he stared down the ivory stretch of beach, remembering. Devil Island had been his childhood refuge, one of the few places he and his brothers had been allowed to sail to alone. Once, Noah had sneaked away to watch loggerhead turtles bury their eggs. Boy, Zach had been in a fine fright when he arrived to find his brother cooking fish over a pile of rocks as if nothing out of the ordinary had happened. Even though Zach had ripped his hair out for a long night trying to find him, in the end he had let Noah stay another night. Heck, they'd stayed together—a deal made *after* the obligatory whipping.

Zach had always been an easy mark; he could be made to agree to almost anything after he gave a whipping.

Dropping to the sand, he tucked his arms beneath his head, staring into the endless midnight. A thousand stars twinkled in a clear sky. The moon was a glowing orb, spilling light over everything. He should have felt content. He had a new wife, the most beautiful, passionate woman in North Carolina—maybe in the whole world. And she seemed to care for him the way he cared for her. It wasn't love, but it felt fine just the same. For the first time in years, he wasn't so lonely that he wondered whether his soul was missing.

Instead, he felt miserable, knowing his family was a scant mile away and that right now he couldn't face them. Not yet.

The small square of leather dug into his hip. Reaching, he shifted, pulling it out of his pocket. It was sweat-stained and smooth from frequent handling, and Zach fumbled with the clasp until it lay open on his palm. The past stared back at him from the faded daguerreotype. *Caleb.* Slightly blurred where he had moved, he had been impatient to get out of there and meet his friends. Noah, with slicked hair and pressed collar, had only been interested in how the tall contraption, like a box on spider legs, worked. Zach had stood there directing them all from behind the man under the black cloth. Hannah had been with him, her arm looped through his, leaning into his side.

Days later she'd given birth to Rory. Zach laughed, recalling how he had tried to push her into the picture. No, no, she wasn't at her best, she'd laughed with an airy wave, declining his suggestion. It didn't matter. He remembered her face as if she stood in the graying picture with his brothers instead of just outside the frame.

The memories hit him, hard and furious. For the first time in years he let them.

It was acceptable to grieve here. He'd come to believe that during the first months after losing Hannah and his child. The taste of tears on his tongue was hauntingly familiar.

Oh, Lord, he prayed, what was he to do? Where would he find the strength to go on?

Savannah was pregnant.

Sitting up, he ripped his hand through his hair, heart pounding hard enough to make him queasy. Gulping in the salty air, he flattened his palms to the sand, digging his fingers in past the knuckles.

She had been asleep when he made it back to the jail after securing another patrol for the evening shift. The look on Ellie's face, and the hints, were too many to overlook. Savannah's sleepiness of late, the bout or two of crying . . . and today, the fainting spell. Zach might not like to think he knew what those things meant, but he did. Of course he did. He had lived through them twice before.

This afternoon he had carried her home, hush-ing her when she tried to rouse herself from sleep. Tucking her into bed, he had left a note telling her he had to go on patrol after all.

Coward.

Digging deep, he threw a ball of moist sand as far as he could, cursing himself, cursing her. He was insane to feel this way, possessive and hungry, wild-eyed and impulsive, about a woman who had tripped into his life only two short months ago. Now she was going to have his child.

Jesus. Arms spread, he collapsed on the sand. How could he rationalize the unbelievable rush of emotion *that* thought channeled through his mind and body? Anger and fear and such unadulterated happiness that he thought he might pass out from the force of it. At this moment, he didn't really care about rationalizing motives and discussing intent. He wanted to go home and make love to his wife with an intensity he had never felt before, an intensity he figured existed only in fanciful tales of love.

Therein lay the triple thrust of guilt. He hadn't felt this strongly about Hannah . . . or maybe that wasn't a good way to put it. He hadn't felt that strongly about her in a *carnal* way. He had loved her deeply, much as he loved Elle, whom he'd grown up thinking of as a sister.

How goddamned depressing was that?

Thirty-four years old and he was just now finding he didn't have *anything* worked out. Did he love Savannah? Had he loved Hannah the way he should have, the way she'd deserved to be loved? Could he silence the nagging voice telling him he was going to lose it all again, and confront the woman who right this very minute was sleeping in his bed?

Who the hell knew? He didn't.

He guessed that left him hiding on an island in

the middle of the night rather than facing the fact that his wife, a woman he couldn't take his eyes off of for more than a minute when they were in the same room—let alone keep from touching—was pregnant with his child.

A woman who had promised not to love him, in a manner of speaking, after—or possibly before—he had promised to do the same.

What a pickle.

Chapter Sixteen

After great pain, a formal feeling comes.
                                    —Emily Dickinson

Zach met Caleb in the kitchen the next morning. After enduring the frown of displeasure on his brother's face, he asked where he could find Savannah.

Oh, that's easy. She was with Rory. *In the tree house.*

Were they all crazy?

"Get down from there," he yelled as soon as he reached the thick oak tree. She could fall and hurt herself or the baby. Thinking fast, he cursed softly, wishing he could call it back. He was supposed to let her tell him the news and accept it calmly. And happily. Happiness—he must remember to include happiness and exclude fear. Though the knot in his belly hadn't got any smaller after spending the night on Devil Island.

Savannah's and Rory's heads popped over the edge: one blond and tousled, the other dark and glossy as a horse's mane. Squinting, Zach lifted his hand for shade, his heart expanding, then tripping into a thunderous cadence.

Did he love her? Was that the problem?

Why her when there were so many uncomplicated women to choose from in town, women who'd been forever bringing him cakes and pastries and cookies with colorful sprinkles to show their interest? They were always batting their eyelashes and simpering prettily when he walked into the mercantile or Christabel's restaurant, making a show of smoothing his cuff or collar when they got the chance.

Didn't God just have a fun time up there, throwing huge boulders in a man's path?

"Pa! Come on up. We're paintin'. You and me can finish hammerin' 'cause I got new nails with Uncle Cale last night. And some strawberry lollies, but I ate 'em all. He let me carry the bag and keep it under my bed. I even showed Vannie when she read me a story." Taking an excited breath, his little chest heaved. "Hey! I almost forgot. I smashed my finger with the hammer and cried a little, but Vannie said that was okay 'cause everybody cries. Not like I'm a baby or nothing."

"Anything," he heard her correct the boy.

Vannie. How long would it be before Rory starting calling her Mommy?

With the question circling, Zach's gaze strayed to hers, and held. The space between them sizzled. He stopped himself from taking a startled step back, hoping no one was going to take a good look at the front of his britches. His body sure did recognize her quickly. "Son, your uncle has biscuits and gravy ready. You need to wash up. We'll get to that hammering after."

Rory pursed his lips. "Oh, Pa."

"Oh, Pa, nothing." Taking his eyes off Savannah,

he nodded at his boy, telling him in no uncertain terms that he meant business.

"Gotta go, Vannie. Big boys have to eat breakfast every day," Rory grumbled and scrambled down the rickety ladder without looking down to see if his feet were going to catch the rungs.

"Inside," Zach said and tapped Rory on the behind. "I'll wait for Savannah." He glanced up as the screen door slammed and his son's excited chatter drifted from the kitchen.

Her head hung over the edge of the tree house; her cheeks were pink. From his look, her thoughts, or her upside-down position: he couldn't guess where the color came from. "Come on down from there. What if you bounce out right on your lovely head? You gotta quit climbing up there with the boy all the time. It isn't safe."

Savannah swallowed slowly. He watched her throat pull, remembering touching her there, kissing her there. "You know," she finally said, her hands clenching around the plank she lay on, her face losing a bit of its blazing color. "*You know.*"

He didn't dispute it; he'd never been much of a liar.

"Who told you?" she demanded, never one to flinch in the face of adversity.

Zach shrugged, arms lifting then dropping to his side. "No one. Took me a while to figure it out, though."

"Because you've experienced all this before." Her eyes glittered when she said it, as if he had done something wrong by figuring out without being told that his wife was pregnant.

Feeling a spark of anger, he took a step forward until he stood directly beneath her. "You coming down so we can talk about this, or you going to sit up there pouting?"

Her head disappeared. "I think I'll hide as you chose to last night," she said calmly, clearly.

"Fine, Miss Connor. Sit up there and stew all day for all I care."

"Mrs. Garrett, you bloody oaf," she yelled. One of her boots flew out, whacking him in the shoulder.

He snatched it from the ground and stalked inside the house, his frown daring anyone to ask why he held his wife's boot with no wife in sight.

Watching the Garrett men race around the back yard in a raucous game of tag eased Savannah's anger by slow but sure degrees. The hesitant glances tossed her way by all of them with the exception of Rory, who remained blissfully unaware of the strife between his father and his new stepmother, helped, too. From the look of it, they had no idea whether she would remain calm or explode like a firecracker.

She hadn't decided that for herself yet, so she couldn't possibly tell them.

They spun and laughed, knocking each other down; tripping and other underhanded tricks were apparently allowed. Savannah sighed, wondering if, as a new wife, she was expected to do all the mending and washing. Zach had a grass stain on his shirt and a piece of pine straw in his hair; Rory had a rip in his britches and smudges of dirt on his face. Caleb was even worse for wear. In contrast, Noah looked squeaky clean, hardly a Garrett—a state Elle claimed he upheld to an irritating degree. At least it lessened the amount of dirty laundry, Ellie had murmured as she left the gathering to deliver books to the school, after asking Savannah to take care of the men's mishaps in her stead.

Never having been a part of a demonstrative family, Savannah felt like an interloper, once again an outsider with her nose pressed to the glass. Sitting on the edge of the porch—she had decided to come down from the tree house after the scent of bacon and eggs drifted in—she swung her legs in time to a scratchy tune blaring from the phonograph in the parlor, a wedding gift from Caroline.

She wished she fit in better than she did.

A bee flew by her face. Shooing it away, she remembered picturing married life as restrictive and encumbering, like a tight corset squeezing your innards until you couldn't breathe. Yet she didn't feel the least bit constricted sitting in a broad band of sunlight, a strong sea breeze lifting her hair from her brow, the sounds of a friendly family scuffle ringing in her ears. She wasn't certain she felt confident enough about her future with Zach to define this warm feeling as contentment, but . . .

Lifting a writing pad to her lap and using the lovely fountain pen Zach had given her, she outlined a resolution she planned to present next week to the town council. They needed additional streetlamps, and to usher Pilot Isle into the modern age, she had contacted the closest electric company about the town's options. Having no idea what funds might be available, she had drawn up a modest plan to erect eight poles and wire lamps atop them, then utilize them from sunset to midnight on moonless nights only. Rather reasonable, at that.

Watching Zach tumble to the ground with Rory clinging to his neck like an impish monkey, Savannah wondered if the town constable would support her resolution. She drew a circle on the paper and a box around it. How could she sway him if he did not seem amenable?

As if he felt her deliberations, he glanced up,

his eyes falling to his gift clutched in her hand. Smiling shyly, he lifted Rory from the grass, turning before she could snag his gaze. She wondered again about this extraordinary lifelong contract she had entered into. And the curious way it had altered Zach's behavior. Overbearing as a mother hen, he had conspicuously placed her under his wing with his other chicks, using every protective instinct he possessed to gather her close. It was by turns insulting and enormously heartwarming. Without doubt, she betrayed her gender, and the causes she had fought so valiantly for, by allowing herself even to acknowledge that she could be pleased by such male authority.

Or perhaps her new husband's stance had more to do with the baby growing inside her rather than his feelings for *her*.

Unconsciously bringing her hand to her still-flat tummy, she marveled at the changes in her life. Why, she had not seen an automobile in two months, smelled the chemical stink of gasoline, or heard the chugging clink and clap as one tottered down a busy avenue. Fizzy cola drinks were scarce in Pilot Isle, as were milk chocolate bars. Heavens, most of her shopping would now be done using a Sears, Roebuck and Company catalog or taking an occasional trip to Raleigh.

Her social calendar, though, was as full as it had ever been. She had accepted an invitation to a candy pull next week, an event she had no idea how to prepare for, or even exactly what it *was*. A church bake sale followed during the next week, then another sewing circle a day later. Throw in weekly meetings with her committee and an average of two classes a day at the school, writing articles, and communicating with her delegation in New York, and that made for an active autumn.

Elle and Caroline had also undertaken to teach
her how to manage a household without a staff at
her beck and call. Her days promised to be filled
with cooking, washing, ironing, and sewing . . . and
soon, with nursing a child. Her fingers tightened
on her stomach.

Saints' blood.

Rory chose that moment to voice his opinion,
sliding into her lap as gracefully as a bull charging
into a china shop. Her writing pad went flying; her
pen dribbled ink on both of them before dropping
to the porch floor. "Goodness, young man, what
is this?"

He turned eyes the color of ash to her, his lashes
quivering sleepily. "I'm hungry. Those biscuits and
gravy worn off. See?" His belly rumbled beneath
her hand to prove it.

"Now what can I do about that?" She couldn't
stop herself from brushing a lock of hair from his
brow, something he wouldn't have dared let her
do if he weren't so drowsy.

He blinked and yawned. "Fix somethin' good."

Leaving the men and their games, she felt a little
peaked when it came right down to it. She carried
Rory inside, remembering the thick slices of ham
and fresh bread she had seen this morning. She
would make him drink a full glass of milk, then
put them both down for a nap.

A salty gust blew in around her, slapping her
skirt against her ankles. It almost felt as if she had
lifted her nose from the glass pane and come
inside—for the first time ever.

Zach watched the screen door slap behind them,
his heart filling his throat near to bursting. Seeing
his son crawl into Savannah's lap and snuggle

against her—something the boy didn't do that often anymore, even with Zach—had made him feel wonderful, and scared as hell. Caleb and Noah hadn't blinked, he'd bet. They accepted Savannah as part of the family as though nothing had changed. Jesus, his entire life had been tossed into a bowl and whipped like an egg. He wasn't at all clear what to do about the mess left behind.

Searching for a sight of them through the kitchen window, he forgot the rules of the game—forgot the game altogether. It came as a surprise when Caleb slammed into him, knocking him to the ground.

His chest heaving against Zach's arm, Caleb panted, "You gonna stand there all day gawking at your wife or play?"

Turning his head, Zach shoved his brother without moving him an inch. Caleb had thirty pounds on him at least. "Get off me, damn it. You're a load."

"Ohh, listen to that. Constance is getting riled."

"Get up, Cale; you look foolish." Noah pushed Caleb to the side and helped Zach to his feet.

"Worst thing you can imagine, huh? How about mooning over a woman like a lovesick pup and doing nothing about it but sighing and frowning all day long?" Caleb smacked his lips against his palm and released the kisses in the general direction of the kitchen.

Zach stopped dusting his trouser leg, his face heating. "I'm . . . *not* . . . lovesick."

Caleb blew another kiss instead of answering.

Stepping forward, fists bunched, Zach only halted when Noah moved in front of him, arms raised to keep his brothers apart. "Will you two quit jawing at each other? This is ridiculous behavior for grown men. One might think you're Rory's age, for God's sake."

"He started it," Zach said, realizing how darned stupid that sounded, yet unable to stop the accusation from tumbling out.

"Holy Mother Mary, Miss Pris, one *might*," Caleb said, yanking a twig from his hair.

"Do you think she looked a little pale? Is that normal this early?" Noah asked, his concerned gaze meeting Zach's. Noah wanted children right away; thus, Savannah's condition interested him to no end. He must have asked her a hundred embarrassing questions today with Elle looking on, aghast and amused.

"She may feel queasy in the afternoons. Hannah did." It surprised Zach as much as his brothers, judging from their shocked expressions, to hear him speak her name freely. His first wife had been a forbidden topic since her death.

"You think you should check on her?" Noah gestured to the kitchen and the figure moving back and forth in front of the window facing the yard.

"Aw, he's scared to do that. If Rory leaves the room, they'll be *alone*."

Zach reached around Noah and shoved Caleb as hard as he could, sending his brother stumbling back two steps.

"Cut it out!" Noah roared, a startling edict from a man who rarely lost his temper. "Cale, let him work this out himself. It's his marriage, not yours. Keep your mouth shut."

"We'd better give him some tips, Professor. What would he know about pleasing a woman?" Caleb danced around them, out of reach, grinning like a kid. "The first time he romanced his wife was in the jail. A romantic story, ain't it?"

The screen door squeaked; a step sounded on

the porch. "Actually, we'd been meeting at the coach house for weeks. The jail"—Savannah shrugged—"a rash decision. I guess I couldn't wait." She smoothed her hand over an apron some-one had given her just before the wedding, rightly thinking all they had at Zach's were Hannah's old ones, and smiled. Zach recognized that spark in her eyes. Mischievous hellion.

"I've made ham sandwiches if you boys are hun-gry," she continued in the same smooth tone, as though she hadn't just shocked the breath out of all of them. The door whapped behind her.

Zach stared, his face burning. Caleb stopped in mid taunt, his arms flopping to his sides.

And Noah . . . Noah smiled. "I knew I liked that woman," he said, leaving his gaping brothers be-hind and hustling inside for a sandwich.

Savannah stretched, rubbing her feet together beneath the sheet. Rain plinked off the roof; a slice of moonlight washed over the bed and directly across her hands and stomach. Patting her tummy, she wondered when she would grow larger with her—with *their*—child. She had never been as tired, or able to sleep so easily, in her life.

The creak of the floorboard near the window made her start, rising up on her elbows in the bed.

"Just me, Irish," Zach whispered, drawing the window higher. A flood of fresh air rushed inside, drying the dampness on her cheeks and brow. The evenings were finally getting cooler, thank good-ness. "Hot as Hades in here."

Yes, she agreed silently, *when are we ever in the same room that it isn't?*

Even now, the few feet separating them fairly bubbled, the air crackling. She felt too restless, too warm for true comfort. What would Zach do if she yanked her thin nightdress from her body and let it drift to the floor at his feet? Her nipples puckered, scratching against the soft cotton, urging her like a tiny devil on her shoulder to *do it.*

"Can we talk?" Drawing a chair beside the bed, he folded his long, lean body into it. His hand went to loosen his collar, unbuttoning it and tugging it off. He had just returned from patrol and still wore his salt-encrusted work trousers. She squinted into the muted light . . . and her favorite shirt, she realized with a sinking heart. Dark blue, it brought out those delicious sapphire flecks in his eyes.

Tangling her hands in the covers to keep them from wandering where they shouldn't, she nodded. She could smell the sea on him. And his peppery shaving balm. Not sure how strong her voice would be, she didn't try speaking but simply nodded again in case he had missed the first try.

"Do you feel all right?" He reached for her hand but didn't grasp it when he realized it lay under the covers. "Anything I can get you?"

She shivered in anticipation. Longing. Fear. The hungry plea sat on the tip of her tongue.

"I'm fine." Sitting up, she reclined against the headboard. "There's water on the nightstand. I brought up a fresh pitcher. I'm just tired." Her hands fluttered, drawing his gaze to her stomach. It traveled to her toes before returning, searing a path a mile wide, or so it felt. "I can't seem to get enough sleep." *Enough anything right now.*

"That'll pass soon enough."

Will it? She drew her arms out and fiddled with the edge of the sheet. "I guess . . . I guess it did with Hannah."

He rubbed the back of his neck, looking less alarmed than she had expected. She didn't want him to run away again, yet they had to get past this or their marriage would fail. "No, she didn't really get over it. Either time. But you're leagues stronger than Hannah ever was. Leagues."

A crack of thunder kept Savannah from replying immediately. It gave her time to watch Zach settle back, steepling his hands over his trim stomach. For a moment in the burst of light, she thought she saw relief cross his face. Then it hit her why.

Leaning over the bed, she touched his knee. He jerked, rocking the chair back on its rear legs. "I'm going to be okay, Zachariah. This baby and I are going to be fine."

The darkness hid his eyes, but she saw his throat draw down as he swallowed. "I know that." A tortured whisper at best. "I know that."

She squeezed his knee, resisting the urge to move her hand up the inside of his thigh. "I don't think you do. And if you don't cast off your reservations"—she weighed how honest she should be—"this is going to be the longest seven or eight months in history."

His head dropped. "It was terrible," he finally uttered in a choked voice, his hand covering hers and gripping tight. "I was helpless, a failure."

Thunder rattled the windowpanes, wind whipping the curtains into a frenzy. Savannah pressed her lips together, wanting to offer guidance and comfort. But she knew she had to tread carefully or risk spoiling the opportunity. It appeared that her husband stood on that cliff, ready to take Elle's leap into the unknown and trust her. To tear down that wall he'd hidden behind for the past few days—for two years, perhaps. That she desperately wanted to kiss away his fear, whisper his name as he moved inside her, and hold him against her breast as he slept didn't make it the right path to take at the moment. "You couldn't be expected to save her. You can't save everyone. Some things are in God's hands, not yours."

"You don't understand. She would rather have moved back home with her folks after she saw what being a wife was—the down-and-dirty reality of living with a man. And I knew it. I did. Bless her heart, she didn't tell me, but every time we . . ." His gaze flicked to hers, glowing like smoking ash in the dim light. "She didn't like it. She didn't want it. Rory was enough; I should have stayed away."

"When are you going to forgive yourself?"

His shoulders tensed, his fingers quaking around hers. Zach ignored her question, asking one of his own. "Why did you admit that, that about the coach house, to my brothers?" She found his stutter and the way he ducked his head utterly charming.

"Because I'm tired of everyone expecting you to be so damned perfect and, consequently, making you think you should be." Savannah smiled, brushing her thumb over his knuckle. She'd done all she could to help him thus far. Absolution rested on his shoulders. "I've forgiven you. After all, you broke our agreement, and I've yet to blame you for it."

His head lifted. "What agreement?"

"You said you wouldn't marry me even if we got caught naked in the middle of the street."

A soft burst of laughter ripped from his throat. "In the middle of a rally is what I said. That all sounds fine and dandy, doesn't it? I didn't think it would actually happen."

The memory of that day, of her hands memorizing a body urging hers into a fury, crowded her heart and mind until she felt she couldn't breathe.

A burst of lightning lit their faces. A storm swirled

in his eyes, as if he too remembered. Devouring her in that brief moment, she recorded the feeling mesmerizing her, tempting her closer. Wild impulses set her skin tingling with impossible desires and forbidden dreams.

He leaned in until their faces were close enough for their breaths to mingle. "Say one of those big words for me, Irish."

Words poured through her mind, ridiculously big ones. Yet she uttered only, "Yes."

Taking her wrists in his hands and pinning them above her head, he poured over her like a scalding flood. His mouth crushed hers, swallowing her gasp of startled pleasure. She met him, letting him possess her from the first instant. Her toes curled beneath the sheet.

He murmured against her lips, gasping a necessary breath of air. "Is that the best . . . you can do? Three . . . little . . . letters?" His hair fluttered around his face. In the meager light, she couldn't make out his expression.

The outline of his arousal dug into her moist folds. She shifted from side to side, searching for the ideal fit. He growled low in his throat and linked their fingers, stretching their arms until their knuckles brushed the headboard. The position thrust her pelvis up and had the maddening bonus—for him—of keeping her from engaging him, changing the direction, or leading their erotic dance.

What had his question been? Something about best . . . somethings. Leaving her lips, he nipped at her neck, her earlobe. Her tortured moan as she struggled for purchase would have to do for an answer.

"I don't know if I have patience for pretty words and wooing." He took her nightdress between his teeth and jerked, ripping it down the front. Air flowed inside the torn garment like a welcome caress.

"I don't want wooing or pretty words." *Or touches meant to ignite.* Her body practically smoked already. She wanted him. Zachariah. Her husband.

Her love.

Her skin tingled; her body ached; her mind spun. And her heart? Zach held that in his hands.

When his lips moved to her nipple, his tongue circling and flicking the taut nub, she thought she might burst into flames on the spot. She jerked her arms from his grasp and plunged her fingers into his hair, raking her nails over his scalp. "Stop toying with me."

"Ah, sweetheart, if I was toying with you," he said, his breath hot and moist on her, "you would know it."

A light sheen of perspiration coated their skin, sticking in patches, sliding freely in others. Hands moving to clutch his shoulders, she thanked goodness for his shirt only because she might not keep a grip on him without it. "Your clothes."

His hand worked its way between their bodies, brushing her mound, sending a shiver through her. Eyes half closed, she threw her head back. "Now, Zach."

Unbuttoning his trousers, he whispered raggedly against her breast, his mouth dragging higher, "How 'bout this time . . . we try it with them on?"

Her eyelids flickered, catching him with such a look of bold longing on his face that her heart fluttered. His shirt lay open at the neck, his chest rising in staggered breaths. She bowed her head, kissing, sucking. Moist skin, crisp hair beneath her lips . . . then his nipple. It hardened slightly under her tongue.

He trembled above her, his hand grasping her nightdress and yanking it to her waist. With a muffled oath and a warning, he entered her in one fluid stroke, stretching her nearly to her limit. She raised her hips, clasping her legs around his.

"I want to feel your mouth beneath mine as I come inside you, Irish." He withdrew to the tip, his lips coming down on hers, commanding and aggressive.

Moving together in a tangle of moist skin, she kissed him, held him to her, and gave him everything she had. Though he did not know it, she lost herself as they became one. It was fantastic. Extraordinary. Remarkable. Heat and bursts of light, a raging storm. Inside her body, outside the windows of their bedroom.

A blinding, white-hot explosion.

He cupped one breast, testing its weight and gently squeezing, thumb finding her nipple and working it in time to his thrusts. One hand went to her hip, lifting her in the same rhythm. Slanting his head, he deepened the kiss, closing in on his climax. She could tell from his frantic plunging and his efforts to bring her with him with whispered pleas. The recognizable sensation started swelling, raising prickles in her lower back.

His hand moved between her legs. "Ah, there, yes." He knew what she needed.

The sound of feet pounding on the stairs barely registered.

The pounding of a fist on the door did.

"Christ," Zach whispered against her ear. His breath charged from his lips. "Not when we're so . . ."

"Zach!"

Caleb. Yelling something about a ship and the shoals and meeting him downstairs. Zach's body

trembled from trying to hold back; his buttocks
quivered beneath her hand. A bead of perspiration
rolled down his cheek to his chin. Angry, he
shrugged it away.

Tipping his head back, he shouted an affirmative
reply and thrust deep, his voice covering the sound
of the bed ropes squeaking.

"You have to—"

He cut her off with a brutal kiss, his hand stroking, seeking. He thrust silently, surely, to the tip
and back, again and again.

"Come on," he murmured, pleading now, "before I . . . have to go."

Close. So close. But someone was outside and
duty called.

"Later. We can—"

"*Now.* I would suck this"—his finger flicked the
nub, circling it—"if I had time. I would make you
shatter into a thousand pieces."

The image of his lips on her body, delving lower,
between her thighs and beyond, something he had
done to her only twice before, lit her fuse.

It was a short one.

The explosion rocked her harder because she
held it back, held it *in*, breathing her shout of
ecstasy into his mouth, digging her nails into his
skin to keep from writhing off the bed. She whispered her hope that he would suck that part of
her body into his mouth. Very soon.

He thrust deep in a lengthy, shuddering release.
A well-timed din of thunder obscured his violent
gasp.

His body trembling, he withdrew, apologizing
profusely and pausing every second to touch her,
to smooth her hair from her eyes or grasp her
hands. Pulling on his boots with an angry oath,
he buttoned his britches, pulling himself quickly

together. Thankfully, they hadn't been completely naked. However, Zach looked bedraggled at best. Sweaty and disheveled and agitated at worst.

Actually, he looked like a man who had just made thorough love to someone.

"Do you think he'll know we—"

"Most definitely," he said, stopping her short with his discomforting reply and a forceful kiss. Then he crossed the room with a shaky stride, his shirttail whipping against his hips. "Stay put," he ordered. "I have enough to worry about as it is."

"Zach . . ."

He swiveled his head, hand on the doorknob, and stood staring, just staring as if he sought to record the night. Or the room. Or *her*. Lines of worry chalked the skin around his eyes. A burst of lightning lit him in a silvery tinge. He quivered, his shoulders shaking.

I love you. Her heart pounded in three beats, saying the words. "My father . . . a boy was all that mattered to him. You. . . ."

"I'll cherish this baby no matter what, Irish. You can count on that." Then he blew her a kiss and was gone. His feet pounded on the staircase. From below, Caleb's voice mingled with his, then the front door slammed as they ran into the stormy night.

"Be careful," she whispered to the empty doorway, feeling as if her heart had left with him.

The boy was young—no more than seventeen, if that. His chin had a pitiful sprinkling of peach fuzz on its round tip; a small crescent scar lay pink and fresh beneath his nose. With skin free of worry or time, he seemed a baby in the scheme of things.

Why, Zach asked, why take someone starting life

instead of someone finishing it? They had pulled an old man from the sea, and not that Zach wished him harm, yet why would God, if He had to take a member of the ship's crew, take this boy? Choking back rage and sorrow, he touched the boy's lips, as blue as the whisper of sky he had glimpsed outside the jail's lone window the day he made love to Savannah. The day his life changed forever. For better or worse, he hadn't yet decided.

The body before him lay still, the soul far from reach. Had he ever felt a woman's touch or heard her whisper his name as he took her? Had he even been old enough to dream of doing that? Had this boy felt anything close to the irrepressible need Zach felt for Savannah?

It was too late to question anything now. Once again, he had been too late.

He placed the boy's hand in a damp puddle, giving it a final, useless squeeze. Shoving to his feet, he wiped his face, tears mixing with rain and sand and salt. Crashing thunder shook the ground beneath his feet, flinging the branches above his head together with a crack.

He felt just as turbulent, unsettled in a way he wished to forget. Was his whole goddamned life useless, he wondered savagely? Was *he* useless?

The anger took him by surprise, the piece of driftwood in his hands before he had time to put into words what he was feeling or to remember picking it up. Smashing it against a tree in the same circle where they'd had their long-ago picnic and now placed bodies from a doomed ship, the impact rocked up his arm in a painful spasm.

"Stop it, Zach." Noah's hand came down on his shoulder and slipped off his slick cotton shirt. Thrown off balance, Zach stumbled, falling to his knees. Rain slashed at his skin. "You're killing yourself," Noah growled. A hard shake followed this pronouncement. "You have been for a long time."

Zach dropped his head to his hands, misery and fear rolling through him as relentlessly as the waves against the shore fifty yards away. He hated death. In any form. From the end of spring when the azalea and dogwood blooms wilted and fell to the ground to the last glimpse of the sun after an awe-inspiring sunset. Those felt like death to him. Finality. An end.

But most, most of *all*, he found he hated the guilt that came with surviving.

"Let him go." Noah gestured to the boy, then sighed. "Let *her* go."

Zach's head lifted, water streaming into his eyes. Lightning lit the sky behind Noah in dazzling flashes. The look on his brother's rain-drenched face reminded him of the look on his when he was worried to death about Caleb or Noah or Rory doing something reckless and endangering their lives.

When he was afraid of losing them.

"Hannah's gone by no fault of your own. You've got to realize that and accept it or risk losing your future. Rory, Savannah, your baby. Do you want them to disappear behind this wall you've erected to protect yourself? Your son won't be a child forever, Zach. What happens once he starts patrolling the beaches with us or moves to a city away from your watchful eye? You plan to cut him out of your life because of fear? Because you don't know what's going to happen? Because you want to dictate every move?"

"Of course not." Like any parent, he didn't like to imagine his child leaving home. The rest—the death and loss that every family had a taste of— he just couldn't imagine in relation to his son. "If you want me to fish a boy's body from the sea and *ever* forget his face or the feel of his chest pushing out his last breath, then you've got the wrong man.''

"When did this happen? Grief has its talons sunk so deep in you that I fret over you ever getting away."

Zach ignored the comment and rose shakily to his feet. With one last glance at the lost young sailor, his stomach churning, he lumbered over the dunes. An angry gust of wind pressed his soaked shirt against his chest. He shivered, watching waves slash the shore in violent spouts of foam. The white-capped swells flung pieces of the ship's hull carelessly about, like a spilled box of toothpicks.

Searching the horizon, he prayed for mercy. For himself and the men on the ill-fated *Augustus.* One of the few they had been able to rescue from the frothy sea had told a tale of a drunken crew and a disastrous decision to challenge the shoals in an area many called the Graveyard of the Atlantic.

"Do you see that last lifeboat we sent out?" Noah asked, coming to stand beside him, hand over his eyes to keep the rain from his vision. They were the only ones left on the beach. The other men in the patrol had taken the survivors across the bay and into town for Dr. Magnus's attention. Zach and Noah had offered to stay. Someone always stayed with the bodies.

Zach shook his head, unable to voice his apprehension. Nathaniel Leonard had sailed away in that skiff. And Homer Jacobs. Both good men, fine men. His hands fisted. Homer's wife was expecting a child in another month or so.

"They'll sail in any time," Noah said, resting his hand on Zach's shoulder. "I'm sure."

A furious downpour pelted his face, running in streams down his neck and into his sodden collar.

Twisting, he turned and snarled, "This damned storm could be the front end of a hurricane! And if it is, God save us all."

Even in the unreliable light, Zach could see the flush settle on his brother's face. "Well, goddamn it, then that's His choice." Noah jabbed his thumb toward the sky. "Not yours. When the hell did you get the irrational idea that you had to control your life—or anyone else's, for that matter? Or that you *could*?"

Zach couldn't have predicted his answer, so the one that popped out had all the earmarks of a truth he should have known but didn't. "When my father left."

Clearly, this answer was unexpected. Noah shook his head, opened and closed his mouth twice before giving up, the stunned glimmer in his eyes visible even in the colorless gloom.

Zach squatted on his haunches, his gaze never leaving the sea. The storm had unfurled a blanket of pitch black over everything, the occasional bursts of lightning the only traces of light. "I didn't ask why he left. Mother told me that he had, simple as that. I had my juvenile ideas about it. I had seen her with your father once in town; I wasn't young enough to miss everything that passed between them. Heck, she didn't even cry when she told me he left. She was probably happy. He wasn't . . . well, maybe you don't remember, but he wasn't an agreeable man."

"I remember. . . ." Noah angled his long body down beside Zach's, his hands going flat to the ground as if he would fall without their support. "Vaguely, like a shadow in this misty dream, I remember him hitting me once when I followed him into the shed. I fell into the dirt, I think. I remember tasting blood."

Zach swiveled his head, amazed he could still hate the bastard after all these years. "Jesus, how old could you have been? Two?"

"Maybe three or so. I used to think about it until my stomach hurt so bad I vomited up everything in it. Not so much because he wasn't there or that I didn't have a father, but because my only memory of him was so wretched. Once I read Mother's diary and figured out whose son I was, a man I never met and never would, I lost all that anger. It was like he didn't matter anymore. He just . . ." Noah shrugged, hands smoothing the sand as though wiping dust from a dresser. ". . . disappeared."

"I shut the door on him, too. Cut him out of my heart so well it felt like he'd never been there. Then—" A crack of thunder obliterated his words. He waited, continuing after a tense, dark moment. "Then I got older, twelve or so when Mother started feeling poorly, the stiffness in her hip the most painful thing I've ever seen a body go through. She couldn't work in Myra's store anymore, taking in alterations and writing up all the invoices and receipts. Someone had to be the man in the family. Mother took in sewing—the little Myra was able to give her, but it wasn't enough. I had to start work. In the mercantile and for a spell in the oyster factory. The piloting came, oh, three years or so later. Captain Hennesey came to me, asking if I was interested. He'd heard about me sailing the shoals like a darned pirate. But damn, the money was good. I couldn't have turned that down if I'd wanted to. The way you were growing, you needed new britches every week, it seemed. Plus books. Piles of 'em. And Caleb, he nearly drove me crazy leaving me pages from that catalog, every blamed fishing rod or knickknack circled."

Noah's hands stilled their brisk movement. "Are you sorry?"

Zach perched his elbows on his knees and peered through the vaporous darkness. *Please God, let my men come in safely,* he prayed. Listening to the rush of the sea and the howling wind, he was thankful for all he'd been given. He really was.

Even if he couldn't come to terms with what had been taken away.

A stretch of time passed in thundering silence. Zach faced his brother in a half turn when he could, when he had himself under control. "I'm not sorry for anything. The first time I held Caleb, this tiny bundle of energy wiggling almost out of my arms, I felt such an overpowering wealth of love. It was such a pure feeling that I didn't even feel stupid or silly for feeling it. I could see myself in his face. Our noses and mouths. How could I argue with that? Then you came along, another wonder, a different wonder. Another brother to love. Why, I would have loved to have half a dozen brothers if I could. And sisters.

"I remember being a pretty little fella myself, just a couple of years older than Rory, but being so proud we each had the same color eyes. Caleb and I would walk you into town when you were old enough to toddle along behind us, and people would stop us in the street and tell us how beautiful the Garrett grays were. So no, I never felt a moment's sorrow for taking care of my family. I wouldn't trade a memory we made together for the world. Admittedly, I may have resented the loss of freedom a time or two as a young man, but that's all I can offer up."

Noah directed his gaze to the sea, where the Garrett men found peace. "Do you think saving

everyone from themselves will change any awful
thing that's happened to us? To you?"

"I know Hannah's gone. Our baby's gone. You
may think I'm living in the past, but I feel their
loss like an ache in my bones every day. That's
unmistakably the present."

Noah's hand started dusting again, the sand
flicking against their legs. "You could love the baby
coming. And its mother. Maybe that'd help the
ache."

"I could," he agreed, nodding. *Maybe I do.* Leaving Savannah with her hair tumbling around her
like a dark cloud and her eyes dazed from loving
had been the hardest thing he'd ever done. Her
body—ah, that magnificent body draped in his
sheets, the teasing scent of her claiming everything
in the room as hers. The sudden squeeze to his
heart had sure felt like love. Perhaps she'd claimed
that, too. However, that was for him to say to her the
first time. Not something to blab to his meddling
younger brother. Telling anyone before his wife
would be a flagrant betrayal, and he wasn't a betraying man.

Noah's gaze cut his way; Zach felt the heat. "Have
you told her you love her and life is smooth sailing
while I'm out here worrying like hell about this?"
He lifted a hand and rubbed his belly. "My stomach
hurts from agonizing over it."

"You and your aching stomach, Professor." Zach
purposely used the childhood nickname someone
in town had made up, one they both despised. It
never failed to rouse the youngest Garrett brother's
temper. "I haven't told her," he added, partly disgusted, partly amused. All parts self-directed. He
should have told her before he left her this evening,
looking so luscious and tempting in his bed. Instead he had let fear shoot him in the foot. *Again.*

"When have we made it easy for our women to love us? You sure didn't make it easy for Ellie. And Caleb, heck, he and Christa may never get married. Fools, both of them. I'm following my siblings' lead, I suppose."

"Don't blame this bit of idiocy on us," Noah said. "The woman is over the moon for you. What harm could it do to let her know you return the favor?"

The wad of balled-up sand in Zach's fist dropped to the ground as his fingers lolled open.

Noah let out a low whistle, then laughed outright. "You don't know? Have you been camping out on the moon?"

"Well, I, I . . ." he began, words seeping from his brain like water from a leaky bucket. His heart thumped hard enough for him to hear it over the splatter of rain and the distant peal of thunder.

"Ah, you're a blind one, ya are," Noah chimed in a mocking Irish lilt. "She lights up when you walk into the room. Sickening, but true. I've seen it. Hell, Christa and Ellie said they knew the first week or two, but they're women and not expected to miss any indication of love. Even Caleb has seen her pining over you. Though he was surprised— we were *all* surprised—to see you'd taken the bull by the old horns and, um, *acted* on the feeling. Getting caught in the jail, whoo-wee, pretty crazy for sensible Zachariah Garrett." Noah leaned back on his elbows and laughed. "I can't believe I'm saying it, but Caleb's worse off than you are where women are concerned. If *he* knew Savannah loved you, you sure should have."

If Zach had been less than certain about his feelings for his wife before this moment, hearing she loved him—*might* love him—firmed everything up quite nicely. To have a woman like Savan-

nah's love. Him, tired old Zach Garrett. Damn
that was something. Scared, yeah, he was scared
Terrified. But ah, hell, to find her when he had
never expected to find anyone ever again. What a
phenomenal feeling that was. And the baby. Lord
how he wanted their baby.

"What do you plan on doing about this, Constable?" The thread of barefaced amusement in his
brother's voice didn't dim Zach's happiness one
bit. "You've got a wife sitting at home—a wife
expecting a child, no less—wondering if her husband loves her. Quite a mess." Noah dusted his
hands on his trousers and rose to a gangly, unsteady
stand. "Quite a mess in-damn-deed, to quote your
missus."

Zach opened his mouth to tell Noah that he was
plenty capable of taking care of the matter when
he saw an arc of lightning highlight a skiff sailing
into shore. And two men working the lines. His
heart rose in his chest. *His men were alive.* Alive to
go home to their families. And he would be able
to go home to his.

His and Rory's new family.

He jumped to his feet and took a fast step forward. Before he made it two feet, with the wind
shrieking in his ears, the world went dark.

Chapter Seventeen

One is not born, but rather becomes, a woman.
—Simone de Beauvoir

The rain slashed to the ground, soaking Savannah to the skin. Fog shrouded the wharf in a filmy white cloud, holding in the oppressive heat. She shivered, despite the warmth, from a dread that chilled her to the bone. She stood with a dwindling group of wives, mothers, and daughters at the end of the oyster factory's pier, the closest point to Devil Island. She was sure Zach would tan her hide when he sailed up and caught her standing like a drowned rat on the docks. Most of the women had left once their men returned to them.

Her man had yet to show up.

Perhaps Zach would be merciful when he saw her because she had not gone to the island as she could have, where the ship lay stranded just offshore. A few women had sailed out there against strict orders not to budge from their homes. But these women had been sailing since they were children and had steady hands, if not steady hearts.

Savannah crossed her arm over her stomach; she hadn't felt it safe enough to go quite that far. There was the baby to consider.

Of course, she hadn't stayed put, either.

Savannah wound a damp strand of hair around her finger. The wind ripped at her clothes and made her sway in place. How could she stay inside their bedroom and remember him loving her only hours before, or pace the parlor floor and listen to the hall clock counting off every single second? When Elle came to tell her the details of the shipwreck, Savannah had listened for a minute, then left the house at a dead run. Men in the life-saving crews often died on these voyages. Horrible deaths, some lost at sea, never to be found. Zach hadn't mentioned that in any of their previous discussions.

As Elle chased her friend to the wharf, she probably wished she hadn't said anything, either.

"They'll sail in any minute." Elle's arm came around her, drawing her close.

They stood there, shivering and peering through the dense fog rolling in from the sea. Waves lashed the pier, sending a salty mist into their faces. Savannah concentrated on the clank and rub of boats edging the dock, ticking off the time in her head. Just when she thought she'd go mad if she stood there doing nothing for much longer, a shout brought some of the men running down the dock.

In the distance, faintly, she could see a skiff cresting a wave and sliding into a hollow, cresting again. One man worked the sails; another sat near the stern, their shapes visible only in a brief flash of lightning not bright enough to tell her who was who.

"It's Noah," Elle breathed, her weight falling against Savannah. Obviously, she had not been as sure of the men's safety as she had led Savannah to believe.

"Zach?" *Maybe Ellie's eyes are better than mine,* Savannah thought, straining to distinguish the faces of the men gliding toward them.

Elle took her hand and pulled her to the very end of the pier, until her toes hung over the misshapen edge. It was only then that she realized she had run to town without shoes. A cool spray struck her ankles, the wind kicking at her skirt as she clung to Elle, saying a silent prayer and telling God she would do everything right from now on—no cursing or drinking ever again—if He delivered her husband safe and sound to her.

A group of men gently moved them aside, apologizing all the while. Savannah murmured her gratitude and patted the wide shoulders of each man. Helping dock the skiff in such a fiery storm as this one took more muscle than she and Elle could offer.

The skiff bumped hard, the hull scraping roughly against the pitted piling. Calling orders and directions, Noah—she could see him well enough now—threw a line to a waiting hand, dancing back to settle the sails. Canvas snapped in the wind, and far away a dog yipped. Dazed by a sudden feeling of dread, Savannah hoped it wasn't Tiger.

"Lift him. Gently," Noah shouted above the roaring wind.

Savannah gasped, recognizing the navy material covering the arm flung limply over the edge of the skiff. She started forward but Elle and a member of Zach's patrol, a man she vaguely thought she recognized from church, held her back.

"Let them bring him up. Then we'll take him . . . home." Elle's voice cracked, upsetting Savannah more than seeing Zach being lifted from the skiff to the dock like a dead weight. Blood oozed from a gash on his temple, a broad crimson river streaking his face and neck. The collar of his shirt showed pink—a mixture of blood and rain—in the muted glow from a lamp hanging beneath a factory overhang.

"Surely, he will be fine," Savannah whispered. Or maybe she simply thought it. A strapping man like Zachariah Garrett didn't get hurt from a bump on the head. Head wounds bled notoriously; even she knew that.

Moving to his side, she took his hand as the men placed him on a wide plank of wood at least seven feet long. Her head pounded; her throat felt flinty, as if she had swallowed a mouthful of sand. Apparently they kept the plank on the docks for just such a purpose. The thought chilled her, and she shivered, her hand squeezing his until her knuckles went as white as Zach's skin. His hair lay in a dark scramble on his brow, a clump of it tangled and bloody. She thought she could see a patch of exposed bone. Swallowing back bile, she knew she must be strong. A constable's wife, a life-saving captain's wife, must be strong.

A jacket slipped over her shoulders. She gazed up into Noah's face, his eyes brimming with concern. "Can't have you getting sick out here," he said. "Zach would kill me."

"He'll be fine, of course." Neither a statement nor a question, perhaps it was a plea. "Simply fine."

Noah nodded, looking less than certain. His eyes moved to Zach, focusing on the bleeding gash, the ashen skin. He drew a long breath. "He has to be. We need him."

* * *

Savannah walked to the window and gripped the sill, the rain blowing inside and dampening her skin. Soothing comfort in a world of little reassurance at the moment. A muted sunrise brightened the horizon in shades of gold and amber and streaks of violet, the promise of a new day. Pressing her brow to the cool pane, she decided that life would go on. It had to. Already the worst of the storm had passed. An occasional roll of thunder sounded in the distance. That and the soft tap of rain against the pine-shingle roof filled their bedroom. Tiger lay on a rag rug in the middle of the floor, his tail thumping lazily. He guarded his master as if he knew Zach needed his encouragement, refusing to come down even when Caleb had called him from the kitchen.

Savannah glanced back, checking as she had every few minutes since they brought Zach home, recording the shallow rise and fall of his chest beneath the thin sheet. If she placed her ear next to his mouth, she could hear him breathe. Raspy but apparent. Yet that also sent warm air rushing inside the canal of her ear, reminding her of their whispering to each other as they made slow, tender love.

Gripping the sill harder, she promised herself she wouldn't cry. Couldn't cry anymore. It had frightened Rory, whom they had spirited away after carrying Zach inside. And it had frightened her. She would like to tell Zach she loved him before he slipped away. What Dr. Leland had cautioned would have to bring what comfort it could: Either Zach would pull out of this deep sleep or he would not. Head injuries were strange things, the doctor had added—a great unknown in medical science. It was a nasty wound requiring stitches, but at least the stark white bandage circling her husband's head had replaced the sight of blood and mangled skin.

Noah had told her about lightning striking the tree beside them. A limb, "thick as a man's waist," he said, had toppled from the sky, knocking them to the ground. He hadn't thought anyone was seriously injured until he got a look at Zach's inert form.

He had also related the tale of the young sailor who'd died in Zach's arms and his subsequent fit of rage.

How terrible, the burden placed upon his shoulders. By himself and every foolhardy resident of Pilot Isle. It had angered Savannah straight to the bone to record the unmitigated confusion and devastation as the men carried Zach along the street and into the house. Townspeople had trudged along behind them like a line of mourners. Sodden hats and bonnets in hand as if they had come to pay their respects. She had shoved her bedroom window as high as she could and leaned out, screaming at them to leave Zach in peace. Elle and Noah and Caleb—one or all of them; she didn't have a clear recollection—had pulled her inside and slammed the window shut.

After that, they had refused to leave her. Until the sidewalk outside the house emptied, except for a scrawny calico tomcat she'd been feeding scraps to and calling—quite originally, she was sure—Tom.

Savannah crossed to the bed, leaning in close to his lips, ignoring the memory his hot breath called forth. She couldn't expect anyone, not even Zach's family, to understand his circumstances. Not as fully as she did. After all, they had laughed about this very matter many times: how no one truly knew him. They thought he was a saint and stronger than any man could be. How could they imagine he carried such responsibility on his shoulders every minute of the day and suffered no consequence? In her mind, he was like a bridge overloaded with weight. He had finally buckled.

Fury coursed through her veins, but it was his hand that clenched in the sheet, fingers drawing into a weak fist.

Savannah gasped and dropped to her knees by the bed. "Zachariah, can you hear me?" She willed him to answer as she checked his temperature. Hot to the touch. Dipping a rag into a cracked basin at her side, she smoothed it over his face and neck. His face looked odd, unnatural. A flush stacked atop pale, pale skin darkened by at least two days' stubble. Moving the sheet lower, she bathed him to the waist, wrung the rag, and repeated the process.

When she hit a bruise she hadn't noticed beneath his armpit, he groaned, a whisper of sound streaking from his lips.

"Zach?" She brushed his hair from his face, smoothing it into a modest tangle.

His hand seized her wrist, more quickly than she suspected he could move in his condition. His eyes flew open. They were fever-filled, glassy, and red. "Hannah?"

Every trace of air left Savannah's lungs, a veritable collapse. The blood in her face seeped away, leaving her dizzy and breathless. She struggled, reminding herself that he was out of his mind. "I'm here," she answered because she was. *Whoever* he thought she was.

"You've been away," he stated feebly, his arm falling to the bed.

She paused a beat, debating what she should do. *Soothe him, Savannah.* So she did, splintering her

heart into a thousand jagged pieces in the process.
"I have."

His eyelids fluttered, too heavy to stay open.
"Happy?"

Savannah glanced at the ceiling, wishing she
could see through the clouds and into heaven so
she could answer honestly. Was Hannah happy?
She had sounded like an angel, or closer to one
than Savannah would ever be.

Angels were always happy.

"Yes." She bathed his face, feeling as if she had
stepped into someone else's body, someone else's
marriage. Surely this was not her own. "I'm
happy."

"Good." He sighed, sinking into the mattress.
"Will you help me. . . ." The words died though
his lips continued to move.

She leaned in. "Help you what, darling?"

He didn't answer, having returned to his cavern-
ous stupor.

Tears falling freely, she sat in his bedroom, morning sunshine scattering across the pine floor. The
room she had foolishly come to think of as *theirs*,
realizing she could never play this role again. The
pain nearly broke her in two.

It was simply unbearable to be second in Zach's
heart, if she resided there at all.

Zach struggled to awaken, desperation driving
him. His body felt battered, his limbs so blamed
heavy he couldn't lift them. And his mind . . .

Ah, hell. Foggy, muddled. Everything muddled.

He wanted to tell Savannah before it was too
late. He had asked Hannah to help him find her.

Was she there? A spurt of panic had his heart
thumping, every movement, every breath painful.

He tried saying it. Maybe that would be enough.
I love you, Irish. Consciousness faded as the words
lay unspoken on his lips.

Savannah peeked through the sparkling window
of the seamstresses' shop. She scanned the brightly
lit room, pleased to see it was empty. After her
tantrum yesterday morning, everyone in town
seemed to be giving her a wide berth. The bell
above the door tinkled, a mixture of fragrances
drifting past, testament to the varied tastes of the
shop's customers.

Lilian Quinn's voice rang from the back, "Just
a minute."

Savannah crossed to the counter, tracing her
finger along the yellow embroidery decorating the
instep of a pair of black-and-white striped stockings.

"Lovely, aren't they?"

She curled her fingers into a fist, flushing as a
knowing smile crossed Lilian's face. Caleb had told
her that the town seamstress had the voice of an
angel and the face of a horse, for her husband to
enjoy in bed so long as the lights were off. Hearing
the comment while preparing dinner last week,
Zach had elbowed his brother in the ribs as Elle
and Savannah burst into shameless laughter.

Zach had bounced them all out on their ears.
Relegated to the yard until dinner was ready as
punishment.

"They'd look right pretty with one of those
riding costumes of yours, Miss Savannah." The
comment brought her back.

"No, no." Hesitantly, she fingered the silk. "Too
fancy for me." Too feminine, she wanted to say.
With her decision made, who in the world would
she wear them for now?

"Zach would love them. As soon as he's feeling up to looking, I mean. I hear he's doing a mite better," Lilian said with a soft smile. Her hair, pulled into a close knot on her head, shone yellow-brown in the warm gas glow. Of average looks, yes. However, she had the sweetest voice ever to grace a church choir, and her skill with a needle provided a handsome income for her family. Too, she was blessed with a husband who worshipped her.

Savannah would have traded places with Lilian Quinn in a minute.

If Lilian's husband traded places with Zach, that is.

"The clothes: are they ready?" Savannah asked, ready to be gone from this place. From this town.

Lilian slipped a pad of paper from her apron pocket, eyes flitting over the page. "Everything but the divided skirt with the braid edging. My fingers can't edge as quickly as they used to. I could have my Elmo bring it by Friday afternoon if that'll do."

She wouldn't be in town Friday. "Can he drop off what you have ready this afternoon? The skirt I can wait for."

Lilian tilted her head, gazing quizzically at Savannah. "Any reason for the hurry? A special event coming up?"

"None at all. Just, well, it's been months since I've purchased new garments." This much was true. Yet she could not stop her hand from straying to the pocket of her cycling trousers and the train ticket to New York folded in a neat square.

The bell above the door tinkled, humid air flooding the room. Savannah released an explosive sigh, knowing a wretched stroke of luck when she saw one. Or smelled one. The distinctive scent could only mean that Caroline Bartram had entered the shop.

Bloody hell! she thought. Wouldn't you know it? She had deliberately traveled into town when most people were having supper, only to run into the one person who looked through any facade she presented as if it were made of glass.

Caroline halted by Savannah's side, lifting her shining blue eyes to her face. Eyes brimming with compassion and understanding. "How is Zach? Woke up this morning briefly, I heard. Christabel says he's on the mend, thank goodness."

"He's better. Not coherent yet, but his fever is down," Savannah replied, neglecting to add that he had yet to rouse enough to recognize her or anyone else for that matter. The wound pained him a great deal, from the tossing and turning and mumbling he did, and the powder Dr. Leland had prescribed kept him far from reach. Savannah's hand trembled. She bit the inside of her cheek.

At least he hadn't called out for Hannah again.

Caroline knotted her fingers together over her draped belt of white satin. "He'll be fine. A tough buck, that boy." She ducked, trying to look into Savannah's eyes. "But what about you? How are *you* doing?"

Tears pricked Savannah's eyelids. She blinked them back. For some reason, this woman's tender air always reminded her of her mother. Fighting the absurd feeling, she spoke calmly. "I'm fine, Caroline. Why? What could be the matter? Zach is getting better, and . . ." She pressed her lips together, struggling to continue. "I have to get back. Everything . . ." She shrugged. "You understand."

With a worried frown, Caroline watched her friend hurry away, hoping she *didn't* understand.

Zach blinked into the bright sunlight, a tiny drummer beating away in his brain. "Lord, help," he groaned, dragging the sheet over his head.

"He ain't gonna help. You're all on your own in this mess."

"Shut up, Cale. Give him a moment to remember where he is, will you? We just stopped giving him pain powders a few hours ago. He's got to be groggy."

Groggy barely covered it. Inching the sheet down, Zach peered out at his brothers, a shaft of pain crossing his eyes. Caleb sat in a chair someone had pulled beside the bed. Noah paced back and forth behind him. "Christ, what happened? It feels like someone took a hammer to my head."

Caleb slid forward in the chair, rocking it precariously on its front legs. Noah tried to cover his mouth, but Caleb knocked his hand away. "A tree limb hit you in the head."

Zach frowned, remembering being on Devil Island and seeing his men sailing in . . . and not much else. He searched each corner of the room, a little disappointed to see that Savannah wasn't in the room.

"Don't be looking for her in here," Caleb said, his mouth sliding into a bitter frown.

"Cale . . ." Noah warned.

Zach felt a stirring of alarm. "Is she all right? Did she go out even when I told her not to?" *Oh, Jesus.* He sat up, nearly passing out from the effort. "The baby?"

Noah moved in front of Caleb, elbowing his

brother aside. "Savannah's fine. The baby's fine. Or they were this morning."

Zach's eyes narrowed. "This morning?"

"That's when your wife left town on a train bound for New York City."

Zach stood in the telegraph office in Morehead City, sweating beneath a suit coat he only wore when he traveled out of town. Shifting from one foot to another, he reread the message. Twice. Then he slid it through the bars separating him from the telegraph operator, a boy no older than sixteen who regarded him with the attentive enthusiasm of a new employee.

"Finished, mister?"

Zach nodded, forcing a smile. "That's it."

The boy returned the smile and began reading aloud, "Daniel Webster Morgan, New York, New York. Sir—"

"Really there's no need."

The boy glanced up, wiping the back of his hand across his nose. "Don't worry, mister. I'm a crack hand with the telegraph."

"Yeah, well, good. No need to—"

"Have to read every message to the customer before it goes. Western Union policy."

Zach rubbed the back of his neck, willing away the headache he had carried around with him since the accident. "Fine. Policy."

The young man nodded and bowed his head. "Dear Sir. Stop. If your daughter is in your po—po—"

"Possession."

"Possession, hold her. Stop. I arrive on the thirteenth. Stop. Keep this between us. Stop. She may not be . . ." The boy glanced up sheepishly. Appar-

ently, reading skills were low on the list for crack
hands with a telegraph.

Zach sighed. "Receptive."

"That's a new one." The paper shook in the
boy's hand as he chuckled. "Receptive to my visit."
He turned the sheet over and back. "No name
attached, mister."

Zach conquered the urge to look over his shoulder. Ridiculous, really. No one in Morehead City
knew him. Not in town, anyway, a full mile from
the docks. He gestured for the paper, found he
still clutched a pencil in his hand, and scribbled
furiously. Guilt, hot and fierce, swept through him.
Savannah would never forgive him for involving
her father in this.

But what choice did he have? She had left him
without giving him a reason—giving anyone a
damned reason. Did she think he would let her go
live in New York and raise his child as a bastard—or
worse, as someone else's if she divorced him and
married again?

Worse, raise his child as a Northerner.

He would die before letting any of those things
happen. The thought of another man touching his
wife or child made the ache in his head almost
more than he could bear and stay on his feet.

The situation, one Irish had created, called for
desperate measures.

Chapter Eighteen

The surest test of discipline is its absence.
—Clara Barton

Since she'd returned to New York, Savannah had found her father's behavior curious indeed. This morning, for instance, he had looked over his shoulder with each block they covered along Fifth Avenue. You couldn't traverse crowded city streets without your mind on your business. You'd get run down by a horse and carriage or trolley car or, worse, an automobile being driven by an inexperienced driver, of which there were many.

Savannah had ended up walking behind her father and apologizing to every person he bumped into or made dance aside in their haste to avoid him.

They didn't speak during the walk from Central Park to their home. This broke no new ground, yet he seemed almost, dare she say, *nervous*. Which made *her* nervous.

He couldn't know about her marriage, could

he? No one in the city did. Unless Zach had contacted . . .

Clutching her parasol close to her stomach, she shook her head, cutting off the thought before it had time to mature. *No.* Zach wouldn't do that to her, knowing how tremulous a relationship she shared with her father. However, would he come storming into town and reclaim her, attempt to drag her back to Pilot Isle under the guise of a committed husband? Perhaps. Men were dreadfully possessive, and as she'd found, Zach was no exception.

Anyway, she hadn't left thinking he would never come and get her, not with *his* baby on the way. Nevertheless, if she could place money on any bet in her lifetime and be sure to come out a winner, that bet would rest on Zachariah Garrett's capable shoulders.

If he came for her, he meant to put her first. If not to love her and forget Hannah, then to commit himself to the best of his ability. She felt as sure of this as she did of the sun's setting in—she threw a quick glance at the endless blue sky—oh, two hours or so. It would go against Zach's code of ethics to take her back to Pilot Isle if he couldn't give her what she wanted. Under those circumstances, it would be against her will.

Because she wanted *him.* Heart, mind, and soul. And she didn't plan on settling for . . . well, not for as little of him as she'd been getting. Although as desperately as she missed him, at this point she may take what she could get.

Her father looked over his shoulder again, nearly running into a lamppost.

"Father, what is wrong with you this morning? You're positively befuddled."

Daniel Morgan fished his watch from its waistcoat

pocket and recorded the time with a mumbled bit of conversation with himself. He never bothered to answer *her.* Typical.

What if Zach doesn't come? Savannah asked herself as she nodded her head contritely at a dapper gentleman her father nearly collided with. What if he found freedom and his old life to be the one he cherished? Her options would run out quickly. Saints' blood, she had relinquished her modest apartment in the city upon acceptance of the position with Elle's school and had no place to stay *but* with her father. And they were a volatile mix: oil and water with a stick of dynamite thrown in for good measure.

Shooting him a side glance, she knew this situation wouldn't last for long.

Once, her life had seemed meaningful—lonely but meaningful. Now, nothing was the same. She loved a man who didn't return the feeling, and with every beat of her heart, their baby grew inside her. Knocking her parasol against her boot, she recognized the ache in her heart. Heavens, she missed Zachariah. His deep voice, his wise, gray eyes, even his maddening certitude.

Too, she missed the camaraderie of small-town life and the simple bonds of friendship. Sniffing the air, she shook her head. She missed the smell of the sea without the taint of diesel fuel or coal.

Wearily, she climbed the stairs leading to the red door at her home's front entrance. James opened it with a flourish as they approached, giving her a strangely shrewd smile before turning to her father and whispering in his ear.

How rude, she thought, frowning as she checked the entry table for calling cards. Habit, nothing more. No one knew she had returned.

Hand pressed to the small of her back, her father

guided Savannah toward the library. At the doorway, he brushed the crown of her head with his dry lips, the most affection he had thrown her way in years, and murmured, "Good luck." Then he shoved her inside, and before she had a moment to contemplate the bizarre turn of events, she heard the tumblers fall as he locked her in.

"Are you insane?" she shouted, banging her parasol once against the door. Tearing her gloves off, she pivoted on her heel. Clearly, her father had lost his mind. Perhaps she should contact the good doctors at Bellevue as soon as she escaped.

She crossed to the window, which sat a good distance off the ground, she noted as she peered out. Not an option in her condition. Perhaps before, she could have risked it.

Quite suddenly, she noticed two things: Music hummed from the phonograph in the corner of the room . . . and cigar smoke wafted beneath her nose. She sniffed. Yes, that was definitely what it was.

Turning, she felt the hair along her nape lift, her spine arch as her skin began to tingle.

Zach.

As if he sensed her awareness, he swiveled around in her father's chair. Electric bulbs, suspended from the ceiling by a tangle of wires, doused light over his face, winking off his spectacles. She took an involuntary step back, bumping against the narrow library table. A vase tumbled to the ground with a shatter of glass.

"Careful," he said, indicating that she should move away from the mess. "I never intended for my appearance here to startle you so badly that you hurt yourself."

She reached around to place her gloves and parasol on the table, her mind spinning. Zach's appearance in the house hadn't been the thing to steal her breath. Oh, my, no. It was the way he *looked.*

Attired as he was in a high-buttoned black frock coat, waistcoat, and striped trousers, she could have taken him into any drawing room in the city— even Mary Astor's. Yet more than clothing captured her attention. He had the look of a warrior about him: caged, restless, feral. His tie dangled limply from his neck; his hair spiked from his ears and brow, arrayed there by careless fingers. Unfashionably dense stubble dotted his cheeks and neck, and his eyes were small gray fires in his otherwise calm, sun-browned face. The inch-long scar on his left temple reminded her of all they'd been through and her foolishness in imagining for a moment that he would let her run.

Conflicting feelings invaded her: anger that he had gone into cahoots with her father; joy to see him well. Joy to see him at all.

And as usual, something potent and wild sizzled between them, as though they were connected with electric wires themselves.

He puffed on one of her father's cigars, his skeptical gaze sweeping her from head to toe and back. A thin wisp of smoke circled his head. "Irish, you're looking mighty expensive."

She glanced down at her chemisette, silk jacket, and trained skirt. Gleaming patent leather boots winked at her. Her grandmother's ear bobs tapped her neck. Leaning back against the table, she crossed her arms over her chest and looked him over as appraisingly. "I could say the same about you."

Mirroring her gesture, he glanced at his clothes, a smile hitching his chapped lips. "Caroline felt I couldn't arrive looking like, as she put it, a country bumpkin."

"I have to ask. Did you travel a thousand miles to lock me in my father's library and critique our wardrobes?"

He raised a hand, his gaze both amused and hard. "Locking you in was his idea. He believed I couldn't keep you from leaving any other way, the damn fool."

She bit the inside of her cheek, holding back her own oath. Saints' blood, she had forgotten about his high-handed manners. Involving her father in her private life. She should kill them both. "What does *that* mean, pray tell?"

Zach laughed around the cigar, spitting out a stream of smoke. "Just because he can't handle you doesn't mean *I* can't. And you know it."

A slow smile moved across those inviting lips of hers, reminding him of that darn cat she'd been feeding and who now hung around the house like an old friend. Did she think it was a game that she'd run off to this godforsaken city, causing him to come after her like an irate papa?

"You're furious with me," she said with irritating delight. He imagined she would clap her hands if she thought she could get away with it. If she didn't look so good—and he hadn't missed her so much—he would go right over there and, well, shake her. Probably end up kissing her, too, and messing everything up for good. Better to stay where he was, so he simply frowned away her statement.

"You are so."

"Ah, hell, no. I love having to board a foul-smelling train and travel for two days all this way only to nearly get run over by some out-of-control engine on wheels when I step out of the station." Ash drifted down to his trouser leg and he brushed it away. His head had begun to pound as it did every day now, a result of the accident. And something Magnus promised would fade in the next week. "And he called *me* an idiot."

She coughed, hiding her laughter. A fresh batch of annoyance lit his blood.

Okay, so maybe he wasn't used to newfangled automobiles roaring right past him with a screech and a belch of smoke, although he'd read a good bit about the contraptions and understood well enough how they worked. Heck, on one avenue, 11th and something or other, he'd actually watched a small set of rail cars chug down tracks running in the middle of the street! Walking the city most of the day, working up the nerve to confront his errant wife, he had seen trains overhead, too, and trolley cars, some drawn by horses and some not. Electric, he guessed. Then there were the dozens of painted advertisements covering entire sides of buildings—buildings with clotheslines hanging out a hundred feet up or more. Add to that flashing signs in the windows of every kind of store, selling gadgets of every kind. And the bicycles, dear Lord, the bicycles! Women, men, children peddling and dodging the other vehicles on wheels. All together, it was complete madness.

Fascinating, too. Yeah, he'd admit that New York City was that, but he couldn't live here.

"I can't live here," he said just in case his Irish devil thought that was a possibility.

"Why would you have to?"

He stubbed out his cigar in a fancy-looking dish he hoped was okay to use as an ashtray. "I know Pilot Isle isn't as exciting as—"

"That isn't why I left." She sighed. "Heavens, you still have no idea."

Zach steepled his hands over his patterned waist-coat—another bit of silly frippery, he thought—

stewing about the jam his wife had gotten him in
Damn it, if she wanted to hear that he loved her
and he said it now, she wouldn't believe it. She
would think he had only said it to get her to agree
to his demands. Maybe she would be so gracious
as to help him out a little. "What *do* you want
Irish?" He felt as though he had asked her the
same question many times lately.

She stared at him so long and so soulfully that
he shifted for a position that didn't highlight his
aroused distress. He was no longer used to celibacy
But it was more than that. It pained him to go
home each night to an empty bed. Loneliness had
been eating a hole in his heart.

Something else he would tell her, if she weren'
looking so suspicious over there.

"What can you give, Constable?"

Everything. Instead of saying what would sound
false to her in this distrustful mood of hers, he
turned to study his crushed cigar, following the
smoldering trail of smoke to the ceiling. "I want
you to come home with me."

"Because of the baby."

"Because of everything."

Shaking her head, she crossed the room. Run
ning her hand over a shelf of leather-bound books
she selected one. "Shakespeare," she said, showing
it to him with a wounded smile.

What the hell?

He answered his own question when she slipped
a small key from inside the pages. On his feet and
behind her pretty quick, he slammed his hand
against the door to prevent her from leaving
"Give me the key. You're not leaving here till we
straighten this out."

Glancing over her shoulder, she took the key

and slipped it down the neck of her frilly shirt. Her eyes glowed, with what, he wasn't sure.

A memory flashed through his mind of kissing her breasts and having her beg for more. "Is that an invitation, Irish?"

"If it was, would that be enough for you?"

He frowned. "Why do I feel like that's a trick question?"

She turned fully then, slamming her bottom against the door and glaring into his face. He felt the wash of her breath on his cheek, and his head pounded harder. "You called out for her when you were ill."

Zach closed his eyes to her hurt expression and the pain in his head. Jesus, so that was the problem. Reaching up to rub the back of his neck, he said without thinking hard about it, "All I remember is waking up and asking about *you*." Clear as day, it was time to tell her he loved her, whether she accepted it graciously or not. Counting to ten and back, he rehearsed a sincere admission. He felt it deep in his bones. Saying that right there in those words should have been enough, but with women it never was. Attractive packaging mattered.

Just when he felt ready, he heard her move away from the door, her boots tapping against the floor and then the rug. "I'm in love with you, Zachariah. Much to my dismay at the moment. However, I assumed my situation might help you understand how difficult it was to sit by your bedside, praying for your recovery, only to have you awaken and call out Hannah's name. It seems you've given me the truth on occasion, wrapped in a ribbon of lies."

Zach thumped his head against the door. He felt like throwing himself on the floor and having a fit that would make Rory proud. Blast, what timing the woman had. He'd be darned if hearing that she loved him didn't make him so happy he wanted to cry . . . but did she have to say it *first?*

Ah, hell.

"What, Constable? No response? No shout of triumph or joy?"

Forcing his eyes open, Zach located her in the shadows. He could see her distress clear across the room. It felt as if a knife had been plunged into his heart when she looked at him like that. "Would you believe me if I told you that I'm in love with you, too? That I have been for a long time? Maybe since the first damned day? More than I ever loved Hannah, which, true as it is, has been eating me up with guilt?"

She swallowed, her hands clenching into fists at her side. Her cheeks paled in rapid degrees, her lips pressing so tight it had to hurt—not exactly the reaction he'd hoped for.

"Would ya, Irish?" He took a step closer. "And that I'm so blamed lonely without you?"

She threw up her hand, panic sweeping her face. "I need . . . time. I can't—this is too much . . . can you . . . ?"

He hung his head, suddenly so tired he felt he might crumple to the floor. His head pounded in time to a ticking clock somewhere in the room. Each second was more painful than the last. "To-morrow," he promised, twisting the knob and yanking the door open. "We settle this then, Mrs. Garrett."

Halting in the archway, he gave her one more piece of his soul. "No matter what you believe, believe this, Irish. I was lost until you came into my life."

* * *

Still up long after midnight, Zach figured he'd better do something or go crazy. Sorting through his suitcase, he stacked the books he'd brought with him on the floor and tossed his underclothes in the top drawer of the hotel room's beat-up chest of drawers. Might as well unpack; no telling how long he would have to stay in this stinking, teeming mess of a city. Because if Irish thought he was leaving without her, she had judged about as poorly as a body could.

"Telling me she loved me first," he muttered and flung a pair of socks to the floor. God, the most incredible words she'd ever said to him. And he believed her. Straight out he did. Of course, she didn't believe anything *he* said. Why did she think he had come, anyway? Spending two days on a crowded train with babies spitting up and children crying, near desperate to see her. Thinking about her with every turn of the wheels, picturing what he would do to her when he got to her. Wondering why she left. The reason, his calling out to Hannah, had never entered his mind. Not once.

He laughed ruefully, closing the case with a snap. It didn't take a genius to see he was in love. After all, Caleb had noticed. And everyone in town knew Noah was the genius in their family. But Cale? Boy, he had it bad.

Tracing his finger down the spine of a law book he'd been meaning to read for some time, he sighed. Getting his wife to cooperate presented a big challenge. He needed to talk to her. Touching her might be a good idea, too.

He needed privacy to do *that* right.

Irish. He smiled, replaying her words for the hundredth time since he left her. Savannah Connor— Savannah Connor Garrett, he revised—*loved* him. That sassy, gorgeous, fascinating woman loved *him*.

What had he done to deserve it? When he had held her off from the beginning, promising nothing but pleasure and friendly companionship. Telling her he could never marry, ever again. And now he'd gone and done it: gotten married quick and ... He settled on the edge of the bed, ignoring the noisy springs. A forgotten pair of suspenders dangled from his hands as he stared at the patched wall, the look on Savannah's face the last time they made love filling his mind.

The spike in his heartbeat didn't elude him. He was excited about the future, for the first time in a long while. Excited to spend it with Savannah. To walk to town with her and hold her hand, to watch her be a mother to Rory, who loved her to distraction already. To raise their baby together. To make slow love all over their house when the children were away.

He guessed the same thing had happened to her that had happened to him. Falling in love wasn't something you planned. It had hit him like that fat tree limb upside his head and fairly knocked the stuffing out of him.

Except that Savannah had said she was ... *dismayed*, yeah, that was it, *dismayed* to be in love with him. Zach wound a suspender around his fist and stretched it until it almost popped. *Dismayed* wasn't too encouraging. In spite of that, she'd also said she felt dismayed *at the moment*. There could be a hint of encouragement there.

Rain pelted the cracked glass panes of the only window in the room in a steady ping. A dim stripe of illumination from a streetlight shot through a moth hole in the faded curtain. It was the only hotel that wouldn't send him to the poorhouse. Shrugging into his jacket, acting on impulse, which was a rare thing for a man like him, Zach gave the

room a quick glance as he left: shelves empty except
for a book or two, a shabby chair with cracked
leather from holding a lot of chubby bottoms.
Quite comfortable, he knew, because he had slept
in it last night. All scarred wood, shadows, and dust,
Zach rather liked it.

It fit his mood.

He slammed the door, whistling to himself as he
took the stairs at a run. If his plan to get Savannah
back worked, he'd be packing up and going home
tomorrow. With a warm, willing wife in tow.

Now, on the walk to the warm, willing wife's
sprawling mansion, all he had to do was come up
with a plan.

Savannah had never felt such contradictory emotions in her life. Joy—unbelievable, pure joy. Fear,
oh yes, that her husband wouldn't return for her.
And sorrow, for hurting the man she loved.

The man who loved her.

Whirling in a circle in the middle of her bedroom, she held back her shout of ecstasy. Head
spinning, she collapsed to the feather mattress in
a sprawl. *Zach loved her.* Not *like* or even *lust,* which
were excellent feelings indeed. But love. *Love.* It
gave her the faith she needed to leave her hometown and go back with him, to be an honest-to-
God true wife to him.

Maybe guilt explained why it had taken him so
long to figure out his feelings. Guilt *was* a powerful
inhibitor.

I was lost until you came.

Heavens. What a thought. She had been lost,
too. Hardnosed, structured Savannah Connor,
freedom fighter and rally organizer, had been so
far astray that when the aching emptiness finally

caught up with her, she wondered if she would have survived. She couldn't imagine going back to her old life. While visiting the women's league offices today, she had said good-bye without actually saying good-bye to her colleagues. How could she truly say farewell when she had not known Zach sat in her father's library waiting for her? Somehow, that connection she had once feared had served her well. Because in her heart she had known he would come. If he loved her. Unspoken, that conviction. Once you loved someone with the depth she loved him with, all else paled. Her life might be harder in North Carolina, but she didn't care. She wanted that life. With Zach and Rory and their unborn child. Boy or girl, its daddy had promised to cherish it no matter what.

Savannah believed him.

A sweeping glance took in every corner of her childhood bedroom: the mahogany wardrobe, the velvet curtains, the Wilton rug, and crystal cologne bottles sitting atop a marble-topped vanity. Framed prints from an artist of world renown graced the walls. Zach's wonderfully homey, welcoming home had none of these luxuries. In fact, it was in desperate need of a woman's touch. Placing her hands on her stomach, feeling an intense connection with the baby inside, she gazed at the wallpapered ceiling, complete *and* content. This world, one she had imagined held everything she needed, didn't seem so perfect anymore.

A stone smacked her window with a dull thump. She jolted to a sit, clasping her dressing gown together beneath her breasts. Another stone struck, harder this time. Scrambling off the edge of the bed, she raced to the window. Sliding it high, she leaned out, suspecting who stood outside. Who else could it be?

Zach stood in the glow of a streetlamp, the world fading to black around him. He wore his spectacles and new suit of clothes, albeit slightly rumpled this time. She watched pleasure seize his face as his gaze centered, locating her a floor off the ground. His lips lifted in a wide smile. There were no chirping crickets or gentle ocean breezes, no surges of the sea in the distance. Nothing familiar to her now except this man. She wanted to go home. And she wanted to tell him that. Now.

"Come down and talk to me," he whispered, an urgent thread to his words. He blinked his eyes. She could see quite clearly that they were strained at the edges.

He thinks I'm still fuming. She needed to rectify that situation. Indeed.

"I miss you, Irish," he added when she failed to respond right away. "Please, please come down."

It *would* be nice to see what he had planned. He had made love to her for weeks without expressing his feelings. Of course, if she were truthful, so had she. Shaking her head, she decided that it served him right if she made him grovel for a few minutes. No longer than, say, ten and she would tell him everything. Gesturing her agreement, she backed into the room. In her closet, the first item of clothing her hand hit was a dress she only wore for painting rally signs. Spotted with black paint, it would have to do. Leather slippers came next. She didn't care to critically examine her attire; she only wanted to see Zach, touch his face, and kiss his lips. To tell him she loved him and hear him say it to her in return.

Unable to help herself, she tugged a brush through her hair and dabbed rose-scented water behind each ear. It was the least she could do when meeting her husband for the first time with love uniting them. Easing her bedroom door open, she crept down the hallway. Her father's snores drifted from his open door and echoed off the darkened walls. She avoided the third and eighth stairs, ones that creaked the most, fondly remembering that long-ago tree outside her bedroom window that had once made escape so easy. At the front door, she reached for a shawl that wasn't there, resolving then to brave the weather without it rather than slink back to her bedroom.

Waiting in the shadows beneath an elm tree in the modest front square her father called a courtyard, Zach rocked back and forth on his heels, hands shoved deep in his pockets. He looked tired and anxious. And determined, she noted as she moved closer. The man had yet to back away from any challenge she threw at him.

Crossing the neat lawn that her father paid a gardener an absurd amount of money to maintain, she halted a foot from her husband, her nerves rapidly taking hold.

"Nice dress," he said, seeming to search for words. He swallowed, his gaze falling to the ground. "You look lovely."

She peered at him, then at herself, patting her still-tangled hair with a trembling hand. He thought she looked pretty? He looked wonderful, as usual, even more so in his sleep-rumpled state. But he thought she looked good that way, too? Her heart soared. "Zachariah, I—"

"No." Ripping his hands from his pockets, he took a fast step forward, stopping just before he touched her. "Not here. I have a place." He threw up his hands in surrender. "I just want to talk to you. Somewhere I can think."

"But Zach, I . . ."

Before she could object—which she wasn't planning on doing—he was there, holding her, kissing her, whispering meaningless words against her lips. Warm, safe, and wonderful. They knew each other so well that passion gained an immediate foothold. Leaning her head back, she let him deepen the kiss until her world, no longer of this place, tilted and spun.

Curling his fingers around hers and holding tight, he groaned and stepped out of the embrace. Shrugging from his jacket, he slipped it over her shoulders. His scent and the heat from his body enveloped her. Not a bad conclusion to their kiss.

Silently he led her down the narrow brick path. When they reached the street, he looped his arm through hers and drew her close to his side—just in case anyone should think they weren't together, she guessed. Also, he placed himself nearest the street, something he never failed to do at home. A simple courtesy in the event a carriage or automobile came along, threatening to splash mud on her skirt. Yet it was a courtesy rarely extended. Or rarely extended to *her*. Perhaps men of her acquaintance had assumed such a durable woman could handle a little mud. To think, Zach had sought to protect this old rag she wore.

"I love you," she whispered, pulling him to a stop at the next corner.

Zach moved her aside as a boy scampered past with a sack of newspapers slung over his shoulder. He gazed into her face for a long moment, looking as if he'd been pole-axed, to use one of Caleb's favorite expressions. "Say it again," he finally said.

She laughed, lifting her hand to trace the scar on his temple. "I love you, Zachariah Dalton Garrett."

His eyes blazed, but he didn't say a word, just seized her hand and dragged her down the street. "Where are we going?"

"Somewhere familiar. I can't do this—tell you what's in my heart—on a blessed street in the middle of this madness. I'd go crazy."

Glancing over each shoulder, she saw a street vendor preparing for a busy morning, and a horse and carriage passing by. In the distance, a train rumbled and a dog yapped. A man rode past on a sparkling new bicycle. She would have to look into getting Rory a new model. Other than that, silence. "Why, there's no one awake yet," she said. "This is hardly madness."

He grunted, his stride increasing. "If I could come out here in the middle of the night and not see a blamed bicycle; I'd be happy, that's all I can say." It amused her to realize how unimpressed he was with the most impressive city in the world. Wondering where he had found comfort here, she followed, skipping to keep up. She would follow him anywhere. He didn't have to lead her or hold on so tight.

He wound his way down an alley that smelled of garbage and across a set of railroad tracks, obviously knowing where he was headed. "You've traveled these streets, I see."

Another grunt. "Yeah, misery makes a man feel like exploring," he said, sounding exactly like Rory when she wouldn't buy him taffy before dinner.

Savannah smiled and ducked to hide it.

"Here," he announced, squeezing between two barrels sitting at a warehouse entrance.

"Are we allowed—"

"It's okay. They know me."

They know you?

She watched in bemused silence as he escorted her into the inner workings of a shipping yard. The stink of fish surrounded them. The ground was slick and grimy beneath her slippers. Men scurried about with ropes hanging from their meaty fists and bundles of netting looped over their backs. A few nodded to Zach; one tipped a ragged hat at her. "How do you know these men?"

He hummed a vague reply, then said, "They recognize a seaman, that's all."

A lumbering bear of a man approached them, a huge grin splitting his ruddy face. A thin scar ran from the edge of his lip, down his neck and into the collar of his shirt. With a sly wink, he elbowed Zach in the ribs. "You found her, all right, mate?"

"I reckon I did, friend."

He chuckled, bobbing his head. "Good, good. Your man's been down here brooding the best of the night. Like a lost pup I had once. Ralph was his name. Poor beast." Laughing outright at Zach's scowl, he added, "Best take care of that hurting, ma'am. A man's heart is a fearsome prideful thing." Then he saluted them both and marched away, a knife of some sort hanging from his belt loop.

She shook her head, gazing up at Zach. "What a strange world you've stumbled upon, Constable."

"Oh, no." Turning between two buildings, he led her onto a narrow pier. Walking to the end of it, they gazed across the Hudson River. Tugboats chugged past, twinkling pinpricks of light from the cabin windows sparking on the water's surface. A faint touch of pink lit the horizon, and beneath that a hint of gold. "This is so recognizable to me that it makes me yearn for home. Homesick, right in the pit of my stomach. I was drawn here like an ant to a glass of sweetened tea." Turning, he grasped her shoulders, bringing her closer. She shivered beneath the warmth of his coat. A moist, heavy breeze fluttered the hair on his head, bring-

ing his scent to her in a gentle caress. "I couldn'
do this without the sea at my back. I just couldn't.'

She tilted her chin, questioning.

"Well . . ." He squirmed, looking as if his clothing had abruptly shrunk two sizes. "Ask you to
marry me."

She sputtered, half laugh, half gasp. "We *are*
married. Or did that crack to your head do more
damage than Dr. Leland led me to believe?"

Digging in his pocket, his trousers riding high
on one side, he extracted a square, dark box. Handing it to her shyly, he rocked back on his heels, as he
often did when he was nervous. "I want a marriage
nothing can tear apart. One you chose. One that
ain't"—he sighed—"*isn't* chosen for you. I know
you. You take responsibility on your shoulders
about as easily as I do. And you're loyal. But I want
more than your loyalty; I want more than your
love." He nodded to the box. "It was my grandmother's."

Staring at him, with the flickering streetlamp
above their heads spilling ivory into the gray pools
of his eyes, and sails flapping and feet stomping
around them—the least privacy she could imagine—Savannah knew that she would do anything
to have him. Slowly she opened the box, the hinges
creaking, until a sapphire blazed amid the velvet
folds in a fervent blue fire. The stone sat atop a
simple band of white gold.

She had never seen anything more lovely in her
life. Tears welled in her eyes. She held them back,
fearing Zach would misunderstand their cause.

"Um, if you don't like it . . . I wasn't sure and
that's why I didn't give it to you before. I know
you're used to nicer jewelry and. . . ." He shrugged,
running out of steam.

Turning the box so he could see the ring, she

held out her left hand. "I adore it, Zach. As I adore you." Spreading her fingers, she said, "Put it on!"

He laughed, taking her beautiful ring in his big fingers. *Heavens, what if he drops it through a crack in the planks?* she thought, breathing a sigh of relief when he slid it on her finger. "Whew, good. I think it fits," he said, sounding like a child who had done well on a test.

She wiggled her fingers, the sapphire shimmering. How dear of him to give her his grandmother's ring without knowing for sure that she'd accept it. "Perfectly." *Everything* fit perfectly. "You said you wanted more. What more can I give you?"

"Your future." His hand slid to her wrist and circled it gently, bringing her fingers to his lips for a tender kiss. The band glittered in the light. His coat slipped from her shoulders and fluttered to the ground unnoticed. "I want babies. I want to read in bed with you underneath those fancy electric lights you're planning on getting, if I know you. I want to spend this winter snuggling beneath the spreads and eating breakfast in bed the mornings Rory is at a friend's. And next winter and the one after that. I want to see your hair turn gray and your skin freckle with age, 'cause it will in the Southern sun, you know. I want you to read me those liberatin' articles like you've done a time or two already. I want to share the weight of those goddamned shipwrecks with someone who understands how much of my heart I cut out each time I pull a lifeless body from the sea."

He lowered his head as he said the last, his arms trembling.

"Oh, Zach." She walked into his arms, forcing herself inside the circle. *His* circle. "I love you," she murmured against his damp shirtfront, inhaling starch and soap and *him.* "I want those things, too.

Saints' blood, I want things I don't even know how to define yet. But with you, I feel sure I'll figure it out. We'll make a list.''

He laid his cheek against the crown of her head and drew her as close as he could. ''One more want I have, now that you mention it. No need for a list.''

''Hmmm?'' She tunneled her hand up the back of his shirt, wondering how quickly they could return to his hotel. His skin felt so warm, and he smelled entirely too tempting. How fantastic, she marveled, to have a husband who was such a marvelously appealing man.

''Well, Irish, to put it plainly like I prefer to, I want a wife who doesn't pounce on every blamed problem in town and end up making troub—''

''Not on your life, Constable.'' She stepped back, glaring into his face to see if he was serious. His eyes held a barely-there spark of amusement, but the lopsided frown on his lips wasn't teasing in the least. ''Being in the same family will not get you special dispensation. You cannot expect me to be anything but unbiased during our future discussions. I know it pains you to quarrel with your wife, but it can't be helped on occasion. Seriously, a little quarreling never truly harms anyone. In fact, it clears the air much like peppermint does for a congested nose.''

Pulling her back into his arms, he sighed against her ear. He sounded content in the final evaluation. If not, she would work on making him happy in the privacy of his hotel room. ''Yeah, that's what I reckoned, Mrs. Garrett. I guess I'm gonna have to learn to enjoy quarreling.''

''Or the making up,'' she reminded him.

''Definitely the making up, ma'am.''

Epilogue

The door to the jail rocketed inward, slapping the wall with a bang.

Zach jerked his head up, his spectacles slipping down his nose. The cargo ledger in his hands hit the floor, coming close to smashing his toes. Hyman Carter stood in the doorway, silent, accusing with nothing more than a finger jabbed in the direction of his factory. A perturbed—Savannah's big word, not his, and why he thought them he guessed was her rubbing off on him after all this time—breath escaped before he could yank it back. Shoving back his chair, he shrugged into his jacket. The air was getting nippy again. You never could guess what you'd get in October.

"I thought once little Regina was born, darling girl, that all this turmoil would be put to bed, Zach. I gotta tell you, I sure thought that."

"Yeah, yeah," Zach muttered, wishing he had a penny for every time he'd heard that opinion come out of some man's mouth in the past four years. Or some old biddy's after they left church and he stood around in the yard waiting for Savannah to finish her business and social dealings. Those were always grand opportunities to give a suffering husband kindly advice about how to handle his misbehaving wife.

"And with her expecting again, why, I can't believe she continues to prance around doing all this equal-female preaching. What I meant to say is, I can't believe *you* allow it."

A nickel for *that* one and he'd be a rich man. "How 'bout this, Hyman?" Zach dashed between a wagon hauling lumber to a new house going up down the street and a fish cart hawking flounder for two cents a pound. Hyman kept up, huffing a bit, bound and determined to watch the drama unfold. "You tell Savannah you think she ought to stay at home and be a proper wife. Hey"— he slapped the startled man's back before turning onto Main Street—"I'll buy the front row of tickets for that show."

"Why, I ... that is, I could never ..." He stuttered, his jowls flushing bright red. "It wouldn't be my place, you see."

"Um-hum, what I thought." Zach left Hyman to his panicky fit, sprinting along the street, dodging through the crowds of people starting to gather. He heard the ruckus before he reached it. Nothing new there. Nothing new with any of it.

"Daddy!" The small projectile charging through the crowd and into his knees, now that *was* a tad different. The greatest difference in his life so far. She looked like something Savannah had spit out, a petite dynamo of a duplicate with his eyes, the Garrett grays. His child all the way, in that way. Damned if that combination hadn't stolen his heart at first sight.

Catching his daughter in his arms, he pressed his nose to her neck and blew moist air against her

kin. Regina shrieked with laughter and wiggled
frantically. This was her favorite greeting when he
walked in the door every afternoon. That and a
butterscotch lollipop. It was his favorite greeting,
too. Because he got to smell his daughter, up close.
Vanilla and the faint scent of lilacs. And glue. Ah
yes, her mother's blessed signs. He inhaled a deep
breath, relishing the moment. She'd about gotten
old enough not to want things like this: babyish
hugs and kisses.

"Daddy, I made a poster all by myself. It's hanging up there on that dirty old wall." She pointed,
and in the distance he could see a rather sad-
looking sign that said, *Equal Pay*. "Rory said it stunk
because I only painted inside the letters Mommy
made. I think it looks good. I cain't get everything
in the lines!"

"It looks beautiful, just like my Reggie-girl."

"Lemme go, Daddy," she said, struggling to get
free, "I have to go help Mommy fight for freed-
dom." When her feet hit the ground, she blew
him a kiss and scampered through the crowd. He
watched her dark head bobbing, faintly anxious
until he saw her reach her mother.

Reggie's tiny hands moved in time with her spirited story. Savannah nodded and smiled, smoothing a tangled lock of hair from her daughter's
flushed, round cheek. Finally, she looked over and
above the crowd, snagging his gaze. The same bolt
of lightning connected them, a storm of emotion
and anticipation that Zach no longer feared. He
frowned at her, just for show mostly. When he
watched his two precious girls, his heart wasn't in
being harsh.

And she knew it, the Irish devil.

Savannah arched a brow and nodded toward the
jail. He shook his head, dipping his chin toward

the modest crowd of women shouting and wavin
signs. The pounding surf nearly covered th
screeching, but not quite, unfortunately. Glancin
around, she studied the crowd, debating to hersel
he could see. Calling Lydia to her side, she gav
instructions that set the rally's finale in motion
Obviously, she had judged *him* to be worth th
sacrifice of a few minutes' bickering.

With a final, intense look, he retraced his rout
to the jail. The wind had picked up, throwing
chill into the salty air. People scurried past, tryin
to make it home for supper. A gull swooped pas
his shoulder, diving for a scrap on the boardwalk
Preparing, Zach ripped off his spectacles and pu
them away the minute his office door closed behin
him. After four years, he and his wife had perfecte
this form of communication to a near-science.

She arrived less than five minutes later, out o
breath, her cheeks flushed, her eyes glowing. He
beauty and the fact that she loved him still had th
power to knock the breath from his body. "Wha
a successful day," she said, closing the door behin
her, and locking it.

"Wonderful." He opened his arms to her, an
Savannah slid inside his embrace, settling her bot
tom on his lap, her head on his shoulder. "Hov
long do we have?"

"Caroline's taking Regina for ice cream an
Rory's at Tommy's house. So, oh . . ." She nibble
on his neck, sending a hot wash through his veins
". . . An hour. Maybe a little less."

"Are you feeling up to this?" She was fou
months along and got sick pretty easily some days
Sinking his fingers into her silky hair, he tilted he
head where he could reach her mouth. Her plump
breasts pressed into his chest. He tugged her skir
to her knee, hoping she'd tell him soon if sh

wasn't up to it. Because he was up, that was for sure.

"You better believe I am, Constable."

"That's my girl," he whispered before claiming her lips. Love poured through him, overwhelming, mind-boggling. "My Irish girl."